Thank you for returning
your books on time.

Abington Free Library
1030 Old York Road
Abington, PA 19001

When a terrorist attack in Tel Aviv violently disrupts his life, Mickey Simhoni abandons his plans to become an artist and instead allows himself to be recruited into the Mossad. Slowly he learns the art of spycraft and the painstaking process of building a cover, becoming someone whom he resembles, who is presumed dead.

His cover story takes him to Toronto where he meets an earlier flame – Niki, a girl he had hooked up with in Tokyo a decade earlier. Mickey is torn between loyalty to the Mossad and his intense feelings for Niki – which the ever-resourceful Niki partially resolves with an unusual decision.

But still Mickey's dilemma persists, as he oscillates between duty and love, his complex operations in the Mossad threatening to kill their love. When his final operation in Algiers goes badly wrong, the rage and hatred engendered, and the utter humiliation visited on them, leads to a traumatic conclusion.

Mishka Ben-David served in the Mossad for twelve years, becoming a high-ranking officer. He is now a full-time novelist living outside Jerusalem. *Duet in Beirut* was his first novel to be translated into English, and received great media attention, which was followed by *Forbidden Love in St Petersburg* (both published by Halban Publishers).

FINAL STOP,
ALGIERS

FINAL STOP,
ALGIERS

A Thriller

MISHKA BEN-DAVID

Translated from the Hebrew by
Ronnie Hope

THE OVERLOOK PRESS
NEW YORK, NY

This edition first published in hardcover in the United States in 2017 by
The Overlook Press, Peter Mayer Publishers, Inc.

141 Wooster Street
New York, NY 10012
www.overlookpress.com
For bulk and special sales, please contact sales@overlookny.com,
or write us at the address above.

Originally published in Hebrew under the title *Tachana Sofit Algier*
by Miskal – Yedioth Ahronoth Books and Chemed Books, Tel-Aviv 2012

Published by arrangement with
The Institute for the Translation of Hebrew Literature

Cataloging-in-Publication Data available from the Library of Congress

Manufactured in the United States of America

1 3 5 7 9 10 8 6 4 2
ISBN: 978-1-4683-1022-1

FINAL STOP, ALGIERS

Prologue

Prologue

The Samurai from Toronto

IT WAS A RELATIONSHIP that began with my spirits – and my eyes – cast down.

Tired of getting lost in Tokyo, I had collapsed onto a bench in a little square outside the subway station in Shibuya. There I sat, focusing on my map when, out of the corner of my eye, I noticed a pair of feet. The toes turned inwards and the heels were slightly apart. Out of pointy black shoes arose two light-skinned legs, lean and shapely, and then my eyes took in her knees, squinting a little at each other. Above these came the thighs, also lean and shapely, but with a space between that made me wonder how they got together up there, under the tiny hot pants.

As I looked up at her face, I guessed what I would see: a pretty Japanese girl. I'd been travelling around Japan for a while, and one of the things that surprised me and that I had grown to like, was the way women's legs turned inwards to face each other. I didn't have anyone to ask, but I assumed that this was prompted by some kind of modesty, and certainly had nothing to do with genetics. When they walk, these Japanese women, both their feet stay on the same narrow path, as if each step must touch a line drawn on the ground. When you stand and walk like that from childhood on, something apparently gets bent forever. But nevertheless, there was something captivating about these slim, utterly smooth legs, slightly muscular and slightly crooked. And now they were standing right in front of me, at a flagrantly un-Japanese distance of only one step away.

I had just completed a walk through the streets around the square, which in no way that I could fathom corresponded to the streets on the map. I was tired of getting lost in Tokyo. When I had first decided to go to Japan after getting out of the army, it hadn't seemed like a very complicated prospect. In fact, in some cases I even managed to reach the places described in my Lonely Planet guidebook. The punctual hi-tech train system carried me all over the central island, wherever I wanted to go, and most of the places I visited were small enough to find my way around with relative ease. The problem was this enormous city of Tokyo, especially when I left the subway stations via a different exit than the one the guidebook writers had meant me to use. At these gigantic stations, this could be hundreds of yards from the exit I was supposed to take, in entirely another section of the neighbourhood, so it was difficult to work out where I was.

That is what I was trying to do now and, not for the first time, unsuccessfully. The huge glass and stone buildings around me looked the same: the names of the shops, even the brand names in English, were not the names of the shops in the book and, furthermore, the narrow alleys full of food stalls and clothes stores that branched away from the square seemed identical. Only a compass would have helped me to find out where I was. But I had no compass, and no more energy.

The Japanese people that I asked at the corners of the alleys and the square, pointing on the map at the place I wanted to get to, were either terrified if they didn't understand my question at all, or very embarrassed if they did understand it and didn't know how to help. I could tell when they were gesticulating in a complicated pantomime instead of simply saying they didn't know. There were also some who just ran away from me to avoid the embarrassment.

As I sat in the square, I wondered whether to give up on my plan and just stroll through the alleys, which looked inviting behind the tall buildings that surrounded the square. I looked at the small statue of a sad dog standing in the centre of the square, a dog that waited for its master every day outside the station, so went the story, and when the master never came back from his daily commute, stayed there waiting until the day it died. And the Japanese, as we know, really admire such loyalty unto death. Around me, a kaleidoscope of a thousand people at any given moment hurried to and from the station, and there was no point in asking them because the chance of finding someone who spoke English was almost zero. Once again I gazed at the map, which for all the good it did me could have been an outline map, one with all the names left out, when my eyes dropped down and those pointy black shoes came into view.

My humbling had just begun. Before I managed to look up,

intentionally avoiding lingering on the slim body and small breasts, I heard
a stern voice in impeccable English:

"May I help you? You seem to be lost."

The impish look came from a face that could almost have been
innately Japanese: sharp chin, thin lips, tiny nose, high cheekbones – but
then, the eyes, instead of being dark and almond-shaped, were green,
thoroughly western, and smiling cheerfully. The smile spread at the sight
of the dumb expression on my face.

The girl before me was, by any standards, very good-looking. Enough
in itself to unnerve me, even if she hadn't seen I was lost, and even without
her chivalrous desire to rescue me. I had already noticed that there were
a number of different tribes or peoples in Japan, some that look a little
like Mongols, some that are a little like Indians or Filipinos, some that are
reminiscent of the drawings of the Edo period, with long, sharp noses,
and others who have delicate, beautiful facial features. But no green eyes.

She grasped my confusion even before she realized how embarrassed
I was but how could she have known that I was an Israeli ex-officer who
didn't relish getting help in orientation from a passerby? She resolved the
confusion at once: "I'm Canadian," she said, explaining the faultless accent.
This of course raised further questions, which for the time being I
refrained from asking. She offered me her hand, and in a friendly,
unaffected way, introduced herself, "Niki. A kind of compromise that my
Japanese father and Canadian mother found for their daughter's name."

I told her my name, Mickey Simhoni, and showed her the place I was
looking for on the map – that turned out to have been upside down,
because Japanese looked the same to me from all directions – and she said
it was on her way and she'd be happy to take me there. That place was a
specialized bicycle shop where I wanted to buy some accessories not yet
available in Israel, like the instrument that measures your blood pressure
and pulse while you're riding and a flashing light that fits onto the back
of the bike. I'd taken up cycling as a hobby after my discharge. I wasn't fit
enough for long distance running, and didn't like it; I was too heavy. But
my combat-veteran friends were in the grip of some kind of a fitness craze,
and I thought that cycling would put me in the picture too.

Niki led me through a maze of pretty alleys, between restaurants and
shops, and I had to make an effort to keep abreast of her. I don't know if
it was my screwed-up military training or my no-less screwed-up male

hormones, but trailing behind a woman bothered me. I told her in a jokey kind of way about the bizarre things that had happened to me here in Japan, and she responded with a clear, loud laugh. But it seemed as if Niki felt shy about speaking to me and she smiled pleasantly enough but also aloofly when it was her turn to say something. She did it with lips that were almost pursed, something that made her look irresistibly cute. All of a sudden, with a captivating smile that spread from her lips to her eyes, she pointed at a three-storey structure devoted totally to bicycles and bicycle accessories.

I did not want to part from her yet. Facing the store was a little Italian restaurant, and I asked her if she felt like a slice of pizza.

"All the way to Japan for pizza?" she laughed, and said, "OK".

There were other restaurants nearby but I didn't want to expose my inferiority again, by having to eat with chopsticks. With Japanese food itself, I got along fairly well. There were pictures of the dishes on the menus, and plastic models near the door that gave a pretty good idea of what you'd be getting. Because there were never menus in English, and no one who could speak the language, I would point at the picture or the plastic dish of the food I wanted, and usually I wasn't disappointed. I didn't know what kind of meat I was eating, but some of the seafood was identifiable, and I always knew that underneath there was a satisfying helping of rice or noodles. I'd never learned to use chopsticks, so I'd ask for a fork, one of the only words in Japanese that I knew, and it wasn't difficult: forku. Straight from the English, with the soft "r" and the Japanese "u" suffix.

I wanted to draw out my time with this lovely Canadian-Japanese girl. For the first time in many days I was conversing freely and at length with someone, and there was something about Niki that I did not want to part with. I hadn't yet put it into words, except for the obvious "good-looker", but later on, when she had vanished out of my life, I defined it for myself: the warmth and the sympathy that she radiated, the grace with which she spoke and moved, the shy smile that never left her lips or her eyes, the combination of openness and modesty that was new to me – all of these gave her a kind of mischievousness that hinted at hidden treasures within.

Over a mound of spaghetti that she sucked in eagerly – my amazement at this made her laugh out loud – Niki asked me about my past and expressed admiration for my having been in the army for so long.

"Like my grandpa when he was young," she said. "He was the descendant of a long line of samurai."

I had more than an inkling of what she was talking about, having visited the castle of a shogun, a military governor of the country in past centuries, as well as homes of his warriors, the samurai. Some of these homes were large feudal mansions and others were small cottages, depending on how close the samurai were to the shogun and the degree of gratitude the shogun owed the warriors. They were built out of wood, with wooden floors and the inside walls were made of rice paper stretched across wooden frameworks. The roofs were constructed from grey tiles, engraved at the ends. Although I didn't enter most of them, because guests were required to remove their shoes and I was tired of unlacing and lacing my trekking boots, I was impressed by their monastic cleanliness and harmonious architecture. These were some of the few structures earmarked for preservation in the building boom that was under way in every city I visited.

This intriguing mixture of old customs preserved in the midst of stepped-up modernization enthralled me. Dignity and respect were evident everywhere. For example, the two lines of people waiting for a train on either side of a stripe painted on the platform to indicate where the car door would be when the train stopped. It draws up exactly there, to the centimetre. No one moves before all the exiting passengers are out, and then they all file in, to the right and to the left, with exemplary order. The blank faces of all the passengers, some of whom are busy playing computer games, ensure that no one will penetrate the private space of anyone else. When the conductor enters each car of the fast train – the last word in fast trains – he bows deeply, and after checking all the tickets and reaching the other end of the car, he turns around and bows again before moving on.

I'd read quite a bit about the samurai codes and their endless loyalty, and I was surprised when Niki told me that her grandfather had emigrated to Canada after what she called "the B". I didn't get it so, dropping her eyes, she explained: "The bomb." When the emperor announced both Japan's surrender as the Americans demanded, and that he was no longer a god, everything her granddad had believed in collapsed. He could not endure the humiliation of the American occupation and decided to desert, not to the ranks of the enemy, but to their close neighbour, Canada, which obliged by granting him a visa, and he settled with his family in Toronto. She tried to explain how harsh the crisis was for her grandfather, and for much of his generation, when their faith in their strength, their religion and their ruler all crumbled away.

Her father, she told me, grew up in Toronto with mixed feelings of belonging and rejection, full of anger at his father's defection, but he had calmed down after he fell in love with her mother. Niki, however, had grown up as a Canadian girl in every sense, particularly under the influence of her mother, "a fifth generation Torontonian".

"On my mother's side, I'm fourth generation Jerusalem and on my father's – third generation Auschwitz," I told her, but I don't think she got it.

From the time she was in kindergarten, she said, she grasped that she was a mixture of her father and her mother, of East and West, and the more she realized that her identity was Canadian, the more she took an interest in her father's heritage, and she asked him to speak Japanese to her. Her elderly grandfather even managed to teach her quite a few samurai sword drills. After he died, her father kept it up, to the chagrin of her mother who hoped that the ties that bound her husband to his faraway homeland would dissipate with time. Now, after graduating from college, Niki had decided to come for an open-ended stay. She wanted to be as Japanese as she was Canadian. She was studying calligraphy, the tea ceremony and flower arrangement. And she was also learning some of the samurai arts: swordplay, karate and judo, and she wondered who would end up on top in unarmed combat: me or her.

I gazed in wonder at the tiny body, the delicate hands, her bony shoulders. Was she being serious? I lay my arm demonstratively alongside hers. My forearm was twice the size of hers, the biceps even more than that, and at the shoulders I was perhaps three times thicker. I was no hunk, by Israeli standards. I don't think an Israeli girl would have been impressed by my physique. On the beach, most of the guys were taller and more muscular than I was. Army service as a combat sapper demanded courage, perhaps, but not much strength and unlike some of my friends, my shoulders, thighs and chest had not grown much during my training. Despite this, I had gone through basic training without too much difficulty, and after that a squad commanders' course and, later, an officers' course. I felt strong, and I was strong, and next to your average Japanese man I must have looked pretty bulky. Some nerve she had, this little thing.

"Let's try it some time," I said, and she replied, "Let's."

I was thrilled. I'm set for tonight, I thought. A judo match between us could lead nowhere but to bed. But then I asked her how she made a living, and it was my turn to gulp down the spaghetti without chewing. "I'm a hostess," she replied.

Before my trip I'd read about the night life of Japanese businessmen and office workers. I knew there were special clubs that catered to them in certain parts of Tokyo. Not many of the salaried workers could afford what they offered, but sometimes their companies paid for a night out as a bonus, or as part of a team-building programme, or as hosts to visiting western businessmen. Niki had wanted to get to know the geisha culture, but quickly learned that to do that she would have had to be a pure Japanese and to study for years. She had to make do with being a hostess in a modern businessmen's club in the Asakusa neighbourhood. She performed the traditional tea ceremony for them there, but what they wanted was mainly to practise their broken English on her. She was especially valuable when they were entertaining visiting westerners: her mastery of both Japanese and English helped the conversation flow more freely.

Niki apparently noticed my astonishment. She knew, as I did, that there were people who confused geishas and hookers, and even those who know better still thought hostesses were on a lower level than geishas. She said this without relish but she certainly wasn't apologetic.

She didn't allow me to pay for her meal. "You're a backpacker and can't have too much money," she said, in a final humiliation, without letting me tell her that in my year as a regular army officer, after my compulsory three years as a conscript, I had managed to save quite a lot. When I asked if we could meet again, she said she was working that night and she never made plans for tomorrow. The next day would take her wherever it took her, just as today had taken her to me for a while, and she was grateful for that.

I was forced to admit that I had failed to leave an indelible impression on Niki, like all the girls I had met so far. But her magic had worked on me and I did not mean to give up.

Holding my bag of bicycle gadgets, and full of hope and expectation, I arrived at the Asakusa district in the early evening. It isn't particularly large, but in Tokyo every neighbourhood is inhabited by hundreds of thousands of people. I assumed that the nightclubs would be close to the office buildings and they wouldn't spill over into the surrounding residential areas. This time, I exited the subway alongside more modern corporate buildings. The nightclubs would probably start coming to life at the end of office hours, I thought, at around five p.m.

Swarms of workers who looked as if they were coming off a mass-production assembly line working at a dizzying pace streamed out of the doors of the steel and glass high-rises. Everyone wore white shirts, cotton trousers and black leather shoes. Most of the men wore jackets and ties. I stood and watched this human river. The assembly line had ensured that they would all be the same height, more or less the same as me, and all have the same straight black hair. From behind, it was hard to tell which of them were men and which were women. The majority flowed towards where I had come from, and were swallowed up by the entrance to the subway station. I trailed after a drizzle of people trickling off in a different direction, but realized this would not take me where I wanted to go. Some of them headed for taxi stands or various garages, and others disappeared down side streets whose neon signs, which flickered on as darkness fell, turned them into a completely different city – night-time Tokyo, all bars and little sushi restaurants, sex clubs, with a barker standing outside each establishment proclaiming the wares available inside and trying to lure in passersby. On each corner, my eyes – and ears – lit upon slot machine arcades, and especially the noisy pachinko parlours where long rows of men sat facing the machines, their attaché cases on shelves above them, with boxes of small iron balls at their feet, carried away by the mesmerizing movement of the balls, over which they had no control, and cheering when they won the prize – more balls.

This, I guessed, was not where I would find respectable clubs of the kind where, I assumed, Niki was working, and I rambled on in the hope that I'd somehow come across one.

In a quiet alley, where most of the buildings were old, a modern, glass structure that didn't belong there caught my eye, with a prominent sign on its ground floor, in English: "Karaoke" and below it a notice – surprisingly also in English – indicating a number of clubs on the upper floors.

I went up one floor in the elevator. To the left and right of a narrow, meandering and gloomy corridor were three heavy, carved doors with some well-tended greenery next to them. At the side of each door was a sign, in English and Japanese giving the opening hours and the prices. I discovered that I was early. The clubs opened at eight p.m., and for the first hour the entry fee was around seven thousand yen – a few dozen dollars at the exchange rate at that time. An hour later the price jumped to ten thousand yen and by the hour.

I went up to the second and third floors, and the same picture greeted me. Only the prices and the decorations on the doors differed slightly. It was here, perhaps, that she worked, this Niki who I felt was being relentlessly driven into my heart like a screw.

I returned to street level, wandered through the nearby alleys, and passed other clubs. Just before eight p.m. I returned to the first building I had found, took up a position in a doorway opposite it, and waited. I knew Niki could be working at any number of other places, but the cluster of clubs here increased my chances.

It was pitch dark. Taxis began arriving sporadically. Well groomed, quiet Japanese women got out of some, and boisterous men, both Japanese and western, from others. My eyes were straining in the dark, and twice I called out "Niki" to someone who wasn't Niki. The third time it was Niki. She turned around, surprised, and came up to me with a stern look on her face.

"You are not supposed to be here," she said, serious and even a little pale. "It's not good for me, and it's very bad for you." There was a warning in her voice.

"The yakuza?" I tried to be funny.

She laid a finger on my lips. "You don't even joke about it," she whispered.

I saw a young man standing at the door to the building staring at us. Niki followed my gaze.

"Now go away and don't come back."

I tried to give her a hug. She was wearing a dark blue evening dress with a bare back, and had a light coat over her arm. Her back trembled under my hands. She was wearing makeup, with scarlet lipstick, a fine line that made her eyes look slanted, her face whitened, and she was taller – under her long gown she must have been wearing high heels. Her hair was braided and held back by a large pin, and it was still damp and gave off a fresh scent of shampoo.

"You are so beautiful," I couldn't resist saying. I felt an intense urge to kiss her, but when I leaned towards her she broke away, muttered "Go now," and hurried with short, quick paces back across the street.

The guy in the doorway began moving in my direction, and another bouncer took his place. I was prepared to take on a small Canadian-Japanese girl, even though she came from a long line of samurai and specialized in judo, but not a trained yakuza thug. I wasn't a combative type and didn't like fighting and avoided it as far as possible; it was not the kind of experience I would choose of my own free will. And now there wasn't even a real reason for it, and I guessed that my chances were not good. The second man would certainly intervene if the first one was in trouble and that wouldn't happen if he had any skill at all.

I turned away and walked up the street at a measured pace. The footsteps that I heard behind me, the heavy steps of steel-tipped boots, quickly stopped, to my relief, and I felt myself breathing normally again.

I went into a small Japanese restaurant. I assumed that in a few hours, Niki's shift would be over and I wanted to be there when she came out. It surprised me that I didn't feel strange. In their desire to respect the privacy of others, the restaurant's customers, all local people, refrained from even stealing glances at me. I lingered over my meal, and then retraced my steps and took up a position outside a house further up the street, with a clear view of the club building, but out of sight of the bouncer. Long nights of lying in ambushes near Israel's border with Lebanon had trained me to stay still in the dark and keep my eyes open. I focused on the strip of pavement outside the door of the building. It never crossed my mind that this would be the first of an endless number of urban lookouts and ambushes that were in store for me across the globe in years to come.

As the evening wore on, the stream of men swelled, arriving mostly in small groups. No more women turned up, and I realized that those I had seen earlier were hostesses. Towards midnight, the flow was reversed, with empty taxis drawing up to collect groups of men, swaying and laughing, and parting from each other with what seemed to me somewhat exaggerated bows. The women were apparently waiting until the last men had left.

It was a hot and humid summer's night, by evening the sky had already clouded over, and all of a sudden a heavy, monsoon-like downpour struck. I got as close as I could to the door of the building where I was sheltering, but I soon realized that this way I wouldn't recognize Niki when she came out. So I came out of my hiding place each time a woman emerged from the club building and scurried with little steps towards the taxi that had arrived for her. Inevitably, I was sopping wet when I saw Niki exiting the building. What now?

She climbed into the back seat of the cab on the side nearest the building, and I had no alternative but to run up, open the door on the other side, and plunk myself down next to her. The driver turned to me, surprised and angry, and Niki was also stunned, but she quickly recovered and said something in Japanese to the driver. He unwillingly turned back and looked the other way, at the doorman, who despite the dense rainfall had apparently seen what was happening and had come out of the building. Niki spoke again and the driver moved off.

"You are crazy, you know that?" she told me, as could only be expected, but instead of shock and anxiety, there was now a broad smile on her face. I moved towards her, but she quickly blocked me with her hand. I understood that she had her limits, and limits were also certainly a part of the norms of behaviour that prevailed here.

"Your place or mine?" I ventured, far more daring than I had ever been with any girl. Niki, or Tokyo, had scrambled everything that I had been before I encountered them.

"Neither," she answered, and said something else to the driver. Again, I was at a loss as to where I stood. The cab stopped, and Niki got out and pulled me after her. Firmly, she ordered the driver to drive off, and she hailed another taxi.

"He was one of their drivers. We couldn't stay with him," she said, without explaining, and looked back to make sure that her employers weren't following. Her nervousness gripped me too.

The second taxi dropped us off in a neighbourhood flooded with neon lights. The rain had stopped, and hundreds of people, perhaps thousands, mostly young, were milling around. It was an astonishing scene. There were droves of punk rockers, boys and girls in leather and amazing get-ups, and all kinds of shops, restaurants and bars, altogether a dazzling sight.

"Doesn't anyone sleep in this town?"

"Not here, in Shinjuku. But don't worry. Everyone will go to work tomorrow morning at 8, in suits. But come let's see what to do about ourselves." She had once again picked up the reins and she led me into a small bar.

"I won't drink, because I've already had at least ten drinks," she said, "but I'll order you something, preferably hot. You're soaked."

The word "soaked" was said in a voice that combined pity and admiration. Apparently her samurai loyalty had kicked in.

As if she owed me some explanation, after realizing that I'd waited for her for hours, she described in brief what she did in the club – which she named – in order to get it out of the way.

"Businessmen turn up after work. Usually groups of a few employees with their boss, who pays. Sometimes with visitors from abroad. They come to relax and have some fun. To drink, to dance. Each group sits around a table, and my boss sends over as many hostesses as there are men. We chat, that's all. The nice atmosphere makes them order more and more drinks, and we also order, and they pay. So I'm already quite drunk."

"Ten drinks," I said admiringly, "and you're still on your feet. I'd already be wallowing in my own vomit."

"My drinks are diluted," she said, extricating me from yet another inferior situation. "Now let's think about us."

Niki suddenly got practical, as if it was obvious that after my noble deed we were going to spend the night together. Very quickly "my place" was ruled out – I was staying at a youth hostel with another three foreigners in my room – and so was hers; she was lodging with a local family. Neither of us had the money for a regular hotel, so Niki suggested we go to a "love hotel". I'd heard the term before, but hadn't yet had the occasion to try one of them.

The sign at the entrance was in Japanese only, and of course I couldn't understand it, but the place didn't look like a hotel, more like an apartment house with the entrance at the rear. In the small lobby there was a sofa and a table, but no desk. A small hatch in the wall next to the price list was knee-high so we couldn't see who was behind it. And they obviously couldn't see anything but our legs.

"How long for?" Niki asked me.

"Till morning, no?"

"It goes by the hour. Till morning, the Hilton would be cheaper."

"Let's start with two hours," I said sorrowfully and hopefully.

Niki quickly opened her purse and held out a 10,000 yen note. An unseen hand gave her 5,000 back, and a key. I took out my wallet to reimburse her, but she pushed it away. "We'll settle up afterwards."

The hatch closed and we walked to the elevator, where I kissed her for the first time.

Niki didn't play coy, and with her tongue in my mouth she gave me a taste of something I had never tasted before. I felt a little dizzy, but a hard bite brought me down to the ground. The elevator door opened.

I thought I'd kiss her some more and begin undressing her as soon as we got into the room, which was simple, sparklingly clean, with two mattresses on the wooden floor, and a robe and towel on each one. But Niki said we must first take off our shoes, and she slipped out of her dress while I took off my wet clothes. The moment I finished, she slithered underneath me, slung me onto her back for a second and then tossed me over her shoulder onto a hard mattress.

"Ippon!" she exclaimed with a little jig. My back hurt from the fall, and I'd also taken a knock to my head.

"This is for all the grief you've given me!" she snarled as she came at me, gripping my throat and squeezing until I stopped breathing. Her eyes glittered like happy green lanterns in the dimly lit room.

I managed to free myself from her grip. In nature, whoever has the greater body mass usually wins, and mine was twice hers. I'm not tall, but still a head taller than her, and with all due respect to judo, it can tip the balance only up to a point.

To an onlooker, what happened next may have looked like rape. It's just not clear who raped whom. When we were finished, spent and scratched, Niki said, "It's never been so good for me before."

"I thought that because of your Japanese half you'd be more delicate," I said, still panting.

"I don't think that applies in bed. And definitely not in a love hotel."

She still had the half-crazed look that I had seen in her eyes, a few minutes before, cat-like, almost non-human, as she approached her climax. She was still hungry, and I also wanted more.

Only after the second time did we calm down a little and begin to gently explore each other's bodies, with our eyes, our fingers, our tongues. It was then that I discovered that Niki had one inverted nipple.

"It can be fixed with a simple operation, if I want," she said shyly. I said I'd make do with sucking it out with my mouth, but that didn't work. For her part, Niki found the scar under my right shoulder, a memento from a fragment of a mortar shell that had been fired at our position in Lebanon and hit me in the back. It was childish of me, I know, but I was really sorry that the wound was on my back. A scar on the front, I thought would have been much sexier, and I was somewhat apologetic as I told Niki about the incident. Then I showed her another lesion, much smaller, from a fragment that had hit me in my buttocks.

A soft bell rang when we were in the middle of the third time. My heart jumped for a moment when I thought the yakuza had arrived. But it was merely a reminder that our two hours were up.

"Now I'll pay," I said as if it was obvious we would go on, and I donned a robe and went down to the lobby.

We'd worn ourselves out with the things that I knew, and with all the things she knew and I hadn't thought were at all possible. It was so very different from everything I'd experienced until then. Apart from one romance that had lasted up until I left on this trip, I'd had only brief affairs, and the sex had been OK, at best. I had been so focused on making it OK, that I'd never even tried any of the things that Niki dragged me into doing and never had nights like this of doing it again and again – each time with innovations and inventions, quite a little carnival of our own.

Towards the end, when I was already sated but Niki wanted more, and was murmuring or gasping "Yes" with each movement, my thoughts wandered to a different series of "Yeses." On the eve of my discharge from the military, I gave my men a lecture on the United Nations resolution of 29 November 1947, when the UN's General Assembly decided on the partition of Palestine, the move that led to the establishment of the State of Israel. There's a recording of that vote, which I'd played to my unit, with the GA's president calling out "Yes" after the names of each country that voted in favour. Those historic thirty-three yeses that brought about the establishment of the State of Israel somehow came back to me every time Niki said yes. I amused myself by counting her yeses, to see if the partition plan would have passed on this historic occasion as well. At the UN, between Australia's and Belgium's votes in favour, there had been a longish pause in the yeses, because Afghanistan voted no and Argentina abstained, and Niki, who was still in low gear, sounded almost as monotonous as the president. But the pauses gradually became shorter, and between Ukraine's yes and Venezuela's, I hardly had the time to murmur the names of the countries. Then, with exquisite timing, after the thirty-third yes, Niki collapsed on top of me, exhausted and the recognition of the State of Israel was reconfirmed in the nicest possible way.

For sex like this, friends of mine have travelled to Bangkok and paid sizeable sums, and here we were just doing what comes naturally. However, after the second two hours, and then another two, the Hilton would have been cheaper.

✧✧✧

The bitter pill came when we were standing outside the hotel.

"I won't be able to see you again," Niki told me, and I choked. I thought that I'd found the love of my life, she'd been so cute, sexy, tender, wild, loving and exciting, all at the same time. And very beautiful, of course. We had spent the last hour locked in an embrace, almost without moving, gently massaging each other's bodies with the tips of our fingers, Niki stroking and kissing the scar on my shoulder, and I felt a happiness and serenity that I had never ever felt with any other girl.

"Say that again?" I muttered incredulously.

Niki's eyes were full of tears. "Don't get me wrong. It was marvellous for me, with you, and I could easily fall in love with you. But you're a complication I do not need in my life."

"Romances are made of complications like this," I came up with, heaven knows how. "I don't want to lose you."

"I left my home in Canada and I came here to fulfil the Japanese half that's hiding inside me. With you, I'd go to completely different places. It's difficult. Don't make it even more difficult, please." And she burst into tears and made off down the road, taking her high heels off and running with the small steps that were all her tight blue gown allowed her to make. Unbelievingly, I stood there, leaning against a wall, in a daze, and watching the love of my life in her blue dress, weeping and gradually disappearing from my sight, with her small Japanese steps.

Osnat, who'd been my girlfriend since the end of my officers' course, had broken up with me on the eve of my trip to Japan. Our romance had survived many forced separations while we were in the army, and when Osnat was discharged and began studying film at Tel Aviv University, I rented a small apartment for us, using my army pay, and we managed to stay together right up until my service ended. But when I was planning my long trip to the Orient, Osnat said that this was too much for her, and I understood, and we broke up without hard feelings. I had in any case seen that her Tel Aviv world, cavorting around the clock with groups of film students doing their various filming and directing assignments, could not be my world.

It had hurt, but not like now. I'd loved Osnat, but not like this. I don't know if an hour of chatting and a one-night stand can be called love, but that's what it was. Without meaning to, Niki had bored her way deep into my heart.

I roamed the streets all morning, feeling sorry for myself and not understanding what had hit me, until I came across a billboard announcing a drumming performance, and I thought the noise and the energy would help me break out of my bubble. I bought a ticket, and found myself in the front row. On the stage was an enormous two-sided drum on a raised platform, looming over me like a sacrificial altar, with three large two-sided drums and a number of smaller ones below it. In the first part of the programme the troupe, called Kodo, reminded me of the Israeli Mayumana dance and percussion troupe. But Niki remained in my mind throughout. In the second part, though, the Kodo drummers put themselves, and me, and the whole audience, into a trance with powerful beating of the huge drum and the other large drums. It was both primordial and spell-binding. I asked myself if I would have been able to beat the drums with such strength, with the two large wooden drumsticks, at that rhythm and for as much time, as those slight but very muscular, perspiring Japanese were doing, a metre away from me. There were three girls in the troupe, one of whom reminded me of Niki and the energy that charged my batteries only made me determined not to give up on her. I knew what I had to do.

When the show was over and I got up to leave, I found that someone was staring at me. It wasn't because I was a foreigner, I knew. For all the weeks I'd been here, not one Japanese had dared to stare at me; my private space was protected by the force of an ancient and rigid tradition. I stared back. I sensed that he was the bouncer who had come out of the club and walked towards me. I couldn't be sure, and the man looked away. Either way, I had taken a decision and I was determined to implement it.

Everything in Japan is expensive, but nevertheless, I did some shopping for things I didn't have in my 80-litre rucksack: first, I bought myself a white shirt and black cotton trousers. I couldn't find a good fit, and both items were too snug – the shirt in the shoulders and the trousers around the waist. I also bought black leather shoes, pointed and funny. And, as all the men who came to the club last night were also wearing jackets and ties, and fearing that this was a mandatory dress code, I also bought a jacket – sleeves too short – and a tie, asking the sales clerk to tie the knot for me because I didn't know how to.

I decided not to turn up at the club early, but only when it had filled up a little, in the hope that I wouldn't stand out so much.

The doorman wasn't the same as the night before, and also not the man who'd stared at me at the end of the Kodo drummers' performance. He gave me a quick once-over, and bowed deeply. Compared to what I'd paid for my outfit, the twelve-thousand-yen entry fee for this hour of the evening was an expense I could handle – on condition, of course, that I wouldn't be slung out.

I was greeted by dimmed coloured lights, like a Tel Aviv discotheque, western music of the 1960s, and a lot of smoke. About twenty men and hostesses, perhaps more, were sitting in the smallish room, divided among three low tables. The atmosphere was relaxed, everyone looked and sounded comfortable as they sat there chatting and laughing. I surveyed the groups, one at a time. Niki wasn't there. I didn't feel that joining one of the tables would be the right thing to do, so I went to the bar, where a hostess was already waiting for me. She was light skinned and turned out to be French. If Niki wasn't there I was wasting my time, but the entrance fee included a drink, so I sat down and order saké. The barman asked me something and the girl translated, "Hot or cold, with an extra dash of alcohol or not?" She called the drink "sakai" and began an explanation in broken English of its history and different types, but then I saw Niki.

On a small dance floor on one side of the room, to the strains of "Oh Carol" played by a small combo, two couples were dancing, bodies pressed close together. Niki was one of the girls. The pang that I felt was intense. My hostess asked me if something was wrong, and I said no, but the drink in the shallow cup had done nothing for me and tasted like ordinary wine, so I ordered a double whisky. The barman asked me what brand, and I shrugged. Scotch or Irish? I didn't care. Single malt? Didn't know what that meant. He poured what he poured, and I swallowed it in two gulps.

The scene was totally surreal. There were multi-coloured lights flashing around the dancing couples, doubled and tripled by revolving disco mirror balls. The whisky had gone to my head and made the already horrifyingly slow dancing even slower, and Niki and her partner merged before my eyes into one, hovering, unmoving body, as the world around them rotated slowly.

When the music ended, her partner ushered Niki towards a corner table, laid for two. He looked like an American, tall and handsome, and she was giggling merrily along with him. The French girl followed my gaze.

"It's the custom to invite one of the hostesses to a meal, if she appeals to you," she said.

I understood that this was another way to separate the customers from their money.

"And also to dance?" I asked.

"Of course. 'Specially if she's your personal hostess for the evening."

She explained that once a month, each hostess had to bring a man with her who hadn't been to the club before, and then she was his personal, exclusive hostess. I realized I wouldn't be able to approach Niki if she was the American's "personal, exclusive hostess" for this evening. Running through my mind were thoughts about the limits of this "exclusivity," despite Niki's assurances that sex wasn't part of this occupation. I wanted to attract her attention, and I asked my hostess to dance with me. The band was playing "California Dreaming" to which I had last slow-danced as a thirteen-year-old boy. It worked: I went afterwards to the men's room, at the end of a short corridor, lined with unfinished wine bottles marked with the names of regular customers, waiting for their next visit. When I came out, Niki was there, pale and frightened.

"What do you think you're doing?" she asked quietly, with pursed lips.

"I thought I could be with you, but I see someone else is the lucky guy."

"Don't be a fool. You've got to go. You're endangering me and yourself."

She looked over my shoulder, and I turned and saw the barman signalling with his head in our direction.

"I'll just watch you," I said. "I'm not here to cause trouble."

She was ravishing, in a turquoise dress this time, with a necklace and earrings.

"Nothing has changed since this morning. And nothing will change. Please go."

Niki's partner needed the men's room too, and raised an eyebrow when he saw us looking as if we were exchanging secrets, but Niki shot him her engaging smile and slipped into the ladies' room. The bouncer was behind him, and I went back to the barman and Frenchy.

The whisky and the saké were swilling around in my head. I asked for some paper, and the barman gave me some napkins. I asked for a pencil, and I got a fountain pen. From the angle I was sitting at, I could see only Niki's lovely profile, and I began with that: her nose, her pointed chin, her small breasts, her slender legs. I drew it all in one line. Then I went on to her hair, gathered behind, and her slender back. Only then did I add the light touches that represented her dress.

The barman and my hostess were impressed. Drawing had been my strong point at high school. I didn't have the patience for oil painting, or even acrylic, although it dries rapidly; I liked seeing quick results. I had a nimble and skilled hand, acquired while still in junior school, when I created the comic-book character Israman, "the first Israeli superhero" as I called him, rightly or wrongly. I copied each comic book by hand ten times and gave it to my better friends and to girls I was interested in.

The barman brought me larger sheets of paper and some pencils and pens. I asked for another whisky. Niki and her partner got up to dance, and now I drew them both. Then, I drew her without looking, from memory. After another few outrageously expensive drinks, I began to be an idiot and drew, for example, some scenes of the previous night that came into my mind. More than that, I don't remember. Only that two tough little guys, something like Oddjob in the James Bond film *Goldfinger* took me downstairs, shoved me into a cab, and tossed my drawings in after me. With the last of my strength, I threw them back. "These are Niki's!" I said in somebody else's voice. I think I saw a turquoise dress and Niki's voice giving my address, and her hand giving the driver a banknote.

When I returned to the club, two days later, the doorman barred my way.

My description had apparently been given to all the bouncers. The door of the elevator behind him opened and in a move that surprised me, and of course also him, I shoved the refrigerator-shaped guy aside and slithered in as the doors closed. I was inside the club before he managed to report the unwanted customer, but Frenchy's wide-eyed look from the bar and a shake of her head told me what I could have guessed myself, and a quick survey of the place confirmed: Niki didn't work there anymore.

The hostess and the barman shot meaningful glances at the security men, clearly signalling to me that there was no chance of anyone telling me anything about her.

"Is she still here?" I asked before the two Oddjobs closed on me. Frenchy lowered her eyes and gave another shake of her head.

I thought I'd wait for her outside, follow her a little and then try to get something out of her about what had happened to Niki. But I was joined by the pissed-off human refrigerators who walked two paces behind me all the way to the subway station, staying close until I was on the train.

Part One

The Double

I.

An Exhibition in Tel Aviv

THE FITZ GALLERY in south Tel Aviv may not be a Mecca for your average Israeli artist, especially not for a Bezalel Art Academy graduate for whom great things had been predicted. But the predictions had come to nothing, and when the owner of the little gallery approached me after seeing my pictures in a group show of works by Bezalel graduates, I accepted his offer and my first solo exhibition was on its way. A mid-September date was set for the opening, just before the Sukkot holidays, when people are looking for things to do. "But don't expect much of a crowd, apart from your family and friends, and don't expect too much from them either," the gallery owner said. "With all the terrorist attacks going on, people don't like going out if they don't have a good reason."

I knew he was right. Without making any conscious decision, I realized that I too hardly ever just wandered around anymore since the Second Intifada – the second Palestinian uprising – had broken out, two years earlier in 2000, and suicide bombings had begun again. I stayed away from places where people gathered, even at traffic lights, in case that gathering became a terrorist's target, and when I had to go somewhere I went by car or I walked, to avoid getting on a bus. I kept my errands brief and quickly got back home or to my studio and, strangely, this also affected my painting style. Instead of frenzied sketching and coloured pencils, I began working in oils, a medium that demands a lot of patience, but I enjoyed the versatility and the effects made possible by the slow-drying paint.

The Fitz Gallery consisted of three whitewashed rooms with arched ceilings in a renovated Arab house on the edge of Neveh Tzedek, an artsy Tel Aviv neighbourhood. In the main room, which faced the entrance and was larger than the other two, I hung my recent paintings. Many of these were depictions of gates and doors and entranceways, windows and porticoes, which I painted with such near-photographic accuracy that there were people who thought that they were actually photographs that I'd gone over with a brush. Whenever I thought I'd do a self-portrait, like any self-respecting artist, I found myself painting the entrance to my house, as if it were only that far and no further that I would allow myself to be exposed. Or sometimes it was the porch, or the view from a window.

In the room on the left, we hung the portraits that I'd sketched. Hundreds of portraits of passersby, old men and pedlars in Carmel Market in Tel Aviv, old women with baskets in Jerusalem's Mahaneh Yehudah Market, Hasidim in buses, girls on university lawns. I sketched very quickly, and after one look I never needed my model any longer, as the lines were already engraved on my mind. Most of the drawings were made on the pages of a medium-sized sketchbook that I took everywhere I went from the time I started studying and began to see myself as a professional artist. I also carried a few mechanical pencils with leads of various thicknesses, and some fountain pens. Sometimes my sketching attracted girls who sensed that they'd been caught by my gaze and my pencil. This could have been a very good pick-up technique, but I never made use of it after my drawings of Niki were tossed into my cab, and I'd tossed them out again.

In the smaller room on the right I insisted on placing my Israman comics, over the objections of the gallery owner. He argued that they were childish, nationalistic, and a lot of other similar adjectives, but that didn't matter to me – precisely because of my social milieu and what was going on in the country at the time. It had taken me a whole semester of my first year at Bezalel to realize that my military service could be a minus, rather than the plus I assumed it would be. Bezalel was, perhaps, a cross-section of Israeli society, but the nature of the fine arts department was a little different, and in the unspoken hierarchy that existed among its students I was only one level above the special forces veterans who were the lowest of the low – and there were very few of those. After another two semesters, I had just about internalized that an officer-artist was a peculiar two-headed creature, a person who had to be afflicted with some degree of schizophrenia. For after all, everyone knows that an artist is a sensitive soul, humane, and a lover of humanity, a cosmopolitan who carries the world's suffering on his shoulders, whereas an officer is an obtuse, misanthropic, nationalistic person who only adds to the world's misery.

Moreover, the former is an absent-minded dreamer, while the latter is a practical, focused man, and the two could never live under one roof together.

No one asked me what I was doing at Bezalel. Just like my army-service, I took art school as a given. What I did best was drawing, what I enjoyed most was drawing, much of the little that I had to say I said in my drawings (after I'd finished with my comics), and it was obvious that what I wanted to study was art. At the best art school in the country, of course, and that's what Bezalel was made out to be. I had an accurate hand and a good eye even before I went to high school, where it was clear that I'd major in art. My parents were more interested in my second major, biology, perhaps because they hoped I'd become a doctor, or an agronomist like my father. But I was only interested in biology because I had a distinct sense, from the time I was a boy, that like any other animal I was a machine: I wanted to understand how that machine worked and what made it go. At the time, I painted a lot of animals, and animal-human hybrids. My apes in funny poses with human faces – especially if they looked like one of our teachers – were a big hit with my friends.

I arrived at Bezalel more prepared than most of the other students in the department, and no one had any reservations about the level of my work, but that didn't make me popular. I didn't understand why they had a problem with me or what attracted them to the opposite type, of whom there were plenty: guys who were all thumbs and had very little talent, but wore long coats and long scarves and preferably had long hair too.

My graduate studies for the most part took place in an artists' workshop complex in south Tel Aviv, which was always abandoned by all its denizens whenever there was some protest somewhere for or against something that was either vital or fatal to democracy or peace. I would go on working alone in the deserted studio, and my fellow students drew their own conclusions about me.

Apparently, it was not only my unfashionable patriotism that stopped me from being "one of the gang" but also my positions on art in general and painting in particular. I'd always believed that an accurate hand and a sharp eye were essential to an artist, whereas here I discovered that these were no more than marginal elements in what was perceived as artistic skill. My teachers and fellow students would speak of "the meeting point between the world of art and postmodernist theories", on "stratification and variation in the world of art" – phrases that found expression in abstract paintings and sculptures or spectacular installations, behind which there was neither skill nor true philosophical depth.

I was a little surprised when I found that the various curators and gallery managers I spoke to about the possibility of showing my work knew not only about my "conservative" style but also more about my politics than I did myself. And it's well known that a conservative or, heaven forfend, a nationalistic-minded person (or a fascist, to use the explicit epithet in use hereabouts), is a ruffian, and his hand must be pretty rough too, so it cannot be that his pictures are beautiful, or subtle, or worthy.

I don't think of myself as a conservative and, although I have never marched in a Gay Pride parade or taken part in any kind of women's-lib or homo-lesbian happening, I am not perturbed by any orientation, religion, "ism" or conduct that doesn't harm anyone else. And at least since the end of my adolescence, when I stopped making my Israman comics, I had never been nationalistic. It was clear to me that I must give my utmost during my military service, because I never had any doubt that without a strong army our state could not survive.

I served in the combat engineering corps because I wasn't accepted for the pilots' course. I never put in for special ops units because I'm thickset and I find running long distances difficult. I didn't want to go into the tank corps because of my fragmentary childhood memories of my father in hospital and the years-long rehab process he underwent after being wounded during the Yom Kippur War in October 1973. Taking all this into account, the best place I could serve was in combat engineering.

I never let my opinions cross my lips, because I knew how superficial they would sound, and I wasn't articulate enough to argue with my colleagues, who were all absolutely certain that the evils of the occupation of Palestinian lands were to blame for the absence of peace and brotherhood in our region. For them, and to a certain extent for me too, the period prior to the Six-Day War in June 1967, before those lands were conquered but when peace was as far off as ever, was shrouded in a fog of ignorance.

But I was "a child of the winter of '73", in the words of an Israeli song. My parents conceived me in pain, after my father came home, a broken, weary and burned man. He had been wounded when his tank was hit. He changed tanks and was wounded again, earning a citation that he never bothered to collect. Secrecy enveloped that period, and the cloud it emitted and that enveloped my childhood contained an anxiety that merged with the anxieties of my father's parents who survived Nazi death camps when they were young and met after World War II in a displaced persons camp. There they conceived twins, only one of whom apparently survived. My father never ever mentioned his brother, and I assumed that he'd died over there, in the camp. For me, as a child, Auschwitz and Majdanek were links in the same chain as the battle to block the invading Egyptian forces in Sinai. My grandparents' survival and the wounding and heroism of my father were only elusive specks of light in a dark continuum of pain.

"We don't speak about that," my father told me emphatically when I asked any question that threatened to penetrate the invisible circle of secrecy. From childhood, I was trained not to ask.

Once, when I was stealing a glimpse at my parents' photo albums, I found a whole package of cropped photographs. In each one, my father was with one of his parents and the other was missing, but here and there a little hand had stolen into the remaining half. I took them to my mother. She put her finger to her lips and I was blocked even before the question left my mouth. During the shiva mourning period after my grandmother died, I found some photographs of her and my grandfather in the drawer of her bedside cabinet, in the "White City" of Tel Aviv in the 1950s. They looked young and lean and were holding two babies but, as I was wondering which one was my father, he came and snatched the pictures away, almost violently. I never saw them again and I never dared to ask about them. I understood only that the death of the twin brother, who would have been my uncle, had happened later than I'd thought and apparently had been all the more painful.

These things happened during my early childhood and my memories of them are blurred. Auschwitz and Majdanek, and the near-destruction of the Third Jewish Commonwealth (as the historically minded call the modern State of Israel) in the Yom Kippur War, were the real story, overshadowing the mysterious details of the family story, which took second place behind the sense of menace, if not terror, that hovered around those events. The cloud that enveloped me from my early childhood was a cloud of existential apprehension that allowed for only one certainty: if we are not strong, if we are not prepared to fight, we will be destroyed.

And so, instead of drawing landscapes or girls, I drew Israman. And although I was slow-moving and a little clumsy, strong but not athletic, I became a combat soldier. For the sake of my father, my grandfather, the state and the nation. "The state" in this sense was my neighbour-hood in Haifa, and "the nation" was my extended family, perhaps also neighbours and friends. For me it was natural, although it might sound a little strange, that my state and nation included my friends from Abbas Street, chiefly Arabs, with whom I spent most of my time. And then we moved away from the street that climbs from the lower city towards Stella Maris, the Carmelite Monastery on the hill. For two years we lived in Canada, where my father did advanced studies in forestry, and when we returned to Israel, it was to a neighbourhood high on Mt. Carmel.

I wasn't concerned with finding definitions for my views, but because I never thought that our country or our people were better than the others, and even on the matter of the occupied territories I had very pragmatic opinions, I certainly was not nationalistic. I could have been defined as security-minded, but only people with fine judgement could see a difference between the two, and my fellow students saved their fine judgement for other matters.

My artistic talents were, needless to say, more clearly seen in my later works, but at the age of twenty-eight, about thirteen years after I drew them and ten years after I joined the army, and when I was almost recognized as an artist, I did not want to give up on the content of my comics. In one of them, Israman appeared on the railway platform, as I imagined it, from which grandpa and grandma were being transported to the camps. He smashed the heads of the Germans and liberated all the Jews gathered there to be sent to die. In another comic, he had apparently arrived late, because he hovered in front of the moving train, blocked it with all his might, and released the Jews imprisoned in the freight cars. And when he was even later, he turned up in the death camp itself, knocking the guards out and leading the inmates through the snowy forest to a safe haven.

I also focused on the War of Independence and the Six- Day War, and in my last comic book on the Yom Kippur War. In the latter, Israman managed to soar over the Suez Canal, bodily diverting the shells that had been mauling the Israeli forces crossing the waterway. Then he used an Egyptian landing craft to scoop water from the canal and douse a certain burning tank and save the life of one of its crew, a man whose face I could have drawn in the dark, and whose groans of pain still echoed in my mind.

I liked Israman, I believed in the goals he was fighting to achieve, and I did not want to give him up. The negotiation with the gallery owner almost fell through, with him trying to explain how much damage it would cause me, but when I stood my ground he agreed.

The photocopies of the comic books were fixed to polystyrene boards and I hung them myself, while the curator of the gallery was responsible for the rest. She was a wild-haired redhead, with large breasts and no bra, who for some reason thought it was a given that while we were hanging the exhibition together at night, we'd also hang onto each other for a while.

Although I'd already been with Dolly for a long time, I didn't think this was so very wrong. Since my marvellous night with Niki I had completely separated sex and love, and what I had was only sex. Casual, student-type sex, and relationships which lasted until the girl realized we weren't going anywhere. And if she stayed with me for a while, it was apparently because, after all, I wasn't bad looking, my face was even quite handsome, and I was also interesting to talk to. They had no reason to run away. But love never waxed, and the sex eventually waned.

Three years earlier I had celebrated my twenty-fifth birthday with my parents and sisters at a restaurant. My mother asked, with extreme delicacy, if I didn't have "someone serious". I said no, and she never asked again. I knew that my parents saw a special importance in generational continuity, but it looked as if they would have to make do with my sisters' offspring. That's what I said, but my sisters were already Ben-Abou and Rosenstein, and my taciturn father asked, "So, what about our name, Simhoni?"

"But dad, it was you who changed the name to Simhoni. You broke away from everything that had gone before, so why does the name matter at all?" I must have been happy with this name, and never asked what it had been back in Europe.

My father looked at me sadly, disappointed that I didn't understand. I knew that he was on the verge of saying that what the Nazis had started I was continuing. But his silence said it all. What was I to do to console him? I simply was not able to fall in love. Certainly not enough to think about marriage and children who would bear his family name. I couldn't think of a logical reason for this, just as there was no logical reason for my sudden infatuation with Niki and that wild sex with her. But logic, it seems, isn't what counts. There, in Tokyo, there had evidently been a kind of convergence of various factors: that "abroad" feeling that naturally intensifies emotions, my distance and disconnection from the person I had been, my loneliness, my sense of being lost, and of course Niki's loveliness, her gentleness and diffidence that contrasted so starkly with her startling openness and forthrightness. Niki was now a distant memory that almost never bothered me but, if it had not been for those thirty-six hours in Tokyo, perhaps I would never have known that I could feel so differently and I would have stuck with one or other of my girlfriends. They were really nice.

It was then that Dolly turned up. She met most of my demands. A good-looking young woman, with both feet (and long, slender legs) on the ground, a captivating smile, and a practicality that was lacking in most of the female artists who'd surrounded me in recent years. She was an investment adviser, an area about which I knew nothing. This did not make her any less otherworldly than the girls of the fine arts faculty, certainly no less exciting a lover. I'd been summoned to a meeting with her by my bank, where she worked, and she told me that it was a waste to leave my money lying in a low-interest deposit account, and that there were much more interesting and profitable things that could be done with it. When I asked what, she asked me if I was daring and ready to take risks. One thing led to another, and we made a date for our next meeting, but away from the bank. I asked if this was standard procedure between an investment adviser and a bank customer, and she said no, but she'd make an exception this time.

After a few months, I had to reply – to her, to myself, to my parents' unasked question – that it seemed to be as good as it gets, and we moved in together.

I am quite an adaptable type, at least when it comes to relationships. My demands from others, and from myself, are minimal, as are my expectations. Most small details don't matter at all to me – what we'll have to eat, what film we'll watch – and I think I'm easy to get along with. Dolly and I got on well. We had similar tastes, she liked my few friends, and I liked the few friends she had. We were a stable couple, and I asked myself if this was enough.

Despite the Niki episode, as I called that affair when I discussed it with myself, I am no romantic, and my attitude to love is quite mundane, one might say. To my mind each of my emotions served a biological purpose: just as my survival was served by fear on the one hand, and anger and aggression on the other, I assumed that this was true about love as well. Clearly, it's purpose was to speed up the mating process (when it emerges as falling in love and as lust) and to make coupling easier (when it takes the form of a calmer and more stable love). There was no falling in love here, there was lust, and there were feelings of intimacy which in my opinion made a long-term family relationship possible. But was this enough?

When Dolly brought it up I told her exactly what I felt. She cried a little, but understood, and she obliged by giving me the time I needed to decide. On the first anniversary of our relationship, she brought it up again. I promised to reply soon. I was busy with the upcoming exhibition, and the school year that had just begun had saddled me with nine art classes a week at the three high schools where I had been teaching since I graduated from art school. I didn't have the time to weigh up my feelings.

The quickie with the redheaded curator was the only time I cheated on Dolly, and strangely I didn't feel bad about it afterwards. But I did feel bad about not feeling bad. As if it was quite natural for something like this to happen if a man and a woman were alone in a small room, in the middle of the night, and they brushed up against each other, once with his head against her buttocks when she was on a ladder hanging something on the wall, and once with her face against his genitals as she was handing him a picture and he was on the ladder. Totally insulated from their relationships outside of this insulated room. Only after it was over – it was done standing up, wild, strong and fast – it occurred to me that I didn't even know if she was married. When I got home late that night, I was so aroused that I made love to Dolly while she was half asleep.

It was clear to me that this incident had, somehow, to affect my decision about the future of our relationship, but I still didn't know how. I put off, for the time being, the possibility of telling Dolly, not because it could have made her get up and leave, but because I thought she didn't deserve to be hurt. And strangely, when it was over and Dolly dozed off on top of me, clinging to me securely and lovingly, I also felt, perhaps for the first time, that I was in love with her. I asked myself if I wasn't confusing it with pity or a need for forgiveness. But at that moment, after two sexual encounters like these, and the day before my exhibition opened, what I felt most was that I needed some sleep.

The opening launch of my exhibition began as a joyful occasion for me, my parents and my sisters, although my mother, embarrassed that I was still unmarried, insisted on telling anyone who would listen that Dolly and I were "getting married, only they haven't yet set the date". They also didn't quite get my attraction to painting and they hadn't really been proud of it, but now they suddenly had something to boast about: a solo show in a Tel Aviv gallery! For them, provincial Haifaites that they were, this was something like a one-man exhibition in an important New York gallery: they even had invited some of their friends to the opening. My sisters and their families, whose celebrations I always attended whereas this was my own very first "event," were very happy and told me they had bought their kids new clothes for the occasion.

Friends from Bezalel were also glad for me and told me they would come. We weren't burdened by baggage from our differences while we were studying, because I'm not the type to bear grudges and they had no cause for grudges – even then I'd lacked the competitiveness that made others fake a smile whenever teachers praised someone else's artwork. We'd kept in touch, perhaps because, as they said about me, "You can always rely on him." In the years since graduation I had helped some of them erect installations all over the country, and others to find posts as art teachers, after receiving more offers to my job applications – with portfolios of sketches – than I could handle myself.

My teenage students at the three Tel Aviv high schools also said they would come. They saw me as an oddball who insisted upon teaching them the craft side of art, but was at the same time open to their own artistic quirks, as long as they came at the right time: my tenth graders knew I was a slave-driver when it came to copying pictures and I wouldn't allow them to do anything abstract; first let them learn how to draw a horse that doesn't look like a donkey and a dog that doesn't look like a fox. To this end, they would choose a work to copy, draw a grid over it and another on their blank paper, and start copying, square after square, only bigger. When they had acquired sufficient skill at this, I would insist that they keep mixing their paints until the shade they obtained was identical to the original. Then I'd work with them on still-life sketches, taking pains with each line, with the perspective, the depth and the play of light and shadow, ensuring that the shades of the greys and blacks were in the correct places; especially so with those who had opted to specialize in drawing, and who could therefore create volume only by means of lines, light and shadow.

In eleventh grade, I allowed them to deviate from realism and precision, but I demanded explanations for what they did: each line had to have its reason. By the twelfth grade, when the students possessed the skills and an awareness of what they were doing, I gave them a lot of freedom, albeit guided freedom. I wanted to see some correspondence between the abstract idea and the execution: the results were excellent.

Our relationship at Shevah-Mofet school, went far beyond the teacher-student paradigm. The students mostly belonged to immigrant families from the former Soviet Union. Close to the end of the 2001 school year, there was a suicide-terrorist attack on a nightclub at the Tel Aviv Dolphinarium: twenty-one youngsters were killed and over a hundred injured. Seven of the dead were from that school, including one of my students, a drawing and graphics major, and one recent graduate, whom I considered to be a fine artist. As most of the students and teachers were not born in Israel, it very quickly became clear to me that I would have to take a central part in the talks with the students that were held in the aftermath of the atrocity. Not only to hug and console them, but also to describe the harsh reality they now found themselves part of, a reality that even I found difficult to grasp. Who could fathom the depth of the hatred and murderousness of a person who decides to give himself an afterlife in Paradise at the expense of kids waiting in line at a discotheque. Some of the youngsters had moved to Israel only a few years before in order to make a better life for themselves, and they now found themselves in the middle of a far worse tragedy than anything that was likely to have happened to them in Russia.

That whole summer I continued to visit the families and the students, consoling, explaining, trying to portray Israel's situation in a manner that would enable them not to regret the step they had taken by coming to Israel, although I myself could not argue that the Zionist dream was worth the life of someone's child. From the broad, national point of view, perhaps it was, certainly for a nation that had undergone humiliations, expulsions, pogroms, and ultimately the Holocaust. But not from the painful, personal point of view of a family that had lost a son or daughter, especially as in some cases these were single-parent families, and the dead boy or girl was an only child.

That summer drew to a close, a new school year began and halfway through, in March 2002, I was called up for reserve duty in Operation Defensive Shield against terrorist cells in Nablus and Jenin in the West Bank. The campaign followed a suicide bomber's attack on a Passover celebration at the Park Hotel in Netanyah that resulted in many deaths and injuries, and I felt that I was fighting for my students. By the time of my exhibition, the operation had ended, and for some of my students I remained the dominant Israeli figure that they had a connection with, and now they were coming to see my show.

Some friends from my reserve unit also accepted my invitation, including some with whom I had also served during my regular army service, and who were like brothers to me and to each other, heart and soul. Like my art student friends, they also didn't understand me, but from an entirely different angle: how could a practical man like me, a brave soldier, be an artist and an art teacher in civilian life, and not the manager of some company, or at least a lawyer.

I also expected to see those of my childhood and teenage friends that I still had, and others I had picked up on the way. I'd also invited ex-girlfriends with whom I was still on good terms.

The Fitz Gallery shared the Arab house and courtyard with a restaurant on the right and an architectural firm on the left. On the evening of my opening, the restaurant put fewer tables for diners in the courtyard, to make room for two long tables, one laden with bottles of white and red wine and plastic glasses, and the other with different kinds of salty snacks. I waived my right to taste the wines and left it up to the owners to choose, because I knew little about wine: all dry red wines were equally unpalatable to me, and all white wines equally OK. Once I told Dolly that to me the whole wine thing, the sniff, the swirl and the sip, was nothing more than showing-off and she told me that I shouldn't judge others on the basis of my own lack of good taste. Hummus, fresh brown bread and pickles are enough for you, she said, and she was right.

But unlike my palate, my eye was discriminating and I could see when

Dolly, or any other woman, was well dressed, although my own taste in clothes was, like my taste in food and wines, simple: jeans and t-shirt in summer and corduroys and a flannel shirt in winter. Dolly forced me to freshen up my wardrobe before the exhibition and for the first time in years I went to the mall and came home with a pair of smart trousers and two smart shirts. Dolly wore a long, clinging, purple dress that she had bought for the opening. She looked wonderful and for a moment I could imagine her in a white dress, under the wedding canopy, and even with a little tummy a little while later. Over her objections ("You're getting it creased") I lay her down on the sofa in the living room, and we produced one of our more successful performances. But when she saw that the dress was soiled she was upset and I could only empathize.

We agreed that I should go to the gallery first, and she would try to remove the mark and come a little later. People would in any case be trickling in gradually in the first hour or so, she said.

Although I arrived half an hour before the set time, I wasn't the first. My parents were already there with two couples of friends; they had all come together by train from Haifa. A dozen students from one of my classes had also arrived. In a trickle, as Dolly had foreseen, more and more people turned up. When the main room in the gallery was quite full, the back doors were opened and the guests went out into the courtyard where the refreshments were laid out.

You don't touch the wine, I admonished my students, but as a dozen or so of my art school pals had also turned up, there was no fear the bottles would stay full. The kids tore into the snacks instead. There was a happy mood, lots of hugs and compliments, and as it grew darker, some journalists showed up. They asked me to say a few words, and I phoned Dolly to ask her where she was. She told me she was at the central bus station and was about to get on the bus to the gallery, but that I should go on without her. Mum told me that Tzippi, my big sister had been held up by her little daughters, but that Aliza, my younger sister would be there in a moment with her baby.

A TV crew, which had already shot my paintings and a short interview with me standing next to the Israman comics, told me they had another event to cover, so I took the mic to make a little speech, and they turned on their spotlights. The crowd gradually quietened down.

"I can see a lot of familiar and friendly faces," I began, surveying my audience until I focused on my parents. "My beloved parents, who allowed me to follow the path laid out by my talents. [Sporadic applause.] My esteemed teachers, who taught me so much of what I know [More applause, mainly from the Bezalel graduates.] My friends from art school, the army, and my childhood. [One of the latter group gave one loud clap, and then stopped.] My dear students, from whom I also learn new things every day. [They cheered when I mentioned the names of their schools.] My beloved sisters aren't here yet, with their husbands and children, and neither is Dolly, the woman in my life. There are also some more dear friends who said they'd come and some students, who are probably on their way. I'll make another speech for all of them later on."

As I looked out at the crowd, I spotted an unfamiliar face, someone who had apparently just come in and was standing near the back – a burly man with a round head and some grey in his hair.

I breathed in, before beginning my actual address, in which I intended to expound on my views on art, beginning, perhaps surprisingly, with Israman, "in whose figure much of what has shaped me so far may be seen, and which may explain why I am here, in the broad sense of the word 'here.'"

Before I had breathed out, the "boom" came.

There was no mistaking what it was. Not in the midst of a series of terrorist bombings, not with the strength of the blast. It could not have been far away, because in addition to the noise, we also felt the shock-waves. Windows rattled, the wine glasses on the tables and the pictures on the walls shifted. And a moment later, before I gathered my wits, beepers started buzzing, the journalists' first, and then the police and ambulance sirens began rending the air, from all directions.

"I'll stop now, until we know what's going on," I said in a totally steady voice.

"Speech, speech!" some of my friends called out, and some others also demanded that I continue. In spite of the bomb, some hecklers insisted, "We mustn't let them ruin our celebrations."

The ability of people to carry on living in a bubble when the liquid on which it is floating is contaminated and mixed with blood had always perplexed me. Perhaps it is normal, and my inability to do so and accept terror as part of life is my own personal problem. This inability of mine had also addicted me to the news. It was as if everything that happened was my concern, as if it happened to me, and as if a great deal depended on me. A kind of sense of responsibility in my bloodstream doesn't let me cut myself off. But this time, the decision was mine.

"A quarter of an hour's break," I announced. "Then we'll see."

I had a very strong feeling that we wouldn't be going on. The central bus station was nearby, Dolly had been there only minutes before, my sisters and their families were passing close by it, my students and friends may have been changing buses there on their way to the gallery. And that was the direction the blast had come from, I was quite sure.

"We can't hang around," the TV reporter told me.

"Off you go, and let's meet again, on happy occasions," I said, in the phrase that Jews use after funerals. Then he leaned towards me and whispered that there had been a suicide-bombing on a bus leaving the central station. That's what he'd just been told on his beeper.

There wasn't a TV or a radio in the gallery, but there was one in the restaurant. The owner was in a tizzy because his three Palestinian workers had run away and left him alone with only one waitress. I drew a chair up to the TV and switched it on. A Channel 1 reporter was describing the scene as he neared the site, huffing and puffing, and in a moment there was no more room for illusions. The charred wreckage of the bus came into view in the distance, in the middle of Allenby Street, near the Great Synagogue. Cars were in flames. Bleeding and burned people were being moved to safety by passersby, and the first estimates of the numbers of dead and wounded were being made.

Next to me, I suddenly noticed the big man with the greying hair.

"I came to see you about something entirely different," he said in a deep voice, leaning over my chair. "And in any case I only meant to give you my business card." I didn't look at the card he gave me. "Call me when you can," he said as he straightened up, squeezed my shoulder with a large, warm hand, and walked away from me with a heavy step and a slight stoop. He looked as if he was in his forties, but was carrying the whole world on his back.

Some of my teachers and friends came into the restaurant.

"Mickey," one of them said, as they gazed at the horrors on the screen, "you've got to carry on. This is the biggest day of your life. Don't let them screw it up for you."

Once again I dialled Dolly's number. If she answers, I thought, and if my sisters turn up, then perhaps I'll be able to continue. But I couldn't finish dialling. The mobile phone networks were down.

"Come on, the opening of your first exhibition is a never-to-be repeated event," said the head of the Bezalel fine arts department. But everyone looked as if they were there to console me rather than celebrate with me; after all, a lot of people had been hurt, and whether they were my relatives and guests or not – they were my people.

I went back into the gallery. The mood was completely different. Many of the guests were trying to speak on their mobiles. All of a sudden I saw that my sisters were there, with their husbands and children, and tears of relief welled up in my eyes.

"I heard you were in the middle of something," said Aliza, after wiping my cheek with a tissue. "You should always finish what you begin."

"A thousand scenarios went through my head because you weren't here," I told her, and only then did I realize that I'd been thinking in great detail about how I'd behave with my parents if we learned that either of my sisters, or any of their daughters, had been killed in the explosion. Would I move them in with me, or would I move in with them? And if a sister and her husband were killed, and not the girls, what then? Would my other sister take them? Would I adopt them? Would Dolly agree? Amazing how many different thoughts run through one's mind at times like these.

Under pressure from the crowd, I returned to the microphone. Without the TV floodlights it was easier, but my words were briefer and very different from what I had planned.

"We are people just like everyone else. People who want to get up in the morning, have their coffee, go to work and do something they enjoy, return home to people they love, and to sleep peacefully. Some of us like working in technology, or driving a cab, teaching, or painting. Each according to his own inclination and ability. We want to live in a country that will provide us with an environment of physical security. But we are not like other people everywhere, and this country isn't like others."

I began to notice perplexity, perhaps some resentment, in my audience, especially among my friends. But the spate of words continued.

"In no other country does an exhibition opening take place in the shadow of a terror attack. There's no other country where an artist can be an artist for only eleven months a year, because in the twelfth month he has to do reserve duty on the borders. And if there weren't enough people like him, nobody would be able to paint here, or do anything else, for those eleven other months."

I managed to refrain from saying anything about those who do paint twelve months a year, oblivious to what I was talking about. Some of them were there in my audience.

"There aren't many artists who began their careers by drawing comics of a national superhero, a hero who doesn't busy himself with saving individuals from danger, but one who saves his nation. And this sprang directly from the biographies of his parents and grandparents."

At this, there was some unexpected applause.

"At a moment like this, I don't think it's right for me to expound on my artistic ideas. I intended to talk about the pictures in this main room, but now it seems that the little room over there with the comics is much more relevant. During that period I never asked myself what the correct style was, or which the preferred style would be, what themes would be a success with curators or with buyers, or worst of all with the arty crowd. It was precisely then, at the age of thirteen, fourteen, fifteen, younger than my students today, that my hand, head and heart worked completely and honestly together."

I signalled to one of the students to bring me a glass of wine.

"Some say, the party must go on. Maybe. That life must go on? Yes, that sounds better," I accepted the correction made by one of the guests. My wine came, and I raised the glass. "I want to drink a toast to that combination of hand, head, and heart, which is also the combination of our roots: personal – our parents; local – this country; social – all the dear people who came to celebrate with me. That is the head, and that is the heart, and it is only from them that the hand that draws should come."

To lukewarm applause, I drank the wine. There was no more happiness. In the last row, the man with the big head stood out. He had apparently decided to stay, and he nodded to me in a sign of respect and agreement. I dialled Dolly's number again, but there was no reply. Some of my pupils told me they'd heard that friends on the way here were on the bus that blew up. The head of the fine arts department asked to speak to me alone. He told me that there were some fourth year students who were coming to the show from Jerusalem and had not been heard from. He and everyone else were very anxious; only a month and a half before students had been killed in a terrorist bombing in the Frank Sinatra Cafeteria of the Hebrew University on Mount Scopus, where Bezalel was also located.

From one moment to the next, the number of people who had been on their way here and with whom contact had been lost, was growing. When Dolly still didn't reply, I said goodbye to my parents and sisters, quickly apologized to my friends and guests, and walked to the site of the bombing, where only the smoking wreck of the bus was standing, and then to the hospitals to which the casualties had been evacuated.

About three hours later, after a nightmare journey full of blood and fear and cries of anger and grief from people whose loved ones had been on the bus, I was sitting on a bench outside the trauma unit of Wolfson Hospital in Holon, south of Tel Aviv. Inside, I understood, doctors were fighting to save Dolly's life. Next to me were groups of relatives of other injured people. All ages and ethnic groups, mothers and fathers, siblings, loved ones. There were also two sets of parents of students of mine who had been on the way to my show and had instead ended up in hospital.

The list of casualties hanging on the door of the emergency ward was smaller than the number of the groups of relatives waiting for news. Most had not found the names of their missing ones on any list but knew that many of the badly wounded and killed had not yet been identified. Some went to Ichilov Hospital, in north Tel Aviv, others had given up and had gone to the morgue at Abu Kabir, to see if their relatives were lying there. But Dolly's name was on the list of wounded although, as I discovered later, by the time I got there she was already dead.

When I was called in to identify her, the doctor warned me it would be hard. "I've seen dead people," I said, and I had really seen mangled and charred bodies. But they had not been the remains of my lover, and I collapsed when I saw the awful sight. The doctor and two nurses dragged me to a cubicle and after I recovered my senses, I left. Not in words, not even in a clearly defined feeling, I vowed that I would take revenge.

Later on, I put my hand in my pocket and found the card given to me by the man with the big head. On it, in a small frame, there was the emblem of the State of Israel, a menorah, and an olive branch, and under it only a name, Udi Barkai, and a phone number.

2.

A small house in the Kiryah

DURING THE TRADITIONAL shiva, the seven days of mourning that I spent with Dolly's family, I gave no thought to Udi and his business card. The Jewish mourning customs of this warm family of immigrants from Morocco enfolded me too, and I got used to the protracted wailing of Dolly's grandmother and even to the chorus of female wailers who turned up for the first few days, until Dolly's father silenced them, I don't know why – perhaps for my benefit. The flavours that Dolly had sneaked, smidgen by smidgen, into the meals she cooked for the two of us made full-blown appearances here, in both taste and aroma. Her parents and brothers and sisters accepted me as if I had married her, and only infrequently a distant relative muttered something like, "It's a pity she never got to stand under the wedding canopy," only to be hushed up, with all eyes turned on me. In the grief that I felt with my entire being, there was indeed sorrow over the way I had dragged things out and denied her those moments of joy that she deserved – yes, wearing a white gown under the huppah, as banal as it sounds, as well as having denied our parents their moment of joy.

I sat with them from morning to evening, and when they spread out the mattresses to prepare to go to sleep all crowded together in their small apartment I left and went to the hospital to visit two of my students who had lost legs in the blast, and a friend from Bezalel who'd been badly burned all over his body. I thought of the way statistics always emphasize the number of fatalities, but the families they leave behind scarred with grief are far more numerous, as are the wounded, some of whom are disfigured and disabled for life. Men serving under me had been wounded in Lebanon. For the first year or two they were war-wounded heroes. But they soon became piteous young men and after a while "cripples" who get

41

in the way and aren't nice to look at. And when they are old and poor, no one will know if they were hurt storming the enemy under fire, or were victims of a terrorist attack, or just had bad luck in some accident. The dead were dead, and that was tragic, but their families and the people wounded by the bomb on the bus would bear the consequences of the terrorist attack for their whole lives, long after the incident disappeared into the overall statistics of Intifada attacks, long after the Intifada itself was swallowed up in the tangled history of the Israeli-Arab conflict.

An old friend of my parents had been in a car next to the bus, and was blinded by the blast. I went with them to visit him, and afterwards my father said, with the harsh realism of a man who has seen everything, that the man would have been better off dead. As I was driving my parents back to Haifa, my mother sighed and said she'd never have dreamed that you wouldn't even be able to have an exhibition of paintings in peace in this country. She then murmured, "In the end it will turn out that Li'or was right." Before I could ask who Li'or was, my father threw a quick look at her, and at me, and rebuked her, saying that they'd had fifty-odd pretty good years here. "True, it wasn't easy for my parents," he said. "They were youngsters and had to begin a new life in a new country after everything they had been through, and I've gone through a few wars, but altogether it's been worth it here. Certainly in comparison with the alternative, we've seen where that led to."

I thought that his fate, and the fate of his parents had been harder than that of my mother's family, but they didn't have an easy time of it either. Her grandfather and grandmother had been murdered in the massacre of Jewish residents of Hebron by their Arab neighbours in 1929, her parents were spared and taken to Jerusalem, but had endured the siege of the Jewish part of that city in 1948. During her own troubled childhood in the divided city, in the Musrara neighbourhood on the border, she couldn't put the light on in her bedroom because of the danger from Arab snipers.

I didn't go back to the exhibition during the shiva, and at the time I didn't really care what was happening at the Fitz. The TV culture crew put together a longish report, in which my pictures were almost hidden from view, and I was shown beginning to speak just before the explosion, and the disconcerted guests appeared on camera. Because of its news value, some of the report was screened in the weekly roundup during the Friday evening newscast. One critic, who had left before the attack, filed a favourable review which ran in her paper's weekend edition. Some of my friends who came to the shiva to console me also said the show was excellent, and the Bezalel people told me I must carry on, as if they realized what was going on inside my head.

During my nights alone in our apartment after my hospital visits, an awareness was taking shape that a chapter of my life had drawn to a close. The exhibition had ended a period during which I had been preoccupied with myself, my dreams, my efforts to refine my talent. I saw no sin in this; my desire to make the most of my artistic ability was only natural, just as that ability was itself natural. Both were part of me, of what I was. But now it was the turn of other parts of me to be fulfilled. I recalled my own words about the roots from which one must set out on one's path, and I knew that from now on my path would be different. I contacted the gallery and asked the owner to pack up the pictures and send them to my apartment. I never looked at the paintings again.

One of the condolence callers during the shiva at Dolly's parents' home was the commander of my reserve brigade. He was a man whose performance during the fighting in Jenin in Operation Defensive Shield I admired, and whom I had got to know when we were still in Lebanon. The admiration was apparently mutual, as he had appointed me commander of the engineering company in his brigade. I told him that if I was needed, I was ready to do a long stint of reserve duty, and what I wanted to have in my hand now was a rifle, and not a paintbrush. He offered to make me deputy commander of the brigade's reconnaissance battalion, which was made up of my company, the recon company and an anti-tank company. These specialized units, he said, did most of the brigade's work. "And in another year, Gadi, the battalion commander will be leaving, and you can have the job."

I toyed with the idea for some time, but wasn't sure I would be capable of commanding a battalion. I doubted I would be physically able to do it, and I was also not at all sure that the military would hold my interest for very long. Most of our activity in recent years had been policing duties in the Palestinian areas, a necessary duty but one that I didn't relish.

The figure of the mysterious burly stranger at the opening began cropping up in my thoughts. Intuitive messages about his possible affiliation flashed across my mind, but I rejected them. He couldn't have known before he appeared at the exhibition what was going to happen, that I would want to change direction. I remembered which pair of trousers I'd left his card in. I hadn't worn them since then. The card had waited there patiently. I called him.

The attractive house was in Tel Aviv's Kiryah – the precinct where many government offices are located. Probably built by the Templers, a German Protestant sect who'd settled in the Holy Land in the early 1900s. The house was surrounded by a high wire fence, and its walls were covered with ivy. A guard at the entrance glanced at my ID card and let me in. A friendly receptionist directed me to the second floor. I climbed the rather shaky stairs and at the top the door to Udi Barkai's office was wide open. He stood up and hugged me, as if we were old pals. At that moment, I felt the ice in my veins beginning to thaw, ice that I had not really identified until then, and a small glimmer of warmth gradually spreading from my chest outwards. Udi was a large man, taller and broader than me, rather heavy, with thick arms and shoulders that looked very strong, and his handshake confirmed this impression. As I had observed earlier, his head was big, even beyond the proportions of his physique, and he needed – and had – a particularly powerful neck to carry it. His face was a web of wrinkles, more than his apparent age warranted, like a man who had been through a thing or two in his lifetime, but he had a pleasant smile and a twinkle in his eye.

"Coffee?"

I thought of the young woman downstairs who would get the order and then have to bring the coffee up, and I wanted to decline, but Udi caught my downward glance and said, "The kitchenette's right here, make yourself a cup the way you like it." It was as if he also knew that there was just about no one who could make coffee to suit my taste. Every size of cup needs a different amount of coffee, and sometimes I add a little or subtract a little, as if I know the precise number of grains, and pour the milk until the exact colour is obtained, taking the fat content into account. "And your coffee, that isn't showing-off?" Dolly's question suddenly popped into my mind, the one she asked when I insisted on making coffee myself, and a tear came into my eye. The steam coming off the cup gave me a good excuse for wiping it away, but the movement didn't escape Udi's observant eyes. He acted as if he'd seen nothing, poured himself a cup, and we went back to his spacious office.

It didn't look like a room where work was done. There was only a large, completely clear desk, an armchair on one side of it and an ordinary chair on the other, a low-slung sofa along one wall and a steel cabinet. The wide-open window, without bars, also didn't fit in with a secret government office. So perhaps it wasn't a secret government office?

"So where do you think you've come to?" Udi asked with a smile when he saw me looking around the room.

I was going to reply, but then I thought, why is he asking the questions and not me? After all, I'm not at some job interview, it was he who had asked me to come, and who was apparently interested in me.

"Let's go back a little," I said, also with a smile. "Why did you come to me?"

"We always go to the people we are interested in." By now I had a fairly clear idea of who the "we" was, so instead I asked, "Yes, but why me? And of all occasions, at the opening of an exhibition, when it looked as if I was finding my feet in my chosen occupation."

"It was important to watch you functioning in a crowd. I'm sorry that it ended the way it did."

"You know that were it not for the bomb I wouldn't have come here."

"There are very few people who we turn to, whatever stage they are at in their careers, who say no to us."

"You still haven't answered my question," I said.

"I'll answer right away. There's just one thing I have to know first."

"Nothing that's said here today will be leaked by me," I retorted rapidly, and Udi laughed.

"I know that. You're also going to sign a secrecy pledge right now," he said, taking a printed form out of a drawer and giving it to me, with the pen from his shirt pocket. I signed after a quick glance. I had no intention of revealing secrets. "But that is not what I wanted to ask. I want to know if you feel you've reached a crossroads and you are ready to take a new road."

"My brigade commander made a condolence call during the shiva. I told him I'd rather hold a rifle than a paintbrush," I said. "He suggested I go back into the army. But I've seen enough of that vicious cycle of terrorist attack, military operation, another attack."

This was true. Only half a year earlier, when my brigade had been called up to take part in Operation Defensive Shield, a bomb was detonated in the Matzah restaurant in Haifa, within earshot of my parents' home, and I was more anxious about them than they were about me.

"The army does a million important things," I continued, "but wars don't happen so often, and I don't like doing what the army does in the territories. I now have a personal score to settle with terrorism. That means, either the Shin Bet or the Mossad. I'd prefer the Mossad. A new road? Yes. For how long? I can't commit myself."

"At your gallery opening, you raised your glass and proposed a toast to the heart, the head and the hand. And your heart and your head are now telling your hand to hold a pistol," Udi summed up for me. His choice of the word "pistol" as distinct from "rifle" was certainly no accident.

This exchange reminded me of a biology paper I wrote in high school, about animals as machines for fighting and survival. All the animals which exist today are first and foremost survival experts, using techniques of fighting, retreating, camouflage, deception and attack. It made no sense to me that when a war was on my doorstep I should forget my own essence as a fighting and surviving machine and give myself over to one talent of mine – painting. But the truth was that I had come here because I had lost my woman. I said this, and Udi immediately replied.

"You've got to understand one important thing about Dolly," he said. "We are not trying to avenge her death. And if you join us, that will apply to you too. We are engaged in a struggle for the existence of the State of Israel. We have many enemies: the Iranians and their nuclear weapons project, the Syrian army, Hezbollah, Hamas. Palestinian terrorism is only one of the threats we face, and from our point of view, not the most important one. The people who killed Dolly are probably in the Palestinian territories, and the Shin Bet, the army and the police will look for them, as part of their efforts to prevent more terrorist attacks. We will not deal with that." Now it was definite: Udi was Mossad, and I was a candidate to join its ranks.

"But the Mossad does kill terrorists abroad. I don't understand what you are getting at," I objected.

Udi gazed deep into my eyes, his expression serious and searching. "I am not saying that when we run into a chance to settle an account we turn away from it. But we do not search for an individual because he has killed someone, we look for him only if he is still a threat. And that also applies to whoever killed Dolly. It is a global struggle, not a personal one. And I have to know that you can function within this framework."

I looked away when I thought that it was not at all sure that I would resist the temptation if at any stage of my job I discovered who'd been behind the bomb on the bus on Allenby, and I could get my hands on him. Udi realized very well what was going on in my head.

"Are you here to get revenge for Dolly's spilt blood, or to fight the enemies of the State of Israel?" was how he narrowed the issue down for me.

"To fight for Israel's survival," I said eventually. "But I'd be happy if that would include settling my personal account."

"And it is clear to you that this would be for the organization to decide, not you, both whether to settle that score at all and who the job should be assigned to?"

"Yes. I can live with that," I said after some thought, knowing full well that if such a moment arose, I would try with all my might, and do everything I could, to be there and to take an active part. But I knew that my joining the Mossad, if that was going to happen, extended far beyond the matter of my own private vengeance.

"Good, so now I'll save us something like eight to ten months of screening," said Udi with a sigh, but he was still eyeing me curiously, and perhaps a little sceptically, "and I'll tell you exactly why we've come to you."

He opened his attaché case and brought out what looked like a waterproof bag. From it, he extracted a passport. It had a dark blue cover, somewhat faded and shabby. I could make out the word Canada printed across it, and an elaborate emblem consisting of crowns, lions, flags and leaves. Opening the passport, Udi turned it towards me, showing me the photograph, with his fingers covering the name. I sat up and gaped. It was me, smiling for the camera. Long hair, which I'd never had, a little younger, wearing a shirt I didn't recognize, but me.

"Take it easy," said Udi. "It's not you."

"Are you sure?" I leaned closer to the passport, but Udi closed it, put it back in the bag, and returned it to his briefcase.

"It's a Canadian guy, around your age, who, let's say for our purposes, died of a drug overdose in a hut in Sinai a few weeks ago. The Bedouin down there sold his passport to some crook, and now we have it."

"But how did you know about his resemblance to me?"

"We have people whose job that is."

"By chance?"

"You still have to learn that chance can be your best friend, and your worst enemy. In this trade, you must never rely on chance. The truth is that we also ran a search through some face-recognition data bases, and found a few other look-alikes for the deceased. We contacted them too."

"And . . .?"

"They weren't right for the job. You are, in principle."

"In principle?"

"In principle. As far as the qualifications are concerned. Age, knowledge, military training. Someone who knows explosives, that's something rare. We liked the idea that you have a good eye and a quick hand. That also has clear advantages. But to know specifically that you are suitable will take a lot of time and a lot of training."

"Because?"

"Because we aren't looking for some company commander to storm the enemy, or some Don Juan who'll get Assad's wife into bed. We are looking for a combination of qualifications that is unique and a combination of sensitivities that is very rare, and only time will tell us if you have those or not."

"And it all begins with a resemblance to this Canadian junkie."

"Correct. Usually, we train a guy and then look for a passport for him. Very difficult today. In this case, we got the passport and looked for the guy. You can't imagine what a great find it is, a genuine passport and someone who fits the picture. Now we have to train you."

"And what about the family of the man in the picture?"

"The stamps in the passport show that he left Canada three years ago, and travelled all over the world. It's not certain that he was in touch with his family. He went to Sinai from Egypt, and there's no Israeli stamp in the passport, which makes it worth so much more."

"And his body? Wasn't it returned to Canada? Won't he be registered as dead?"

"Let's assume that the Bedouin buried him deep in the sand. They don't want to tangle with the Egyptian police and to have to explain things. The passport got separated from its owner, who from our point of view and for all practical purposes, has disappeared off the face of the earth."

"But, you can't leave the family not knowing anything. He must have parents, perhaps a wife, siblings, people who care about him?"

"You're a nice guy, and that's something we'll have to iron out," said

Udi, and this time there wasn't even a hint of a smile on his lips. "We didn't kill him, we didn't bury his body, we have no responsibility for him."

"Yes, but we know he is dead – and it's unthinkable not to notify his family!"

"As an intelligence operative, you'll have to be careful of the words 'we know'. Also of the word 'unthinkable' or 'impossible'. You are about to enter a world where 'we know' means we've seen it with our own eyes – and you haven't seen the body and neither have I. And 'unthinkable' is a dirty word in our profession. Of course it is thinkable. To notify them would mean getting entangled in some way with responsibility for his death, and it would also mean the passport would be dead and buried. At the moment a living passport is preferable to a dead body."

"But we aren't speaking about him, it's about his parents," I objected.

"I don't want to get into an argument over what's better – parents who don't know what happened to their son, or parents who are told their son is dead. In any case, the decisions about this have already been taken. Get it out of your system."

I took a deep breath. I knew this was a critical moment for me. This little incident, this minor moral dilemma, probably embodied the character of the world at whose portal I was standing. The dilemmas down the road were liable to be far more weighty. This was a world in which, according to the books and films and rumours, one lied, deceived, framed, blackmailed, blew up cars and buildings, killed people in cold blood. I had to take a decision in principle. It was clear to me that there was no point in being stubborn about this specific situation. I breathed out. My decision was obvious. I was here to fight people who blow up buses. This could not be done pleasantly and politely.

"OK. It's out of my system. At least for the moment," I met myself halfway.

Udi stood up and gave me his hand. "We'll discuss that moment down the road. But I'd rather have to work with good guys and make them bad than the other way round." He looked me straight in the eye and I looked back at him. His grip was long and robust. "We start right now," he said. "This is a one-man course, suited to your requirements. How much time do you need to get organized before we start?"

"I have to keep on teaching until the end of the school year. The course will have to fit in with that."

"OK. Make whatever other arrangements you may have by Sunday, and report here. And for starters, I want you to leave this building without the guard or the receptionist seeing you."

I went to the window and studied the branches of a nearby tree.

"That's a sure-fire way to get kicked out of the course even before it begins," I heard him say behind my back, and I was sorry because I had thought of that just before he spoke. I wouldn't want to take the risk of passersby seeing me and calling the cops and alarming all the security officers of all the surrounding government buildings.

"Does anyone care about this?" I asked, pointing at my empty coffee cup.

"Don't think so," said Udi with some curiosity in his voice.

"And that one?" I asked, pointing at his.

"I'd sacrifice it for my country's sake," he smiled.

"Are you in on this game?" I asked

"I am a ghost," he replied.

I took a look at the hallway and saw a little niche, covered by a curtain, off the staircase landing.

I checked it out, and it was empty. I smashed Udi's cup on the floor outside his room and quickly hid in the niche. Seconds later, the alarmed receptionist came running up the stairs, past the niche. I ran down to the entrance, smashed the second cup on the floor, and hid behind the door. The guard dashed in to see what was happening, noticed that the receptionist wasn't at her desk, and went to the staircase to look for her. This gave me time to slip outside.

I looked up and saw Udi at the window. He was shaking his head. I understood that he wasn't pleased with the method I'd chosen. It probably wasn't the office budget that worried him, but that he thought there were more elegant ways of leaving. I still had a lot to learn; actually, everything.

My course took place on the three days of the week that I wasn't teaching. One morning I spent at the firing range; on the second, in a gym doing hand-to-hand combat, and the third day I spent in a language laboratory. Right at the start of the language course, it became clear that my English had picked up a Canadian accent during the two years that I'd been at school in Ottawa, where my father was studying forestry; this made my instructor in the lab very happy, but she still had a lot to teach me.

At most of the course, I was no more than mediocre. I didn't become

the fastest gun in the Middle East, and despite the long time I took to draw
and aim, my scores were only middling. "Hand and eye, hand and eye,"
the instructor yelled. "Aiming and firing is like pointing at someone. It's a
movement we make from the age of one!" But my hand worked better on
a drawing pad than on the firing range.

And as someone who was not in any way particularly athletic, I never
became a Bruce Lee. My kicks and punches were all right, but the
combinations weren't fast enough and, in the instructors' opinion, they
also didn't have enough energy behind them. "Isn't there someone you
hate, so you can imagine you are punching or kicking him?" my karate
instructor asked, and I had to tell him there wasn't. I didn't even hate the
man who sent Dolly's killer to blow himself up in the bus. I wanted to kill
him, because that's what should be done, in this conflict we were
embroiled in. But I felt no hatred. The only time I had was as a child, when
I hated Germans.

Luckily I was strong enough to take the physical punishment meted
out in the hand-to-hand combat course without breaking. I was also
determined enough not to give in to the instructors, who tried every
possible dirty trick on me, including punches on the nose, and knees in
the testicles. The problem was that I didn't know how to drop this very
conspicuous determination in street situations, and substitute some
elegant flexibility.

In the afternoons, I would walk around the streets of Tel Aviv and
execute various tasks that Udi gave me. Some of them were peculiar, but
I felt that I was getting better at them. Udi was trying to root out the
sapper officer in me who kept popping up, and to implant some subtlety
and finesse instead.

"You don't force anyone to do something, and you don't threaten," he
told me often, when I tried to get what I wanted in too assertive a manner.
That's what happened when he ordered me to examine the locking
mechanism of the door to a certain balcony, and ruled out my suggestion
that I climb onto it from the outside. He also vetoed my idea that I do it by
posing as a municipal employee who had to measure the apartment for
taxation purposes. Eventually, I did as he ordered by pretending to be a
representative of the Beautiful Israel Association, which wanted to renovate
balconies in the building, and this led to rapid and willing co-operation on
the part of the residents. Another time, my assignment was to photograph

from a certain high balcony two people meeting in the street below, and Udi nixed my idea of posing as a private eye. Instead, I used the cover of a student taking part in a photography competition titled "Tel Aviv from on high" and the amiable occupants even advised me what to shoot from their balcony, and then left me alone there.

I learned how to tail people, and grew to love this dance in the streets of Tel Aviv. It took some time to shed my combat-ready manner, and to grasp that my adversary was not only the person I was following but also everyone else in the street. I learned to adopt a normal, almost casual gait, aware of everything around me and keeping the back of my target or "object" (as subjects of surveillance, intel gathering or even elimination are called in Mossad parlance) in view out of the corner of my eye and at a suitable distance.

I was good at the drill for discovering when I was being tailed. To do this, I set up a little trap, entering a shop just after a corner and looking through the display window as the person following me came around the corner, showed surprise that I'd disappeared, and called up his surveillance team on his radio, unaware that I was a few metres away. Sometimes, I'd draw the tail after me into a main street, say Ben-Yehuda, and then duck down the passage by the cinema there into Ruppin Street. I knew that the team would have to put someone in right behind me, and if someone emerged from the passage half a minute after me and looked right and left to see which way I'd turned on Ruppin, I'd know I had a tail. Then the cat and mouse game of getting rid of it would begin.

"Stop being Rambo, because they can call in a whole army," Udi rebuked me after I'd learned for myself, during the early exercises, how quickly a lone follower walking twenty or thirty metres behind me could become a whole team closing in on me from all directions. "And don't behave like a thief, because they are the cops," he added, when I tried evasion tricks like shinnying up a drainpipe on to a roof, and very soon saw the place surrounded by patrol cars. "You are always, but always, the innocent law-abiding citizen, going about your legitimate business, and everyone who sees you knows that's what you are," said Udi, trying to teach me the ABC of spy-craft, which was hard for me to digest.

"When you notice that they are following you, it's a sign that they aren't sure you're a spy, otherwise they would arrest you, or they want to see who you're going to meet, and to uncover the network one by one. So you go into innocent-activity mode. Make things easy for them. Go into a big shop, and pamper yourself with a nice shirt. Or go to a good restaurant, and chew everything really slowly. They'll put someone in to see if you're meeting anyone, and that guy will, incidentally, get a meal out of it, and thank you for that."

There were many layers of the soldier in me that I had to peel away, a lot of roughness that I had to smooth out, before I could acquire the elegance of the secret agent. "You can't sit at a bus stop and keep a look-out in the opposite direction from the one the bus would be coming," Udi scolded me. And he also rebuked me when I took up a position for a night look-out, in the dark garden of the house across from the one I was watching. "You can't put yourself at the mercy of some neighbour who in the best-case scenario would think you were there to take a leak and lose his temper, and in the worst case take you for a thief and call the police."

In the evening, I read up on the history and geography of Canada, and practised my English until after midnight, as ordered. After that I read material on the countries of the Middle East. Now and again, I had sessions with experts on various subjects. I learned to take photographs secretly. I learned to dismantle and assemble locks and safes. I learned clandestine communications. I performed adequately at these crafts, and I didn't need lessons on making and defusing explosive devices.

The months rolled by. During school vacations, when I had no teaching duties, I underwent intensive courses involving intelligence collection and simple operations. My less polished aspects came to light again towards the end, during the part of the course that dealt with inter-personal relations.

For some reason, I had a positive opinion of the way I got on with others. I thought I was interesting to talk to, even pleasant. I used to have lively conversations with my friends, teachers and students, and I knew quite a lot about a lot of subjects. On painting and art in general, obviously, but also on literature, science and politics. I also was familiar with places all over the world that could be the basis for conversation. After everything that happened in Japan, and after taking a brief break, I made a thoroughgoing tour of South and Central America, and in a separate journey, after my first year at Bezalel, I "did" Thailand, Myanmar, India and China. After graduating, I toured Europe several times, visiting most of the great museums in the capital cities, and as an architecture buff, most of the important palaces and cathedrals. I could talk freely and interestingly about all of the above.

But now, it became clear to me that I was actually shy. If someone approached me, or if the situation was suitable, I was able to hold a conversation amiably enough, but if I had to initiate the approach, it was difficult. And when, moreover, I had to lie to that someone – and I would always have to lie, whether about my identity or about the reason for my approach – my stomach turned over. It was easier for me to follow him, to watch him, to break into his home, than to start talking to him.

When I got dried up, time and again, wondering how to get a conversation going, or hesitantly began and got the cold shoulder, it seemed to me that Udi was about to give up on me. In a discussion half-way through the course, Udi told me that he had his doubts about me. I was still too tough, more the sapper than the spy. Too much of the company commander, too little of the secret agent. I reminded him that he'd told me he'd rather spoil a good guy, and that Moshe Dayan had said of Ariel Sharon that he preferred to have to restrain a wild horse than to whip a lazy mule. But Udi said the problem was that I hadn't internalized yet that the spy was the weak man in the field, and as such had to adopt different habits and a different personality.

"There'll be enough moments, at the critical stage of each operation, when you'll have to be a superhero. Israman," he smiled. "But until that moment, you must be the most ordinary person on the scene, to merge with the shadows on the wall, and you don't get that by sticking your chest and chin out. Up until the time when there's no more cover and you have to be a hero, you must play everyone you meet to your own advantage – the hotel receptionist, the housemaid, the taxi driver, your target's assistant, your target himself – and this can't be done if you're too shy, or if you're too fussy, but only if you're a schemer."

But apparently everything I had learned, plus my resemblance to the Canadian guy buried in the sands of Sinai, were enough of a reason for Udi to keep on trying, and for my part, I tried even harder.

As I'd discovered in the long runs during my basic training in the military, and the stretcher-carrying marches, which I found very difficult, I was able to stretch my limits further and further. If the first lie was hard, by the tenth lie my satisfaction at having accomplished my task was greater than the discomfort, and by the twentieth I even felt quite triumphant.

Once I had managed to acquire the required amiability and smiles, I learned how to drag anyone into a friendly chat, adapting myself chameleon-like to the person in question, and the responses were surprisingly quick and positive. With an elderly person, I would stoop and talk softly, with a woman I was the perfect gentleman, with shorter people I could decrease my stature by drooping my shoulders and drawing in my chest, so as not to project a threatening image, and with tough businessmen I was an ambitious, self-confident alpha male. I had become an actor.

The country was aflame throughout this period, and I was ready to do anything to finish my training and begin actively fighting terror. One day, during the early stages of my training, I was in the middle of an evasion exercise at Tel Aviv's new bus station, a place with innumerable exits and entrances that could be used to shake off a tail, when there was a terrorist bombing at the old bus station, not far away, that left twenty-three people dead. I called Udi and asked for permission to break off the exercise and help evacuate the wounded. That would be against all the rules, he replied angrily, and I had to carry on with my getaway game. In the middle of the course, while I was on another exercise, I heard about a bomb on a bus in Haifa with seventeen fatal casualties, and I decided to break the rules. After executing the procedure for discovering a tail, I called my parents from a payphone; they or either of my sisters or their kids could have been on that bus. I reported my deviation and I was rebuked, but Udi understood and allowed me to go on.

In the final months, when I was not teaching any more and free to get on with my training, I carried out complex operations all over Israel, many of them in Arab communities, first amongst Israeli Arabs in the Galilee and later amongst Palestinians in Jerusalem and the West Bank. As a soldier and officer, I had done my stints of service in the Palestinian territories, and now I could hardly overcome an instinctive sense that I should be armed, and instead rely on a cover story. I tailed, watched, photographed, and prepared intelligence files on people and buildings, and Udi seemed particularly pleased with the drawings I made. In a matter of seconds, I would sketch the village, the alley or the home of my target, and sometimes the man himself. This was especially useful when I had no photographic equipment, and sometimes I could capture a perspective that a camera could not.

I penetrated installations, laid dummy explosive devices, sniped at targets from a distance with blank ammunition, fired point blank with a cap gun at Mossad personnel I had trailed, and executed planned getaways. Luckily, none of the targets died of a heart attack or drew a real gun and shot me as I made off. To my surprise, neither did passersby. They stood by, shocked, or called the police. Now I understood what Udi meant when he spoke of the moment when there was no more cover and you had to be a hero – and all the moments before and after that when you had to merge with the shadows.

I established contact with various bodies, some of them hostile to Israel, like straw companies that channelled funds to Hamas, using the Canadian identity that I had not yet polished, and forged firm ties with them. The butterflies in my stomach had gradually settled down, and in any case didn't stop me from putting on the show as required. Udi decided that I was ripe for field assignments.

In a summing-up talk, after almost a year of training, Udi told me he had never had to peel so many layers from a trainee, and that there had been times when he'd almost given up. It was my good luck, he said, that he liked the very integrity which had made it so difficult for me to become the chameleon that a secret agent has to be, and he had faith in me. "I never thought it would be so hard to take an honest guy and teach him how to lie," he said.

I had grasped that the usual trainees were types that screening had shown to already possess the suitable traits, whereas in my case my main qualification was that I resembled the dead Canadian. Without that, I might not have made it to trainee status. But Udi did let me know that some of my own abilities and not only my face, also helped him come to a favourable decision about me. "Not everyone manages to overcome his fears and to walk around Arab villages in the West Bank," he continued, and I realized that my army service had also worked in my favour. "Not everyone is capable of keeping a lookout and sniping, and for sure not everyone is capable of storming a target and firing at him point blank." So apparently Udi too, and not only Moshe Dayan, preferred to tame a wild horse.

In this talk, for the first time, Udi was telling me I had successfully completed my training, and I was to become a fully-fledged Mossad operative. I was also informed for the first time what I had been recruited and trained for. "It's your good fortune that Iran's support for terrorism is increasing, as is the progress in their nuclear weapons project, and that I was ordered to recruit and train a squad to be assigned to this subject," Udi told me, giving me to understand that the urgent needs of the state had tipped the scales in my favour.

I did not know then who the other members of the crew were, and what stage they had reached in their training. What I did know was that Udi would also be our field commander, and I was happy about that. I sensed that I could trust him. He was a taciturn type, not overly congenial, but obviously a consummate professional, and that's what was important here. If Udi was to head up the team, clearly he was more than a mere recruiter and instructor, but an experienced operative, someone who had already done all of the things that I had been prepared for, I thought to myself. He was ten years older than me, I guessed, and at least twenty pounds heavier. His clothes were a little rumpled and sometimes he turned up for our meetings unshaven and with bloodshot eyes.

He didn't seem physically fit enough to be operational, but when he was teaching me I saw how capable he was. Sometimes we did target practice together, and he always drew seconds faster than I did and emptied his magazine before I'd fired a single shot. When we walked up to our targets, I peeked at his and saw that his hits were tightly clustered on the heart. Now and again, he'd watch me doing hand-to-hand combat with the instructor and then step in and skillfully smooth out a movement of mine until I got it right – a punch, a kick or a shoulder throw. "Why go for the chin if you can sock him in the nose, or poke your fingers in his eyes, and turn him into a punching bag?" he asked once, proving that he was not exactly a stickler for fighting fair. He was always a few score yards behind me the first few times I went into Arab villages and he seemed quite tranquil and merged with his surroundings in his sloppy clothing and ponderous gait.

I noticed the great respect with which Udi was treated by the various specialists we met, but it was never slaps on the shoulder or mutual friendly insults, the way the instructors related to each other, not even simple manifestations of camaraderie. Udi was aloof, and I didn't forge a personal relationship with him during that entire year. We never just chatted, and he never said a word that didn't arise from my training programme. I didn't even know what his rank was in the Mossad's hierarchy. All I knew about him was his name as it appeared on the business card he'd given me, and which was soon to turn out to be false: he remained a mystery to me.

Straight after the summing-up talk, there was a brief initiation ceremony, in which apart from myself, the participants were Udi, some of the specialist instructors who'd taught me over the year, and Orit, the cute receptionist at the small house in the Kiryah, who'd forgiven me for the shattered cups. There were also two men from Mossad HQ, one of them a small, stern-looking man who didn't say a word and was introduced as the intelligence officer who would be working with Udi's team. The other, tall and smiling, would serve as the case officer working with operatives on their cover stories and liaising between the team and HQ when we were in the field. Orit poured white wine into plastic glasses and there were plates of pastries and pears on the table. Udi said some nice things about me, the case officer welcomed me on my joining the ranks of the organization – pending the completion of some necessary forms – and wished me well on the "long and winding road full of ups and downs" ahead of me. He informed me formally that my operational codename would be Boaz. The name Mickey Simhoni, my true identity, would never be mentioned within the walls of the Mossad, neither orally nor in writing. Everyone would know me as Boaz from now on. That's when I realized that the name Udi Barkai was also a pseudonym.

Udi told me to come to the small house at ten a.m. the next day, to start work.

I was happy and proud, and on my way home it felt very strange that I had no one to tell about it. I was of course barred from sharing my happiness at launching my new career with my parents. But in any case, I would never have told them. They had been shaken by what had happened at the opening of my exhibition. The time until my sisters showed up after the blast had aroused old anxieties, and since then they had not returned to their usual selves. Knowing what I was up to would only have added to their fears.

Arriving home that evening, Dolly's absence hit me really hard. Ours may not have been a great love, but now with joy and pride filling my heart, and with the empty rooms of the apartment, I felt a profound loneliness. Some of Dolly's belongings, which her family hadn't taken, were still there, and for the first time since she died, I touched and stroked them. I even laid out one of her evening dresses on our double bed, but then I quickly pulled myself together and put it back in the wardrobe.

During the past year, I had dated a few women. Generally these were casual encounters, and after an even more casual screw, there may have been another two or three meetings, and then it was over. Apparently I never made enough of an impression on these women, who were as lonely as I was, to make them want to keep the relationship alive. For my part, I wasn't very keen on any of them. My mind had been focused on the course which didn't leave me time to grieve for Dolly or to wallow in loneliness.

The sudden loneliness that engulfed me now must have been connected to the need I felt to celebrate and not having anyone to do it with. I decided to do so on my own and went to a nearby bar, had a little too much to drink and ended the night in bed with a woman who was several years older than me. She was an immigrant from Russia, and at first light she sent me on my way, saying "See you again, my little shpion." I racked my brains to try and remember if I'd said anything I shouldn't have said.

I decided to report the encounter to Udi when we met, as agreed, in the little house. He was stern but sympathetic, and quoted the Bible at me: "It is not good that the man should be alone," adding, "especially if he's a spy." But after ascertaining that the Russian woman didn't know who I was or where I lived, he said that no harm seemed to have been done, but that drinking was out, "at least until you find a partner who can look after you." But I shouldn't bring him any new immigrants from Russia or anywhere else, because if she didn't get the right security clearance, I would have to decide whether to split from her, or from the Office, as insiders called the Mossad.

Then he went on to describe the next stage in my career.

This, it turned out, was a serious matter, known in the jargon as "establishing cover". For me, it would involve travelling to Canada to pick up the trail of the unfortunate druggie, whose name was now given to me for the first time, and to study and take on my new identity. His passport said he was born in Toronto, and that's where it had been issued, but this was just the beginning. I would have to find out where in Toronto he was born and grew up, where he went to school, who his friends were, what family members of his were still alive and where they lived, and gradually become Ronald Friedlich.

"What does that mean, 'become Ronald Friedlich?'" I asked, rolling the name – which sounded both close and distant at the same time – on my tongue. It felt as if I was being asked to merge with an alien being who was about to become part of me, or I part of him.

"It's a lot simpler than it sounds," Udi replied, and then he made me even more worried: "Wherever you go in the world, you'll introduce yourself as Ronald Friedlich and if you get into trouble and have to verify your identity, you'll have to be able to reply to any question that he could have answered, including the smallest details of his biography."

Really very simple, and very encouraging, I thought to myself. How would I get to know "the smallest details" of his life story, even if I do go hanging around Toronto? Where would I find information about his parents, his friends, the schools he went to: the concrete events of his life? The kind of things I could tell my interrogators, that they could check and verify. . . .

The attempt to take the general outline of my assignment as given to me by Udi and break it down had suddenly made it seem very complex indeed.

"I may look like the guy whose photo's in the passport," I said, "but what if the investigators send his family a picture of me?"

"It will be identified by them as a picture of their son," Udi answered with a calm that seemed to me like indifference to my fate.

"And if they know he's dead?"

"They don't. And they won't come to a Damascus lockup to see if you are him," he replied sending a red-hot dart into my gut.

The language lab in which I'd spent dozens of mornings over the year had polished my accent, the many books I'd read about Canada had given me more knowledge than the average Canadian has about his country's history, geography and politics. I don't know how many Canadians would have been able to describe and explain the national emblem that I'd seen on the cover of Ronald Friedlich's passport. Its formal name, the "Arms of Her Majesty The Queen in Right of Canada" was as complicated as the thing itself, but I could explain it all, from St Edward's crown at the top, to Canada's maple leaves at the bottom.

Memories of the period I had spent as a child in Ottawa began to surface, and could add some shades and aromas to my cover story, but I still had more than a few questions about my Canadian identity. I decided to put them aside for the time being. I had undergone training, there were many things that I could do and this was no time, before my first mission, to ask too many questions and display a lack of confidence. But nevertheless, I had one more question.

"I can't be the first to ask this," I said. "What about my being a Jew? I mean, circumcised?"

"In Canada, no one will examine you. And if they strip you naked in some Syrian lockup, you won't be the first man they've seen without a foreskin. They're all like that over there."

"Yes, but . . ."

"So you'll make up some story of a circumcision for medical reasons, or even of having a Jewish background. It's your job to come up with answers for establishing your cover," Udi growled with distinct impatience. Clearly, he hadn't expected this flood of questions from a graduate of his course who was facing a relatively simple assignment. I could imagine the words that were probably going through his head: "If this is what he's asking now, what's he going to ask me before his first real mission, in an Arab country."

I was full of curiosity and excitement before my journey, which was open-ended but which Udi estimated should take two to three months, to meet up with my double's life. More than that, it was a journey to meet and learn a life that was going to be my own life on any mission abroad. A feeling began to grow in me that I was also perhaps going on a journey to meet a life that could have been my life, if history had taken a slightly different course.

3.

First Stop, Limassol

ACCORDING TO THE operational orders Udi had drawn up for me, I was to sail from Haifa to Cyprus, to carry out some lookout and intelligence-gathering assignments against Palestinian agents located on the island, to transmit my findings via secret communications to Mossad HQ, and only then to head for Toronto. At first I didn't know what the purpose of the stopover was, and I assumed it was meant mainly to give me a taste of working abroad before I reached my destination and before I could endanger the precious passport by making some novice's slip-up. But the briefing I received before setting out convinced me that it was serious: the intelligence officer I had met a few days before at my induction ceremony, who I now learned went by the name of Moshik, sat with me for a few hours. First he taught me about the island and the way things happened down there, and then about my targets, or "objects". He showed me detailed intelligence files on each of them, with photographs of the men, their families, their homes and neighbourhoods, their vehicles and their regular haunts. The files showed me that these people were kept under constant watch, and I understood that the photographs I was to take and my reports were intended to bring the files up to date.

This time the briefings were held at our squad's base, and there I met Jerry and Ronen for the first time. They were operatives Udi had trained and had been engaged in intelligence-gathering assignments all over the world, while waiting for me and other recruits to complete our training and identity-establishment before we could start operating as a team.

The base was part of a disused army camp outside Tel Aviv, with a central structure where we lived and adjoining buildings that were used for various purposes. There was a basketball court with crooked tiles and an old obstacle course, neither of which we ever used; storerooms where

62

models could be built and trained on, and a firing range. Every now and again, shots were heard from the range and we guessed that other parts of the base were being used by other teams, hidden from us by modular concrete walls.

The main building housed Udi's office, which was empty most of the time, as were the rooms used by Moshik and the tall case officer, who introduced himself with a broad grin as Avi, when they visited our base. The other parts of the structure were our living quarters, a briefing room, classrooms, and a fully-equipped gym where we worked out between other activities.

Moshik explained the importance of my planned recon assignment: "Some of these objects are recruiters and controllers of actual terrorists. There's no knowing when one of them will summon a member of his gang from Gaza or the West Bank, who we'd then be able to identify and arrest on his return. For this, it's vital to keep an eye on the controllers. Sometimes we have no more than twenty-four hours' notice."

He never even hinted at where the tip-offs about the summons came from, or how the Office knew about the upcoming meetings. I presumed that a lot of intelligence capabilities were in play here. Terrorist attacks were still occurring regularly, with suicide bombers blowing themselves up in buses, markets, and cafés. The importance of my assignment was clear, and I accepted it gladly.

"Among the objects there are functionaries of Fatah's Al-Aqsa Martyrs' Brigades, Hamas's Izz ad-Din al-Qassam Brigades, the Islamic Jihad and the Global Jihad," said Moshik, listing the main terrorist groupings. "There are moneymen and weapons purchasers. If we get info on a weapons deal, we may want to stop it, or after some terrorist attack we may want to settle scores, right away. To do this, we need updated intelligence files."

For the first time, I felt that I was actually about to start the job for which I had given up my truncated, bleeding career as an artist. I couldn't help thinking that perhaps one of those objects was the individual who recruited or dispatched the suicide bomber to the No. 4 bus on Allenby Street, the man who murdered Dolly. Eventually, I couldn't keep it in and told Moshik.

"Oh, haven't they updated you? In fact, we've known for quite a long time who they were. The suicide bomber was a guy called Iyad Radad, and had been recruited by a Hamas operative from Ramallah by the name of

Mahmoud Sharitakh. The army captured him some time ago, and a few weeks ago a military court sentenced him."

Just like that, and all this time I'd known nothing. Udi and the rest of the insiders apparently sincerely believed that the matter of my personal revenge was all over. But in my heart, I never felt that. I had mixed feelings about the capture and imprisonment of the man responsible for Dolly's death. I would've liked to have been involved in capturing him, and I wanted him to be dead, and not spending his time in prison with his comrades, eating, drinking and playing backgammon, until being freed in the next prisoner exchange.

"What was he sentenced to?" I asked

"I don't really remember, I think a number of life sentences, as many as the people who were killed by the bomber."

"Six people were killed, and more than 80 were wounded."

"Right, I remember now. He got seven life terms, the seventh for the wounded."

I thought about my injured students and the other victims, who would have to bear their disabilities for the rest of their lives, about the distraught families I'd seen at the hospital. There was no death penalty in Israel, but it should at least be life with hard labour, I thought, in return for their daily sufferings.

"Do you know how they caught him?" I asked.

"Yes. He sent another suicide bomber, to a Tel Aviv café, but this one was caught, and his interrogation led to Sharitakh."

"And did they manage to go further up the chain? Do they know who controlled this Sharitakh?" I hadn't given up on my hope of finding the other end of the chain in Cyprus. My desire for revenge had not died, it had just lain dormant inside me, and now it had awoken.

Moshik, who had turned out to be a friendly fellow who did not make an ideology out of secrecy, apologized. He only happened to know about Sharitakh's arrest and sentencing, as well as the name of the suicide bomber, because he read every scrap of information about the terrorist organizations, and remembered it all. But it was not part of his direct duties.

I sensed that the capture of the recruiter diminished my motivation ever so slightly. But I well remembered my first talk with Udi. I was not there for personal revenge, but for the general good. I forced myself to overcome that slight drop in motivation. I studied the intelligence material until I knew it by heart: the faces of the objects, the maps of the vicinities of their homes, and the pictures of their houses. Fortunately, this was not a problem for me, as my visual memory was excellent, and just to make sure I also made quick sketches of what I saw in the pictures, sketches that put smiles of satisfaction on the lips of Moshik and Udi. But this was my first mission, so Udi sat with me for hours, going over all the actions I was to execute, stage by stage: what to say at my hotel, how to leave it, how to reach each location, how to photograph my targets, how and when to transmit the material to Israel. Only when he was sure that I had fully grasped my tasks and how to implement them, did Udi send me on my way, with a "See you in Toronto." I had almost forgotten that the Cyprus assignment was just a stopover, and when I asked him when and how we would meet, he told me he would take care of that. The only rule was that I should not seek him out, but wait until he contacted me.

I knew I'd be away from home for a long and unbroken period of time, during which I would have to refrain from communicating with Israel, except for one phone call to my parents every two weeks, at the most. To do that I'd have to go to a different city, execute the drill for ensuring I wasn't being tailed, and use a public payphone. Knowing this cast an additional shadow over my separation from mum and dad, and as my departure neared I felt a deep sorrow: I already sensed the imminent loneliness that would be my lot in the coming weeks and months.

Because I would now be making many more trips abroad, usually for short periods, it was decided that my cover story, as far as my parents were concerned, would be that I was still an artist and I was participating in various exhibitions. My few friends were not close enough for me to have to explain my absences to them; Dolly's death had made most of them feel uncomfortable in my presence, and this led to a weakening of whatever links had existed between us.

I told my parents I'd been invited to show my work at a little museum near New York, and I would have to be there to set it up and stay for the duration of the exhibition, some two months, and then to dismantle it before returning home. I did not know what I'd be living on, and they shouldn't expect me to call home too often. When my mother said, "You really don't have to call every day, it's too expensive," and I replied that it wouldn't even be every week, there was an uncomfortable silence.

"Two months is a long time," she said. "Please don't be stingy with your calls. Reverse the charges." My father, as usual, was silent. I didn't respond to mum's generous suggestion, which I knew I wouldn't be able to fulfil. There was nothing I could say.

My dear, long-suffering parents. Since Dolly's death they had not spoken to me of marriage and kids, but I knew they were dreaming about it. Now, before their eyes, the dream was growing more remote. I understood their longing for "a little Simhoni" to keep the family name alive. From my dad's extensive family, only his parents, miraculously, had survived the Holocaust, to produce him and his brother in the smoking ruins of Europe, with their past consumed by the flames and their future shrouded by fog. Smoke and fog, into which his brother had also melted away.

My father told me once that there was no way his parents had survived without a purpose. He knew no more than I did about his father, but at night he'd heard his cries and seen his mother – who had also undergone her share of agonies – placing cold compresses on his father's forehead, holding his hand and consoling him. He also picked up something about their experiences from their conversations. I suppose that it wasn't easy for him, growing up in the Israel of the 1950s, the son of Holocaust survivors, feeling more committed to them than to himself, and never trying to fulfil his own potential. Yet, his forestry seemed to satisfy him completely and he saw it as a contribution to his country. I thought that it was easier for him to be with his trees than to be with people.

Because it wasn't possible to discuss the Holocaust and the wars in our home, I recoiled from dealing with them in any way while I was growing up, and I couldn't feel any empathy with my grandparents or my father. In the "My Roots" project at school, I focused on my mother's family. This attitude changed only after I myself faced the tangible possibility of being killed, and even more so, after I myself had killed.

By the time I enlisted, in the early 1990s, the Israeli army had retreated from the heart of Lebanon, which it had invaded during the first Lebanon war in 1982, in an attempt to drive Palestinian rockets out of range from Israeli communities which were frequently fired at. The forces had withdrawn into a "Security Zone" in southern Lebanon, just north of the border between the two countries, but by now the enemy had become Hezbollah, the Lebanese Shia militia backed by Iran and Syria. After we completed our advanced training, my engineers' unit was sent to support the Golani infantry brigade that was holding the line of fortified positions along the Litani river, the northern border of the security zone. We were responsible for maintaining fences and minefields around the positions, defusing mines that had become exposed or washed away by rain and, because of a shortage of manpower, we also had to do sentry duty. Over time, against standing orders, we were also called upon to provide reinforcements for the ambushes that were laid each night outside the fortresses.

About a month after our deployment along the line, as we lay in a routine circular ambush covering all angles of approach at the foot of a fort's sand rampart, I felt a blow on my leg – the signal that a suspicious movement had been detected. Together with the rest of the platoon, I wriggled into a straight line facing the direction of the movement. Night vision equipment had picked up three armed figures working their way through the bushes towards the fortress. We knew the combat procedures, but the platoon commander nevertheless pointed out the targets. The section on the left, including me, were to aim at the third man in the approaching enemy squad. The other sections aimed at the other two. The open-fire order was given when they were about twenty yards away from us. I squeezed the trigger of my rifle, together with all the others. I saw my target fall. The noise of the firing was frightening. I wasn't ready for it and I almost jumped up. The man next to me held me down, and perhaps saved my life. The explosives the three armed men were carrying blew up and the fragments flew over our heads. When we went up to where they had been, only charred body parts remained, scattered around. It was a shocking sight, and the image of the falling militiaman, a split second before the racket deafened me, kept coming back to me for many nights a long time afterwards.

When I went home on leave, and saw my parents, whose eyes were bleary from lack of sleep because they knew where I was and what was happening there, and my elderly grandparents, I told them about it. At first I had wanted to say that I had been at a base inside Israel, at Biranit or Metullah, far from the events that were filling the news, firefights that also led to the loss of many Israeli soldiers' lives. But I felt the need to share my frightening experience with them. Then my grandfather told me about the first time he had killed a man.

It happened soon after the end of World War II, when the men of the

Jewish Brigade, a British army unit made up mainly of volunteers from among the Jews of Palestine, came across this young man who spoke German, and enlisted him into a unit that was engaged in doing away with Nazi war criminals who were still at large. His task was to talk to the suspected Nazi and make sure that he was the man they were looking for, a death camp commander, say, or an SS officer, or a camp guard. The Germans never suspected the slender youth who spoke their language, and willingly identified themselves. At granddad's signal, the Brigade soldiers moved in, took the Nazi to a nearby forest, read him his death sentence and executed him.

"The first time, I felt really bad, like you," my grandfather told me, "and I stepped aside and vomited. It is a terrible thing to see the fear in a man's eyes, even if he is a war criminal, and then the hole in the forehead and the body crumpling like a sack. But I got used to it, and after a few executions, I even asked if I could be the one to squeeze the trigger. They let me do it. I did it once for my mother, once for my father, and three more times, once for each of my brothers."

Only then did I see for the first time that my grandfather still possessed the hardness of someone who had escaped, hidden, lived from hand to mouth, survived, fought, and avenged by killing with his own hand people whom he believed shared the guilt of murdering his family. And with this storm raging in his breast, he had married, started a family, migrated to Israel, and joined – as a young man of barely eighteen years old – the forces fighting for the establishment of the Jewish state, and fought again in the Sinai Campaign of 1956, and the Six-Day War of 1967.

This hardness had passed on to my father as well. He had fought with his father in the Six-Day War, a young tank officer and an old reserves officer, and a few years later it was granddad who was the first in the family to hear that his son had been seriously wounded in the 1973 Yom Kippur War. My father never volunteered any information about what had happened to him.

All of a sudden, my grasp of the ties between these two taciturn men changed completely; of their withdrawal, even their self-denial, which I had until now interpreted as meanness. People who have been through all that they had don't see the point in having and spending money, in luxury apartments, in fine furnishings, in going out and having fun. All at once, I felt a deep kinship with them. Now I too had joined "the fighting family". Now I had been accepted into it. My feelings about my own deed, only a few days before, on the banks of the Litani River, were totally transformed.

In a similar way, I felt proud of my mother, who had been conceived during the siege of Jerusalem and grew up in the gun-sights of the Jordanian army snipers in the eastern part of that city, which had been divided until the Six-Day War straightened the backs of her generation. I was glad that despite her life of deprivation and anxiety, there was still softness and joy in her.

I was a gentle and easygoing man, like her; at least that's what I tended to believe. Not taut and strict and tough like dad. I also thought that I was open and congenial and forgiving, like her, and not secretive and silent and grudging like him. Although I had inherited his facial features, it was from her that I had received my rotund physique. If my childhood had not been enveloped in the dark clouds arising from his injury, the treatments, the changing of the bandages, that went on for years, something that cannot be kept out of the life of a small child; if that war had not been shrouded in secrecy; if this commitment had not seeped into me, drop by drop, a word here and a sentence there – perhaps I would still have been an artist. Without that baggage borne on my shoulders since my childhood, perhaps even Dolly's death would not have diverted me from the path that had been hewn for me by my clearest and most manifest talent. Perhaps I would actually have had to settle a score with dad – but even with all of this in the background, all I felt for him was kinship.

But now I was leaving my parents behind, albeit with my sisters, who lived nearby, and their loveable grand-daughters, but without a little Simhoni. "Just don't bring us some shiksa from over there," mum surprised me by saying, using the Yiddish word for a Gentile woman. I knew her as an open, liberal woman, but that little Simhoni would have to be, from her point of view, a Jew, born to a Jewish mother. In the context of my parents' biographies, I could definitely understand why.

I spent the evening before my departure with them, drawing it out until their eyelids, and mine also, drooped with weariness. My sisters, who'd come to say goodbye, had already left, and then, with a heavy heart and heavy eyes, I said goodbye and drove back to my apartment in Tel Aviv, glad that I was too tired to think. In the morning, I went to HQ for a last briefing, and then travelled back to Haifa, to the port, where my journey was to begin. I felt a pang in my heart when I passed the turnoff to the French Carmel, the way I always took to my parents' home, a pang that stayed with me as I boarded the ferry. Out of the corner of my eye I spotted Udi, standing in the crowd on the quay.

The ship set sail at sunset. I put my suitcase in my cabin, which was small, with a porthole, and went out onto the upper deck. To the west, the sun was sinking over the horizon, but I took a seat at the stern, where Haifa was growing ever more distant from me, a white city with a green mountain, a darkening sky and a strip of sea serving as a picture frame. The windows flashed the setting sun's rays back at me. I sought out my parents' house from this unfamiliar angle. The Sail Tower skyscraper with its billowing sides and pointed spire served as a salient landmark from which my eyes moved up and southwards. The golden dome at the centre of the Bahai gardens shone in the waning light and, on both sides of the garden, chains of street lamps flickered on, marking out in yellow the descent of the German Colony towards the sea. The aura they created was swallowed up by the glow of the port's lights, and I pictured in my mind the cafés and restaurants opening their doors for the evening.

I identified the buildings and radar installations at Stella Maris, and from there my gaze wandered to the haunts of my childhood. The buildings of Abbas Street, built on the hillside slope with half of their six or eight storeys below the bridge leading from the street to the apartment block and the other half above it, were blurred in the advancing dark. Really blurred, as were those childhood years when I played on the bridge level overlooking the port, together with the children of the new immigrants and the children of the Arab families who lived down the road. When we returned from our stay in Canada, we moved higher up the Carmel and there, right above the broad green swathe that remained in the centre of the mountain, we could see the houses which stood between one street with the rather obliging name of Zionism Avenue and the smaller Jubilee Road, where we lived. In the evening mists, the houses merged into one lump, but I could see our home, the one on the end, painted a pinkish-orange, and another lump, made up of melancholy and emotion, echoed it inside me, beating like a tom-tom.

When the whole of Mount Carmel was nothing more than a dark smear with only the towers of the Panorama Buildings and Haifa

University flickering above the skyline, and my eyes had shifted from the gradually shrinking lights of the port and the glowing halo over my hometown, towards the greying foam in the wake of the ship, I walked to the bow. On the horizon, there was still a reddish glimmer, and the clouds hanging high above had pink and yellow linings, the last remnants left by the sun, whose light was still marking out the course of the vessel on the surface of the sea. A cold gust of wind ruffled my hair and the last of the passengers left the deck and descended into the warm belly of the ship. It was late in September, autumn, and I had a clear sense of leaving one phase of my life, which had encompassed almost thirty years, and sailing towards a new phase. But I didn't do any summing-up. Instead I allowed a pleasant, poignant melancholy to float around inside me, as if I had just drunk a strong and tasty liqueur. I wondered if Udi had chosen this form of departure for me so that I could take my leave from my life so far, and enter the new world of espionage gradually and not in one abrupt hop in a plane. I stayed like that until the darkness engulfed me and the cold sent me shivering indoors.

In the passenger hall, gaiety reigned. A small band was playing Greek tunes, some couples were dancing, people were sitting around at tables eating the light meal supplied by the ship's galley. A lot of them were migrant workers speaking different languages, mostly Greek, and there were also young Israelis and backpackers, who had chosen this inexpensive way to leave Israel. I found a seat in a corner, next to one of the portholes that looked out into the darkness. My heart contracted as it occurred to me that this could have been a romantic evening. Being alone in a happy crowd only intensified the feeling of loneliness that was overwhelming me, or was perhaps draining me. I skipped the meal, went down to my cabin and fell asleep.

I awoke to the blast on the ship's horn that heralded our arrival at the port of Limassol. As I stretched my limbs, I could actually feel the energy generated by my upcoming mission coursing through my veins. I quickly got my things together and went on deck. It was dawn, and mists covered the city and the tops of the Troodos Mountains that formed its backdrop. As the passengers prepared to disembark, the sun began breaking through the mists, warming my body and my soul. I felt invigorated and ready for action. I knew this feeling from the army: the apprehension and gloom of the night before a battle, dispelled by the adrenaline pumping through your bloodstream the moment you set out.

The passport stamping procedure went quickly. This was the first time I'd used a passport that wasn't my own, and I had a queer feeling. I stood outside the small terminal and a taxi drew up. The driver put my suitcase in the boot, and I climbed into the backseat. As I sat down, the radio blared out, "Yossi calling Shlomo" – in Hebrew.

I caught my breath. What could this mean? Some kind of a trick? Was the Office trying to see how I would react?

My driver turned on the ignition and asked, in English, where I was heading. "Holiday Inn" I said, and as he drove off, Shlomo answered Yossi over the radio. My driver ignored them, and called in something in Greek. I heard him reporting his destination, "Holiday Inn." Then Yossi and Shlomo spoke in Hebrew about a fare, and it dawned on me that my Limassol taxi was on the same wavelength as a Haifa cab company. I chuckled to myself.

The taxi entered October 28th Avenue, which ran parallel to the seashore, with palm trees and flowerbeds on the central reservation, hotels on the one side and parks, beaches and more hotels on the other. In a minute we were in the Holiday Inn parking area. The hotel was a long, five-storey building right on the beach.

I asked for, and received a room facing the sea. It was still very early in the morning, and I had to pay a surcharge. I decided to act like a regular tourist and as soon as I had unpacked my bag, I donned a swimsuit and a hotel robe, and headed for the pool, which was located between the lobby and the beach. I put my toe into the water, and it was still icy. I stretched out on a deckchair, closed my eyes and dedicated myself to the morning sun. What a great start to the first chapter of my new life.

For the next few days I divided my time between the hotel pool and my assignments, until I had executed them in full. These agents of terror didn't shrink from living the good life. They resided in villas, luxury apartments or the best hotels, something that made my job easier. I devoted several hours to each one of my objects, verifying their addresses and the vehicles they were using. Sometimes I found newer models than those on my list, and then I kept up my surveillance until I was sure that the target was using that car. I updated details about family members that

I observed, and in some cases I tailed the object in a car that I'd rented to his first stop, and I added it to the list of their regular haunts. I drove carefully, not feeling too comfortable on the left side of the road, a relic of British rule. Sometimes I misjudged my distance from the kerb and bumped into it.

I gave the Hamas representative special attention, gathering intelligence information about him that I hadn't been asked for. Places he visited, cafés where he drank, people he met with. Perhaps it would still emerge that he had been behind the bomb on the No. 4 bus. In that case, I would want to lead the team sent in to eliminate him.

The Fatah agent was staying at the Four Seasons hotel, at the end of the promenade. I invited myself to the hotel's private beach, and I saw him twice, once with the Hamas man and once with a call girl who looked like a Russian. In most cases, people don't look very much like their photographs, with the angle from which they are seen different to that of the camera, or their hairstyle may have been changed, as well as their attire. Pounds may have been added, or lost. Nevertheless, my practised eye picked my objects up quickly. Back when Moshik had shown me the pictures, I had noted characteristics which I could now identify. I took a photo of the Fatah man with his Russian, in case the Office would want to make use of it sometime. As my orders said nothing to the contrary, I decided to indulge myself with a girl like her. After months of sexual deprivation, I thought I deserved it. For a few days running, I'd noticed a good-looking young woman sitting in the lobby of my hotel, and a quick exchange of glances was enough to get her to follow me to the elevator. I already had a raging erection on the way up, and as soon as we were in my room I began to unload all of my accumulated excess baggage, from all possible angles. Only after the third time did I ask her how old she was and where she was from. This abundantly endowed female turned out to be a Moldovan, and she was seventeen. I gave her double her asking price and sent her away.

I remained naked and ashamed in my bed. So now I was not only an accomplice to human trafficking, I was also almost a pedophile. I realized that after more than a year without Dolly and only isolated and hopeless sexual encounters – there was nothing romantic about them – I had reached rock bottom. The thought that the demands of my job wouldn't allow me to find a genuine companion and to build a significant relationship made me really despondent. It would be like it had been in the army, when no relationship could survive my protracted absences. When I met Osnat, things seemed to be settling down until I told her I wanted to travel to the Orient after my discharge. Now, I would have to lie, on top of everything else. As long as a girl wasn't a serious partner, I wouldn't give her details to the Office for a security check, and even when and if I did so, it would take months before a clearance came through and she would discover I'd been lying to her about my profession since we met. Then, either she would realize this had been a necessity, and accept it or not. But what could I do about it? It looked like the new road I had chosen was a dead end when it came to finding a mate.

Down in the dumps, I switched on the TV.

When I had first checked in, I discovered that I could get Israel's Channel 2, and as soon as the picture cleared, my blood ran cold. This time it was an attack on Maxim's restaurant in Haifa by a female suicide bomber, and by late that night the death toll had reached twenty-one, with scores wounded. Many of the less badly injured were interviewed in the extended live broadcast, as were relatives of the victims, and I sat there for hours facing the screen, trying to identify familiar faces.

Again, I was in a dilemma, and again I chose to call home. I waited, sleepless and tense, until the morning, drove to the Sheraton at the marina, and called from a payphone there. My father was awake and answered immediately. All my relatives were all right, but a family who lived near my parents had been badly hit. I had known them all since I was a child.

I transmitted a message to HQ. Islamic Jihad had taken responsibility, and I knew precisely where their man in Cyprus lived. I could execute a retaliatory hit very quickly. I was ready. In the reply, I was thanked for my reports and told to get set for my trip to Toronto, that same day or the next. The matter was being taken care of. I bit my lip and booked a flight. I could only hope that if they wanted me off the island by the next day, others were on the way to settle scores with whomever necessary, and that I had done my bit by updating the intelligence. I also hoped that when I had completed establishing my cover and could travel the world as a genuine Canadian I, too, would be among the executors. With or without a woman. Apparently without, I had to admit to myself, regretfully.

4.

Toronto Debut

TORONTO GREETED ME with bright but icy weather. When I landed there, in early October, the skies were clear but strong winds from Lake Ontario swept through the streets that led up from the waterfront, and at around five p.m. when it grew dark, emptied the central area and sent people hurrying home. The cold, colours, smells and winds evoked dim memories of the two years I'd spent as a child in Ottawa.

I bought a long woollen coat, fur-lined gloves, good shoes, a scarf and a hat. When I had been told to get a suit and tie in Israel I felt as if I was masquerading, and now I looked like someone else entirely. The warm clothing made it easier for me outdoors, but the weather still crimped my ability to do what I had to do. At eight a.m. it was still dark, offices opened at nine, and my activities were limited to the mid-day hours.

After a few days in Cyprus as the Canadian Ron Friedlich, I'd resumed an Israeli identity. I checked into the Town Inn Suites, an apartment hotel near the intersection of Bloor and Church Streets, at the north-eastern end of the central area. Between it and the main tourist attractions stood Toronto University campus, which I had to visit. But first I intended to spend a few days as a tourist both to explain my stay here and to learn as much about the city as I could before I began my enquiries regarding Ron Friedlich, so that later on I'd be able to pass myself off as someone who had grown up and lived in Toronto.

Relying on the blue of the sky and misjudging the temperature, I started walking along Yonge Street, which has been called the longest street in the world. I walked towards the centre, getting used to the way locals pronounced its name, as in "young". The street ran all the way down to the lake, and the wind froze my ears, poked icicles into my eyes, and found its way up my legs, so I went into a clothing store and bought some

75

thermal long-johns. Despite the cold, the street was a lively place and I felt quite elated as I walked along it. It was quite narrow, teeming with cars, streetcars and hurrying pedestrians, and lined with shops of every conceivable kind, with people of different nationalities and skin colours selling goods from all over the world. There was a mixture of older, English-style brick buildings, newer stone-faced ones, and modern steel and glass structures. Music blared from the record shops, smells wafted from the eateries, and multi-coloured items of clothing hanging outside clothing stores waved in the wind, creating a feeling of a perpetual street party. Later on, I understood that the locals tried to enjoy themselves as much as they could as long as there was some sunlight and before winter arrived to put a dampener on everything. When the first sunny days of spring came around, they'd burst out again, in shorts and sandals, openly defying the persistent cold.

I was about to take refuge from the wind in the Eaton Centre, a large mall flanked by two impressive silvery glass buildings. But just then I spotted the Hard Rock Café hidden away on a corner of the square opposite the mall, and that's where I hurried to thaw my freezing limbs.

As I entered, my ears burning with cold, it struck me that since leaving the hotel I hadn't executed any moves to detect if I was being followed. Although I wasn't exactly engaged in an operation, I felt I should make sure I was clean, if only for reasons of protocol. I sat down in a corner facing out towards the street and made a mental note of the people looking at the café, those who stopped outside, and also those who entered, especially if I saw they had first surveyed the people sitting inside. Any chance of spotting a tail among them was small.

I did it again when I left the Hard Rock Café, as soon as I'd turned the corner into Queen Street. Two people came around the corner after me moving fast, one of them a young woman who had also come into the café behind me. She caught my eye, gave me a sweet smile and kept walking quickly. A tail wouldn't have smiled at me, so I decided I was clean, and because the street was protected from the wind coming in from the bay, I began enjoying myself even more. This was apparently a really old street and it was lined by two- or three-storey brownstone buildings housing little shops and a vast array of restaurants, as well as more modern blocks. Soon, my wandering led me to the Old City Hall, a magnificent palace built of light brown stone, resembling a huge basilica.

Crossing a large plaza, in the centre of which workers were setting up an ice rink, I headed for the New City Hall, a low, round structure flanked by two curved towers with a space between them, forming a kind of bisected semi-circle. Near the entrance there was a sculpture by Henry Moore, whose work I knew from the sculpture garden at the Israel Museum in Jerusalem. I went to the information desk, and asked when the building was erected; the architecture was so modern that I suspected it was completely new, but I was told it was built in 1965, which meant it had already been standing for some time when Ronald Friedlich was still alive and living in Toronto. I was given some maps of the city, including one of The Path, which is actually a kind of underground city for pedestrians, living and breathing beneath the aboveground one. I decided my ears had suffered enough, and that I'd continue on my way via The Path. But just then, out of the corner of my eye, I spotted the girl with the sweet smile huddled with two men next to one of the side exit doors of the underground thoroughfare.

I crossed over to the Sheraton Hotel on the other side of the square, from which I would be able to keep a lookout in the direction of City Hall, and only after no one had come from that direction for a good few minutes, did I descend into the maze of underground tunnels. There were miles and miles of passages that made it possible to get from place to place, sparing pedestrians the need to contend with the weather and traffic in the streets above. The passages were tiled and spotlessly clean and the shops, clubs, bars and cinemas were immaculate.

It was clear that in order to follow me effectively, a large surveillance squad would be necessary, with one of its members waiting for me at every intersection, and that their only hope, at the morning and evening rush hours, would be for them to stick right up close to my ass. These, therefore, were the hours that I chose when, in the next few days, I used the passages to get to most of the must-see attractions, like the CN Tower, the city's most familiar landmark – though I assumed that the chances that the local secret service would have me on their lists were minimal.

My interest in architecture took me to St Andrews Church, a sandstone building to which a modern wing had been added that fitted in nicely with the older part, and to the magnificent Ontario Legislative Building, site of the provincial parliament, a structure that reminded me of the splendid buildings erected in Europe in the nineteenth century.

For my cover as a tourist, it was important for me to have in my pockets stubs of tickets to various sites, and when the temperature sank I took refuge in museums. I visited AGO, the Art Gallery of Ontario, as well as the Toronto Art Gallery. The first was undergoing renovations and was partly sheathed in a glass covering, with corridors and staircases of planed wood leading inside, and the second was a strange, black and white checkered box standing on coloured iron legs, atop the original building, something like a futuristic alien who'd come to visit. The outside of the building, it seemed to me, was more interesting than the interior and the contents, and that's also what I felt about the ROM, the Royal Ontario Museum, on Bloor Street near my hotel, where the architect had designed an annex to the old stone building comprising a striking cluster of lopsided, asymmetrical aluminium and glass triangles.

I didn't see the girl with the sweet smile and her friends again, and I assumed they had not been following me, and if they had, they'd been satisfied that my behaviour was that of a tourist and struck me off their list, had I been there to begin with.

I went to these great, rich museums to help establish my cover story, and only when I was inside did I remember that I had actually been an artist. A painter. A Bezalel graduate. And for a few hours, I went back to being what I had been. Perhaps that's what I still was, deep down inside, and what I could go back to being, if the world around me would return to being normal. As I was somewhat detached from the avant-garde atmosphere of Bezalel and the artistic scene of its graduates, I found myself interested in and enjoying the pictures by native Canadians, who'd painted in oils or watercolours or made black and grey drawings of scenes from their lives in the northern territories, bear hunts, shark fishing. These were more appealing to me than works made up of, say, boots cast in metal and welded together to create a distorted female form, or a bicycle that had been dismantled and reassembled to look like an elk.

As part of my plan to build a cover story, I had brought with me a few pictures that I'd made especially for this purpose, nondescript landscapes based on pictures from Canadian magazines, and signed "RF". I went to some small galleries to try and place them there until they were sold. Success came sooner than I had anticipated; so soon that I had not even rented an apartment, something that my operational orders called for, and I had to give the gallery the address of the apartment hotel. Later, Udi rebuked me for this, and rightly. But I was so elated by this renewed recognition of my artistic ability that at the time I didn't relate to it as seriously as I should have. I painted more pictures, because the city was speaking to me with all the colours and sights of autumn and early winter, the like of which I had never experienced. I took them to galleries, and they were gladly accepted.

Only after a week of being a tourist and getting to know Toronto did I turn to the matter of Ronald Friedlich. I began my search in open, accessible sources, like phone books and municipal records, and went about it very cautiously, after preparing a fairly convincing cover story. I found his parents' names and their current address, as well as the address of the house where Ron – as I had taken to calling him in my mind – had lived as a child.

That childhood home was a small two-storey house, a couple of miles from central Toronto, in a neighbourhood that seemed rather poor, and was partly inhabited by Greek and Indian immigrants. The house was on a main street, where streetcars and buses passed by on their way to the eastern suburbs. The houses were close to each other, and were fronted by patches of untended lawn. The Friedlich's house, now home to an Indian family, was built of dark bricks and had a small attic under its roof.

I walked around the house, taking photographs and sketching. A boy and girl from the next-door house, with the suspicion of immigrants lacking in self-confidence, asked me what I was doing. I told them I was moving into the neighbourhood and asked where the school was. They were happy to point the way.

Before going into the neighbourhood elementary school, I decided that if a teacher thought I was the Ron who'd graduated over ten years ago, I'd simply deny it. But that never happened. The corridors were full of immigrants' kids and the commotion reminded me of my elementary school, which had also been largely populated by a mixture of children from immigrant families and Arabs whose parents wanted to integrate into Israeli society. The atmosphere was nothing at all like I remembered of my two years at the polite, conservative school in Ottawa – mainly the school uniform and the blond hair of my classmates, and one girl with very blue eyes, who gave me my first kiss, the day before my father's assignment was over and we flew back to Israel. It was a kiss that transformed Canada from a geographical concept to a secret desire, a dream realm which I thought I'd never visit again. And here I was once more, walking around freely in a Canadian school, quite excited.

On a wall, I found photos of the graduating classes. Despite the ten years that separated the photo of the long-haired twenty-five-year-old Ronald Friedlich in his passport and the kid in eighth grade, his face jumped straight out at me. Had it not been an impossibility, I would have thought that the chubby, nice-looking boy smiling at me from one of the frames was me. Perhaps I shouldn't have been surprised; if we were so similar now, it was logical that we were also similar when we were little. Nevertheless, it was a peculiar sensation.

A bell rang and the kids scurried into their classrooms. Teachers who passed by looked at me, and eventually one of them asked if I needed help. I said I was moving with my family into the area, and looking into schools for my son, who would be going into first grade next year. This led to an invitation to the principal's office, something I hadn't wanted, but I did learn one important thing there for my cover story: the current name of the school dated back about a decade, and before that it had only been a number. The principal called in the teacher who would be taking first grade, and the two posed for a photo for me in the main corridor and again at the entrance, so I'd "have something to show my son". I also took a picture of Ron's class photograph, and I memorized the names of some of the teachers, the homeroom teacher, the then-principal, and a few of his classmates. I asked what high schools the graduates went to and I was given the names of two, which helped me focus my search.

At the high school, it would have been difficult to deny the resemblance between me and the eighteen-year-old graduate, and I decided to cut my visit there to a minimum. Luckily, at the first one I went to I found two photographs of Ron. The first was of the graduating class, at the exact age at which I was inducted into the Israeli army. I was still umbilically linked to my feelings and memories about the induction, and in Ron's picture I saw a more successful version of myself. The eighteen-year-old Ron was a lot skinnier than the pleasant kid of fourteen. His cheekbones were prominent, his face seemed longer, and his jaw more clean-cut. The look in his eyes was also different. No longer the nice friendly boy, but rather a predatory young male, with a look that I had never had.

The second picture shed some light on the change. Hanging next to the class photo was one of the school football team, taken after it won the Toronto schools' championship. In the centre, smiling proudly, holding the trophy, was my double: a robust young man, the puppy fat of childhood replaced by muscle.

A special ops guy, I thought to myself. If he'd been an Israeli with that physique, with the strength and fitness needed to captain a football team, he would have got into the elite commando unit, Sayeret Matkal. When had the chubby kid decided he'd had enough of the softy image, and that he wanted to be captain of the school football team, perhaps the number one aspiration in the culture of North American youth? What had he done to morph from a puffy fourteen to a beefy eighteen?

It reminded me of all the workouts I did in the eleventh and twelfth grades, in the hope of getting my combat fitness rating high enough to be able to join one of the elite units. Just as we, the students of Leo Baeck High in Haifa, saw ourselves as smarter than the kids at Reali High, we also tried to show that we were more militarily gung ho than they were, despite their affiliated military boarding school. But I gave up too quickly. By then I was already aware of my not particularly positive trait of not seeing anything as important enough to devote much effort to it. During night runs in the deep sand along the seashore, and then up the French Carmel to the state of the art gym facilities that Leo Baeck High had put at our disposal, I used to huff and puff like an antiquated steam engine, curse, spit, retch – and simply break down. Fuck the paratroops, fuck the Golani recon unit. So it'll be artillery or engineers. As long as it wasn't the tanks, for obvious reasons. And if I had tried a little harder? Would I have become a guy with a body like Ron's?

So why did he succeed, I asked myself, where I didn't? Was there something in the Canadian air that led him to set the goals that were right for him and to act to achieve them in a more focused way than I had? Perhaps football was to him what art was to me: the things we were good at, where our talents showed through. But, in the meantime, my road had been blocked by my "surroundings". By the messy nature of the part of the world where I grew up. And what had happened to him? What had he gone through before becoming a homeless wanderer, and then dead and buried in the sands of Sinai, without anyone knowing what had befallen him?

I felt a need to get to know him better, and not only for cover purposes.

There was something about Ron that was signalling to me, again and again, that he was a relevant alternative to myself, if I could only decipher those signals properly.

I decided to take a look at his parents. It wouldn't do any harm for me to know what they looked like, so that if necessary I could give an accurate description of them. I devoted three days to this, at first without results. The Friedlichs were now living in a neighbourhood of Toronto known as The Beach, on the shore of Lake Ontario, down the road from where they had lived before. I took the streetcar, and the trip along Queen Street took far longer than I'd expected. As it turned towards the lake and the houses began to look more cared-for, the road itself became the dividing line between a more expensive area, to the right of Queen Street, and the less well-off part, to the left. I alighted and walked along the road, which was like a street in a seaside village. The trees were covered in autumn foliage and the small buildings, one or two storeys high, housed shops selling souvenirs, beach equipment, clothing and all kinds of food.

The Friedlich's street ran from the main road towards the lake, ending at a large park along the shore. It was lined by small, wooden, two-family duplexes that could have all looked the same, but each was painted a different colour, green, yellow, orange, blue or brown, and each had a garage in the yard painted the same color. It was a cheerful sight, and my first thought was how much I would like to live in such a house, close to a park and a lake. When I remembered it was Ron's parents who lived here, I thought how much I would like my parents to live in a house like this and in a place like this, free of the anxiety over national existence that casts such a dark shadow over everything that happens to them. But Ron's parents had lost their son, I reminded myself. Nobody would want to change places with them. Nobody deserves such sorrow.

I knew the house number, but I didn't want to stake out their home from nearby. In fact, I couldn't do so, for fear of arousing their suspicions or that of their neighbours. In the half-light of dawn or in the evening, observation from a distance is not effective, so I did mine during daylight hours. Some of the time I sat on a bench in the park looking up the street, with a freezing wind blowing on my back from over the lake, and the rest of the time I sat at a bus stop on Queen, with a view straight down the street. I couldn't stay there too long without getting onto one of the buses, so I also spent hours in one of the restaurants on the corner, from which

I couldn't see the house but could see everyone emerging from the little street. I decided to rent a car, something that would make things easier, and would enable me to follow the Friedlichs if they left in a vehicle.

With the motor running and the heat on, the discomfort of stakeout duty was relieved, but the difference in the temperature between inside and outside caused condensation on the windows, and the white fumes emitted through the exhaust pipe into the freezing air formed a pillar of cloud that signalled something irregular was afoot. I didn't feel comfortable, although I moved the car around and changed it for another one on some pretext after a couple of days.

On the fourth day I saw a couple aged around sixty coming out of the house. I had no doubt they were the Friedlichs. Ron's father had a grey beard and his mother was an attractive woman. I had seen her before, when I was watching the end of the street and she had walked by to do some shopping. But then I'd had no way of knowing she was Ron's mother. Arm in arm, they walked to the bus stop. I took several photographs of them, and got ready to follow their bus. Obviously, I wasn't about to show myself to them because they would immediately think I was their son.

I asked myself, if they didn't know their son was dead, what did they know? When had they last seen him? Not for the past four years, judging from the stamps in his passport, unless they had travelled to meet him somewhere. How often had he called them, and what were they thinking now? I pictured my parents in their situation, and tears came into my eyes. Did the Friedlichs have other children, who just maybe could be some kind of comfort? Did they have grandchildren, impish little sources of consolation? If Ron was their only child, their situation was too horrible to contemplate.

Nature has designed us to separate from our parents, when the time comes. From the time they help us to come of age, they gradually wither and we become prepared for the moment of parting. But for parents to have to part from their son forever? It's not only that he is supposed to carry on your genetic presence in the world. After you have brought a son into the world, raised him in joy and in pain, loved him unconditionally, watched his every stage of development, worshipped every clever thing he uttered, seen him grow older and smarter, become a teenager, the captain of the football team – and all at once it is all over?

I recalled a conversation I had with Udi in the little house in Tel Aviv, when I raised the matter. Then, I'd put it out of my mind, but now the horror of it was clear. Growing old like that, without knowing. It was a terrible thing for me – for us – to know and not to tell them. I knew very well that if and when Ronald Friedlich was registered as deceased in the Canadian registry, the passport would become worthless. Any check carried out by the authorities would expose our bluff and put me in considerable danger. And as Udi said, we hadn't killed him, we hadn't concealed his body, and we were not even sure what had actually happened to him. We also couldn't own up to having his passport – and a passport like this, in the hands of a trained operative, was invaluable.

So why was I feeling so lousy about myself? I felt I couldn't go on watching them. Let them go wherever they were going, in any case it was unlikely to provide much information.

But then, something else occurred to me. The house was empty now, and in it might be the answers to all my questions, even to questions I hadn't thought of. I knew I would have to get the Office's approval for a break-in, to submit an operational plan, to think of escape routes, contingencies and responses. What if they were to come home suddenly, or if the cleaning lady turned up, or if I bumped into a neighbour? What cover did I have for any such occurrence, especially in light of my identical resemblance to Ron? For one moment I thought that if I was surprised by a neighbour I could pretend to be Ron, but ruled it out immediately. How would his parents be able to live with the news that Ron had appeared and then vanished again? I could say I had the wrong address, and if that didn't work, I would have to stun the person, and clear out quickly in my car. And after that, of course, I would have to explain everything to Udi.

There was no chance I'd get approval for such an operation, and even if I did, I'd probably lose days waiting until they left the house again. As the bus with Ron's parents on it drove away I got out of the car and headed for the house. I'll either get a medal or get busted.

I didn't see any sign of a burglar alarm, closed circuit TV or extra locks. It looked as if the door simply locked when you closed it. Anything more, and I would have needed special equipment. Looking both ways, and with my heart beating 180 times a minute, I went to the door, rang the bell – to ascertain there was no one inside – took two plastic cards out of my wallet, shoved them between the door and the jamb and pressed with a small pen knife. The latch slid in and the door swung silently open.

I knew what to look for: any information at all on my Canadian double, his childhood, youth, parents and other family members. Pictures, documents, anything that would enable me to be him. That was on the operational level. But I felt I was here for another reason as well, and this was what had led me to violate the rules. I was here to check out the alternative to my own life. What I would have been, had I grown up under the conditions in which Ron had grown up. The closeness I felt for him, because of our great resemblance, aroused in me a strong urge to get to know him, inside and outside, not only as Ron Friedlich, but as another way that Mickey Simhoni could have lived his life. Just as a tree would grow differently if planted in different soil, I was curious to know how I would have turned out if I'd grown up here, and not in Haifa.

I pushed the locking button on the latch with my knuckle, so as not to leave a fingerprint. Inside the house the curtains were drawn and I had to wait until my eyes grew accustomed to the dark. It smelled like a home: the breakfast toast, the flowers in the vase. On the wall facing me, in the hall, I made out some framed certificates and pictures. Leo Friedlich, doctor of dental medicine, was printed in large letters on one diploma, under the name of some Anglican university in elaborate lettering that was hard to read: its emblem had a large cross at its centre. It had been awarded to Leo on his graduation with distinction in 1980. The other certificates were in smaller letters; I rapidly photographed them to be examined later.

On another wall there were family photos. Even in the faint light I could recognize myself, that is Ron, and his parents, at different ages and in different places. There was a girl in the pictures too, probably Ron's sister. Leo always had an unkempt beard that grew greyer as the years went by. In contrast, his clothes were always impeccable. He was wearing suits and ties that I had never seen on my father or his friends in Israel, where informality in dress reigned. I even remember dad saying, "I don't understand how all the geniuses in the field of men's fashion have come up with nothing more than the same jacket in almost the same colours everywhere." And I understood even less this idiocy, the tie, a piece of cloth, a colourful decoration, hard to knot, that chokes you and yet everyone feels that they have to wear one.

In other photos, from more recent years, Ron was absent. Here were his father, his mother, his sister and a balding young man who was apparently her husband, and a baby who grew older in each picture.

Despite my accelerated pulse, common sense told me I wasn't in danger, for now. They had taken a bus in the direction of central Toronto and were likely to be away for some time. I was about to climb the stairs to the second floor when I saw a chest of drawers against the far wall, and on it a pair of tall candlesticks, a large seven-branched menorah and above them, a wooden plaque carved with the word "Shalom" in Hebrew and English.

My insides quaked. They were Jewish. For a moment, I felt weak-kneed. Here I was, Mickey Simhoni, a Mossad operative, an agent of the Jewish state, posing as a dead Jew, and breaking into the home of his parents, Jews like me.

Actually there was nothing about this situation that should have astonished me, certainly not to the extent that it did. No one had ever told me that the dead Canadian in Sinai was not a Jew. He could have been a Jew just as much as he could have been anything else. The only thing that interested the Mossad was that he was a Canadian. Was I adopting a Jewish name? But Friedlich was not necessarily a Jewish name. Perhaps only one of the parents was Jewish. This could also be the reason that there was no mezuzah on the doorpost. If only the mother was Jewish, the family name wasn't, and if only the father was a Jew, then Ron wasn't one. And anyway, why should I care about it?

But care I did. I felt my betrayal all the more strongly, if the identity I was stealing was that of the son of a Jewish family, and I was leaving that family in the dark about their son's death. I also felt my kinship all the more strongly. This too should not have happened to me, but it did. Just as I was a "patriot by default" I was also a "Jew by default". I had never thought there was any special value in my being Jewish, I never thought Jews were better than any other people, but I knew where the concept of "Germans of the Mosaic faith" had led. Other nations weren't willing to accept us as part of them – and I couldn't even define myself as being "of the Mosaic faith". Ever since I could think for myself, as a teenager, I had never given even a shadow of a chance to there being any such thing as what believers of all kinds call "god". But I also knew what the fate of unbelieving Jews had been, those who thought they could somehow tag along with the ostensibly supra-national, ideological, classless collective of Soviet Communism. And beyond all this, I was the grandchild of survivors of death camps and the son of people who had been conceived in a displaced persons camp and in besieged Jerusalem. I had imbibed with my mother's milk the certainty that in order to survive the Jews had to have their own country.

To the same extent, I too felt the estrangement my father felt from all those Jews living outside Israel "who don't see the situation they're in" and who "are ready to give up being a free nation in its own land" and "to live under the protection of the Gentiles" – all dad's phrases, and he never spared those Jews his tongue lashings. I however, didn't feel the same way about those whose fate had taken them elsewhere and offered them different possibilities, those who were able to live under the illusion of merging into other surroundings, as was apparently possible here, in Canada and the United States, each a place where immigrants from many lands were creating a new nation.

My father was even more vituperative whenever the matter of Jews who left Israel came up. "Rabin was being gentle when he called them 'a fallout of nobodies'," I remember him saying. "They're simply traitors." When I challenged him about this, he replied, "If ever mum and I are in big trouble and you, instead of lending a hand, desert us, you would be, in my eyes, a traitor." Sometimes he reminded me of the terrifying father in one of the stories I'd read as a child, who preferred his son to die in battle rather than come home without winning.

All of this ran through my mind in seconds, but it seemed as though my confusion had rooted me to the spot facing the Shalom plaque, the candlesticks and the menorah for too much precious time. I began to feel an urgency, and I hurried upstairs.

There I found Ron's room. It was quite dark, but I didn't want to turn on a light. Next to one wall there was a weightlifting bench with a barbell and heavy weights on the rack, and next to it dumbbells that also looked pretty heavy. Along the other walls there were a double bed and bookshelves, containing mostly travel books, science fiction and sports magazines. On a small desk, there was a pile of letters, which I made out to be from Ron. I switched on the desk lamp and photographed the one on top, and a random sampling of the others lower down in the pile. It would have taken too long to photograph them all. I saw some photograph albums underneath the desk and leafed through two of them, taking care to touch only the outside edges of the pages. One contained pictures from Ron's childhood, the other was from his teenage years.

Here are Ron and his parents in the garden of the old house that I'd visited only a few days before. Leo is grinning, standing by a barbecue and little Ron is taking what may have been his first steps towards his mother's outstretched arms . . . And here's Ron again, perhaps three years old by now, wearing a sailor suit, on the deck of a cruise ship. I remembered a picture like this one, in my own album, of myself in an almost identical sailor suit, on the beach in Haifa, with the ships in the port in the background. I turned the pages, enthralled by my alternative childhood, a green childhood amongst little cottages and forests, lakes and rivers. I and the bearded man – Ron that is, with Leo – swimming in a river, sailing on a lake, climbing a hill and skiing down it, with his pretty mother in the background. I photographed two of the pictures and moved on to the second album.

Until now, I had been gripped by the nostalgia of someone looking at photographs of his distant childhood, with landscapes clouded by mists of oblivion and youthful parents, both belonging and not belonging there. But the second album hit me with an awareness of my own unfulfilled youth. For page after page, I saw how the little boy shed his puppy fat and morphed into a sturdy, handsome teenager. His parents appeared in fewer photos, replaced by friends. And the more Ron stopped being Mickey, the more his muscles thickened and his facial features became clearly defined, the more friends there were around him, as he became the centre of the photographs, the focal point.

What had made him like this? What was it about Canadian life that had not allowed him to remain what he was, and what I had also been, the chubby, friendly-looking boy on the sidelines? Or more to the point, what had enabled him to escape from this genetic trap in which I had remained ensnared?

I had always been one of the gang, but never its focal point. Never the leader. Different qualities, or a different appearance, were apparently needed to be at the centre, somewhere that I had never aspired to be, either because I knew I couldn't or because it simply wasn't my natural position. Is an alpha male born to be an alpha male, or does his environment make him one? Does every soldier, in Napoleon's adage, carry the marshal's baton in his knapsack or are there those who are meant to be marshals while still in their mothers' wombs, and others who are not? I didn't have the answers, but I did have a clear sense that the toddler in the sailor suit on the cruise ship and the toddler in the sailor suit on the Haifa beach carried the identical kit in their rucksacks. Something had caused them to grow up differently.

The gap became still more tangible when my browsing brought me to the period when Ron's male buddies were replaced by girls. They were all so pretty, all these leggy, Waspy blondes with blue eyes that surrounded him, first in cheerleader uniforms around the football captain, and then, one at a time, clinging to his arm, or cuddling up to his chest. Ron, you fucker, I whispered to my dead double, you fucked all the beauties in your class, something I could only dream of.

I photographed some of the pictures. After transmitting the material to the Office, I'd be able to make prints of some to carry in my wallet as part of my cover.

The phone rang, and I jumped. I went out into the hall, and stopped to hear the message on the answering machine.

"This is the home of Dianne and Dr Leo Friedlich," said a pleasant female voice and after the request to leave a message, I heard a young woman saying, "Hi mom and dad. Where are you?"

A little girl's voice could be heard in the background, and then the message continued: "It's Marcy. I took Bonnie out of school because she didn't feel well, and we're on our way to you."

Time for me to clear out. But an almost irresistible urge made me peek into the parents' bedroom. The curtains were open and the room was bathed in sunlight. An ordinary bedroom, with an en suite bathroom, an unmade bed, a cupboard, and a bookshelf. As I turned to leave, my eyes went back of their own accord to the books. Did I see right? Hebrew letters? There was a Jewish prayer book, and beside it a slim volume, in Hebrew. The title caught my eye, *Memories of a Beloved Land*. And underneath that, in small type, *A Lament*. The author's name wasn't given.

I opened the book. I must be crazy, I said to myself. What a great news story it would make: "Israeli Spy Nabbed in Break-in Reading a Book of Hebrew Poems." But what the heck was this little book doing here? Did someone give it to them? The Friedlichs apparently must have some connection with Israel, I thought as I scanned the first lines which seemed to be predicting an Arab conquest of Tel Aviv.

Downtown Tel Aviv, and Ramat Gan, looked like a little Manhattan
From Tel Aviv U or from Ayalon freeway (now Istiqlal Highway).
Splendid skyscrapers, Azrieli's towers, white on blue, kind of Zionist;
anyway, the bombs wrecked it, they say.
Nothing left but a bent steel skeleton, a monument screaming to
    heaven.

I was enthralled and horrified. I wanted to take the book with me, but
couldn't. I had no idea how important it was to them, or whether they'd
notice it was missing or not, and in any case I couldn't have anything in
Hebrew on me.

The front door could have opened at any minute, and I would be in
big trouble, but I quickly photographed several more pages.

A car outside blew its horn.

I leaped up as if I'd been bitten by a snake. Idiot! I wiped the cover of
the book with my sleeve, in case I'd left prints, shoved it back into its place
next to the prayer book, and zipped downstairs to the front door. A fast
peek through the eyehole showed me the coast was clear. I pulled my
sleeve over my hand and turned the door handle, pushed the latch button
and went out, closing the door behind me.

I tried to walk away slowly, so as not to arouse the suspicions of passersby,
but I wanted to be clear of the place as soon as possible. If it had been
Marcy who blew the horn and she'd seen me she'd probably think I was
Ron. But it wasn't her. I walked away from the house towards my car at
the corner of the street when I heard a car drawing up behind me. Like
Lot's wife, like a novice at espionage, I turned around. It was a red mini-
van. Marcy, who I recognized from the photos, was manoeuvring into a
parking space, but her six or seven-year-old daughter saw me.

"Mommy, look," the childish and rather hysterical voice reached me
as I quickened my pace. I could barely breathe as I slid into the car, turned
on the engine and drove off into the traffic. Only after a few blocks, when
I saw the mini-van wasn't following me did I take a deep breath and try
to get my heartbeat down to normal.

It was obvious that I had to report my actions, so I transmitted a message to HQ describing what I had done. The reply came within minutes: Udi is on his way. Remain in your hotel room until he arrives.

It sounded ominous, as befitted my departure from regular procedures. For doing things like this they threw trainees out of their course without blinking. I thought I'd have to stay in the room for at least two days before Udi showed up, and that didn't seem reasonable to me.

I had a bottle of Glenfiddich single malt, on which I had spent fifty Canadian dollars, and I wasn't sorry. This was what I needed to settle the raging in my mind. When I finally managed to gather my thoughts, I transferred the photos from my camera to my laptop and began to decipher the certificates, the pictures and the letters.

At the end, there were the poems in Hebrew. On the screen I read one about nightlife in Tel Aviv, ending with another allusion to the city under Arab rule:

> *Tel Aviv at night was amazing*
> *The promenade between the hotels and the sea,*
> *The sea of people, walking, jogging, juggling*
> *Bauhaus buildings on Rothschild Ave., restaurants all around.*
> *The Sheinkin area, the Florentine neighbourhood*
> *And the women*
> *Right out of Toulouse Lautrec.*
> *The Old Port compound with its*
> *Cafés, wooden promenade, and all those people.*
> *Like London's Docklands, like New York's Pier 17*
> *Like the waterfront.*
> *The beach, the bars everywhere.*
> *But booze is banned in this new*
> *Sharia-law land.*

The shock that hit me had nothing to do with the quality of these poems, if they were poems at all. It was connected to the dual realities depicted here: the one the poet was familiar with, and that I also knew, although I wasn't a Tel Aviv night owl, and the one that he or she was imagining, but was depicting in the same realistic way, that made me see it actually happening. A similar future was foreseen for Jerusalem, I discovered when

I clicked on the arrow to the right of the poetic depiction of Tel Aviv, and this text came up:

> *There were full bars in Jerusalem too,*
> *All the alleyways around Nahalat Shiv'a*
> *Are crowded, bar, restaurant, bar, restaurant*
> *Also the whole of downtown*
> *Girls strapless and in hot pants,*
> *A city full of booze and sex.*
> *That's what kids do today, old man*
> *You think these are your times*
> *With your campfires and sing songs?*
> *They are not, but neither are they the youngsters'*
> *When a girl can go out only if she's wearing a burka.*

Whoever wrote this, perhaps some Israeli street poet, perhaps someone Leo Friedlich met at his synagogue, must have done so before the Second Intifada, perhaps in the lull between the First and Second Intifadas, because now the cafés were empty, in both Tel Aviv and Jerusalem. The songs described some time past, and a remarkably scary future.

I decided to move on and examine the photographs.

There was Ron skiing on snow and on water, riding a water scooter and waving; sitting on a big Honda motorbike, with a beautiful girl behind him whose hair would soon be blowing in the wind. The man knew how to live well, something I had never learned.

Suddenly it dawned on me: I did what was necessary, what I was good at, and what attracted me; this included being in the army, being an officer, and being an artist but simply enjoying life wasn't something that had ever occurred to me. Not that I don't go to the beach. I do, and I like sunbathing and swimming. And it's not that I don't go to restaurants. I do, and although I'm no connoisseur, I like food. And I watch films and sometimes plays as well, but all of these were a kind of light dessert to the so-called "real" things in life. How was it that I'd never just hung out with the gang in a bar or a café, just to kid around and laugh at life? Why shouldn't the most important thing be to get some fun out of life?

I had no answers. To be like that would have required a reboot of the disc which had programmed my upbringing. It had never crossed my mind that I could live without commitments, to my surroundings and to myself, simply so that I could enjoy life. But it seems as though my Canadian double had, and had a really good time doing so.

✧✧✧

I read the letters from him that I'd photographed. The oldest was from Katmandu, right after he'd completed a twenty-day trek around the Annapurna range, and he wrote that he felt like "the king of the world". In the next, from Vietnam, he said it was simply unbelievable what the Canadians had allowed their American neighbours to do there, and what for? For another scrap of influence? "The generals should be hanged. All the generals," he wrote.

So maybe he wouldn't have become a company commander . . .

Three letters were from India, and in them I was dismayed to note a clear mental deterioration. The first was a balanced, philosophical epistle from Dharamsala after attending a Vipassana meditation workshop for beginners, combined with an introductory course on Buddhism. Ron distinguished clearly between what he got out of it – it seemed to him a good way of looking at life (how to avoid trying to hold onto things, because everything changes, both the holder and the thing that is held and holding on brings distress) – and the spiritual concept of reincarnation which he perceived as totally detached from reason. ("How can I spend an hour meditating on the gratitude I feel for being a human and not a cat in this incarnation, when the whole business of reincarnation seems absurd to me?" he wrote, winning another plus mark from me.) India had been an unfulfilled goal of mine ever since my pre-army days, and I thought that this was exactly how I would have reacted had I been sitting there like him on "a slanted wooden stool that relaxes your legs but kills your ass".

In the second letter he wrote that he'd made friends with a beautiful Danish woman, the loveliest woman he'd ever met, and after two days with her he'd discovered that she'd been living there for months, making a living by dealing in drugs. She travelled freely around the villages of the stunningly beautiful Parvati valley, where high-grade hashish was grown, and he'd fallen in love with her beauty, her daring, and he thought he'd found his ideal partner. The third letter was quite confused, the handwriting jerky and judging by what could be understood from it, the

Danish woman had not returned from one of her expeditions and he was trying to get rid of the drugs she'd left in their room, but he did not exactly understand what was happening to him or what he should do.

I felt a pang in my heart. I knew what had eventually happened to him, starting in India and ending up in Sinai. How rapidly he had fallen from the heights of insight in Dharamsala to his lonely death in a Bedouin shack!

I felt sorrow gradually spreading inside me. How easy it was to fall. And what a waste it was. Now it was no longer the death of some Canadian junkie who looked a lot like me. Now it was the death of the alternative life that could have been mine if, for example, my grandfather had taken advantage of his service in the Jewish Brigade of the British army and migrated to a Commonwealth country instead of going to Palestine, where one bloody war awaited him, then another, and yet another for him and his son, and finally a war that almost killed his son. There was plenty still to come for his grandson too, for me.

Sitting in an armchair, with the mellow Glenfiddich warming my throat and my chest and my belly and my thoughts, I began to feel that it was the dead Ron Friedlich flowing through my bloodstream and trickling into my brain. Ron had exposed me to a different reality, one that could have been my own. It could have been me. I was who I was, that couldn't be lost. The son of my parents, the grandson of my grandparents. I was born in a hard country, one for which we will always have to fight, we and our children after us, unless what was hinted at in the frightening poems by that anonymous poet actually transpired, God forbid. But nevertheless, there was no reason for me not to take from Ron the things that I could, the things I liked about him. Tomorrow, I thought, I would enroll at a gym. It would even be good for my cover, and the Office would pay.

I went back to study the photos I'd taken, trying to reconstruct Ron's family life, focusing on the pictures of Marcy, his sister and her daughter, who may have recognized Ron in me, and while I was doing this, there was a knock on my door. I thought for a moment of deleting the pictures, but instead just closed the computer. To my amazement, it was Udi. Only then did I remember that the knock had been an agreed signal.

"You fucking idiot," he said as he came in. "You don't know how much I feel like punching you in the nose."

Udi placed his bag by the wall and shut the door with his foot. I saw an Air Canada sticker, with the codes YVR and YTO on the bag, and I understood he'd arrived at the inland flight terminal here from Vancouver. He undid his sloppily knotted tie, took off his jacket, which wasn't an exact match with his trousers, and tossed it onto the back of the nearest armchair.

"Your luck I happened to be in Canada, or you would have been grounded, and perhaps sent back to Israel for a disciplinary hearing."

I replied by relating to the part of the sentence that suited me more. "I see you came from Vancouver."

Udi followed my eyes and understood. "So now you're not only a hero, but also smart. Nice. Get me a drink and start talking."

I recounted everything I had done so far, stressing all the considerations that led me to break into the Friedlich place. To persuade him that the risk had been not only reasonable but also worth taking, I showed him the copies I'd taken of the certificates, photographs and letters, which had almost completed the puzzle. I now knew almost everything about Ronald Friedlich that could come up in an interrogation, apart from his time at university.

When I came to the poetry book, Udi tensed up.

"Erase them all right away."

"But it's strange, isn't it?"

Udi didn't see it as I did.

"As strange as finding a book of poems in Italian or French. And as you've told me they are Jews, it's even less strange. Now, erase it. You don't want to have to explain what it is, do you?"

"Perhaps it means the family has some connection with Israel. Don't we want to know?"

"You erase it. We know what we want and need to know. And erase it not only from your computer but also from your head."

There and then, before his eyes, I deleted the poems, one screen after the other, picking up, as I did so, a few lines here and there.

"Now, reformat. If there's anything important on your disc, send it to the Office."

"All the pictures are on the D drive, the rest's on C," I said and I entered the reformat order.

"I don't know what to do with you," said Udi when I'd finished, pursing his lips. "Your information gathering has been going very well, and I have something to compare it with." I assumed he was referring to some other operative establishing cover in Vancouver who had evidently not collected as much as I had, but was sticking to the rules. "On the other hand, you're a loose cannon. I don't know what to expect next. And that we cannot afford."

I explained all the contingency responses I'd prepared before the break-in, but Udi cut me short because that wasn't the issue.

"A wild horse . . ." I tried to remind him, but Udi replied with the Talmudic epithet for an ox which has gored someone and must be restrained.

"You are on the verge of getting fired," and he really meant it. "You can now assume without any doubt that you cannot do anything like this again and stay in the organization."

I was relieved, and sensed from his expression that Udi actually appreciated what I had done. Perhaps he would have done the same.

"OK, before you kick me out, can you tell me if anything came of the information I collected in Cyprus?"

"You really are cut off here, huh?" said Udi suppressing what I imagined was a hint of a smile. "Keep abreast of the news. Two of your clients over there were preparing explosives to be shipped to Gaza on a fishing boat. You tipped us off about the link between them. They had already done it a few times, with the Hamas naval force picking the stuff up. This time we doctored it and they had a "work accident" in Limassol port. The two are off our list now, as is another dear friend, who we didn't know about."

A huge feeling of satisfaction filled my chest. My very first operational expedition had yielded results. Less weaponry in Gaza, and fewer weaponry dispatchers in Cyprus.

"Good, so I earned the cost of my ticket and upkeep," I tried my luck, when Udi failed to compliment me directly.

"You're not in a position to joke or to collect citations: you have a large overdraft," he warned. "From now on, I want a double message every evening. What you did that day, and what you've planned for the next day, and you don't do what you've planned without an explicit go-ahead from me."

I felt slighted, but had no option but to live with it. I didn't respond.

"I'll try to see you next week. Until then, do not stray even an inch from the straight and narrow. Dir balak," he added using an Arabic phrase meaning "be careful" that's found its way into Israeli slang.

"By the way, how did you feel when you saw the parents?" he asked, as he donned his coat.

"Awful," I replied. I didn't want to let him into the complicated emotions that the sight of the Friedlichs had aroused in me, and neither into my thoughts about the alternative life that had revealed itself to me. Udi was a man whose motivations were clear-cut, and not abstract.

""Bullshit," he said.

Before leaving, he turned to me at the door and said, "Personally there's nothing that pisses me off more than two-faced morality. I'm an asshole who has killed people, blown them up, burned them, framed them. You name it, I've done it. But I don't allow myself to cry over the people I did it to. Not only when they were shits who deserved it, but also when they were the innocent people I used for the cause. You have to do that reckoning before and not after you pull the trigger. You don't cry for someone and shoot him at the same time. If you're crying, you don't shoot. So don't blubber about the poor parents, and then break into their house so you can do your job better, the job that in the end is preventing them from knowing what's happened to their son."

I closed the door behind him.

I picked up the camera to delete the pictures, something I should have done as soon as I'd transferred them to the laptop. While doing this, I came across the poems that were still on the camera's memory card.

I called each of them up onto the screen, one after the other, reading and erasing. I don't know how many I'd skipped when I was photographing, and what had transformed their content from memories of a beloved, occupied land to descriptions of the war in which it was destroyed. The lines were packed close on the small screen of the camera, and it was hard to read them, but I took in the harsh words as if I'd been hypnotized.

My wife wouldn't leave without the boys.
The young one, who'd just enlisted,
Called from the Valley

To tell us that tanks from Syria and Jordan
And Palestinian police from Jenin
Were racing to get to Kfar Tabor,
And our big boy, a reservist,
Texted us from the Ramon Crater,
That quite a large force of ours is forming there
And looks like there's going to be
An inverted Masada.
What an eye for an image he has.
My wife wouldn't leave without them,
Not on evac day number one
Nor on day two or three.
Later on they said the Americans
Themselves are getting out.
Holders of US passports
Should come to the roof of the embassy
And the sooner the better,
but my wife wouldn't, not without our boys.
What would you have done,
In our place?

I had no answer. But I heard the anguished cry:

My sons, my sons,
What is life without you?
Your splendid curls, my young one,
That you shed before enlisting
On the eve of the war.
And you my big boy
You took on your lean shoulders
All the weight of
The eternity of Israel.
But eternity let us down.
My sons, my sons,
Why am I still alive?

Half-drunk after another shot of whisky, I continued reading the appallingly, shockingly understated accounts of the last days before the country fell. I don't know what happened to the poet's sons in his vision, his nightmare, but I know what he did in the end, because he asked

> *And when we suddenly meet*
> *If we suddenly meet*
> *In a Brooklyn side street*
> *Shall we hug? Laugh? Cry?*

Tears came into my eyes. Alone in the Toronto hotel, far from my family, the thread of events depicted with almost no lamentation was too hard to bear. Precisely because they seemed so plausible.

There was nothing I could do with the emotional baggage these words burdened me with. I could only go on with what I had started.

5.

Encounter at Trinity College

THE NEXT DAY, I headed for the university.

I was not at all sure that Ron Friedlich had gone to university in Toronto. There was no bachelor's or master's diploma on the wall of his parents' home, and perhaps he had studied at some faraway college that gave him a football scholarship, or perhaps he hadn't studied at all after graduating from high school. If indeed he had gone to college here, it could have been at any one of the three campuses in the city. I decided to begin my search at the St George campus of the University of Toronto.

The entrance was on Bloor Street, very close to my hotel and almost adjoining the Royal Ontario Museum, with its new ultra-modernist glass and aluminium entrance building. Two stone pillars topped by clusters of lamps on iron pedestals stood on either side of the gate. From there, a paved footpath led to the heart of the campus, wending its way between green lawns and leafy trees. The path was called Philosopher's Walk, and it really had that kind of a quality. Within a few paces, the glass and steel structures of the city were left behind and instead, on either side of the path, there were the brown or grey stone buildings of the different colleges and faculties, with pillared porticoes and bas-relief cornices, and American ivy that was changing colour from red to brown before shedding its leaves covering the walls.

I decided that unless I found evidence to the contrary, this would be where Ron had studied. All I had to do was to pick a college and a faculty. It would of course be better if I discovered the truth, and that's what I was there for, but it wasn't an easy task. I had already learned there were seven colleges on the campus. Where to begin?

A large, grey stone building loomed ahead, its fourth floor built into a tiled roof, also grey. A path that forked off from Philosopher's Walk led to a wide entrance in the middle of the ground floor, and my feet led me there.

Just after passing through the entrance, I found myself in the quadrangle of what seemed like a castle, consisting of four buildings almost identical to the one I had passed though. The courtyard was made up of perfectly symmetrical rectangles and flower-shaped patterns resembling the Greek letter "chi" which represents Christ, delineated by greenery and narrow pathways.

Several students sitting on benches in the corners of the courtyard followed me with their eyes, and I decided to go through a doorway in the building furthest from them. I found myself in a long, white, arched corridor with niches in the walls, hanging lamps diffusing a yellow light, and a floor paved with small red tiles. It was empty. At one end was an office and from the other end came the pleasant sound of singing voices. I went in the latter direction. On the way, I passed a large noticeboard with pictures of twelve smiling young people on it and "Trinity College" in big letters at the top. There was a crest with an elk or a moose and a unicorn on either side of a shield with a cross painted on it, and underneath that, in smaller letters, University of Toronto. Over the pictures was the heading "Academic Dons".

I continued down the corridor and the singing grew louder until I found myself entering a chapel, a tall, splendid structure made of white marble. At the far end, in a loft, a small choir was singing. I was standing in Trinity Chapel and a plaque on my left informed me that it was dedicated to members of Trinity college who fell in World War II.

The pure voices enthralled me, and I sat down in one of the pews. Despite my atheism, church choral singing had done that to me before. A young man sat next to me. He looked at his watch and muttered that he was waiting for his girlfriend, who enjoyed her choir practices too much. From him I learned that unlike most North American universities, the colleges here were not educational frameworks but rather organizational ones. It was at their colleges that students resided, ate, had social functions, belonged to sports teams and so on. Academically, the thousands of students affiliated to a certain college belonged to one of the various university-wide faculties, such as arts and sciences, engineering, or business.

This would make my search still more complicated.

When I left the chapel after absorbing more of the sublime singing, I called at the office at the opposite end of the corridor. Next to the heavy wooden door was a bench and on the wall above it a tapestry of the college emblem and the sign "Registrar" in large letters. Where to begin if not here?

Here I would not be able to evade my resemblance to Ron. If he had been enrolled here, he would have left only a few years before, and certainly would not have looked different from the way I looked now. If someone remembered him, or if they took out his file with a photograph in it, the question would arise. I was his cousin, and yes, people always said we looked alike. I decided to set aside the claim that I was Ron himself. I would try to stay with the cousin version. It would be better. It would stave off unwanted questions about the resemblance, and would, at most, elicit a smile.

I took a deep breath and went into the reception area, with chairs for people who were waiting. I told the woman behind the counter that a friend of mine was applying for admission to Cambridge and needed a copy of his diploma and his transcripts, a word that I'd made a point of learning. She asked me if I was sure he'd been a student at Trinity College and with a pretended bashfulness I gave her the reply that I'd prepared: he'd given me the name of the college three times and I'd forgotten each time. But how many Ron Friedlichs could there be?

"The thing is, I've only got the lists of students who were at our college. And in any case, the diploma and transcripts would be at the faculty in which he studied, but I'll do what I can. Meanwhile, make yourself a coffee," she added, pointing to a small kitchenette, as she began making phone calls.

I was standing with my back to the kitchenette door, stirring my coffee, when my blood froze.

"I thought I recognized that voice, and the accent, although it has improved somewhat."

I turned around slowly, my coffee cup trembling in my hand.

"Take a sip, or you'll spill it," said Niki, with a hesitant smile. "And maybe you'd better sit down," she said, and indeed, my knees were feeling a little weak. I was overcome by a mixture of joy and horror, and a thousand butterflies were fluttering around in my stomach. The best thing that could happen to me was happening, at the worst time. Who would I say I was? What would I tell her? I didn't want to tie myself, the Israeli that

Niki knew, to Ron Friedlich and the documents in his name that I had asked for.

Niki herself seemed unshaken, although slightly pale, and just as lovely as she had been when we parted nearly a decade before. She looked me up and down, and stood there, as if waiting for the next move. A big hug? A muttered evasion?

We glanced at each other's hands. There were no rings on my fingers, and she wore one that didn't look like a wedding band. Her body bore no signs of having given birth; she was still slight and girlish, wearing a shirt with buttons down the front and a skirt that covered her knees. I stole a glance at her feet, and her toes were still pointing inwards, though not as sharply as then. Niki saw my glance, and her eyes became distant, remembering, warm. She took a small step towards me.

Before I could move, the woman who had been on the reception desk appeared in the door of the kitchenette. "Ron Friedlich was enrolled in the Arts and Science Faculty, and they're ordering up a copy of his BA diploma from the central registrar, but you'll need a power of attorney from Mr Friedlich." At that point she took in the situation. "You know each other?" she asked.

"A little. I'll handle this," said Niki, signalling to me to follow her into one of the rooms leading off the main hall, from which she had probably seen me approaching the reception desk.

I thanked the woman in a faint voice, and walked behind Niki, in a bit of a tizzy. I really did not want her to handle it, and make me have to lie to her as well.

The drab walls of the office were covered with shelves of box files. Near the window were some pretty bonsai trees in pots. This wasn't a room for receiving the public, because apart from Niki's chair on the other side of the desk there were no other chairs. I put my cup on the desk, trying not to let my trembling hand spill coffee on the piles of paperwork, and went to get a chair from the hall. As I turned, I saw on the wall next to the door one of the sketches I had made, with a passionate yearning, of Niki in the club in Asakusa. I walked up to it. There were marks and creases from what it had been through. I ran my finger over the outline of the sketched figure. For a second I was back there, drunk, in love, heartbroken. I turned around slowly. Niki was sitting upright, biting her lip, tears in her eyes.

My heart was pounding and a wave of emotion rose inside me and was about to burst through my throat. But Niki looked at me, even more upright, and put a finger to her lips, signalling to me to be quiet.

"I understand you need someone's paperwork," she said, her first words tremulous but her voice gradually settling down. "But you don't have a power of attorney from him?"

I shook my head.

"And I understand you need it now?"

I nodded.

"I'll get it for you," she said. "Will you follow me?"

I nodded again.

"Would you like to drink your coffee first?"

All I wanted was to get out of there. I took one sip and said, "That will do."

"So let's go."

Niki picked up a short fur jacket and beckoned me to follow her. I stopped at the drawing once more and again stroked it lightly with my fingers. We left the room and I headed for the exit.

"No, it's this way," said Niki, pointing in the opposite direction, and just as in that previous incarnation in Tokyo, I found myself scurrying in her wake.

We left by the main entrance doors with its grandiose portico with marble pillars, and the building's spire soaring over it, and descended the broad stone steps crossing a lawn where a large sign bearing the name of the college stood, and came to a wide and busy avenue, Hoskin Avenue. Niki suggested we make our way to the faculty building through the subterranean passageways to get out of the cold.

She still had the same way of walking with those short steps, her calves were still smooth, muscular and shapely and her skirt was tight enough to outline her cute little bottom. I hurried to close the gap between us, just like then. In one of the semi-dark passages, with no one else around, Niki stopped and turned to me.

"I don't know, and at the moment I don't want to know, what brought you here," she said. "I don't know, and at the moment I don't want to know what you've been through until now, if you're married, if you've got kids. I just want . . ." and then, throwing herself into my arms she continued ". . . for you to hold me, hold me tight." She pressed her face into my chest. "Tighter. As if you'll never let go."

Her small body was shaking in my embrace. She began to cry.

For a long moment we stood there. I wondered if I was dreaming. I couldn't believe this was actually happening to me, to us, but Niki in my arms was so real.

She turned her face, wet with tears, up at me and I leaned over to kiss her, but she broke away and blurted, "No. I'm so sorry. I actually don't know a thing about you. Perhaps I shouldn't."

I wanted to shout out loud, "I have never stopped being yours, even though I never believed it was at all possible. I have had no other love since you."

But I couldn't say anything. Once again I was tongue-tied and awkward, and I didn't know what I should say, or what I could tell her and do with her in my peculiar situation here. Niki wiped away her tears and tidied her hair, and then said just one word, "Come," as she began walking away.

When we emerged from the passageway she said, "Wait here. I'll call you if I need you." We were next to the main library on the campus, a modern two-storey building faced with grey stone slabs and glass windows that protruded from the walls.

"No. I'm coming with you," I said and followed her to the nearby Faculty of Arts and Science, a combination that I had not yet understood. The modern structure, at 100 George Street, was five storeys high with large windows. Inside, we took a corridor that led us to a wide glass door with the words "Departments & Administration" on it. It struck me as an odd term.

"I'll go in by myself," said Niki, quietly but firmly, pointing to a nearby cafeteria where I should wait for her.

As a confirmed coffee aficionado, and a freezing one, I gladly ordered a cup and sat down in one of the black leather armchairs that were placed around the little tables. I regretted not having thought of ordering coffee for her, but before I could return to the counter, or even take a sip from mine, she appeared with a rolled up diploma and a sheaf of transcripts. She asked nothing and said nothing as she handed them to me in a rather formal manner. And then she gave me her hand and said, "I suppose you can find your way out without my help."

"Niki . . . when do you finish work?" were all the words I could find.

"At four."

"Where should I wait?"

"Be in the lobby of the Four Seasons at seven."

"I'll be there."

And she walked away, looking ethereal and as if she was walking on water. I watched her, stunned, until she vanished into the gloom in the corridor. Once again, I had allowed her to walk away. She had come back into my life again so abruptly, so similarly to our first encounter, that all the assertiveness I had developed, all those days and nights during which I had trained to take control of situations and to adapt them to suit myself, had melted away the moment she approached me, again, just like then, offering effective assistance and then disappearing.

But we had fixed a meeting for the evening. And I knew where she worked. This time I would not let her get away from me. But it had all been too sudden, and the surrounding circumstances were really not ideal.

Although getting Ron Friedlich's paperwork was a simple mission, many major operations have fallen through when a routine task like this failed, and many troubles have ensued. If I'd been asked to provide ID before obtaining the material, if someone's suspicions had been aroused and the university security people called in and only a superficial investigation made, there would be no documentation for my cover, and Ron's disappearance would have been linked with us. Who knows what diplomatic and other difficulties would have arisen – not to mention my own plight. I had my good fortune to thank for producing Niki at precisely the right moment, for her not asking any questions and simply performing this service for me. It probably could have got her into trouble and perhaps even cost her her post in the university. But I had a job to do and this wasn't the time to pursue a courtship. The documents I was carrying suddenly seemed red hot. I had to get rid of them right away. I went to a post office in a nearby building and after photographing the papers, I put them in a padded envelope and mailed it to one of our safe addresses in Canada, from which it would find its way to the Office via undercover personnel.

I was curious to know what Ron had studied, and before I transmitted the pictures to Israel as backup for the original documents, I took a look at them on the screen of my camera. The courses he had taken seemed diverse and not particularly challenging. Among them were Environment and Behaviour, Forest Conservation Science, and Nutritional Science, which fell under the heading Life Sciences. There were also Humanities courses, including American Studies, Aboriginal Studies and Buddhism, as well as social sciences courses, including Anthropology, Canadian Studies – I couldn't fathom why that was separate from American Studies – and others that I assumed did not demand too much of an effort, like Environmental Ethics, and Human Geography. There was clearly a common factor, concern with the Earth and culture, and another common factor was the grades – all were average or lower.

Later on I realized why. There was a whole set of fairly high grades under the heading "Varsity Blues", which meant nothing to me. But the following day, when I left the hotel, I noticed a sign saying "Varsity Blues Football Team" outside a sports stadium right across the road. I realized that this was what Toronto University's sports teams were called, and that Ron had apparently made his life easier by accumulating credits for his performance and training on the football squad.

At first I tended to belittle all this, but then I thought that his choice was not all that different from my decision to study art. The guy had a talent for sports and he focused on what interested him and did the necessary minimum of everything else; or perhaps not the minimum – he studied precisely what he wanted to study and invested precisely the time and energy he wanted to invest. "Ron the Jock" seemed to have taken life quite easily. Hats off to you, my dear deceased double.

The Four Seasons was a short walk away from the Town Inn Suites, but after showering, shaving and even applying some aftershave lotion, which I didn't usually do, and donning for the first time the suit I had brought with me, I decided to take a cab. The Pakistani driver pulled a face when he realized it was just a quick hop, but was grateful when I let him keep all the change. He spent the short time trying to find out where I was from. I asked where he was from. "I'm from here," he said. "In Toronto everyone's from Toronto." "So am I from here," I said, concluding our brief conversation. At six o'clock I was already in the hotel lobby.

I couldn't really settle down in the luxurious space, a separate structure from the multi-storey hotel. There were a lot of designer stores around a large marble floor with a thick, expensive-looking carpet in the middle. A few stairs led to a seating area with several identical clusters of a sofa and two chairs around a table, all close to a counter with a selection of pastries and cakes, and a waiter behind the counter. A bad place for a secret meeting, and not exactly right for a romantic rendezvous either. You couldn't sit there without ordering something but I had no appetite. I spent most of the hour in the shops, amazed anew each time by the price tags and by the fact that there must be people prepared to pay so much for the leather and fur coats, handbags, and items of jewellery, all of which seemed to me to be entirely superfluous.

What did I think would happen now? I asked myself. What did I want to happen? I corrected the question. Of course I couldn't know, because I knew nothing about Niki. She may be married, married with kids. And even if she were single, I was here on a mission, I would have to leave soon, and I would not be able to tell her why or where. There was no chance here for a normal relationship. And even if there were, what did I feel about her?

In the years that had gone by, I thought I had overcome the magic, the craziness, the spell that had gripped me during our previous encounter. "Eruption" may be a better word. Something that had occurred suddenly and powerfully, without any explanation that I could articulate. I knew very well that no relationship of mine, pre- or post-Niki, had taken me to the heights of excitement that she had elicited in me, and no night had been anything like the night of wild sensuality I'd had with her. But then I'd been on my post-army travels, borne upon a euphoric wave of freedom from military discipline, open to such a crazy adventure. Since then I had become more settled in my ways. I would probably not be able to feel like that again. Not even about the same woman. For years I had not even been searching for anything like those feelings. I had been seeking a woman I could like and live with, and I had found someone like that, but she was one of the thousand victims of the Second Intifada. What seeing Niki again had aroused in me was mainly confusion, I decided. Emotions apparently take longer to awaken, and it was not certain that what a pretty, girlish figure aroused in a twenty-odd year old guy would work the same way when he was pushing thirty. She, I saw, had hardly changed. I, on the other hand, was about twenty pounds heavier. I would probably not turn her on the way I had then, if I had turned her on, that is. She was the one who cut me out of her life and, when that didn't go smoothly, she had simply disappeared.

Just before seven, I went up into the sitting area, took a chair facing the entrance, ordered a coffee and waited expectantly.

All of the reservations that had gone through my mind melted away the second Niki entered the lobby. She was wearing the same dark blue dress she had worn that night in Asakusa, with a fur coat now covering her bare back. She must have been wearing high heels because she looked quite tall. My heart almost stopped beating. I stood up to welcome her as she came towards me with those small steps of hers. Her hair was gathered at the back, her face was white and a line of black lengthened her eyes. She was stunning. This was the most beautiful woman I'd ever laid eyes on. The excitement that overcame me was stronger than I was. I knew people were watching us. I knew it wasn't done, but I couldn't stop myself. I took hold of her head, her high cheekbones cupped in the palms of my hands, bent over her and kissed her lips. I meant it to be a long kiss, oblivious to everything, but she gave my lip a quick, hard bite and when I pulled my head back, surprised and hurt, she said, "Good evening to you too," her expression icy cold.

Embarrassed, I put out my hand to shake hers, but Niki ignored even that formality and sat down.

"What exactly do you think you are doing?" she asked quietly.

What exactly was I thinking? That I could walk up to a near stranger, not knowing anything about what had happened to her since that far off night in the Tokyo love hotel and kiss her as if she was still mine? The plain truth is that I didn't think. I simply did not think, and that's what I told her: I sat on the sofa and she was on one of the chairs, our knees not quite touching. The waiter, who must have witnessed the entire scene, came over. Niki ordered a cocktail I'd never heard of and I said I'd make do with my coffee.

"Please see this as just an ordinary date," she said when the waiter left us. "We had better get to know each other a bit, no?"

My insides quaked. It wasn't a "yes" – she had not fallen into my arms again as if she'd been waiting for me all these years. But neither was it a "no" – here she was, gorgeous, made-up, well groomed. There was a "perhaps" that fluctuated in my mind between the possibility that she was here out of good manners, like a woman meeting up with an old friend, and the possibility that she was contemplating me as a potential partner. Like an ordinary date. Despite her momentary breakdown in my arms in the dimly-lit university passageway, what was now occurring would not simply close the wide-open gap that had been left between us in the nightclub in Tokyo. I would have to adjust myself to this, but my insides were quaking so deeply that I knew my feelings were coming directly from that place and time, skipping over the almost ten years that had elapsed since then.

For the next hour, we told each other about our lives over that decade, stories that were marked mainly by what had been missing: love. I told her about art school, my painting, teaching, relationships in which I'd found no meaning, journeys around the world that skirted Japan, carefully avoiding her magnetic field, until Dolly appeared. How I had thought I could make a life with her, without being deeply in love. My description of her death made Niki's tears flow freely, while my eyes remained dry. That's where I ended my story.

Niki told me her life had changed abruptly after that night, but she didn't want to go into details about why and how. She'd returned to her parents' home and her father was disappointed because he'd hoped she would be the magnet that would draw the family back to Japan. She tried to keep up the samurai culture here in Toronto by persevering at her judo and swordplay training at a Japanese centre, and she was also teaching a course in calligraphy. After a while she'd understood that she couldn't go on living with her parents, moved out, and enrolled at the university to study literature and editing. To make a living, she'd taken the low-level job at Trinity College and she also worked as a reader for a small publishing house, as well as doing occasional editing jobs.

"Mostly, I like editing romantic novels," she said with a shy little smile. "There are so many ways to love."

"What about men?" I asked rather gruffly.

Niki sighed.

"Some. But Canadians."

The question mark on my face made her finish the sentence: just as she had not come to terms with the stupid traditional machismo that Japanese males couldn't shake off, and which made it impossible for them to accept her for what she was, so she also could not reconcile herself to the overly polite men of Canada, who were scared of women like her. Apparently, I fit in exactly between the two types. She said she'd had one boyfriend who reminded her very much of me, and my heart skipped a beat: I even thought that she was watching me for a reaction but at no point did she ask me why I wanted Ron Friedlich's documents.

Without noticing it, our knees touched and then our legs were entangled and once again I had to ask, "Your place or mine" and this time she said, "Either" and we left the Four Seasons hugging into the cold night and made our way to my warm hotel room.

Niki smiled at the mess and my hurried attempt to tidy it up, and said, "Anyway it's going to be a mess again soon." Her eyes, still shining with a suppressed smile, soon became the crazed predatory eyes of the alley cat, eyes the like of which I had seen in no other human but her, as all those years of pent up yearning and lust flooded together into a single tempestuous night.

6.

The Morning After

THE DILEMMA I'D wanted to spare myself hit me hard next morning. What was I to do now? What was I to do after the most exciting night of love I'd had since the last time with Niki? Actually, there hadn't been a night since then that I could call a night of love. I had simply never been in love, even if the sex was good, and even if I felt affection for the woman I was with, as I did mainly with Dolly. There had been nothing like the spate of feelings for Niki that rushed through me when the dam inside my breast finally broke.

Even when it seemed that there were no more emotions to emerge from the depths of my heart, a whole spectrum of sensations kept on welling up while Niki told me, tears streaming from her eyes, what had happened after I was thrown out of the club in Tokyo. My taxi had driven away, and the moment after I hurled my drawings out of the window one of the guards shoved them into Niki's hands, and another placed her coat around her shoulders. There was a brief, harsh exchange of words in Japanese, someone barred her from going back into the club, and a few minutes later a black Lexus sedan drew up. She was pushed in and a guard sitting next to her said only, "Your apartment." Niki told them where it was, realizing she was in trouble. The missing top part of the driver's little finger left her in no doubt as to whose hands she was in.

She was given five minutes to pack her things under close watch. Her suitcase and two open bags were put in the boot of the Lexus and, with her and the guard in the backseat, it took off. No one said a word to her during the rest of the journey of hundreds of miles all the way to the city of Kyoto, where they arrived at first light. The car stopped in a narrow alley lined with old houses, and Niki had no problem knowing where she was: Gion, the city's geisha district. Another guard was waiting at the doorway of one of the houses, and after some words of welcome and perfunctory bows, as required by the rules of etiquette, she was led to a room at the back of the house. It was here that she was to begin the new chapter in her life as a hostess. Her cell phone was taken away. On the futon mattress on the polished wooden floor her new outfit was laid out. The madam of the house stood over her as Niki stripped off her old identity and replaced it with a new one.

"The clients were mostly local men," Niki told me. "I was still a kind of traditional hostess, something like a warm-up act before or instead of the actual geisha. It was more or less the same kind of work as in Tokyo; all they wanted was to distance me from you."

Scared and anxious, she did what she was told to do for a few months before she dared to run away, from Kyoto to nearby Osaka, where she took the first flight to Canada.

I felt terrible. Niki's Japanese dream had been wrecked by my infantile and idiotic behaviour. If I could only turn back the clock. . . . But I didn't really want to do that. I was here with the sobbing Niki in my arms, and I was as utterly in love as I could be.

So, what was I to do now?

On the face of it, the answer was plain, if only we'd been in a normal situation. A couple of lovers who'd lost each other and had just found each other again would stay together and do what they felt like doing. He'd paint, she'd edit romantic novels. But like the yakuza with the truncated finger who'd taken Niki from Tokyo to Kyoto, I felt Udi, my bulky controller, breathing down the back of my neck. I knew no one would force me to do anything if I chose Niki. I wouldn't be pushed into a black Lexus and whisked away in the dark of night to another city. It was the yakuza in me that didn't allow me to follow this dream, the most natural dream that any young guy and young girl could – and should – dream together. So, what was I to do?

I wrapped myself around Niki and I wrapped her around me, trying to draw a little more heat out of her body to stop the icy tentacles in my mind from spreading, but Niki picked up on my silence and asked, "What do we do now."

"I don't want to lose you again Niki," I groaned with genuine passion, without the faintest idea of how to avoid that happening.

"Do you have to fly back to London? Or Cambridge?" she asked. And before I realized what she was talking about she added, "To give Ronald Friedlich his paperwork?"

I searched for the right words. How could I both avoid lying and avoid confessing, both leave the door open for more and hint that the door could close at any time.

"Ron Friedlich and London are only a small piece of a big puzzle," I said. "And you are a big piece in a very big puzzle that is my life." I said no more, and Niki, very attentive to my words, didn't ask any more questions. We made love again, and then Niki said she had to get up, go home, put on normal clothes and get to work on time. We arranged that I'd pick her up that afternoon at five.

After she'd left, I felt confused and lost, exactly as I'd been back then, but this time, ostensibly, the decision was mine. Ostensibly, because a long and tortuous past that I could not cut myself off from, stretching back way before the day Niki had first come into my life, was haunting me, and I had to satisfy it before I could satisfy the fresh lust and love that had awoken in me.

I decided that in the meantime I'd say nothing to Udi, and that I'd continue getting to know the presumed city where I had grown up, but from now on with Niki.

The days before Udi's return to Toronto were among the most magical of my life. And I could also draw up an exhaustive daily report on the parts of the city I'd visited, and where I'd be going the next day, places known only to the locals. One evening Niki took me to Gerard Street, the site of Little India, which I very quickly learned was actually little Pakistan, but with the same cultural accoutrements as India: restaurants serving chicken tikka masala, shops selling silk scarves, songs in Urdu over the loudspeakers, and posters advertising Bollywood movies.

We strolled around Chinatown, along Spadina Avenue, with signs in Mandarin and shops selling Chinese remedies, but it was Japanese food that we wanted. Nearby, Niki showed me Kensington market, a short colourful street with small wooden buildings and magnificent roofs painted in gaudy shades of red and turquoise blue – with each bottom floor housing a delightful little shop. There were all kinds of paintings, textiles and clothing from India and other Far Eastern places, lots of Buddhist writings on wall hangings, oriental carpets, as well as the sorts of clothes that people used to wear in the Sixties. I thought it would have suited us to be hippies, had we been around then. Especially Niki, and perhaps I'd have tagged along after her. I was glad Niki thought I'd like what I saw, and I really did: the people, the atmosphere, the textiles – which were far from cheap, to my surprise. Nevertheless, I bought her a floral blouse, and with the coming winter in mind, a thick colourful shawl.

"And what about you?" Niki asked.

I stammered something. I didn't see myself wearing these clothes. A sorrowful expression flickered across her lovely face, slight disappointment perhaps. Me and my stodginess, I rebuked myself. No, I could never have been a hippie, even if I'd been around then. But why shouldn't I walk around in a sarwal? What was stopping me from looking like a New-Age type? Well, I told myself, because I wasn't like that, regrettably. Regrettably? I wasn't so sure. I was too rational, too rooted in the ground. I didn't really want to be different. Perhaps if I'd been Ron.

We wandered in the direction of Jenny's bar-café, from which sounds of music were emanating. In the doorway stood an elderly man with a guitar, perhaps a relic of the Sixties, and another oddball in a kilt, and some black guys who were tapping the beat with their feet, and once again we were in heaven. I can be different. In the right circumstances.

The sun was setting, pink clouds were gathering in the sky and all the colours of the street glowed in the spectacular twilight. I asked Jenny, the ageing hippie who owned the place, for a sheet of paper and coloured pencils and she brought me some. On a little table outside, with the guitarist, the Scot and the black guys looking on sympathetically, I drew the street in quick lines, and Niki, in a shop full of vivid Chinese wall hangings, spreading out one inscribed with: "The past is history, tomorrow is a mystery, today is a gift."

This made me into something of a tourist attraction myself, and soon a little crowd gathered around to watch, and some snapped photos of me as I drew. An instinct told me to get away, but, on the surface at least, it fit in with my cover so I kept going. Nonetheless, I was jolted when I feared that one of the tourists taking pictures of me was the girl with the sweet smile from the Hard Rock Café and the City Hall. So they were actually tailing me? Was it possible that I had gone and reawakened the suspicion of the authorities when I was sniffing around the Friedlich residence, or making inquiries at the schools and the university? The girl's face was obscured by the camera and then she turned away, so I couldn't verify my apprehension. A professional tail, on the other hand, if it really were the Canadians, would have photographed me surreptitiously, without attracting my attention. No, it must have been my imagination.

At not too late an hour, after the by now customary "my place or yours", we began our nightly lovefest.

From the first time I went to her apartment I saw that it was a far better love nest than my hotel suite. Niki lived in the Old Town neighbourhood, on the corner of Adelaide and Church, opposite St James Cathedral and a few hundred yards away from the lake, no more than a stone's throw from anywhere we wanted to go. Her building was one of a few huge apartment blocks thirty or forty storeys high, made of a steel skeleton and giant bluish windows facing the lake.

Access to a brightly-lit lobby, faced in brown marble, was gained by punching in a code. There were a few sofas in the lobby, a mirror and another door, which required a key to open it. A key was also needed for the elevator, which whisked us up to the 32nd floor and opened onto the hall of her apartment. Sometimes we couldn't wait until we got to the bedroom and made love on the soft, thick, white carpet, or on the designer sofa overlooking the stunning lake.

I wondered how Niki could afford an apartment like this in a lake-view building, and she told me her father paid half the rent because he wanted her to live in a good place. I also wondered how Niki lasted in her job, because we never slept at night, and only in the morning, after she left for work, did I fall into a deep, exhausted sleep.

When I woke up, and there wasn't much time left before she was due to get back, I dared to step out onto the balcony and the way I felt there reminded me why I wasn't the right material to be a paratrooper. At times, I'd buy groceries at the nearby St Lawrence Market, which was situated in an old brewery building and was full of people and activity all the time. At other times, I would have lunch at one of the food stalls there.

Occasionally, to salve my conscience, I performed a manoeuvre to see if I was being tailed, but I never detected anyone. That doesn't mean I am clean, I told myself. Clearly I wasn't a target who justified a twenty-four hour surveillance operation by the Canadian Secret Service. Perhaps I was just being "sampled" every now and again, but even that seemed unlikely to me. Why should they? Thinking about it unsettled me, but that feeling melted away as soon as Niki showed up, with the glowing green gleam in her eyes. It was like a traffic light telling me, "Go. The coast is clear. You can get to wherever you wish."

When I stayed put, I surfed the Internet, visiting Israeli sites and updating myself on events at home, and sometimes I'd switch on the camera and like someone poking around in an old wound, I couldn't resist the exquisite pain and read some of the poems that I hadn't deleted.

It was hard to read on the little camera screen and I quickly skimmed through those whose first lines didn't grab me, erasing one after the other. The mystery of the writer preoccupied me. It could be a triviality, as Udi had said. Some friend of the family, an Israeli expat perhaps? Maybe not. It must have been there, on the title page and on the cover. What a pity I'd been in such a hurry and hadn't noticed it.

As I went on reading it was clear to me that these words had been written here, in Canada:

Of course there was no choice
But to get a state, and
It wasn't just the Holocaust:
Herzl was right,
I must admit, from my American exile,
A people must have a land.
What Zionism did was a great triumph
In the annals of human endeavour.
One plank after another, we found in the waves
And some rope, and we tied them together
And we had a raft
And then a dinghy
And then a sailing boat
And then a ship,
A destroyer, with guns.
Nothing to be ashamed of,
A home for millions of refugees.
We made deserts bloom
Won Nobel Prizes,
A stable democracy
A high-tech powerhouse

And a light unto the farmers of the world.
I was happy to be part of it,
Until it was no longer there.

My heart was caught in a vice of amazement and anxiety. I didn't have the strength to read further. I was sorry that I had begun. I knew the poems were telling me something, but I didn't know what. Could I surrender? Just drop out? Not be part of that enterprise that I loved so much and believed in, and was even proud of? Be a dejected emigrant, listening to Israeli pop music on CDs?

I debated endlessly, the way they do in Israeli youth movements, but with myself: to live with a bent back in exile, or to die upright in the homeland? This was the choice those lines laid on my doorstep, by forecasting the collapse of the Zionist dream, of Israel. The author, apparently, had made his choice: he had fled to America.

When Niki remembered I was an artist, and I told her that I'd already visited the big galleries, she suggested we go down to the Harbourfront Centre, a complex of buildings on the lake. Here, unlike Pier 17 in New York, or London's Docklands, or even Tel Aviv port and the lively marina in Herzliyah, artists' workshops were the main element and not shops and restaurants.

I'd stayed away from the waterfront so far because of the icy winds blowing in over the lake. Now we walked as quickly as we could to the complex, trying to avoid the gusts. The tourist yachts were battened down for the winter and moored along the stone promenade, though a few were still making the trip to the nearby islands. The restaurants by the shore were mostly empty.

At the entrance to the complex, under the Harbourfront Centre sign, there was an ice skating rink, overlooked by popular restaurants. Niki told me that in summer it was a sea-water pool, with boats.

We hurried inside and I saw that the entire length of the structure was one big space housing workshops for artists and craftspeople. We watched ceramicists, painters and sculptors at work. It was a concept that was new to me, and it seemed a little odd. But when I saw my counterparts doing their thing, my fingers itched.

"You can make yourself a little gallery here, if we stay in Toronto," Niki whispered, and I felt a cold shiver, because I had told myself exactly the same thing a moment before, and had immediately rejected the idea; but the temptation was so great that I feared I would not be able to withstand it. In order to clear the thought from my mind, I dragged her to the ice rink and agreed to skate, although it was something I'd never done before.

Niki slipped into her rented skates with ease and glided gracefully out to the centre of the rink where she executed some pretty dance steps while she waited for me. There were other beginners but they moved gingerly along the railing and I decided to plunge in and slid directly towards Niki, something that of course ended in a painful crash onto my backside and a loud, unrestrained peal of happy laughter from her. Once I had gained a little steadiness and confidence, I tried to imitate her steps, but that, too, ended in another few painful encounters between my butt and the ice, and now some of the other skaters permitted themselves to laugh at my expense. I was amazed at myself. I'd never been so liberated as to paint in the street in front of a crowd and certainly not to make a fool of myself in public. Something in me had changed. The nail driving into my heart had broken through the hard shell that had encased it, revealing a new being, a happy being, as colourful as the scene at Kensington Market: the charcoal sketches of the Nazi trains and the burned out tanks had been left behind.

We ended the evening with a hot chocolate at one of the cafés and with the usual question – your place or mine – but this time, after we'd decided on my place, and I'd paid and we got up to leave, I spotted a burly figure in a dark corner of the café. I needed no more than a split second to recognize that big head with its close-cropped, grey-flecked hair. We stepped out, and I asked Niki to wait a moment. I went back into the café and approached Udi. His blank expression stopped me in my tracks, and only then did I recall his orders: he was a ghost. Only he could come to me, never me to him. I turned around and left.

"Do you have something to do with that man?" Niki asked.

"Not at the moment," I replied rather opaquely, and she didn't press the point. Udi would certainly want to talk to me tonight. Should I return alone to my hotel? Resentment surged inside me.

"Come, we're going to your place," I said, abruptly changing the plan.

"So you do have something to do with that man," she said, but I didn't reply and again she let it drop.

"You're not the same," said Niki, after our first love-making. "Not at all," she added after the second. There wasn't a third time. My spirits had clouded over, and I was torn. When Niki went to work, I went to my hotel, a decision taking shape in my mind. I would not break up with Niki, and if Udi insisted, I'd tell him that this was the end of the connection between us. I would go to Ron Friedlich's parents to tell them their son had died in Sinai and had been buried by the Bedouin. I felt that this unfortunate couple was burdening me with a heavy weight.

Udi was sitting in a wedge of sunlight shining between two tall buildings and illuminating a narrow space near the entrance to the café across from the Town Inn Suites, wrapped in an overcoat. In front of him was one full cup of coffee plus two empty cups. He caught sight of me a moment before I saw him, and signalled to the waiter. I went into the hotel without waiting for him, and just after I'd locked my door, came the knock we'd agreed upon.

"No thank you, I've had mine," said Udi, though I hadn't offered him anything, "but pour yourself one. You look exhausted." Then he glanced around the room and added, "Your room resembles that of a smelly old bachelor. Not surprising you went to her place and not here."

"Actually, she doesn't mind being here," I saw fit to fire back at him.

"Bravo. A man's man. Now, start spilling the beans. I've read all your reports and there wasn't a word there about a girl or about you sleeping somewhere else."

There was a clear tone of rebuke there, and I remembered that I was still in a kind of trial period.

I poured coffee for both of us, tidied the room a bit and sat facing him at the table in the kitchenette.

"I'm waiting," he said.

I decided to begin with Japan. Clearly, that was the only way I could explain how my connection with Niki in Toronto had happened so quickly, and had been inevitable once we met. Udi listened in silence, now and then writing something in a notebook made of rice paper, which would disintegrate in a glass of water.

"Yes, after I saw you humiliating yourself with her on the ice rink like a little boy, I understood that the two of you were in love."

When he said that, I realized how right he was. We were kindred spirits: Niki had brought me great joy and I had the feeling that this was a good foundation for a life together.

Udi looked alternately at me and at his notes, and said, "So the girl knows you're an Israeli, and knows you asked for Ronald Friedlich's papers so you could take them to him in Cambridge. What else does she know? Your full name? How long you are here for? What for? What you do for a living?"

It was obvious that he was interested in the security angles, and not the romance.

After I satisfied him that I had kept my Mossad status a complete secret, and that Niki never asked difficult questions, he said, "I had her checked last night. There's nothing in the files about her. Apparently she's clean."

"How did you check her?"

"You went to her place, right? And there's a name on the mail box, right?"

It was very naïve of me to assume Udi wouldn't have had me tailed.

"Didn't you notice anything?" He threw an envelope onto the tabletop.

The first picture was of Niki holding a wall hanging in Kensington Market with me in the background, drawing. It was obvious who'd taken it. The girl with the cute smile.

I stammered something. What was I to say? That I suspected something but didn't do anything about it?

"She's a novice, but she ate you up without salt. She's a trainee with another squad, and you were her target for a few days. From her reports I know quite a few things you didn't put in yours during those days."

That's probably what brought him here. After the Friedlich residence episode, I'd thought Udi was going to fire me, and I was thinking the same thing now, but I was in for a surprise.

"About your complacency, and your idiosyncratic way of interpreting orders, we'll speak another time. But about the girl, I have weighed it up and it actually suits me. She can give you excellent cover."

"What do you mean? How?"

"We have to think about it together. What exactly the story will be, what the stages will be. In any event, we have to reach a situation in which, if you run into trouble and they search for someone in Canada who knows you – Ron Friedlich, that is – you can give her name, and she'll know what to say to fit in with your cover story."

"Are you crazy?" I allowed myself to raise my voice in anger. "I am not going to mislead her, and I'm not going to introduce lies into our relationship."

Udi remained calm. "The lies are already there, my friend, from the moment you told her what you told her about Ron Friedlich. Now we have to give her to understand that at times you have to pretend to be Ron, and that she'll have to back you up. In exchange, you'll keep your lovey-dovey thing going."

"Never. I am not going to manipulate her."

"'Lies and manipulate' are not nice words. You are going to recruit her."

"Not on your life!" I was really losing it now, so much so that I was on the verge of throwing him out of my room. In the end, I asked him to leave.

"Young man," he cut me down to size again. "This isn't your room, you're not here on your own documentation, and you are much less of a *jabaar* than you think you are." He used another Arabic word – for "he-man" – that has entered Hebrew slang. "Now, get a grip on yourself."

I knew, whatever Udi said, that I would not recruit Niki, or lie to her, or manipulate her.

"I am ready to tell her the whole truth," I said finally. "Namely, that I, Mickey Simhoni, belong to the Mossad and in Arab countries I'm Ronald Friedlich. But no half-truths and no lies. And if she agrees, well and good."

"Forget it," said Udi. "The word Mossad is not to be uttered. We don't know enough about her yet, and what if she says no? A salesman doing business in Arab countries, maybe."

I was aware that Udi had come more than halfway to meet me, and I realized why I couldn't tell Niki the whole truth. But none the less, I didn't want to tell her a half-truth. When my fury at Udi had died down it was also clear to me that I was not going to repudiate the commitment I had undertaken, that this commitment came from a deeper place than my love for Niki. I felt utterly lost.

Udi grasped my predicament. "You've got until this evening to make up your mind. Meanwhile there are a few things that you're going to set about doing right now: rent an apartment, buy an answering machine, give your new address to the galleries selling your work, check out of the hotel. In other words, you've got a day to do what would usually take a week, and what you should have done long ago. Get moving. We meet here at five p.m."

Five o'clock was when I was supposed to meet Niki. I assumed Udi knew this and was intentionally sabotaging our meeting. This, and the chores he'd given me, were probably meant to nudge me back into the course he'd plotted for me, and to stay there – but could also just pave the way for my replacement. He gave me a list of addresses. "These are rental apartments in houses we have checked in the past. They're good security-wise and also as far as their size and the amount of rent we are prepared to pay are concerned."

My mind wasn't on my duties when I took the first flat on the list. In retrospect, I realized that my head wasn't on my shoulders at all, because the apartment was only a few hundred metres from the Friedlich home, albeit in the poorer part of the Beach neighbourhood. The three-storey white stucco building was on Woodbine Avenue. A red brick basement level was partly above ground and on the front wall there was the logo and phone number of the rental company, Signet Group. Before calling, I checked the names of the tenants next to the intercom – there were no Cohens or Levys or Abous – and then pressed the button for the superintendent.

She was a woman in her fifties with a pronounced Hispanic accent. She showed me the three vacant apartments in the building. They were almost identical, with parquet floors, a kitchenette, a bedroom and a living room, with basic furniture. She told me some of the tenants were Canadians who lived there during the summer months only, because of the proximity to the beach, and I liked that, because I too would not be there all the time. I took a third-floor flat, where my neighbours all had perfectly Canadian-sounding names and I signed the lease after scanning it quickly. I knew the woman wouldn't be able to detect foreign shades in my accent, and I preferred finalizing the deal as Ron Friedlich then and there rather than with some official of the rental company.

Within an hour I had a phone line and had purchased an answering machine. I recorded a standard message, something like "This is Ron Friedlich. I'm abroad now. Leave a message and I'll get back to you when I return."

I was already quite familiar with the neighbourhood, but I ran through the checklist Udi had given me: bus and streetcar stops, shops, entertainment sites, laundries, names of nearby streets, and everything a person needs to know about the vicinity of his home. Then I did the rest of my chores, extremely unwillingly. Even hearing that two of my RF pictures, as I now called them, had sold, and the money I made, didn't make me as happy as it would have before, and I returned to the hotel.

Nothing changed during the hours before our rendezvous. Pictures of Niki passed through my mind, and of my family, and of the burned-out bus, and pictures of Dolly and Dolly's body, and of the practice drills during my course when I felt on top of the world, and of the suicide bombing at Maxim's restaurant just before I came to Canada. "Recruiting" Niki, against the backdrop of all this, might have seemed a reasonable thing to do, but I didn't want to drag her into this murky world. I could exist in it without her, or with her and outside it. Combining the two of them seemed utterly impossible. Not to mention the fact that Niki would have to agree, and I had no reason at all to assume she would. This was not the lakeside studio she had spoken of. And it would also mean living in Israel for periods of time, something that we hadn't ever discussed. I couldn't decide rationally. But the closer five o'clock came, while I was winding up my list of chores and on my way back to the hotel for my meeting with Udi, instead of heading for my rendezvous with Niki, I knew that a decision was taking shape in my mind.

✧✧✧

I arrived at the hotel one minute before five. Out of the corner of my eye I saw Udi approaching ponderously wrapped in a voluminous coat. I knew my decision had been made and that Udi knew what it was. Otherwise, I wouldn't have been there. Otherwise, I would have been meeting Niki now, as we had arranged, and to hell with everything else. I'd texted her that I couldn't make it, without an explanation. There was no explanation I could give that she would understand, without unveiling my cover.

Udi waited for me to go up in the elevator, and he took the next one. I left my door open and he kept his coat on after he entered the room. Instead of telling him that I was sticking to the position I'd taken before,

I detailed the things I'd done that day. Udi looked at me in scowling silence. When I'd finished my report, he said:

"If you'd told me you were choosing her, I'd have said goodbye. If you'd said you accepted my proposal to recruit Niki, I'd have instructed you to do it delicately. But you haven't chosen either of them, and I take it that you are staying with us, without her. So now, get moving and pack. We've got a plane to Israel to catch."

Stunned, in a state of grief, I grasped what a cowardly act Udi was making me perform, but it was the only thing that I could do at that time, and I did it with eyes wide open. As deeply in love as I was, I could not disavow everything that I was, my beliefs, the decisions I'd made and, consequently, leaving with Udi was my default choice. Niki, I knew, would remain a scar on my heart as long as I lived.

Udi stayed by my side, watching me pack, just like the Yakuza guard in Niki's room in Tokyo, and he escorted me to the black taxi waiting at the entrance to the hotel. I didn't examine the car logo, lest I saw that this was also a Lexus. At the airport, a mysterious man who could have been Israeli handed us our tickets. I didn't look back. I preferred to believe I was dreaming.

7.

New Life

THE NEXT DAY I reported to Eli, head of the Mossad's special operations division, at his office at HQ in Tel Aviv. Eli was fiftyish, of average height and with a pleasant face. Also there were his deputy, Jack, a man with a sharp face and a stern expression who looked hostile from the start, as well as Avi, the case officer, the intelligence officer Moshik, and of course Udi.

Udi had told me such meetings were held after a new operative's cover had been established, in order to decide on his future. At this stage, he said, the new person's superiors knew not only how he'd performed in training, but also how good his cover was and how he'd executed simple missions abroad. I assumed Udi meant the intelligence-updating I'd done in Cyprus, and the tracing of Ron Friedlich's background in Toronto.

Eli asked me to give an account of my activities, and I started off with some self-flagellation, taking in my misconduct with the Russian woman in Tel Aviv and the Moldovan in Limassol, the break-in at the Friedlichs, ignoring my sweet-smiling tail, and resuming my ties with Niki. When Jack asked sarcastically "Is that all?" I threw in the way I'd obtained Ron's diploma by using Niki.

"Was there anything positive?" Eli asked with a slight smile.

"I think the collection in Cyprus was quite good, and I also know a whole lot about Friedlich," I replied.

"Let's hear what the professionals have to say," said Eli.

Moshik was the first to speak and he said the intelligence I'd supplied from Cyprus was highly accurate. All the subjects had been identified and photographed, as well as their homes and cars, and I'd also provided new material on their contacts "which proved significant for Operation Sea Dog". In addition to the photographs, I'd supplied accurate and illuminating three-dimensional sketches that had "helped the force that broke into the subject's house and booby-trapped the explosives".

Avi said all of my reports had come in on time, and were coherent and satisfactory and that I'd adhered properly to timetables and budgets, and there had been no credibility problems, except for my loose interpretation of the order to report everything by failing to say anything about Niki.

"I'm afraid this is a problem that crops up with more than a few operatives, and we haven't yet found the right way to get into their underpants. That's something you'll have to settle between yourselves," Eli told his subordinates. I felt massive relief.

After that Udi spoke at some length, analyzing my deviations from the orders and the times I had taken unnecessary risks or been too complacent, but also describing the precautionary measures I'd executed and the "for and against" considerations I'd outlined for him. He added that in countries like Cyprus and Canada, or more or less friendly "bases" as he called them, using Mossad lingo, what I'd done was within the boundaries of the permissible. The big question was whether I understood that things like negligence in spotting and shaking off a tail and even more so the break-in without preparation or instructions, were not to be contemplated in hostile "target" countries.

All eyes were on me. "I understand that," I said. "But of course it depends on the circumstances."

"That is not good enough," said Jack impatiently. "There's a lack of internalization of the risk here. I believe that in the first stage Boaz should be confined to base countries."

"Your opinion, Udi?" asked Eli.

"We have a few months before all the squad personnel wind up their preparations, and in any case I was thinking of keeping Boaz busy in base countries, except for one 'baptism' in a soft target."

The use of my operational codename confirmed that from Udi's point of view I was in. From now on he would use my own name only to express special intimacy – or a rebuke.

"Then OK, I agree," said the chief, ignoring his deputy's remark. "Let Boaz get some rough edges smoothed out in base countries, preferably with you around, Udi, and possibly also in some team exercises with Ronen and Jerry, so they'll learn to work together, and then have his baptism in a target country."

Eli leaned over to shake my hand, and signalled to me to remain with him as all the others got up to leave.

"You are entering a world of make-believe reality," he told me. "With every step you take, the moment you leave this country on a passport that isn't yours, you are serving Israel, officially and legally, but you are breaking the law in any country you land in. The more significant your mission is to your own country, the more criminal it will be in the country where you are operating. Extreme actions, whose aim is to save lives in Israel and perhaps even to save Israel itself from destruction, will be considered grave crimes by the enemy, and if you are caught you will be sentenced to long jail terms or even to death. In difficult places, it's unlikely that we'll be able to rescue you. It's also unlikely that we'll acknowledge that you belong to us, and your death will be inglorious."

He looked me straight in the eye. Nothing that he'd said was new to me and I didn't react. He continued: "Here, in the offices, facing the sea and under the fluorescent bulbs, it's easy to be heroes. Determined. Patriotic. Big Zionists. On the steps of a plane heading for a tough target, with your stomach churning – and believe me it will churn, as it has done for everyone – there's also a tendency for your mind to turn over. Suddenly, the goal isn't worth your life. Or doesn't justify the means. Suddenly, there's a whole lot to lose. Or a great deal to gain if you turn around, and after a moment of great shame, say that it's not for you."

Again he watched my response, and when I heard a noise behind me I turned around and saw that Udi had remained in the room and was listening.

"That has rarely happened," Eli continued, "not only because we have chosen the right people and trained them well, but because the right people chose us. On the steps to the plane to Tehran or Beirut or Damascus, it isn't adventurism that makes you go on, or experience or self-confidence, but only faith in the justice of our cause. The deep understanding that without you, and without people like you, the Arabs and Iranians would long ago have acquired the means to destroy us, and against which neither tanks, nor fortified positions and apparently not even warplanes would have helped. Only lone warriors, brave and resolute, who know how to get to the core of a reactor and to make sure it won't work, or a centrifuge plant, and to make sure they won't spin the way they should.

"We believe you're made of this kind of stuff. For each mission, you'll also get the best preparation and intelligence that we can supply, but ninety-nine per cent of your success depends upon you. Because when you're there, sometimes with a few good people around you, sometimes on your own, it is you alone facing your fate, and facing the fate of the State of Israel."

The chief shook my hand again, and busied himself with the papers on his desk. Udi signalled to me with a jerk of his head to leave together with him.

"Well, OK. Everyone has to go through that," said Udi with a slight smile when we were outside. He gave me a wink and a pat on the shoulder and chuckled. That was the first time I'd seen him laugh, and he looked ten years younger. His laugh, wink and pat on my shoulder meant far more to me than the chief's rhetoric. They told me far more clearly than the flowery phrases, that I'd been accepted, that I was in. And furthermore, I was now part of the band of operatives, on Udi's side, the side of the doers. But as Udi emphasised, ahead of me was a long period of simple, almost routine activity and only after that – perhaps – would I be a full partner to operations of the kind that "You'll never be able to tell your grandkids about," and he laughed again. But just then something sad stole into his laughter, which ceased immediately.

I was torn. Although I was happy about finally joining Udi and his team, the break with Niki was destroying me. She was in my thoughts all the time. I'd clear her out, but she'd come right back in. I missed her all day, and I dreamed about her at night. What did she make of my mysterious disappearance? How was she explaining it to herself? She certainly couldn't be imagining that something similar had happened to me as happened to her in Tokyo. She must be angry, and perhaps even hating me. Rightly so. Because I couldn't hide behind Udi's orders. I could have refused to leave with him. It was up to me. I chose him and his organization over her. I chose my country, my parents, my obligations to my nation, over the promise of great pleasure and great love, the likes of which I would never have again without Niki.

And I felt a need to tell her this. I couldn't just leave her in the dark. But I couldn't call her on the phone from Israel, and I couldn't send her a letter, and when I consulted Udi he told me that I couldn't send her an e-mail either. If she were to go to the Canadian security services, they could find out where it came from. I kept pressing, and Udi agreed that on my next trip abroad I could phone her from some stopover point. But there was no trip planned, and I was left to wallow in torment.

Sometimes I woke up at night in a panic and at other times it was the first thought that assailed me when I opened my eyes in the morning. What had I done? How could I have done it? To her and to myself. After all, this wasn't a temporary sacrifice, like stopping painting. How had I allowed myself to be dragged into an insane choice like this?

The thought that the love of my life was sitting there, across the Atlantic Ocean, weeping and waiting, was intolerable. Knowing that it had been my choice, and that I was still bound by it, was unbearably frustrating. Getting her back in my life would be a wish come true, something out of a fairy tale. The way we had bonded together again seamlessly, as if oceans and rivers hadn't passed between us since we separated, was nothing short of wondrous. Her touch – ours – was magical. I could not believe we'd been together in Toronto for only a week. The happiest week of my life. In a way, I wanted to believe that Niki was furious, hating me, and even that she would never agree to see me again, ever, that there wasn't a way back any more. Believing that was the only way out of my dilemma. Nevertheless, when I asked myself if I wanted to turn the clock back, I knew that I didn't. I could not have given up what I was doing, and I could not have got her entangled in it. I also would not have sullied our love with all kinds of lies and tricks. It seemed as if I was doomed to fulfil one side of my personality and beliefs, and pay a high price on the other side, in personal happiness.

A few days of routine in the training facility went by before Ronen and I were summoned to a briefing in Udi's office. In the meantime, I'd made friends with Ronen and Jerry, the two members of our squad who'd been there longer than I had. We'd gone through some hand-to-hand combat drills with the trainer and they both turned out to be tough opponents, especially Ronen, a former naval commando. He was thin, but he had long powerful muscles and sinewy arms, and all the training had made his blood vessels stand out under his skin. He was supple and agile, and always managed to hit me with two quick blows before I could get in one. Jerry, a former attack helicopter navigator, was a smiley guy and, like me, not particularly physical. He did the training because he had to and not because he enjoyed it, like Ronen. We spent long hours pumping iron in the small gym, and my body mass proved critical in helping me lift a hundred kilograms, while Ronen eked out ninety, not bad for a lanky type like him, and Jerry smiled with satisfaction when he lifted eighty. The rest of the time we boned up on material that Moshik the intelligence officer compiled for us, mainly the history, politics and geography of Middle Eastern countries, as well as a course in spoken Arabic. We also had individual lessons in the Mossad HQ's language laboratory, each in the dialect and accent appropriate to his cover story.

Moshik and Avi were also at Udi's briefing, along with Ronen and me. "There's a job for you two," Udi told us. "A case that's cropped up in recent days, and you are leaving tomorrow morning to deal with it." Even before he outlined the mission, I felt jitters of excitement fluttering around between my stomach and my loins. This was it. No more playing around.

"Alex – that's a codename – is an asset that our agent-recruitment and handling division, 'Junction', has in Russia's missile directorate." As Udi spoke, Moshik placed photographs of Alex in front of us. "Don't study the pictures now, you're going to spend a few hours with Moshik and he'll give you all the intelligence you need. Listen to the big picture." Moshik took the photos back and Udi continued.

"Alex usually transmits material via a secret communication channel. In the last few days, he's seen some Zil vans with antennae on top cruising around his place, and he's worried that they've picked up his signals and are trying to triangulate them. He's got some stuff he says is 'top grade' on a disc that he can't transmit because of this. Our research people and his handlers in 'Junction' think it may be the answers to some queries they gave him on data the Russians have given Iran, to help them build their Shihab-3 missiles. These missiles can reach Israel, and our top priority is, of course, to prevent them from completing that project."

Udi looked at us. I squinted at Ronen. While I was tense and attentive, he was drumming on the table with his fingertips. Apparently he sensed this was a secondary assignment. He, too, was a long way from being sent on "very vital missions", but couldn't wait for that to happen.

"In two days' time," Udi continued, "a delegation from Alex's plant is going to Poland, and he has managed to get himself onto the list. There'll be a lot of security men with them. That's the big picture. Your job is to get to him, to get the disc, and to get it back here. The adversary is not only the security men but also the other delegation members, who will be briefed and alert and wary of strangers; the Polish guards who'll be assigned to the delegation, and the hotel security staff, as well as local cops and, in the widest sense, every civilian in the vicinity."

I felt mounting apprehension. There was still so much we didn't know. How would we locate the delegation? How would we make contact with Alex? How would we communicate with him to set up the hand-over of the disc? Would we have to break into his room? What happens if the security men confront us? What escape routes would we have?

"Now you'll go to the briefing room and Moshik will give all the intelligence we have on this assignment, and then Avi will go through the procedural matters. Meanwhile I'll prepare your operational orders, and go to HQ to get the OK from the division chief and the Mossad's director. When I get back, we'll sit here as long as it takes until you've got every detail down pat, and if there's anything left over we'll take care of it on the way to the airport."

I felt a heaviness as I left for the briefing room. Although Poland was not a hostile "target" country, neither was it really a "base". The security services there had probably not yet freed themselves from the ways of the communist regime.

Moshik showed us the pictures of Alex. "They are not up to date," he warned. "They were taken when the 'Junction' guys were still following him, before he was recruited. He's about five years older now." He gave us some details about the man's habits and character. Then he spoke about the nature of the delegation, what the schedule of such groups usually was, and the places where it was expected to be. Some of the time, they'd be at the visitors' facility of the plant that they were heading for, about an hour away from Warsaw, "and you'll stay away from there". Later on they would be at a hotel in Warsaw. He had a list of the hotels where such delegations had stayed in the past, and he gave them to us in detail, projecting pictures of them, inside and outside, onto the briefing room screen: corridors, doors, locks, housekeepers' rooms and security officer's uniforms. To wind up, he gave us a comprehensive briefing on the Polish security forces, and screened pictures of their uniforms. "You'll have to memorize this stuff because you won't have the files on you there," he warned.

After three hours, Moshik left us with the thick files to study and we went to grab a quick bite, for which I didn't really have much of an appetite, but Ronen wolfed the food down hungrily. Then came Avi's briefing. We were told we'd be flying into Warsaw together, after a stopover in Vienna, but staying at different hotels close to each other, "And in another hotel across the road," Avi told us, "will be Udi."

It's hard to describe the feeling of relief that overcame me when I heard Udi would be there. All at once, my frozen insides thawed, my heavy heart felt lighter and I knew everything would be all right. I saw no change in Ronen's expression, as if it was obvious and he'd known it all along or it made no difference to him, but he didn't miss the glow on my face.

"What are you so pleased about?" he muttered. "All it means is that we'll have to get his OK for everything and to keep him posted all the time."

Ronen, together with Jerry, had already been on three "base" operations, and he wasn't as excited as I was. It was also easier for him to tell Avi his cover story for each of the phases of the mission: What he'd say at the airport, in the hotel, and so on. Avi worked on my cover stories with me until I felt comfortable with them, and he also coached me on how to reply to questions immigration officials or hotel security officers might ask me.

When Udi came back from HQ, he told us the plan had the green light. He let us read the operational order which went into minute detail, defined the goal precisely, the limits of what was allowed and what forbidden, and also gave examples of problems we were liable to run into and suggested possible solutions.

"And that's exactly what we are going to talk about now," said Udi, referring to the "incidents and responses" section of the order. What could go wrong, and how we were to react. When we were finished, late that evening, we had a real live operation before us. I said as much and Udi looked me straight in the eye and spoke in utter gravity:

"You're living now in an operation that we've built here, in the briefing room. There, in Warsaw, you are going to come up against an entirely different operation. It's reasonable to assume that nothing will happen the way we've planned it, and that things we haven't dreamed of will crop up. What we've been doing here is no more than warming up our ways of thinking about how to handle such occurrences."

We were sent off to say goodbye to our families and, because we were due to take off early next morning, we were ordered to return to the facility for the night. Ronen lived with his girlfriend, and he said he'd be back sometime before we were due to leave. I prepared for a quick trip to Haifa, about an hour's drive away. Jerry left with me, after spending a long day learning about some African states where he was due to go on an assignment which I knew nothing about. He was married and the father of twins, but he was a conscientious man, and had kept on studying until late in the evening.

"You're in good hands," he said when we parted. "Your own," and he laughed and gave me a surprisingly limp handshake. I was astonished at how different the three of us – Jerry, Ronen and myself – were from each other, although it was also easy to pick out common personality traits.

The visit to my parents was a brief one as they were already on the way to bed. I didn't want to tell them that a new exhibition had been arranged for me, in Europe this time. My failure to call them from Canada and the way I'd avoided mentioning my exhibition since returning had seemed very odd to them, and I didn't want them to worry. This time, the trip was going to be short and I didn't need to tell them a complicated cover story or make a dramatic farewell. This was just a visit, not a goodbye.

I stopped off at my apartment in Tel Aviv and picked up some items I thought I'd need in wintery Warsaw, including woollen socks and the thermal long-johns I'd acquired in Toronto. There were also some that had the Hebrew letter tsadi, for "Tsahal", the Israel Defence Forces, printed on them, and those I left behind. Who would have thought that instead of needing such things for a reserve stint in Lebanon or the Samarian hills, I'd be wearing similar clothes on an espionage operation in Warsaw. I didn't stay in my apartment longer than necessary. Tonight, more than other nights, I preferred not to reminisce about Dolly or Niki, and I headed for the base camp.

Udi had been there when I left and he was still there when I returned, perusing a sheaf of papers which may have been our orders, or the contingency plans. It didn't look as if he was planning to go anywhere.

"Get some sleep," he told me when he saw me sit down in front of the TV in the dining room, which also served as a mini-clubroom. "Better to be awake on the flight and not half asleep when you get to Polish border control. Apart from that, in future make sure that you have all the clothes you need in your room here, and a suitcase and carry-on bag, in case you have to scramble. This time we had a twenty-four hour advance notice. We don't always have such a luxury."

"Udi, I know this isn't the time, but it never is. We have to talk about Niki," I said. "You gave me permission to call her when I'm abroad, and that's about to happen, but I want to know if I can give her – and myself

– any hope. The way I left her was lousy, and I feel lousy. It has to be solved one way or another, before she decides that it's over for her. I want to explain why I disappeared."

"We'll do it, but not now," Udi replied. "Now I only want you to tell me precisely what you are going to say to her. It has to be brief. It can't be a long conversation between lovers. You'll be in the middle of a mission."

"That I decided to enlist in a government organization and I couldn't stay in Canada?" I ventured.

Udi looked at me in amazement. "Why not just tell her you're Mossad?"

"I'm not going to tell her my grandmother passed away suddenly," I said, with some anger.

"Kill off whoever you want to, only not your cover."

"I'll say that something happened that I can't explain, and that I am very sorry."

"That's OK from my point of view. But you can't give any explanations beyond that, and no promises or timetables."

He went back to his papers, signalling an end to our talk. I thought about what he'd said. Did he really not get how much this mattered to me? Or did he think that my inner struggle had been decided at our last meeting in the Town Inn Suites and that everything that followed was merely the death throes, like a fish flapping on the beach?

Avi woke me at five a.m. When I was dressed he told me to change my tie, and then he fixed the knot and said I had to learn to do one properly. I had been told some general stuff about my team-mates – family status, military service, etc – but not about Udi, Moshik, or Avi. I knew absolutely nothing about them or about what they had done in the Mossad before their present postings. As Avi was our squad's liaison with Mossad HQ, I had been told not to fall off my chair if he suddenly turned up at my hotel, something a case officer may do if orders have been changed or more intelligence has come to light.

When we were due to leave, we heard a motorbike roar and Ronen appeared out of the slanting rain that had begun to fall. Without speaking he took off his biker's garb and gave it to Avi. Underneath he was wearing his travelling clothes and all he had to do was go to his room to get his bag which was already packed. He remained silent and seemed upset, but Avi whispered to me not to worry: Ronen's partings with his girlfriend were always difficult.

We climbed into an Office mini-bus. All the way to the airport I was thinking about Niki. How was I supposed to live in total separation from her without showing the strong emotion that Ronen was showing over this brief separation from his woman? I couldn't believe that he simply loved her more. I didn't believe that was possible but somehow this short break seemed to be affecting him more than my long break from Niki was affecting me.

At the airport we split up. Udi said goodbye to us, with a pat on the shoulder for me and a few light slaps and a pinch on the cheek for Ronen, like a well-known Israeli rabbi-politician, Ovadia Yosef, used to give his disciples. "Come on. She'll get over it, and on Friday night you'll be back to fulfil your duties," he said, managing to raise a thin smile on Ronen's lips. The two of us checked in for our flight to Vienna, and Udi went to stand in line for the flight to Frankfurt.

When I called Niki from Vienna, it was two a.m. in Toronto. I was prepared to apologize for the late hour, but Niki didn't pick up. I felt a chill at the thought that my beloved was out enjoying herself, perhaps with another man. In an icy voice, I left a brief message on her machine, saying just that I was sorry I had to leave so abruptly and sorry I could not explain.

I felt dejected until the moment we passed immigration control and went to the boarding gate for the flight to Warsaw, when a blessed calm overwhelmed me. The calm of an operation, with which I was familiar from my military service. In my seat on the plane, I remained absolutely calm. Ronen misinterpreted my silence and said, "An operation is like a pickup. You find a girl, observe her, approach her carefully, pay her a compliment, chat with her, invite her to a meal, dance with her, and after a few days and nights of that, you get into bed with her, a quarter of an hour passes, and it's all over." But these words only brought back the heartsickness that I'd managed to overcome, and it quickly gripped my soul with frozen fingers. Everything about Niki and me was the exact opposite of what Ronen was saying.

8.

Warsaw in the Winter

WE LANDED IN Warsaw at around the same time as the Russians, but they continued on to their first destination so we had two or three days to get to know the city and the hotels the Russians were likely to stay at. Our orders specified exactly what we had to do. Each one of us had to check everything there was to be checked at his hotel, and we arranged to meet for coffee and meals at the others on the list. Both our hotels were on a street designated for conservation: the buildings were all four storeys high, with chimneys that had been repainted, each in a different colour, introducing a cheerful element into the otherwise rather drab scene. At the other hotels, which were scattered around an area not far from the city centre, we watched each other's backs as we did our scouting. Nothing much had changed since the intelligence files we'd been shown were made, but it was good that we were seeing it all with our own eyes. We spent the remaining time getting to know the city, driving around in a car Ronen had rented, and plotting escape routes for use if anything went wrong.

Ronald Friedlich, if he didn't want to proclaim his Jewish ancestry, had no reason to visit the site of the Warsaw Ghetto during World War II, but I didn't want to forgo the historical route, studded with memorial plaques and monuments to the Jews who were concentrated there before being dispatched to their deaths, and to the young men and women who rose up to battle the Nazi army. Ronen didn't accompany me, preferring to take a look at other parts of the city in his car. I took the subway to the start of the route, walked along Zamenhof Street, and at the park in the middle of what had been the ghetto, I crossed the snow-covered lawn and came to a large monument. The figures sculpted on it looked familiar. When I read the name of the sculptor, Nathan Rapoport, I realized why. They reminded me of his statue of Mordechai Anielewicz, commander of the ghetto uprising, at kibbutz Yad Mordechai in southern Israel, as well as the memorial to the defenders in 1948 of Kibbutz Negba not far from there. On one side of the monument were heroic figures, and on the other Jews being led with bowed heads, holding Torah scrolls, and behind them, helmets of German troops. The bronze sculpture was framed in a massive rectangle of stone blocks. Across the road, a few dozen yards away were nondescript apartment buildings which now probably housed the children and grandchildren of the men and women who had watched the ghetto in flames two generations before. Watched and, in all likelihood, didn't shed a tear.

I continued on to the other memorials, stopping to read the plaques dotting the route. At one point, to escape the cold, I entered a small courtyard, surrounded by some of the few buildings left standing after the ghetto was razed. Dismal, cramped five-storey buildings: it was easy for me to picture the way Jews lived there, crowded together, drawing strength from each other, turning their backs on the storm raging outside. Less tangible but far more terrible than the actual snow storm swirling around me, blowing flakes into my eyes, making it hard to breathe.

At the end of the route I came to the Umschlagplatz, the square where Jews were herded together before being transported to the death camps. I tensed up when I saw a row of blue and white Israeli flags. Then I heard the sounds of Hebrew on a loudspeaker, and I saw that a group of Israeli schoolchildren, dressed in blue and white and probably freezing, were standing in the square and holding a memorial ceremony of their own. I didn't get any closer, and I didn't know if the shiver that ran through my body was because of the cold or the powerful effect of what I was witnessing.

From the ghetto I went straight to the hotel, where Ronen and I had arranged to meet and plan our next moves. I tried to warm myself up in the lobby, where the heating was quite effective. While I was waiting for the bowl of soup that I'd ordered, I was happy to see Udi walk in. He joined me without any unnecessary ceremony, and Ronen came in directly afterwards. Their handshake showed me there was a closeness between them that I had yet to develop with Udi.

My soup came, and they had a little laugh at my expense, with remarks like, "What does the son of a Polish mother order when he's in Poland" – a Polish mother being the butt of many Israeli jokes. I wanted to tell them that my mother was in fact a Jerusalemite through and through, but we were, of course, speaking English, and I didn't know the English words for through and through. Neither did I want to say the word "Jerusalem" out loud, so I took their teasing in silence.

Their coffee arrived, and Udi moved on to business. The Russian delegation was due to arrive the next day at the Metropol Hotel, which wasn't on our list. He had not only inspected it, but had also checked in there. "It's a three-star hotel, right in the centre of the city, not as nice as yours," he said, letting us know that the Office had been generous by putting us up at four-star hotels. "Looks like there are cutbacks in Russia, and also prices here are going up as Poland's entry into the European Union approaches." He wanted the two of us to pay a visit to the Metropol as well. His room there would be our base from which we would set out and to which we would return after doing what we had to do. There we would also practise on the lock, and do whatever else was necessary.

The Russians had taken a whole floor of the hotel. I was sitting with Udi in the lobby when they came in, while Ronen was outside in the car checking the delegation's security arrangements. A Russian security man and a Polish police officer came in before the group, and surveyed the lobby, taking a good look at us as they did so, and then the Russian went out and signalled to the others to enter the hotel. Udi drew my attention to the way the cop asked the receptionist who we were, and we assumed he was told that Udi was a guest at the hotel. There were some twenty men and four women in the delegation, with five security men and two police officers watching them. They waited patiently in the lobby while their keys were handed out and then they waited silently for the small, rickety elevator to take them up to their rooms. I didn't want to watch them too blatantly, but I was curious to know which one was Alex. From the glimpses that I took, two or three looked something like the pictures I'd seen. It was actually a glance that he threw at us that helped me to identify him. He apparently assumed someone from Mossad would be there, and although he didn't know who Udi and I were, he didn't look too pleased.

When the last of them had gone, a Russian security man and a police officer remained in the lobby.

"I'm going up to my room," said Udi, "and to take a look at what's happening on their floor. We'll meet at nine in the evening in the café across the street."

We stood up and shook hands. Ronen picked me up outside and we drove away.

"Their security sticks to them like sheepdogs. Not one of them can make a move," Ronen said irritably. "I don't think we'll be able to get close enough to Alex for him to hand us the disc anywhere but in his room."

When we met Udi at nine, he told us Alex had managed to get a message through to HQ. He was in room 428, with a roommate, and that he'd leave the disc in the narrow space under a cupboard, on the right hand side.

"Why couldn't he leave it somewhere neutral, like the cloakroom off the lobby?" I asked.

"I also would have preferred something like that, but our connection with Alex is one-way," said Udi. "He transmits to HQ, but there's no way of replying or giving him instructions. That's what he chose, perhaps because he didn't want to take unnecessary risks. That's the way it is, and having to get into his room isn't the end of the world. I peeked into their corridor twice, when they were still in their rooms and when they were downstairs having dinner, about an hour ago. When they were in their rooms, there were two guards in the corridor, and when they went down there was only one. The other one went down with them."

The delegation left the hotel, apparently to sample Warsaw's night life, and Udi sent me to check the situation on their floor. The moment the elevator door opened, the guard was facing me, a very suspicious look on his face. I pretended I'd made a mistake, and went back to report. Udi decided we'd do the job the next day. "I'll keep the guard busy, and you two will break into the room," he said.

"What do you mean by 'keep him busy'?" I wondered aloud.

"Nicely, but if that doesn't work, not nicely," he replied and it was obvious that he didn't like my question.

We met in Udi's room after the Russians left for their morning tour. "I counted them, and there were two missing, but our Alex got on the bus," Udi told us. "So apart from the guard, there are two people still in the rooms. Take that into account."

"That means we may have to deal with one in Alex's room," said Ronen.

"Right. The odds are about one in seven that you will. I've consulted

HQ. Alex has reported that the Russians' departure has been put forward to this evening. That means it's now or never, and HQ wants that disc."

"Why don't we wait until they leave?" I asked.

"I brought that up, but it was decided that we do not wait. We have no way of contacting Alex, and he may take the disc back to Russia, or destroy it. Since he suspects they are listening to his transmissions and are trying to zero in on him, if we don't pick it up now we may never get another chance to get the information. HQ has decided it's worth the risk."

"What do we do if we find his roommate there when we break in?" I asked.

"What did you do for a whole year during your course?" Udi asked, but it turned out that he wasn't relying on our hand-to-hand combat skills. He produced two compact stun guns from a compartment in his suitcase. "They may look like the vibrator you gave your girlfriend, but they pack double the voltage of a regular stun gun. Use only if there's no other option." He gave one of them to Ronen, and he gave me a short length of rope, for strangulation. He kept the other stun gun, probably to use on the guard. He also gave me a key he'd fashioned to get into Alex's room. "It may stick a little but it should work. Just do it quickly – I don't know how long I'll be able to keep the guard busy."

Then he gave us small two-way radios with wireless earpieces, and we tested them.

We rehearsed the operation twice, once entering Udi's room and getting the disc without opposition, and once with Udi "surprising" us.

"Any questions?"

"The escape route from here, if there's a hitch?" I asked.

"As per the operational order," Udi chided me. "What does it say?"

"We go back to our rooms, check out properly and take the first flight back to Vienna," I said, "and if necessary, the first flight out to the west."

"You reckon we have to change that?"

"For us, not . . ."

"And for me, don't worry," Udi interrupted me.

We left his room, which was one floor below the delegation's. Udi took the elevator and Ronen and I the stairs. We heard him breathing over the radio, the elevator groaning and its door opening. We stood by the door from the stairwell into the hallway, and we heard Udi's voice addressing the guard. He said the drinks dispenser on his floor was broken, and asked if the guard knew if there were cokes in the machine on this floor. The two apparently walked over to the machine which was at a corner of the hallway, and we heard the click that was Udi's signal for us to get going.

I went first. Room 428 was the second door on the right. The elevator was about five rooms away and Udi and the guard were moving further in the other direction. If the key worked, we would be in the room before they got to the dispenser.

I took rapid, careful paces, the wooden floor creaking under me, and in the distance I saw Udi putting his hand on the guard's shoulder, probably to distract his attention from the noise Ronen and I were making behind them. At first, the key didn't turn, but then the lock gave and we slipped inside, me with fists clenched and Ronen with the stun gun at the ready. The room was empty. Ronen closed the door and bent over in front of the cupboard, holding a bent wire that we'd prepared. It looked to me that he wasn't managing to hook the disc. I leaned towards him, when suddenly we heard the toilet flushing in the bathroom. "We are not alone," I notified Udi over the radio. It was clear what we had to do, and I didn't think about it, even for a second. Because I was closer to the bathroom door and Ronen was still on all fours next to the cupboard, I quickly took up a position next to the door. The moment it opened, I saw a naked man standing there and I punched him in the gut with all my strength, exactly as our instructor had taught us, imagining my fist going all the way through his body. I heard the wind wheezing out of his lungs as he fell forwards and began retching. I whipped the cord out of my pocket, looped it around his neck and pulled it tight, pushing in the other direction with my knee in his back. He fluttered helplessly, made horrific gurgling sounds as he tried desperately to suck air into his lungs. Ronen put the stun gun to his temple. He stopped moving.

Ronen checked the man's pulse and signalled he was dead. Then he knelt down again by the cupboard, and pulled the disc out.

Ronen clicked and Udi clicked back, the sign that the corridor was clear. We left the room and saw Udi standing over the unconscious body of the guard.

"He heard the noise and began running towards the room," he said. We dragged him into the room.

Then it transpired that Udi had a back-up plan. He switched on the dead man's laptop and plugged in a USB stick.

"This will tell the whole story. The guard caught the 'agent' red handed while transmitting classified information, and in the fight that ensued they killed each other." He went up to the guard and stomped hard on the back of his neck. The sound of crunching bone was heard, and I felt a wave of nausea rising inside me. Udi moved the bodies so that it would look as if the two men had been fighting.

We cleared out, after hanging the Do Not Disturb sign on the door, and without pushing the lock button. The sign would attract the attention of the next guard when he came to begin his shift.

"See you at the airport," said Udi and he went to his room. Ronen and I left the hotel, with an interval of two minutes between us. Only when I got to my hotel room did my legs begin to tremble.

I was in a really awful mood. We'd just killed two innocent men. I could call it bad luck, I could call it dereliction in our intelligence gathering or mission execution. The end here had justified the means, and that was an approach to which I did not entirely subscribe. It may be that in the situation we found ourselves in we had no alternative, but I shared the responsibility for that situation.

There would apparently always be aspects and phases of operations that the commander would know about, and I wouldn't. I wasn't aware at all of the plan to incriminate another member of Alex's group, with that USB stick that Udi had produced. I had no idea what was on it. Perhaps some of the material Alex had sent us in the past. Udi kept that to himself, leaving only the "clean" part of the mission to us. That's what was planned, at least.

I could come to terms with the way I punched and strangled the Russian, as well as Ronen's lethal use of the stun gun on him. Perhaps, in retrospect, there was also justification for breaking the guard's neck. But the cold-bloodedness with which Udi had done it appalled me. I remembered his words in my hotel room in Toronto: "I'm an asshole who has killed people, blown them up, burned them, framed them" and his assertion that he did the crying before the deed itself, and not afterwards. From that day on I didn't believe what he said about the crying. There was something in him that was beyond the stage where he would cry. The only point I could find in his favour was that he had done it himself, without saying anything, without waiting to see what we thought about it. He could have ordered one of us to do it. I wondered if I would have been able not to cry after doing it. I wondered if I even wanted to reach his level of toughness – or was it obtuseness? A maelstrom of emotion was raging inside me.

On the way back, when everything seemed to be behind us, Ronen tried to correct what he had said about missions being like picking up women, and once again he got me wrong. "And sometimes, there are quickies that get you into trouble, and affairs that blow up out of proportion. But in any case, in a few hours' time, when my head's stuck between her thighs, I'll forget everything."

For the first time in days, I thought about Niki again. While Ronen would head straight for his waiting girlfriend, I'd be going to my empty apartment, alone with all these sights and sounds, and Niki, on the other side of the globe, as far away and as unattainable as if she were on the dark side of the moon. And in truth, it was I who had been on the dark side.

9.

Getting Ready to Go Solo

THERE WAS A sense of failure when we returned. I certainly felt it, and I think I detected it in Udi and Ronen as well, although they didn't speak about it. A minor mission to pick up a disc had turned into a fully-fledged double elimination. On top of all that, for me, came my return to an empty apartment where I felt so alone that I travelled to Haifa, quite late in the evening just to sit with my parents for a while, and when they went to bed I surprised my two sisters with unannounced visits. One of my nieces was still awake and when I hugged her I almost burst into tears. Never before had I felt this need for a little girl of my own.

My mood improved when I heard about the reaction at the technical branch of Military Intelligence, after they deciphered the material on the disc. This included all the specifications for several types of missiles that had been supplied to Iran – the technologies used not only in the Shihab-3, but also in anti-aircraft and sea-to-sea missiles that Syria had received, and would in all likelihood get to Hezbollah too. The data was detailed enough for Israeli hi-tech specialists to begin working immediately on ways to counter and jam the missiles.

"You've saved the lives of many civilians, as well as pilots and seamen," said Eli who'd invited the head of the MI tech branch to tell us what was on the disc. I was sure that he mentioned the "many lives" we'd saved in order to minimize the fact that we'd taken two lives – but it turned out that the old-time MI colonel was quite pleased about that too. One of the dead men, Leonid Sholokhov, was one of Russia's top missile scientists and had been personally responsible for training Iranian technical crews.

In the debriefings, Udi took the blame for what he called "the lacuna" between the information we had and our plan, a gap which led to our not knowing that Alex's roommate had remained in the hotel. We could have remedied this with a preliminary move, such as calling the room on the phone, or knocking on the door after distracting the guard.

Somewhere deep inside me, I suspected that Udi didn't see it as an operational or intelligence defect. Since he had prepared us for a fight in the room, and readied himself for a fight with the guard, I presumed he had taken the risk knowingly, out of the assumption that if we'd known the room was occupied, and reported it to HQ, our mission would die and the disc would return to Russia or be destroyed. This was why he'd also provided us with suitable accessories. I also assumed that in order to overcome the robust and well-trained young guard so elegantly and quietly, it had been necessary to plan several steps in advance. The actual killing was ugly but I had nothing prettier to propose.

I asked if we'd received any message from Alex about what had happened when the delegation got back to Russia, and I was told that communications with Alex were the concern of "Junction" and they only told us what we had to know. There had been an item in the Polish press about "mysterious deaths in a hotel" and that official intervention had prevented local police from investigating, as it was "an internal matter of a friendly country".

Udi complimented us on our work. Our quick thinking and neutralization of the roommate had been professional, he said, but we had slipped up by not making sure the whole arena was clear, including the bathroom. It sounds pretty basic, but it was somehow neglected in the briefings and the preparatory run-throughs we'd had in Udi's room, as well as in the actual operation.

We returned to a routine of training and studying. Jerry got back from his African trip, and a fourth operative, Dudu, joined our squad after completing the preparatory stages. He was a plump, friendly guy who'd immigrated from Argentina some years before and had done his army service in the artillery.

Then, one day, Udi summoned me to his office. "The time has come for you to carry out a solo mission in a target country," he told me.

"What's known as a 'baptism'?" I asked.

"A little more than that," he replied. "About a year after the unsuccessful Mossad attempt to assassinate Khaled Mashal, head of

Hamas, in Amman, King Hussein kicked all the Hamas leaders out of Jordan. He died a little while after that. His son, Abdullah, the present king, has been ruling ever since and there's constant talk of the return of the Hamas leaders to Amman. Fatah has filled the vacuum left by Hamas, and the suicide bombing on a No. 19 bus in Jerusalem last week was the work of their Al-Aqsa Martyrs' Brigades. Shin Bet intelligence tells us Fatah is drunk with victory and is planning to do more. We know nothing at all about their infrastructure in Amman."

I had indeed been wondering if we were going to sit with our arms folded after that bus bombing, in which eleven Jews were killed, but I knew there was no point asking because I wouldn't get a reply. We were only one of many squads, and perhaps another one had been assigned to take retaliatory action.

Udi continued: "We do not want to find ourselves in the same situation we were in before the Mashal incident, when our operatives didn't know the arena or the actors and where they hung out. So we've been carrying out occasional surveillance ops on the Hamas people who remained in Jordan or returned to Amman, as you did in Cyprus. Updating addresses, filling in gaps in pre-op intelligence files. This time, we want to get to know the Fatah functionaries as well. They are providing quite a lot of funding and weaponry, although their high command is here, in the West Bank."

I had no doubts as to the importance of this mission. Udi saw fit to stress that, "Amman is what we call a 'soft target' but it must not be taken lightly. We've already had one phenomenal cock-up there. The main difference with Limassol is that you'll be walking around in areas that are totally Palestinian, suspicious and sensitive, and you'll stand out far more than you did in Cyprus, with everything that this implies. You'll start working on the intelligence with Moshik, and then Avi will go over the plan and your cover. I'll define the goals for you. Oh, and it's important for you to know that you'll be there on your own."

I had the same feeling as I had before going to Cyprus and on the way to Warsaw: this was for real. How long would I have these butterflies in my stomach before missions? After Amman there would be the really tough targets, Beirut perhaps, or Damascus or even Tehran. It was clear that Udi was preparing me for that stage by stage and, as in every selection process, the constant examination and screening boosted my hunger for

success, my desire to make it. Somewhere deep inside my mind a thought
was taking shape that didn't dare come to the fore: when I finally did
perform the critical act, the one for which I had been trained and for the
likes of which I was posing as Ron Friedlich, and following which I would
feel I had justified the investment in me and had repaid my moral debt to
the organization and to the state, only then would I feel free to go back to
my Niki. If she still wanted me.

"You'll go when you are ready," Udi told me. "But we always set a tentative
date, and that's one week from now."

I felt like someone who'd been told to come back in a week for his
biopsy results: not necessarily a death sentence, but the possibility of one.
Of course, it wasn't really the same thing, because I'd chosen a job that
included high-risk missions in target countries and that meant something
to me.

I knew what the two great crossroads in my life had been, when I had
made a certain decision that had closed off other possibilities: when I had
abandoned art and when I abandoned Niki. Since childhood I had set
being an artist as my goal in life. Because drawing and painting were the
most natural and primal thing to emerge from me, and on the very day
that my career as an artist took off, at the opening of my first exhibition,
I had been diverted onto another path. When I rediscovered the lost love
of my life, that path led me away from her. I knew I would continue on
the path I had chosen. This sprang from an existential need that charged
my life with greater significance than had either art or Niki.

I wondered why. After all, I wasn't a believer in grandiose ideas like
the eternity of Israel. In a few thousand years' time, our people wouldn't
exist. In a few decades' time, I myself wouldn't exist. Only what I did in
those few decades had any significance for me. In the light of all this, was
it right for me to devote my life to defending the Jewish people and its
state, and to sacrifice on this altar the things that sprang from my own
inner forces – my artistic talent and my love for Niki? Were the genetic
links that flowed from my grandfather to my father and to me, and my
membership in the Jewish "flock", stronger and more deserving of
realization than my talents and emotions? All of these elements had
genetic-biological aspects, not merely the sense of belonging to the
collective. My love, like anyone's love, was also a kind of biological-genetic

attribute without which we wouldn't exist today. And to a certain extent, so was my artistic ability. So what was it that determined which of these took precedence over the others?

I'd never have thought that my biology studies at school, my major subject which gave me a good understanding of the logic of nature, would place me in such a concrete dilemma. The solution was by no means clear cut and unequivocal, and the fact that I, nonetheless, was making an unequivocal choice bothered me a lot. I felt overwhelmed by events, and that I was losing control over my freedom to choose. This wasn't right for the judicious, rational person that I thought I was, until then. I was used to evaluating situations and then making decisions, and not to being dragged into them.

Moshik slave-drove me for days on end. The quantity of material he fed me in the briefing room, and the files he left for me to study in my "free time", were inordinate and insufferable. The field intelligence on the Hamas personnel was good, and the main difficulty I had was learning the routes to the homes of the Fatah men, where all we had were the addresses and a few partial descriptions obtained by various Shin Bet agents or compiled by our intelligence from open sources. There was nothing visual that my eyes could absorb and memorize.

To save time, I didn't go home. I had everything I needed at the base. There were showers, a TV, and a kitchen, and I avoided both the trip in the rain and having to be in my place, which evoked memories and longings I could do without.

It was quite strange, being alone in the large barracks, with the only sound coming from the rain lashing the roof and the gusts of wind whistling outside. The solitude sent light tremors running through me which I mistakenly and willingly took to be caused by the cold, and I warmed myself up with another cup of coffee, or a quick workout in the gym. Because my room was the only one in the building that was heated, I made these sorties brief, and returned to sit by the radiator and painstakingly study the intelligence files, until weariness overcame me and I went to bed.

When Moshik tested me after a few days, I had mastered the map of Amman and the traffic arrangements there, everything I had to know about the various security forces, and the names and addresses of the

Hamas and Fatah personnel. The thought that one of them may have been the recruiter, the dispatcher or the mastermind behind "my" terror attack was abruptly cut off by Moshik, my channel of communication to what was happening in the outside world, as soon as I raised it.

"It was on the news. It can't be that you didn' hear it," he said. "No time ago at all, at the beginning of December. The Shin Bet located some of the top Hamasniks in the West Bank. One of them was Hamdi Hasanin Rumana, who recruited Mahmoud Sharitakh. They must have shaken it out of Sharitakh. Anyway, one night they tried to pick some of them up, and Rumana resisted. He was killed."

Once again I felt a slight drop in my motivation. The circle had been closed, without me. But it wasn't a circle, it was a spiral. Someone had recruited this Rumana, and perhaps that someone was living in Amman.

I began working on my cover, as the Canadian Ron Friedlich, whose main occupations were painting, photography and travel. When I sat with Avi he tripped me up with some questions and I had to hone a lot of the details of my story. I practised sketching Bedouins, camels and horses, so I'd get them right when I carried on drawing in Jordan. I decided it would be easiest to make outline drawings and then colour each one in pencil. I equipped myself with some pencils and Pilot pens to make the outline sketches, and a set of Caran d'Ache coloured pencils. At this point, Udi arrived with my operational order and the specific tasks I was to carry out. As he had said, it was similar to my Cyprus mission but in an Arab country and, what was more, most of the addresses were in Palestinian neighbourhoods, some even in areas that were considered refugee camps. "Learn every detail of the assignment, picture the contingencies and your responses, and add another contingency of your own, something that may go wrong, at all stages of your trip, and how you'll get out of it. That's how I'll know the mission is in your head and not just on paper."

It seemed to me that Udi was relating rather nonchalantly to my mission, perhaps because it looked simple to him, or he was preoccupied with another operation, with Ronen, Jerry and Dudu. In our little squad, although we lived together some of the time, each of us dealt solely with his own duties, and I had only a rough idea of what they were doing. I understood their mission involved gathering pre-op intelligence in some African country which served as a stopover on the weapons route from Iran to Gaza. It was the continuation of Jerry's previous mission, which had apparently yielded good results. My own trip was even put off for a week, until Udi had the time to give me a comprehensive briefing. Obviously, he never had the time to speak about Niki, although with a great deal of discomfort I raised the matter time after time.

"Didn't you leave her a message? Isn't your thing all sewn up?" Udi asked almost truculently.

"I left the message, but things are not sewn up at all," I replied. The feeling he gave me was that I was being a nuisance with my pettiness amidst the important activities of the squad, and the in-depth discussion I wanted was put off once again.

The four of them left a few days before my scheduled departure. I took leave of Udi and my three buddies, feeling a twinge of sorrow that they were going together and I'd be alone. Udi said goodbye with some warm words and added that he was confident about me. "When we get back, we'll talk about Niki," he said, taking my hand in both of his. "Promise."

I was amazed at how pliable I was in his hands. I was moved by his little gesture, but someplace in my head an old Arabic saying was floating around: This is my life that you're pushing off. My happiness, which wasn't as important to you as another minute of prepping for your mission, about which I knew next to nothing.

I wound up my own preparations and Jack, the deputy division head, who I thought didn't like me too much, came to the base to give me a final briefing. He told me that Udi and the others had completed their mission successfully and were on their way back but I shouldn't wait for them and was to leave according to plan. It wouldn't be good to make more cancellations and re-bookings on Royal Jordanian Airlines and at the hotel.

At most I'd lose a few more points with him, I reckoned, and told him I'd wanted to speak to Udi about the Niki matter. His elongated face became even longer, and his thin lips pursed.

"You'll forgive me for not going into that, OK? I know there's an issue to be dealt with but I'm not familiar with the details. I have four teams in target countries right now, so you'll have to take that up with Udi, when you get back, in a week's time. If she dumps you in the meantime, take it as a sign that she wasn't worth the effort."

I don't know what it is about the Mossad and its hierarchy, and the awe that it inspires in its own insiders that stops a guy like me from saying,

"So go and get fucked, you and your mission. First solve my problem for me, then I'll go." But the fact is, I kept quiet and that ate my heart out for hours afterwards. I made do with leaving a note on Udi's desk: "Reminder that we have to speak about Niki, as soon as I get back. There must be a solution to this."

I meant it. Let HQ OK an exception to the rules, so I could tell Niki exactly who I was and what I did, and then we'd see. If she allowed me to go on, I'd go on, otherwise . . . otherwise, what? My cover would be burned and I would be back at the starting line, where I had already once been.

The evening before I left, I visited my parents and my sisters and they all complained that I was cutting myself off and they could never reach me. "You're also never at home, your phone just rings and rings. And that Orange mobile phone of yours just tells us, 'The subscriber cannot take your call.' Well, really!" fumed Tzippi, my big sister. She was right. At the base, all mobiles were switched off and I was almost never at home.

The story about exhibitions abroad wasn't holding water any more. Tzippi's husband had guessed I was working for "the Shin Bet or the Mossad" and Aliza's husband thought I may be an El Al sky marshal or with a cabinet minister's security guard detail. He also said he saw I'd been working out, that I'd "developed shoulders" and my belly had flattened out. My parents, although still quite alert for their age, were too old to trouble their minds with this question, and I was surprised at how they aged from one trip to the next.

Tzippi put her girls to bed and her husband Amnon and I watched the evening news. The lead item was a news agency report about an attack by unidentified warplanes on a convoy of container trucks on the Sudanese coastal road north of Port Sudan. In all likelihood Israeli planes had knocked out an arms shipment on its way from Iran via Egypt to Hamas in Gaza, said an analyst. So that's what Udi and the boys had been setting up. I felt a wave of pride rising inside me and had to restrain myself not to show or say anything.

"Lucky you're here," said Amnon, "otherwise I might have thought you were involved."

"Really lucky," I replied. "Otherwise you'd give my parents ideas and they wouldn't sleep at night."

"Sometimes I think you don't really know your parents," he said. "In my opinion, if your father knew you were involved in such things he'd only sleep better."

I returned to Tel Aviv, full of motivation.

The next day, Avi took me to the airport. He shook my hand warmly. "Funny to be flying four hours to Paris and then four and a half hours back in the same direction just to reach a place you could get to in half an hour on a direct flight," he smiled. "What can we do? Our lives are complicated."

"I'm a little envious of Dudu," I said. "Just arrived and already been on a real operation."

Avi, tall and slender, hesitated for a second, and then told me, "Dudu wasn't actually there. He got a bad case of diarrhoea on the way. We almost sent you instead, but Udi decided he could make do with what he had, because your mission is also important."

"There's medication for diarrhoea, no?" I wondered.

"It was his belly speaking in his name. It's not a stomach problem, and he wasn't the first. Usually, they don't get a second chance."

I had the evening free in Paris, and decided to spend it in a Pigalle striptease joint. This didn't exactly fit in with the operational orders, but I justified it by telling myself, "That's what Ron would do, wouldn't he?" The truth was that I needed a woman more than I would admit to myself. Here would be far easier than in Tel Aviv.

Reality, as usual, did not chime with my imagination. I had to be quite firm with a rather unpleasant Moroccan hostess who joined me and insisted that I buy her a drink. When voices were raised I cleared out without getting any thrills out of the breasts and backsides that I'd been fantasizing about.

I walked along the avenue, which seemed more like part of Casablanca than Paris. There were almost no hookers on the street and those there didn't appeal to me. It surprised me that my need to get laid was almost divorced from my need for Niki. The gap between my raw, impulsive desire and the combined love and passion I had for Niki was real. I could feel my longing for her and I could feel my as-yet unfulfilled need for a Parisian whore, and the two things didn't clash with one another at all. I mused over whether the ability to compartmentalize like this was one of the qualifications for being a spy, and I decided that it was actually an ability possessed by most men. Civilization had compelled us to stick with one female, while nature was pushing us in the other direction. Or perhaps I was just a bastard. Or perhaps all men were bastards.

At my hotel, there was a message waiting. Moshik would be coming the next day with fresh information. I had to work out the time and place for our rendezvous using our usual codes.

The next day, according to plan, I purchased a suit and wore it to my meeting with Moshik, who was similarly togged out and looked so bizarre that I almost burst out laughing.

"Hey, you also look like a monkey at his wedding," he growled at me.

We went up to his room, where he ran through some updates about my targets that had come in the day before.

"Too bad, the Shin Bet case officers don't co-ordinate timetables with us; only yesterday they finished debriefing a source who arrived from Amman."

After giving me all the relevant info, the diminutive intelligence officer permitted himself to have a little personal chat with me. He, like everyone at HQ who worked closely with us, was familiar with my story and, not knowing that it had been kept a secret from me, he told me that all the Mickey Simhonis in Israeli phone directories had received a call "from that girl you left in Toronto, what's her name?" and also that a Tel Aviv private investigator had been hired to find me, but a terse warning from a high Shin Bet official had made it clear he could choose between the fee that he'd been offered and his PI license.

"So what did he do?"

"As far as I know, he told her there isn't a Mickey Simhoni in Israel who answers to the description she gave him."

"Are you all nuts?" I barked, stunned and frustrated. "Why didn't you tell me?"

"Whoa! I'm not your case officer, nor your commander, and I don't have to deal with this, but I gathered that you'd decided to give her up, no? So what did you expect they'd do?"

Correct, I had resolved to give her up, at least that had been my decision then, but I'd not been happy about it, and it certainly wasn't what I wanted now that I knew she was fighting for me. The HQ guys should have told me.

"Udi's not going to get away with this," I muttered.

"Hey, I never told you anything!" Moshik quickly warned me, but he went on to say that the Foreign Ministry had also been involved, because "that girl of yours went to our consulate in Toronto and notified them that her Israeli boyfriend had disappeared, and she thought something had happened to him, that perhaps he'd been abducted, because she had a key to his room and she'd gone in and that was what it looked like."

My Niki!

I remembered exactly the mess I'd left in my hotel room after moving my stuff to my rented apartment, and when I returned to meet Udi, the place looked like it had been burgled.

"Have you got a way of contacting Udi?" I asked. "I've got to talk to him."

Moshik took out his scrambled mobile. "I think he's already back in Israel," he said, handing me the phone.

"I saw your note," Udi told me, "but this isn't the time and it isn't a matter for the phone." He was right, of course, but I didn't want to keep it all in, nor was I capable of doing so. I didn't even care if he was in the middle of some stupid ceremony at the facility, with Jack or even with Eli, in honour of his team's successful operation.

This was the first time that I'd put my feelings for Niki into words. Feelings that had intensified now that I'd heard she wasn't prepared to give up on me. Strange, but apparently that's how things work even with this thing called love. Action, response, action.

Udi realized he couldn't send me into a target country without first having a proper conversation.

"To tell you the truth, I don't know how to handle this," he confessed. "The decision has to be yours. Clearly a man with a torn heart, who isn't focusing on his mission, is very bad, something I can't afford to allow. You didn't want to recruit her, and that's what would have enabled you to keep on seeing her."

"You're still telling me to lie to her," I shot back. "And I'm surely not going to do that. Anyhow, that would also have exposed that I was using you know what." I decided not to mention, even on a scrambled phone, Ron's passport.

"Right, but as I told you back there in the north, and it's a pity you didn't listen to me then, the question is, using it for what. For business in places where you couldn't do business as what you are. It's not all that far-fetched."

"And again, that means lying to her. We've already had this conversation. The answer is still no. I don't believe a relationship can be based on a lie and subterfuge."

"You aren't leaving yourself many choices. It is your decision. But I'd like you to make it after you get back."

From his point of view, the matter of Niki was in abeyance and the only item on the agenda now was my mission. From my point of view, it wasn't like that. Instead of being preoccupied with my assignments, or getting cold feet, or an upset stomach like Dudu, I took my flight to Amman and spent the time thinking about Niki and how much I loved her.

It would have been nice and convenient if I could have told myself as I had in the past, that nature had given us a biological screening mechanism that enables us to find suitable partners, zeroing in on those who are more or less suitable for us, or else we would all be hopelessly in love with Michelle Pfeifer or with Claudia Schiffer, and we aren't.

I was compelled to emphasize to myself that nothing about the way Niki and I had bonded seemed logical. The screening mechanism had gone crazy. And the moment these feelings of mine towards her had awoken – once in Tokyo, then again in Toronto, and again today in Paris, en route to Jordan – a magic that seemed to be utterly un-biological also awoke in me: Love – precisely what had been missing with the hookers in Pigalle the evening before. And throughout my life so far, this love had awakened, with this intensity, only towards Niki.

So, biology – with all the respect that I harbour for it, and the high marks I got for it at school – is one thing, and love is something else entirely.

10.

Alone in Amman

I FELT STRANGE landing in Amman. Although I'd been there twice before, this was my first time under a false identity. My first two visits were after my discharge from the army when I'd stopped over on my way to and from Japan. Before and after Niki. Royal Jordanian's flights to the Far East were the least expensive of all the airlines. I was sure that on the previous trips I had not felt the rumbling in my stomach, a rumbling that if it had been one or two degrees more acute would have put me in Dudu's situation. Some Israeli tourists visit Amman, but I was there undercover, and if I were to be caught it would be very unpleasant for me, and very embarrassing for the Israeli government.

Apart from the rumbling, border control went smoothly. There was no way that a border guard was going to link me with the young Israeli with the cropped hair who'd landed there twelve years ago and returned with slightly longer hair.

Then, I'd only seen Amman from the air. This time, on my way to the Intercontinental Hotel in the city centre, I was surprised by the many palatial villas, built out of what Israelis call Jerusalem stone, surrounded by high walls and gardens in bloom. Only after I got to know the city did I realize that the road from the airport went through an enclave inhabited by wealthy members of the regime, many of them belonging to the Hashemite royal family. There were also homes owned by rich residents of certain Gulf emirates who often came to spend weekends of pleasures forbidden in their home countries. Other parts of Amman looked like East Jerusalem, Ramallah or Nablus, typically Palestinian.

I spent my first two days working at being a tourist. On the first day, my Lonely Planet guidebook led me to the Roman amphitheatre on a hill overlooking the city, and the museum at its foot, as well as the Sheikh

Hussein Mosque, the market and to the well preserved Hellenist palace. Two taxi drivers addressed me in Hebrew, freezing the blood in my veins. One of them even mumbled in disbelief when I replied in English that I didn't understand what he was saying. It was apparently not easy to deceive our cousins, especially those who'd come here from the West Bank or Jerusalem and could identify the features and manner common to many Israelis. But these drivers didn't want to make a big deal out of it and my Israeli appearance didn't bother them for long.

On the second day I travelled south in a rented car to Madaba, site of an ancient mosaic map of the Holy Land, Mt Nebo, and Petra, the Nabataean city carved out of red rock cliffs. It was actually Mt Nebo that moved me most, as I looked out over the northern part of the Dead Sea and the southern Jordan Valley, from the spot where Moses had stood thousands of years before, according to the Bible. There was something exciting about standing there, posing as a foreigner amongst the locals and the few tourists, and gazing at my own country. It was easy to pick out Mt Karantal, the hill overlooking Jericho, from which I had, as a soldier, done observation duty in the opposite direction, and the slopes of the mountains all the way up to Jerusalem. There in the desert I began filling my sketchbook with quick drawings, and taking photographs, of the wadis and hills, horses and camels, Bedouin girls with water pitchers on their heads, desert vegetation and flocks of black goats. I found that the cheap Pilot pens did the job in the quickest and most precise way, and it was simple to use them to fill in the black clothing of the Bedouin, while the coloured pencils filled in the background in several different shades of brown, with a little green and yellow.

On day three, I began carrying out recon for my pre-op intelligence-gathering mission. The following two days went by exactly according to plan. First, I drove along the streets where the targets lived, trying to spot their houses, something that wasn't always easy because many of the houses didn't have numbers, and also because I had difficulty making out the names of the streets, which were in Arabic. The small tourist map that I kept in my pocket with the guidebook wasn't much help in the winding streets where our "objects" had chosen to reside, but fortunately I'd put a lot of time into studying the more detailed maps and the aerial photos, and had them pretty much down pat. The material Moshik had brought to Paris was useful and I was able to navigate my car relatively confidently along the route I had mapped out. I located the addresses according to landmarks I had set for myself beforehand and I drove on past them, without stopping or slowing down. I didn't think I was arousing suspicion, although rental cars must have been a rarity in these neighbourhoods.

After driving past some of the addresses in two of the neighbourhoods, I returned to the main street to take a break in a restaurant. The intense concentration and high state of alert that I'd summoned up to reconstruct the routes in my mind and drive along them had been exhausting.

After another swing past further addresses on my list in a third neighbourhood, I called it a day and went back to my hotel. In the evening I went to the city centre where I indulged myself with a shwarma and aubergine with tahini and yoghurt – a combination that wasn't kosher but was absolutely delicious. I took my coffee onto the terrace, where people were smoking hookahs. It was cold outside, but my coat, the coffee and the water-pipe would take care of that, I reckoned. It was my first hookah since the army, and I coughed a little – I'd lost my knack for it – but the satisfying smoke filled me with serenity.

I sat up half the night writing reports on what I had seen. I drew a few three-dimensional sketches, photo-graphed them and sent everything to HQ in an encoded message. The next day, I changed my car, got my camera ready, and set out on a second round of more detailed observation. This time I stopped at where Fatah functionaries were assumed to be living, checked that I was at the correct site and took pictures of the numbers over the entrances. I also photographed the cars parked outside, and here and there I snapped people entering or leaving the houses. I did it all covertly, from inside the car. I managed quite a bit, and that evening I drove out to Kan Zaman, a tourist village on the outskirts of the city which houses a variety of arts and crafts workshops, souvenir shops, cafés and restaurants in restored old buildings.

When I got back to the hotel, a wedding party was taking place around the pool. I found a table, ordered another coffee and enjoyed the cool air and the pretty location. I also enjoyed that special Invisible Man feeling, with no one there aware of who I was, as if I could see everyone and no one could see me. All the men were in suits and ties and the women were in evening dresses and there was a kind of genteel, calm atmosphere, very different from the noisy Israeli weddings I was used to. I assumed it was a high-class affair, people from the Hashemite nobility, but I could quite easily picture them as partners with whom we Israelis could live in harmony.

That night on CNN I saw a report of a terror attack in Jerusalem – a burned-out bus, injured people, bodies, paramedics, police, a scared crowd of onlookers. The background looked familiar and after a while I realized it was Liberty Bell Park. Then came the announcement by the perpetrators: Only three weeks after their last suicide attack, the one on the No. 19 bus, Fatah's Al Aqsa Martyrs' Brigades were admitting responsibility for this one too. Eight people were dead, including students on their way to school. It had happened in the morning and, who knew, perhaps I had been driving around by the homes of the very people who had supplied the explosives or had raised the money to purchase them.

I couldn't fall asleep. In addition to my daily report, I relayed: "Please notify by return if any of the targets I observed today is connected to latest attacks, if there is any intention of acting against him, and if you want me to prepare a full field file."

The reply came: "Carry on as usual. They may be more wary today."

Pictures of the bombing were still on my mind in the morning. Before going out I saw on CNN parents of the casualties, stunned and grieving, and a few seconds of footage fro m a memorial assembly at the Experimental School, where one of the murdered children had been a student. When I was at Bezalel, I'd rented an apartment on Rabbi Akiva Street, where the school was located. Every morning, I'd walk along that street on my way to the old Bezalel buildings, where the fine arts studies were held before their move to Mount Scopus, and often it would be at the same time as the parents bringing their kids to the Experimental School. I always thought these parents were rather special, an unusual mix of yuppies, former hippies, and plain, good-natured Jerusalemites. I'd also watch them on my free mornings as I sat in the Aroma café at the other end of the street, or as I lunched at the Focaccia Bar, right opposite the school gate. Sometimes I surprised some students sharing a joint in the yard of my building, instead of being in class. This, I thought, is what good parents generate when they give their kids a little too much freedom by sending them to "democratic" schools like the Experimental.

The tearful faces of the children on CNN took me back to my own students after the Dolphinarium attack, two and a half years before. It's strange, I thought, how the bombings at places I knew affected me in ways that other attacks didn't. Terrorist outrages in Hadera, Pardes Hanna, Nahariya, Afula, Beersheba, left me less moved, as if they had happened in another country. Even the huge atrocities, with hosts of casualties, like the bombings at the Patt Junction in Jerusalem, the Megiddo Junction, or the Old Bus Terminal in Tel Aviv, with at least twenty people killed in each, did not arouse the same emotion in me as those at places I was familiar with, or where I had even spent time, like the Sbarro restaurant, or Moment café, or Café Hillel in Jerusalem. Not to mention the bus bombing in which I'd lost Dolly.

I couldn't help but intensify my intelligence gathering, push the risk a little more. Fatah had taken responsibility for the bombing, and not Hamas, as in Dolly's case, but at the higher echelons of activity – planning, weapons purchase, money matters – they could well be the self-same people. I became a little more daring and decided to do some recon on foot around those places where, from the car, I had been unable to ascertain unequivocally who lived there. Twice, when apartment blocks were involved, I photographed the mailboxes with the names of the tenants. I did the same thing at the entrance to some smaller houses as well. When I saw I was attracting the attention of children playing there, I got back into the car and drove off.

My downfall occurred elsewhere. I'd stopped in a narrow street at the northern edge of the neighbourhood where three known Hamas activists lived, although I didn't have to check their addresses, as well as two Fatah members whose houses I'd snapped earlier. I had the feeling the camera hadn't clicked and wanted to see if the pictures had come out, so that if necessary I could change the battery and go back and take them again. I saw that they were fine, but the battery did have to be changed. I decided to stay in the car and make some of my 3-dimensional sketches of the houses and streets that I'd just passed by, while they were fresh in my memory.

The further I drove away from the activists' homes, the more my adrenalin level dropped, something that apparently made me less alert. I didn't see who was paying attention to me, or why – the rented car, my foreign appearance, busy with a camera, sketching . . . Catching me off guard, a police patrol car drew up behind me and an armed officer climbed out.

I'm not sure my face didn't give away my alarm. I stammered a little when he asked what I was doing, and it took a few seconds before I selected the cover story that would fit best, but it didn't account for the camera and the sketches. The cop asked politely for my papers, and I took my passport out of the pocket of my jacket, which was lying on the seat next to me. Just before I handed it over I thought of putting my foot on the pedal and speeding away. I might have got away but they would have called in reinforcements and in the narrow streets it would have been easy to block me. Escape on foot after that, on the edge of a refugee camp, was not an option. It was also clear that the number of my car, which had probably already been checked by the cop who'd stayed in the vehicle behind me, would lead them straight to my hotel. And actually I had done nothing serious enough, as far as they were concerned, to warrant endangering myself in a chase through the streets and then having to steal across the border back to Israel and totally invalidate my documentation for future use.

I handed over my passport and, while the officer was examining it, I surreptitiously erased all the photographs in my camera. This meant losing a full day's work, and I was glad that I'd already transmitted the pictures I took the day before. But I didn't have time to remove from the screen the last command. The "Empty card?" and "Yes" option.

Neither did I manage to hide the sketches. I'd meant to push them under the seat, but before I could I hear his voice: "Artist?" I nodded and quite surprisingly, I found this definition quite heart-warming.

"May I see?" He held out his hand through the car window and signalled to me to give him the drawings that were in my hand. I gave him the sketchbook as well, open at the pictures I'd made in the desert. He ignored them, and looked at the sketches of buildings.

"I think I know these places," he said. "They are houses in the street below here, no?"

"Houses that I saw and I want to remember. Perhaps they are mixtures of more than one house."

"No, no, they look very exact to me," he complimented me. "And may I see your camera please?"

That was what tipped the scales. The cop asked me to get out of the car and accompany him to his vehicle. Again the option of running for it occurred to me and again I ruled it out. I believed I could explain to him – and if necessary to the chief at the station – that I was no more than a tourist, an artist, seeking out places that seemed exotic without having any idea what went on inside them, drawing them, and then taking the drawings home to Toronto where I made paintings of them that "sold not at all badly".

But clearly, my having emptied the camera would work against me.

The other cop had finished getting details from the car rental company. They saw that my passport checked out against the information they had, asked where I was staying, and then called the Intercontinental as well. The officer with the camera showed the "Empty" command to his partner, and the drawings as well and that, apparently, convinced him. They told me to get into the patrol car.

"But why?" I asked indignantly. "And what about my car?"

"Lock it, and after further questioning at the station, we'll bring you back to it," said the cop, still politely, but firmly.

"Why shouldn't I drive behind you to the station?" I asked innocently.

"Lock your car and come with us," said the cop, with increasing impatience.

I did as I was told and sat in the backseat of the police car. Even before they drove off, I thought I could waste both of them, or at least knock them out and run away. I could punch one of them in the back of his neck, which would stun him for a good few seconds, and then strangle the other one until he lost consciousness, or gave up the ghost, and then go back to deal with number one. There was almost nothing moving outside, and nothing would move inside the vehicle either. I would get out, start my car, and drive away. If they were dead, I'd have enough time to get out of Jordan in an orderly fashion: it would take time before someone would be able to check and discover that their last communication had been about me. Friedlich's passport might be spoiled or even burned, but I would be somewhere safe.

But I knew this wasn't a real option. The killings in Warsaw still lay heavily on my conscience. No one had authorized me to liquidate two innocent Jordanian cops to get myself off the hook. Jordan wasn't an enemy country and my chances of persuading their superior officer of my innocence seemed reasonable.

A few minutes later we were in the courtyard of the police station. The moment we entered, all the possibilities for violent action that were still running around in my head melted away, and I forced myself to switch from combat mode to the cover story that fitted the situation I found myself in: an innocent Canadian tourist who had no idea why he had been picked up.

I was led into the duty officer's room, which was behind the reception desk in the entrance hall of the small station. The cop who had brought me in gave the officer a lengthy explanation of the reasons for his action, pointing at the camera and the drawings. The officer sent him out with the drawings, apparently to check out the houses I'd sketched, and sat me down facing him for the preliminary interrogation.

The duty officer, a man of about fifty, with a neat moustache and a freshly pressed uniform, was still polite at this stage. I assumed this wasn't his own office, because the walls were full of pennants and photographs of many different men in police uniform. In polished English, and an accent very reminiscent of the late King Hussein's, he asked me for my personal details, my reasons for visiting Jordan and what I was doing in the refugee camp. I gave a brief account of my cover story, and wound up by saying I had no idea that I had been in a refugee camp and what I pictured when I heard the words "refugee camp" were rows of tin huts or tents with strips of bare earth between them. In my eyes, it had been a residential neighbourhood, full of interesting little houses, and I'd simply been driving around in my car seeking out exotic places that I could draw. And, while we were about it, I wanted to get my car out of there urgently if it really was a refugee camp.

The officer listened attentively, made notes on a form in front of him, and then picked up the phone.

"You are right about the car. I have just ordered a tow truck to bring it here," he told me. "I need your keys."

"Why don't you just release me, and let me get it myself? And why don't you tell me why I've been detained?"

Apologizing, he said, "We haven't yet finished your investigation."

"I intend on remaining in Jordan for a few days. I can come back here if there's a need. I don't see what the problem is."

"As you apparently do not realize, the problem is that you erased everything in your camera when the officer approached you, and you have made very precise sketches of a number of houses, and we want to find out who lives there. This activity of yours does not seem innocent. But if it turns out that there are no problems, you'll be released forthwith."

"I don't understand all this. Am I under arrest?"

"You are detained for questioning."

I handed over the car keys, and the officer left me. If he discovered that Palestinian militant activists lived in the houses that I'd drawn, the noose would tighten around my neck. Again, I weighed up the chances of escape. I could see the desk at the entrance to the building, around which a number of cops with nothing better to do were clustered. I couldn't walk out without them noticing me. To run away from a police station with armed cops on my tail was not a reasonable thing to do, and besides my cover story could still pass any test of reasonability.

I could hear the officer talking on the phone. From the little Arabic I had acquired, I understood things were getting grimmer. He returned with a serious expression on his face.

"Do you know whose houses you were drawing?"

"No. Just interesting buildings."

"More interesting than you think – or want to say. I'll have to pass you on to the chief interrogator. I have summoned him and he's on his way."

"You're wasting your time and mine."

"Very sorry about your time; as for our time – this is why we get our salaries."

He asked me to follow him and this time there was an armed cop behind us. We walked along a corridor lined with apparently empty offices, until he opened the door of one of them and asked me to wait there. Inside was a table and two chairs, the walls were whitewashed, and there was a small barred window. I sat down and the door behind me was slammed shut and locked. From the sounds outside, I concluded that the officer had left, and the cop had remained outside to guard me.

When the door opened, I seemed to wake up from a little nap because I had no sense of elapsed time. This didn't surprise me much, because I remembered what had happened once when I'd been arrested during my training and taken to a police station not knowing what to expect and how long I'd be there. For some reason I was locked into a toilet cubicle – perhaps there were no vacant holding cells – and to gather my strength I sat on the toilet seat, put my feet up on the door handle, and fell asleep, something that raised quite a few laughs when they came to get me. "The daddy of all the don't-cares" said the cop who opened the door, and he didn't stop telling anyone who would listen.

The interrogation officer was a different type from those who'd been dealing with me so far. He was young and energetic with a hard face. He was wearing a jacket, an open-necked pink shirt, blue trousers and sports shoes. His English was excellent.

"What does the name Halil Abu Zaweid mean to you?"

I didn't recognize the name from my list of targets, until I realized that he pronounced it differently from what I thought it was. I kept silent, while I was working this out.

"Jamal Zakhut?"

My response was the same.

"Mustafa Shehadeh?"

This time he pronounced the name in the same way as Moshik, the intelligence officer.

I looked my interrogator in the eye and said, "I have never heard any of these names."

"These are the names of the people whose houses you have drawn. And do you know what they have in common?"

"That they have nice stone houses, with bougainvillea and flowers in pots," I said. A grimace flickered across his face.

"Don't be smart with me. Who sent you to draw these particular houses?"

"They caught my eye as I was passing through the neighbourhood. I hadn't any idea who lives in them."

The interrogator placed my camera on the table.

"Can you explain this?" and he pointed at the "Empty card?" query and the "Yes" command.

"Yes I can. At home I inserted an old card by mistake. It was full of pictures from my previous trips, and I decided to empty it so I could take pictures here," I rattled out the reply that I had cooked up since being detained. The "contingencies and responses" that I'd worked on at the facility had not included this situation.

"Wouldn't it have been more logical to buy a new card?"

"I wouldn't have found my way back to the place, and anyway I'd uploaded the whole card onto my computer at home long ago, so I wasn't losing anything."

One might have thought that would satisfy him, but I was aware of what he wasn't telling me – that he knew that I'd made drawings of the homes of three Fatah key officials with whose identity he was certainly familiar. He began questioning me on every move I'd made since arriving in Jordan. Again I thought that I was convincing, telling him at length about all the sites I'd visited, my trip to Petra, the restaurants I'd dined at.

Obviously, I said nothing about my preliminary recon of my targets. But the matter of the Fatah officials was still unexplained. He began to ask me about my home, my studies and what I did in Canada.

I gave him all the details, even adding the names of the galleries where my pictures were sold. I mentioned the drawings I'd made in the desert. When he asked about my family, I told him that, as he could see from my passport, I had been travelling outside Canada for years, my parents were no longer alive and I was not in touch with any relatives. For a moment I had a blood-curdling thought: the deceased Ron Friedlich was killing off his very much alive parents. The thought of his parents was enough to reawaken that pity I felt for them. I felt Ron Friedlich in my bloodstream. When I told his story, I was Ron Friedlich.

"But you were in Canada last October," said my inquisitor after studying the passport. The Mossad had made sure I'd have the right stamps there, to fit in with my renting the apartment and the other cover-establishment activities I'd undertaken in Toronto.

"Right. I was thinking of going back and settling down there. Since then I've been invited to several places on photographic assignments."

"So I see. Rather strange variety of destinations, no?"

"I am a painter and photographer of nature. I like drawing in exotic places, and I have photographed bird migrations from Eastern Europe to Asia and the Middle East and back again."

His face remained blank. I had no idea what impression my cover story had made on him, and whether my explanations for my travels held water, whether birds actually migrated to and from these places and at those times. He told me everything would be checked and if it was all true, I'd be released. Until then, I had to remain in the detention room.

I really didn't like the idea of being detained not least because I would have to explain afterwards why I hadn't managed to talk myself out of it.

For a moment I thought of demanding that the Canadian consulate be contacted. Six or seven years ago, after the abortive attempt to do away with the Hamas leader Khaled Mashal, the Mossad operatives who were caught also had Canadian passports and they had done just that but, after speaking to them, the consul had told the cops that "Whatever these guys are, they aren't Canadians." I was confident this wouldn't happen to me, that I could pass a brief questioning and the consul would back my story, but didn't want to take the risk. It could easily develop into a situation in which the consulate would locate the Friedlichs, who would ask to speak to their missing son, and the whole structure would come tumbling down.

My detention lasted longer than I thought it would and even when everything I said had checked out, after almost two full days, I was still being held. Twice I banged on the door and demanded to be released. I knew this wouldn't help, but I didn't want it to look as if I had accepted what they were doing and thereby indicate that I was guilty.

Luckily, the detention conditions at the police station were tolerable. I was placed in a regular office room, with a camp bed, a table and a chair. There was a small window, through which came mainly cold air and occasional drops of rain. A jug of water and a glass were on the table, and a bucket in the corner served as a toilet. It was emptied once a day, and the rest of the time I had to live with the smell, but I soon discovered that a person learns to live with his own odours and it's only the odour of the excreta of others that is repellant.

Three meals a day were brought to the room, and they were reasonable for prison fare. The cops didn't treat me as an enemy, and not even as a criminal detainee: In fact they seemed to be quite indifferent, and that suited me. The problem was time, which went by at an excruciatingly slow pace, especially at night, when it was too cold to fall asleep. I had too much time to reflect upon all the things that I would have been better off forgetting, under the circumstances. Mainly, of course, Niki, and where I would have been now, if I'd gone with my love, and where I was now because I didn't.

It is failure that designates the limits of our abilities, I mused. And to be imprisoned in Amman, in a semi-friendly country, clearly showed the limits of my ability as a secret agent. A cautious man, more versatile and skilled than me, would not have ended up here. It was clear to me that my potential for contributing to my nation as a secret agent was inferior to my potential as a painter or a lover.

Above all, I felt personal failure, but I also had a sense of being covered by a protective layer. It was as if these things were happening to someone else and, at the end of the affair, I'd be freed. The most unpleasant thing then would be having to explain what happened when I returned to HQ. I had after all executed almost my entire mission.

They kept me locked up that night, the next day and a further night. I was beginning to feel weighed down. Something had gone wrong. They wouldn't do this to an innocent Canadian tourist.

And then I was taken back to the interrogation room, and the same officer appeared. He was wearing a pink shirt again. I couldn't complain because I was also wearing the same clothes, except mine, unlike his, were creased and sweaty.

"We have verified most of your details," he said, "and you may even be happy to hear that one of the galleries – one second," he looked at his papers, "'art gallery' is all I have here, said they've been looking for you because they've sold two of your pictures. They asked us to inform you that they're holding three thousand Canadian dollars for you."

It's a subject for psychological research, how a marginal detail like that can make someone happy, in a very unhappy situation like the one I was in. Nevertheless, I began to feel a little optimistic. I had learned two things, both about myself and in general: firstly, receiving recognition as an artist made me very happy, even though I really didn't need to have any doubts on the matter; and secondly, I had a natural tendency to assume things would work out. Not only for myself, with the detention and the investigation, but generally. In Israel, we believed the Intifada would come to an end and there'd be peace with the Palestinians, although no one knew how; cancer patients believe they'll be cured, and people in general think they'll never die – everyone else would, of course, but not themselves, through some miraculous means which they never bother to try to clarify for themselves. And now, somehow, the little compliment I'd received gave me a distinct sense that soon I'd be a free man.

"I'll be honest with you," said the officer. "We don't have too many problems with you, apart from your having done some unreasonable and suspicious things, and your explanations are not completely satisfactory. You know what they are. Apart from that, you look and sound OK. It's fifty-fifty from our point of view. Lucky for you this is the Hashemite Kingdom and not one of the other countries around here. There, you'd never get out, but for us to let you go, we do need a tiny drop more than what we've got."

"Like what? You've already held me here for three days for nothing. Soon my visa will expire, and then you'll arrest me for that."

The officer smiled. "Don't worry about that. What we need is something definite, some totally positive identification, and we haven't got that."

"And what can I do about that?"

"You think about it. What can give us that positive identification that you are who you say you are. Not some answering machine that gives your name in your voice in Toronto, but someone who knows you, who'll speak to you and then tell us you are who and what you say you are."

"And if there is no one like that?"

"Again, I'll be honest. In that case, we'd tend to take a graver view of the case."

"What do you mean?"

"If you haven't got it yet, let me make it clear: your case borders on being a security incident."

"Me? Security?" My voice was choked.

"I'm not supposed to tell you, but I'll tell you anyway. The neighbourhood you were driving around in is a bad one, one that our intelligence keeps an eye on. And the houses you drew belong to people who are intelligence targets."

"I'm sorry, but I don't understand. What's an intelligence target?"

"What you've understood, you've understood. And what you haven't, you haven't. The problem is that they can also be intelligence targets of foreign espionage agencies. And that's why we tend to play it safe."

"And what does that mean?"

It means that we won't decide by ourselves whether to release you, which is what I would do right now, but we'd hand you over to the Mukhabarat. They would decide what to do with you."

"Listen, Mr – what's your name?"

"Na'im. Call me Na'im."

"You've been holding me for three days and my patience is at an end, Mr Na'im. It's not legal, it's not reasonable and it's not acceptable. I understood that you had some sort of a problem, but that's it. You've got all the answers you wanted!"

It was self-evident that I must avoid at all costs being handed over to the Mukhabarat. They would treat me very differently.

Na'im rubbed his chin as his mind worked. "I have only two ways of letting you go without giving you to the Mukhabarat. One would be to ask your consul to come here. The truth is that it would be embarrassing because we should have done so when you were arrested and I want to avoid a diplomatic incident. The other way, as I have said, would be for you to think of somebody else who could verify your identity over the phone. A brother or a sister, a neighbour, someone who knows you. Even the owner of that gallery, anyone, I don't care who."

It was just as important for me that the consul shouldn't be called in. The chance that the gallery owner would recognize my voice was small, but I had to try it. There was no one else who knew me as Ron Friedlich.

"All right. I'll call the gallery," I said. "but bear in mind that the owner has seen me only once."

I dialled the number. There was no reply.

"Of course. It's the middle of the night there now."

"I realize you haven't been living in Toronto for the past few years, but isn't there a single soul there who knows you?" Na'im asked sympathetically. "A friend? A girlfriend? Someone who would recognize you in their sleep? I can't wait with this until it's morning there."

Niki.

She would, of course, recognize my voice immediately. She was also the only one who could link me with the name Ron Friedlich. Actually, all she knew was that I had asked for his university paperwork, but, if I identified myself straight away as Ron Friedlich, wasn't it possible that she would connect that with my sudden disappearance and my asking for his documents, and realize that I had to pretend that I was he?

Of course she might not catch on straight away, and say something like, "What's all this bullshit, Mickey?" Or that she'd been contacting all the Mickey Simhonis in Israel, thereby dooming me to years in prison. That was the most likely reaction. She was also liable to grasp the situation, but not to cooperate. I didn't know what she felt about me after I walked out on her.

"OK, listen to me," Na'im's voice cut in. "If you fall into the hands of the Mukhabarat, I really pity you. You will stay with them until you see the consul which will take another week and which won't be as pleasant as your time here. I'm going to call the consul. I'll have to do some explaining about the departure from proper procedure, and I hope they won't accuse me of false arrest, but I hope that in a few hours you'll be a free man."

"Wait. There is someone," I said. I had to prevent an encounter with the Canadian consul. "Someone who may be able to confirm my identity."

"So what have you been waiting for?"

"It's a little sensitive. It's a woman I met when I was back in Toronto recently. We had a little fling, and the problem is that I left without saying a word. She may be furious at me."

"May be? If I did something like that to my woman, I'd lose my dick." Na'im had decided to move onto more intimate ground with me.

"She may make things difficult for me. You've got to take that into account."

"Worth your while to try, no? Perhaps she'll be prepared to take you back, after we let you go."

His words fell on the most fertile of grounds. All I wanted was to fly out of there straight into her arms.

"I'll try."

I was putting my fate into her hands. I knew I was wagering not only on her speed of comprehension and her good will, but also on my ability to manoeuvre the conversation correctly. While Na'im asked his exchange for an international line I was working out exactly what I would say.

"There's something else," I said. "It's the middle of the night over there. She may be confused. And of course she may be with another man. So please take that into account as well."

"Yalla, dial." Nai'im turned the phone towards me.

My heartbeat must have been audible across the Atlantic.

I heard the ring-back tone from across the seas and the continents. And then a surprised and sleepy "Hello" that seared my heart and my guts.

"Hi Niki, it's me, Ron," I said, trying to suppress the eruption of emotion that overwhelmed me and to conduct the conversation exactly as I had planned it, with all the responses to all the possible contingencies.

I knew it would take her a moment to connect the familiar but unexpected voice with the totally unexpected name, and that her first reaction would be what it in fact was:

"Who is it again?"

"It's me, Ron. Ron Friedlich. And I owe you a big apology for the way I left."

I wanted her to hear a full sentence, so that she would have no doubt that it was me speaking, and that she would hear the name twice, so that she wouldn't blurt out my real name.

"I'm sorry, who?"

"Ron. Ron Friedlich."

Niki was really confused, and I heard some alarm in her voice.

"Ron? I never thought I'd hear your voice again."

I wasn't sure that she knew she was talking to me. I had to make things clearer.

"Niki, listen. Do you remember when you went with me to get my transcripts and BA diploma? And then we spent a few days together and I left without saying goodbye? I'm terribly sorry about the way I did that. There were good reasons."

"Yes . . ." her voice sounded hesitant, waiting for me to say more. And then, "Do you know what time it is?"

That's exactly what I'd expected.

"I know it's the middle of the night, and I'm terribly sorry. But I've got a problem. I've been arrested in Jordan, and my interrogators here told me to call someone who could identify me. I hoped . . ."

Na'im grabbed the phone. He looked a little angry. I had apparently said a little too much for his liking. I could only pray that Niki would pull herself together and understand and be prepared to go along with me. I was no longer in control.

"This is Captain Na'im speaking."

I heard the echo of Niki's voice resonating from the handset, and a moment later Na'im's face softened, and a smile spread across it and turned into an actual laugh.

"She's asked me to give you a couple of slaps, not in the face but on your butt, for what you did to her," he chuckled. "And I'm liable to do just that," he told both of us.

I couldn't share his mirth.

"I have some questions for you, if I may," Na'im continued with his identification process, and when he got her permission he asked her what my occupation was and what I'd studied. She was able to say that I had majored in Anthropology and Earth Science – as she'd seen the transcripts – and then she must have added that I'd played football for the Varsity Blues, as he asked her what kind of a team that was. He asked her to describe me, and burst out laughing again.

"She says she hopes that our treatment will shrink your swollen chest, shave off your wavy forelock and pull out the curly little hairs on your chest and arms, one by one . . ." Na'im dissolved in sheer enjoyment. "Well, there's no doubt you made quite an impression on her," he said as he ordered me to open my shirt and roll my sleeves up.

Things seemed to be going in a positive direction, despite her weird humour. She hadn't given me away, but there was no way of knowing how the phone call would end.

To complete her description, Niki apparently suggested they pluck out my two green eyes, make a hole in my other cheek as well, because I had only one dimple, and slice off my straight and rather longish nose. I deduced this by the way he looked at my eyes, signalled me to show my profile and smile, and expressed surprise at my single dimple. He couldn't know that it was the result of an unlucky fall on a sharp object when I was a kid. Her description was perfect, and seemed to satisfy him, as did her performance as an injured party – if it was in fact a performance. I felt that the whole lump of tension that had been building up inside me was beginning to melt away and that an internal sea of love was welling up instead.

I hoped that he'd let me have another few words with Niki, but he thanked her, apologized for the intrusion, and hung up.

The sea of love overwhelmed me. My wise and good Niki. But was she actually mine? Although she had decided to save me and had gone along with my cover story, did she really mean it when she wished all those tortures on me? And Nai'm's conniving, somewhat lecherous laughter evoked a dubiousness in me which straight away I understood was a kind of jealousy, and which was immediately replaced by desire. I felt pressure in my trousers. Just hearing Niki's voice on the phone, even now, as had always happened when she called me from work, was enough to make me hard.

"Well, Mr Friedlich, you are a free man," said Captain Na'im, and he shook my hand. "I'm sorry you were detained, but don't do any more silly things now. Stick to the places where tourists usually go. Your car is parked in the station courtyard." He walked with me to the duty officer, signed my release forms and made sure that my camera and car keys were returned to me.

I drove to the hotel and there I was greeted with considerable surprise, because of my unexplained absence. While I was waiting at the elevator, I caught sight of a tall, slender man get out of an armchair in the lobby, look at me, and then give me an almost imperceptible nod. It was Avi, our case officer. The blanket of isolation enveloping me was lifted. I was no longer alone.

I went to my room and straight to the shower. I took into account that I might be under surveillance, and decided not to make any calls or send any secret messages. Everything I did may be transmitted by cameras concealed in my room before my release. I hoped Avi wouldn't come knocking at my door, and he didn't. He'd apparently been sent to sniff around after I'd failed to communicate for three days.

I guessed that the report on my release would reach Jordanian intelligence soon and I didn't want to be in Amman while there was an argument going on over whether I should have been let go or not, and why the Mukhabarat hadn't been told about me. I phoned the airline, and was told that planes to Paris and Brussels were full, so I booked a flight to Amsterdam for that afternoon. No one would be amazed that a tourist who'd been jailed for three days without having done anything wrong would want to clear out as quickly as he could.

As I left the hotel and picked up a taxi, I couldn't see any untoward activity around me. Neither did I see Avi. In the plane, a moment before takeoff, before we were asked to switch off our electronic devices, I thought I'd send a coded message to HQ. Held for three days, released, leaving now. But I decided not to take the risk. Avi must have reported. Only when we were in the air did I feel the tension easing.

The route surprised me. I hadn't known that the peace agreement allowed planes leaving Amman to fly over Israel. All of a sudden, with a surge of joy, I saw Jerusalem and the Temple Mount, and then we veered to the north and flew over Mount Carmel and Haifa Bay, and when I looked back a little, I saw Haifa itself. I had to keep my happiness pent up but it felt as if it would burst through my chest.

And then, at that moment, I knew I wouldn't be going home anytime soon. There was a far more important matter I had to settle first, and a new and different tension, a sweeter one, began gathering anew in my now relaxed limbs.

If I'd been able to, I wouldn't have left Amsterdam airport at all, but simply bought a ticket to Toronto on the first flight out. But I could not enter Canada as Ron Friedlich. I had no idea what was listed under his name at Canadian border control, or whether the Jordanians had queried their Canadian counterparts about him, and I'd had enough of interrogations. I had to pick up the documents I'd left in a locker at the Gare du Nord. It was late, but I didn't want to spend another night as Ron Friedlich: there was just time to buy a ticket for the last train from Schiphol airport to Paris.

I climbed into an empty compartment, and prepared to catch up on my sleep. Just after the train left the airport and began picking up speed, the door opened, a shadow fell over me and a large form was reflected in the window, through which I was watching the receding lights. I turned my head. Standing in the doorway was Udi. In his hands, there were two paper coffee cups, giving off steam.

Contradictory waves of emotion flooded over me at the sight. My first, instinctive, urge was to throw my arms around him – metaphorically, of course, because that's not what they expect us to do, and straight after that the opposite urge kicked in – to gather up my stuff and move to another compartment, without exchanging a word with him. Clearly, his presence here was going to make it difficult, or even impossible, for me to fly off to Niki, as I had already set my heart on doing.

Udi sat down facing me and placed the cups on the shelf next to the window, pushing one in my direction.

"I saw you the minute you came out of customs. You didn't even take a minute for a cup of coffee. I made it the way you like it."

Again, the warm feeling welled up. Udi had been my home for the past year. But he was also what was keeping me from a real home.

"How did you know my whereabouts?"

"Avi accompanied you to the airport. I'm glad you never noticed. It's also no big problem to scan the lists of passengers departing from Amman."

"And how did you get here?"

"I was in the neighbourhood."

We were silent for a while.

"I think you can start talking. There's no one in the car with us."

"I'll start at the end," I said. "I'm going to Toronto. To Niki. So let's not waste our breath talking about it."

"OK, so that's the end. Now let's go back to the beginning."

For a number of hours, until we arrived in Paris, I told Udi what had happened. Here and there he asked a question, to help him grasp the situation better.

"You had more luck than sense," he summed up after I'd told him about the call to Niki. "And she's proved she's worth returning to."

I thought I hadn't heard right.

"You know what that means."

"No, I don't know. And neither do you," he replied with his

characteristic serenity, which hadn't left him since he entered the compartment. Actually, since I first met him.

"It means I'm choosing her and leaving you."

"That's what you are thinking now. But you don't know where she's at today, nor where you'll be at tomorrow."

"So that's how easily you're giving up on me? Was I so lousy?"

"You've been really bad. We can't afford foul-ups like this one, but you got out of it, and I'm not giving up on you, yet. Problem is, you haven't chosen us, yet."

I remained silent.

"You deserve a chance, and so does she," he said. "You owe her a lot."

"I know."

"You don't know. An hour after you left, Captain Na'im Aziz called her again."

"Na'im Aziz?"

"Right. That's his name. His brother is in Toronto and he wanted to fix him up with her. You could say, she threw him down the stairs and told him that if he doesn't let you go right away, and make sure you get to her the same day, she'd take the matter all the way up to the Canadian foreign minister."

I gawked at him in amazement, both at the story and at the level of the intelligence he had at his disposal.

"I've just read a book of short stories by Savyon Liebrecht. It's called *A Love Story Needs an Ending*," Udi said. "Most of the stories in it actually don't have an ending, and your story also doesn't have one yet. It's neither this way nor that. It has to be wrapped up, one way or another."

Deep down somewhere, hidden in Udi's bear-like body, inside his gruff apathy, there was a soul!

He rose, shook my hand warmly, and left the compartment.

I got out at Gare du Nord which was almost empty at this hour of the night, and caught a glimpse of him alighting from another car. I walked past a couple of cops who gave me a quick once-over, and went to the locker feeling enormously secure. Somewhere behind me, Udi had my back covered.

I took my Israeli documents out of the locker and left Ron Friedlich's there. Was this goodbye forever?

I I.

"A Love Story Needs an Ending"

BUT I HAVE an apartment in Toronto, I remembered when I was thinking about booking into a hotel on my way into town from the airport, although I'd rented it as Ron Friedlich, and living there as an Israeli would be contaminating if any situation arose in which I had to identify myself. Damn it, I shook myself, I'm behaving as if I've chosen to stay in the Mossad. And I had not. I'd had six hours on the plane to rearrange my order of priorities. My wonderful luck had given me a woman whom I loved with all my heart and who apparently also loved me with all her heart. All the rest came after that. "Therefore shall a man leave his father and his mother and shall cleave unto his wife," I recalled. The wisdom of the Bible had grasped it long before I did, even though cleaving to Niki meant not only leaving my parents, but also my country, my homeland, and obviously the Mossad as well. I didn't want to think about it too much. I only wanted to be with her.

I adjusted my watch to Toronto time. It was twelve noon and Niki would be at work. I'll surprise her there, I decided. But because I had a suitcase and hadn't changed my clothes since leaving Paris and was in need of a shower and a shave, I decided to check into a hotel.

Just before four p.m., I arrived at the registrar's office in Trinity College. I was refreshed and smelling of aftershave but too lightly dressed for late February in Toronto. The winter coat that I'd reckoned would do for Amman couldn't keep out the freezing, dry cold here. There were two good thick coats in my, or Ron's, apartment, but I decided it would be better to buy myself another one rather than collect them.

My teeth were chattering, and I had goose bumps, but didn't know if it was the cold or the excitement. I soon discovered that I'd wasted energy on the excitement – Niki didn't work at the College any more.

I took the subway to her apartment, imagining the surprise in her beloved voice, as it had resonated on the phone in Captain Na'im's office.

It was already dark when I emerged from the subway, the temperature had sunk way below zero and a piercing wind was blowing in from the iced-over Lake Ontario, only a few hundred yards away. Without a hat on my head, I felt my scalp and my ears freezing and an icicle forming at the tip of my nose. I didn't come across any clothing stores on my way or I would have bought at least a thick sweater, a hat, a scarf and a pair of gloves. My trembling increased. I hurried towards her building, a few blocks away, holding my breath against the cold.

I rehearsed what I would say to her, but when I pressed the bell there was no reply. Niki wasn't home.

I had no idea when she would return, since she'd changed her place of work. Perhaps she was running errands after work? Or she was on a date? But I remembered the entry code and I decided to wait for a while in the lobby where I was at least protected from the wind.

Sitting in the unheated space, endlessly waiting, I began to sweat. My body temperature was soaring. An ache in my throat, a shivering back, a first cough, a running nose all heralded what I already knew was happening inside me. The seed sown in the cold police detention room in Amman, had sprouted in the gusts of winds from Lake Ontario. If I didn't leave right away and get to my hotel room, I would end up with pneumonia, I thought, and I got up to go. I headed back to the subway station, teetering a little and almost bumping into the few people coming towards me.

"Mickey?"

The soft, startled voice came from behind me. I stopped. A little figure that I had passed by seconds before, bundled up in a coat and hat turned around and stepped in front of me.

"Mickey. Is it you?" she yelped gleefully.

I felt like a polar bear buried in snow, unable to move. Niki immediately realized how sick I was, took my arm, turned me around and lugged me back to her house. All I felt was the trembling getting worse and, hardly able to move my legs, I let her drag me along.

✧✧✧

This was not the way I had imagined our first few hours together. Niki put a thermometer in my mouth and was shocked when she saw my temperature was 104° Fahrenheit, which I couldn't convert in my mind to Celsius, but I guessed it was about 40°. She didn't know whether to give me a hot cup of tea or to put me in a cold bath. I mumbled that tea would be better and she added a couple of pills and led me to her bed.

When I woke up in the morning, she wasn't there. The clothes I had slept in and the sheets were drenched in my sweat, but I felt a lot better. On the table in the kitchen was a list of instructions, ending with "Love, Niki."

"Love" in American, and therefore probably in Canadian too, is a very general concept. I'd have to wait until she got back to find out what she meant by it. Meanwhile, I gladly did everything on the list: breakfast, which I had only to put in the microwave for a minute, so the bacon wouldn't be cold (if my religion permitted it); a towel, soap and shampoo were in the bathroom, and I could use her robe (if it fitted); some clothes that I'd left last time, were washed, ironed and folded at the foot of the bed; the TV could be switched on with the green button on the red remote (she didn't think we'd ever switched it on last time), and she'd call at noon, but anyway here's what there is for lunch . . .

The heating was on and I felt nice and warm. As I was doing battle with the TV knobs, after showering and breakfasting, and dressed only in a pair of boxer shorts that I'd left last time, the door opened, and Niki came in. Despite the gust of wind that came with her from the hall, I felt a wave of warmth. My misgivings about how she would feel melted away as she charged at me and kissed me passionately.

"I couldn't wait until the end of the day to see you," she said, radiant, and she took a step back to check me over. "You've really recovered!" She jumped at me again.

At first I was surprised at the level of her confidence in me, in my feelings, that I was back with her, until it dawned on me that last night, of which I remembered nothing, had been a night of feverish talk and such deep confessions of love that I couldn't imagine myself uttering them in my normal state. In her bedroom, she told me that I had made a clean breast of everything, of the little half-lies that I had told ("Ron Friedlich and London are only small details in a little puzzle . . ." she reminded me with a reproachful smile), of my unwillingness to live a lie with her, and on my choice of her over my other life.

"I hereby release you from all the commitments you made last night, and erase everything you said," Niki told me when she saw I was alarmed. "Even the declarations of love, which I am sure were sincere, and all the secrets. And I'm open to hearing everything again."

The impish smile that appeared at the corners of her mouth when she uttered the last sentence filled me with a lunatic happiness. I hurled her right onto the bed. "You've got too many clothes on", I felt no need to say more about my love; what I'd whispered during the night was enough for Niki too and she gave me her all.

"So, what now?" Niki asked later in the evening, when we felt that our bouts of love-making had released the tension in both of us. We were still marvellous together.

"Well, I don't feel a need to go to some restaurant right now," I said.

"That's not what I'm asking about, fool."

I knew what she'd meant the second my clumsy response came out.

"OK, let me tell you in an orderly fashion what's relevant, so we'll have some common denominator. I really don't know what I told you last night."

"No, I'll tell you what you told me last night, and then we'll really have a common denominator."

Then, in amazing detail, Niki recounted the entire story of my life that had led to the situation I was in now. She told the story of my parents, which from her lips sounded like a fairytale; the first time I had killed, in that ambush in Lebanon; my rather odd position in Bezalel; the bombing at the Dolphinarium, where I'd lost some precious students, and the bombing of the bus on Allenby Street, in which I'd lost Dolly, "Who you were going to marry," she emphasized, on the day my exhibition opened. And then she told me about my decision to join the Mossad.

I had linked it all, even in a state of delirium and fever, to my theories about we humans being survivalist pack animals, about survival being the real history of the natural world, and I had not spared her my talk about my duty now to fight for my people, my pack, which were in danger. And about which Niki now said to me: "That's what you look at, so that's what you see. I see a completely different history of the world, a history of love: all the animals that have lasted this long, have the astonishing ability to love; that is, to multiply and to nurture their offspring. For this purpose, they decorate themselves, paint themselves, sing, dance, woo, suckle, caress, lick . . ."

Yes, that's another aspect of nature, and being next to Niki it was no wonder that it was also possible to see things that way.

Shocked, I also heard the details of my course, about my cover as Ron Friedlich, "who the Bedouins buried in Sinai and you think it's awful that his parents don't know about it." And then also about the missions I'd been on in Cyprus, Poland and Jordan. I had left nothing to her imagination.

"What's clear is that your bosses shouldn't send you on missions without a coat, a scarf, gloves and a hat," Niki laughed. I didn't think it was so funny. All right, I had a high fever, but something had unlocked my innermost secrets, and I'd told her everything, down to the smallest detail. What had been done could not be undone.

She recounted it all as she lay on top of me, her two sharp elbows sticking into my chest, her small beautiful face cupped in the palms of her delicate hands, her hair tumbling over her shoulders and the sides of her face, her eyes glued to mine, deadly serious. I sensed that yet another link had been forged between us, making us a single entity.

"And what did I say about us?" I asked.

Niki slid off me, turned her back to me, and I turned onto my side and hugged her.

"You blabbered something about love being a biological ability, like defending the nation and like painting, and whoever has it must fulfil it, and all kinds of nonsense like that."

"That's it?"

"No," she hesitated. "You said you don't understand how you could have made the mistake of leaving me, and that you'd never do it again, ever." She was speaking without looking at me. I held her closer. I knew she was avoiding facing me because she didn't want to embarrass me nor watch as I retracted that statement.

"It appears I was telling the truth all night," I said, and only then did she turn around and kiss me hotly, pushing her little body up against mine and holding me as tight as she could with her slender arms.

And then, she asked the same question again, "So, what now?"

"We'll begin with what's obvious," I said. "I am staying with you. All the rest is details that we'll deal with later on."

A sigh emanated from somewhere deep down in Niki's belly, and after it came some abrupt gulps that were her attempts to stop herself from crying, and when she saw that she couldn't, she wanted me to make love to her again. Now that I had said what I said while in perfect control of my senses, and knowing that I was ready to stand by my word, whatever happened, I could also abandon myself to our loving. I think that this was our best time ever. It was a bond that did not spring from the joining of our sexual organs, but from the intertwining of our souls. Eye to eye, mouth to mouth, breast to breast, heart to beating heart, arms and legs tangled together, and yes, the organs of our pleasure were also there, and through them everything erupted from one body into the other.

What came into my mind later was a close combat lesson back when an instructor had tried to explain how a short punch to the body of the opponent begins a long time before, deep inside the belly and passes through our whole being, while the blow itself is only the external manifestation of the movement. I then understood that this was also the way that love passes through our sexual organs.

I was sweating, and Niki took my temperature again. It had gone up a bit so she brought me a pill and a glass of water. Then she told me about the anxious days she had gone through after my disappearance. At first she thought something bad had happened to me, but after checking with the police and the hospitals she realized that wasn't the problem. She went to the Town Inn Suites where they told her that I'd checked out, "rather hastily" they said, accompanied by a man who "didn't look very nice". Later on she'd recalled the documents belonging to Ron Friedlich that I'd requested and received, and put two and two together.

"I remembered news items about how the Mossad uses Canadian passports. There was that business in Jordan six or seven years ago. It occurred to me that you were trying to pose as some Canadian whose passport had somehow fallen into Israeli hands. If you actually were a Mossad agent, then maybe you'd been killed, or kidnapped. I was terribly worried and I turned half the world upside down trying to find out what had happened to you. None of the Mickey Simhonis I called were you, at your consulate here they didn't care, and when a Tel Aviv private detective, to whom I'd offered all my savings, informed me he had to drop the case, I realized it must be a government thing, and I'd better drop it too. That I could even get hurt. I came to the conclusion that actually, you looked like you could be in the Mossad."

Just like the compliments I used to receive about my art, I also found it very flattering that Niki was saying I looked like a Mossad agent.

"Later on, you left me that weird little message on my machine, that you were very sorry but you couldn't explain. I realized that my guesses were probably right, and that I didn't have anything to wait for any more. But I couldn't calm down and to try and solve another bit of the puzzle I called up Ron Friedlich's parents. Don't get alarmed, I already knew them, and later I'll tell you how, and I did it without giving anything away. I heard from them that he'd been travelling around the world for years, that he'd been in India and got involved with drugs, that his father had gone there and been with him for a while and had placed him in some rehab centre because Ron wouldn't come home. But after that he'd vanished, apparently in Sinai. They didn't think he'd kicked the habit and they were quite sure he'd not enrolled on any course in Cambridge, which made it clear to me that there was another story behind the transcripts you asked for," she said reproachfully.

Hearing that she'd spoken to Ron's parents, with whom I felt a special connection, rattled me, more than it alarmed me. I asked her to tell me more about them. How each of them sounded, what she felt about them, what she thought they were feeling.

"I can see that it really bothers you," she said, this time sympathetically.

"Of course. Both the idea that I know their son is dead and they don't, and also my guilt, that part of the reason for their not knowing is that I'm pretending to be their son. And that pretence does something to me. For days and weeks I am Ron Friedlich in my mind. Their actual son. There under interrogation in Jordan, I felt it in a very tangible way."

Niki stroked my arm, and said nothing. She wanted to get back to talking about us. She told me that as the days passed, and she didn't hear anything, it became an actual process of mourning. To get over it, she felt she had to change some things about her life. She left the registrar's office and devoted herself to what she really loved doing, editing books, which now involved her full-time. She'd also thought of moving to another apartment but didn't because of the vague hope that I'd come back, and if I did I wouldn't find her. She was clever, my Niki.

I sang her a Hebrew song about a sailor's sweetheart who lit a candle in her window each night to signal that she was waiting for him but, the night his ship came in, the wind blew the candle out while she slept, and he sailed away again. I translated the words for her, and she said, "That almost happened to us. Tell me, what would have happened if that Captain Na'im, that flirt, hadn't allowed you to call me?"

I didn't have a good reply for her. I believed at some time or another my longing for her, or my loneliness, would have risen to the surface and overcome me, but I had no way of being certain.

"We've got to thank Na'im, or even the cop who arrested you," she said.

This world is full of peculiar twists and turns.

We were besotted with each other. Over the following days, Niki brought home manuscripts that she read and commented on, and that meant we could be together every moment that she wasn't working. She could enjoy this flexibility because she worked for her mother, who owned a literary agency, and her father owned the printing press that produced some of the books that Niki and her mother selected and edited.

"We prefer bringing our books out through big publishing houses, but when work we believe is good is rejected, we have the means to print and publish it ourselves. So we are also a small publishing house, and we work with a publicity agency and a distribution company that do the rest," she explained.

I began to feel at home in the elegant apartment high in the sky. But every now and again, mostly when Niki was busy or when she had to go into the office to return or pick up new material, my thoughts drifted back to the Mossad, to the few things I had done for it so far, and which were only the prelude, in my mind, to the real thing. TV news broadcasts took me back to the gloomy reality of Israel, and phone conversations with my parents and my sisters, and even more with my little nieces, awoke a longing in me. From time to time I recalled lines from that slender volume, and my mood darkened:

How long, I wonder, can this American exile last?
A century and a half so far, they say, and thank God, all's well.
A century and a half? That's
How long our Golden Age –
The one in Spain – lasted
Before the expulsion.

But in New York alone there are three million Jews
I'm told. Three million? As in Poland, on the eve of WWII.
They'd been there for six hundred years
Until one day . . .

I kept reading, and there was a sentiment that gripped my heart so tightly
that I thought it was about to seize up:

It's so sad, saying goodbye to all that.
So sad it's all over.
It was hard, but good to be together, and alone.
I loved my life, and living there.
Pride, and fear
The swell and the ebb.
Everything possible
All in one capsule.
How sad to say goodbye.
How sad it's all over.
My heart, my broken heart.

Wasn't what I was doing contributing to the realization of that terrible
reality the anonymous poet was depicting? I bit my lips. I had, after all,
decided on my life's priorities: Niki, art, Israel, Mossad. In that order.
Whatever didn't fit in would be dropped, depending on its place in that
order.

Niki had seen inside me and understood, and one day she told me, in
preparation for a surprise she was going to spring on me later: "Do you
know that you are actually a samurai?"

"Meaning?"

"You are a warrior. You have chosen to fight. For a country, a leader, a
nation, whatever. You have chosen to devote your life to this. Any other
Canadian woman would have thought you were a primitive, militant
fanatic. But I am a descendant of samurais. I wanted to be a samurai
myself. But here there isn't a reason, a cause, so all I do is train. But I can
understand you."

That's how I discovered that Niki was a student – at Toronto's Japanese
Canadian Cultural Centre – of what she called "the way of the warrior",

the old samurai arts of judo, jiu-jitsu, swordplay. Then she showed me the secret sign, which only a graduate of warrior training was entitled to bear. A small samurai sword had recently been tattooed beneath her navel. "Here, where you stick the knife in when the time comes to perform hara-kiri," she said with a faint smile.

"How the heck didn't I notice it?" I wondered.

"You must have been busy with other parts of my body," she taunted me, and I realized that this was true, and that since my return I hadn't gone over every bit of her again, with my tongue. "I'll put that right, this minute," I said, and I did. But what she'd said echoed inside me, and later on we would get back to thrashing it out.

"I was a warrior. Or more correctly, I tried to be one," I was attempting to respond to what she'd said. "And while I was, I came to understand a few things. I know what my capabilities are, and what their order is: loving you and art come first. Being a warrior comes much lower down."

"I've given it a great deal of thought, so don't dismiss what I'm about to say," Niki said. "Being a warrior isn't last on your list, even if at the moment you think it is. True, you are an artist and a lover, but being a samurai is first and foremost to belong, and only after that to fight. And when necessary, fighting climbs up the order of priorities, overtaking the other concerns that are so important to you today."

She gave me a minute to digest this. I did indeed belong, and I felt that I belonged, my whole life. For one month a year, I had demonstrated this in practice by doing my army reserve stint, and the rest of the year I'd been an artist and an art teacher, and I'd looked for love. But when Dolly's death told me that the "necessary" time had come, I left everything behind and became a warrior again.

"I know what agony it was for a samurai to abandon those he'd been loyal to. And I see it in your eyes, even though you don't talk about it. I know what my grandfather went through when he left Japan and came here. I do not want you to undergo that same anguish. I've told you that I wanted to be a samurai. I believe that a samurai is loyal not only to his shogun or to the place where he lives. Wandering samurais used to seek out masters for themselves. I've heard your story, and your parents' and your country's stories. I've read a lot about Israel, way back then, after we met, and mainly in the last few months since you vanished."

I am truly a sort of samurai, I thought. I and my fellow soldiers, the tens of thousands of youngsters who join the combat units of the Israeli army – we are a nation of samurais. And more than I was aware of it was, perhaps, imprinted in me.

I thought I knew where she was heading. Would she be prepared to come to Israel with me, to live with me there, and let me stay in the Mossad? Or did she want to be the woman waiting for her warrior here in Toronto, with me changing the hub of my life, coming and going from here instead of Tel Aviv? Both possibilities intrigued me, although what I wanted most was to be with her and to be an artist. But Niki had taken a step further than my imagination allowed me.

"You had to do some weird stuff to get a borrowed Canadian identity. I have an authentic one. And I'm also a samurai, like you. What do you think about . . ."

She didn't finish the sentence, and it already seemed too good to be true. To my amazement, my artistic career dropped away, in light of the new coalition formed between Niki, the Mossad, my country and my parents. I had no idea what Udi and the organization would make of it.

"Whoa, wait," I said. "It's too early to speak about this. And please forget about the samurai thing. If you want to follow me, to join me, and I were to be here with you and you'd let me carry on with my missions, it would have to be because we are very much in love. Not because of any romantic samurai traditions, please, with all the respect that I have for them."

Niki listened in silence. Then she responded:

"I don't know how to separate the two. My culture is part of me. For me to be loyal is cultural. It's not preordained. To follow my man is cultural, not preordained. The same goes for being a warrior. And even to love like we love is cultural, to some extent. Not everything is biological, as you tend to believe. If we were living in another place and at another time, perhaps we wouldn't be able to give our feelings the expression that we can here and now. I feel the way I do now because my feelings have erupted. I feel the way I do because that's the way my life has pointed me, and what has shaped me to a certain degree has been the culture I received from my father, and to a certain degree the culture I received from my mother and from the kids I grew up with. Don't try to make me separate these things, because I can't."

As I digested this I realised that the same was true for me. I would not have been who I was – and I certainly would not feel the same burden of loyalty to my country and my people – if it had not been for my parents' past, and the history of my nation, and the society I grew up in. Even my having fallen so powerfully in love was perhaps the product of social concepts that I had been exposed to. But now all that didn't matter. What mattered was how I felt, and what Niki was enabling me to feel, to do, to be. She was enabling me to live enormous parts of my life. As for the art – it could wait for the evenings and the weekends. And it was up to me to enable her to feel what she felt and to do what she wanted to do.

I was at a loss for words to express my gratitude. I just held her tight.

"I think it's time for me to meet your parents," I said.

"I've already set up a dinner date. It's happening on Saturday. My mother insists that it be at their home."

This step up in our relationship accentuated the fact that I had not set any kind of a timetable with Udi. The matter had been left open-ended. Even though he'd said we had to find an ending for my love story, I nevertheless felt as if I was living on borrowed time. It wasn't at all reasonable to expect Udi and the Mossad to let me carry on like this, without even officially seeing my contract through. I didn't assume that they would simply let me go, although they had perhaps classified my performance in Amman as a failure.

I decided to wait for them to take the initiative, and in the meantime to work on my love story, whose actual ending couldn't be foreseen.

We agreed that I'd take Niki's parents a painting, and I spent the next few days working, in watercolours, on a portrait of her that I called, *Girl with Green Eyes*. Although I could sketch her in a minute, and although I had worked most of my coloured paintings in oil when holed up in my studio for hours and days, or in acrylic, which dries quicker, I thought that in aquarelle I'd be able to better capture her translucent skin and her radiant eyes and the invisible aura of joy that surrounded her. The delicate combination of the transparent watercolours and the shade of the paper would also enable me to express Niki's spirit and spirituality more faithfully. I would have to wait before applying the paint for each colour until the one before had dried, but I was ready to lovingly devote all the time in the world to it.

Because I didn't have the necessary supplies I went out to buy a few sheets of heavy, absorbent, paper and soft sable-hair brushes. The brushes, made from the fur of that rare Siberian animal, were insanely expensive – 200 Canadian dollars for the fine brush, 300 for the medium and 400 for the thick. The firm of Winsor and Newton had originally made the Kolinsky sable brush for Queen Victoria. They were out of reach for hard-up artists and I didn't know if I'd ever use them again but, I too, wanted the very best. Neither did I compromise on my watercolours, and I selected a Cotman set whose little squares of paint looked softer and more delicate than the German Schmincke. The Canadian supplies were different from those I was familiar with in Israel, and I thought I'd have to do a certain amount of improvisation, something appropriate to this medium which enables both maximum precision and spontaneity.

I sat Niki down facing me and I painted her directly, using the fine brush, with transparent and translucent colours, dispensing with a pencil sketch, although I knew that I would have almost no way of making corrections. I began with an off-white outline of her face and upper body, and when it looked sufficiently accurate, I waited for it to dry and in the meanwhile mixed the paints that would catch the radiance of her skin: white, ochre, pink and orange, and then I filled in the face and throat, leaving spaces for the eyes. I enjoyed creating the fine, transparent layers of colour with the brush, and the shades and tints that formed on the paper and were absorbed by it, looking as if they had grown out of it, not placed onto it.

Before the paint dried, I dabbed in pink highlights on the cheeks, and the touch of paint spread as a gentle blush without a clear outline. Then I began working with slightly darker paints, carefully and delicately, on her beautiful throat and collarbones. I felt that I was managing, with a small number of pigments, to build Niki's soft and vivid harmoniousness but, in order to obtain the ivory shine of her skin I used moist cotton-wool to brush over her cheeks and forehead, thereby lightening them to get the gleaming radiance just right.

I also felt that I was conveying her internal essence, by elongating her eyes a little and giving them the brilliant green tint that shone through them. Then I worked on her smile, both restrained and captivating, in a bright red, and with a few more touches of cotton-wool I completed the brightness surrounding her image. Niki posed for many hours, an obedient, contented model. After I let her get up, she whooped with joy when she saw the final result. "Am I so beautiful in your eyes?" she asked, hugging and kissing me.

I continued painting applying dark shades to her hair and bright colours to her dress. But I left the background of the room and furnishings dim and lacking in detail, the more to highlight her lustrous image. Next day I took the finished portrait to be framed at one of the galleries where I'd placed my work. When they saw it, the owners immediately said they could sell it, or any similar work for not less than twelve thousand Canadian dollars.

Once again, I donned my suit, and Niki said I looked "just perfect". She wore trousers, a thick turtleneck sweater and no makeup: she was the perfect petite and beautiful girl-woman.

Niki drove us in her little car northwards, out of the city centre. We passed the high-rises, along Mount Pleasant Road, and into a more residential area. The homes here were single family residences and the further north we drove, the larger they became. Still two-storeys high, some were constructed of red and black brick, others of brown and light-coloured brick, with roofs that were less pointy and gardens that were bigger and better tended. Niki turned into a street of really large homes, some of them reminiscent of small castles nestling deep inside expansive gardens, and reached by private driveways. She drove into one of these, up to a large house with a roof of grey tiles set at varying angles that immediately reminded me of the tiled roofs of houses in Japan. Niki saw what I was looking at and said, "Welcome to Little Japan."

She gave a short toot on the horn, and lights went on in the front of the house, the door opened and light from the inside silhouetted a tall woman and a stocky man.

Niki's mother looked like your typical WASP – blonde and blue-eyed, tall and slender. "Emily," she introduced herself, coming up to me and air-kissing both my cheeks. Her father was the short, strong-looking type of Japanese, with a handsome face. He said "Yoshima" and bowed deeply. I did the same, a little shallower. I'd read up on Japanese etiquette, and Niki had briefed me, and it seemed to me that by doing this, I acquired both his trust and his affection.

"So, I understand you met back in Japan," he said when we were inside the large entrance hall, which gave off a Japanese warmth: the ceiling and the floor were both made of wood, and the walls were partitions of paper in wooden frames, which served as wide sliding doors. We both confirmed what he'd said, and when I saw Niki slipping her shoes off I remembered that she'd warned me I'd have to do the same.

"A ten-year friendship is no small matter," said Yoshima, apparently unaware of the almost decade-long break. His wife put him right, saying, "But it was pure coincidence that you met up again here, I gather. When you came to sell your paintings in our galleries."

"Though we actually met at the university," Niki said. "He came to get some papers for a friend."

I gulped. What else was she going to divulge? But it turned out she just wanted to get the facts straight.

I handed my gift to Niki's parents. The way they opened the wrapping was mannered but their outburst of admiration for the portrait was spontaneous and genuine. So was mine, when I saw Niki's painted form, with all my love reflected in her face, a rendition which to my eyes was a marvellous combination of Niki herself, of my love and of my handiwork.

Emily took down a reproduction of Jan Vermeer's *Girl with a Red Hat* that was hanging on the living room wall. It was a painting I was familiar with from my theoretical studies at Bezalel, but only in recent years had I gone deeper into Vermeer's work, after the publication of the novel by Tracey Chevalier, *Girl with a Pearl Earring*, inspired by a work which Vermeer himself called *Girl with a Headscarf*.

Emily hung my painting in the place she had vacated. The three of them clapped hands enthusiastically at the radiant effect, and Niki gave me a shy kiss on the cheek.

We went into the dining room, where there were both a conventional, long western-style table and a low Japanese table, with cushions around it. I was glad when we sat at the normal one. During the meal, Emily asked me a host of questions about my painting. I didn't tell her much. I found it easier to talk about the picture she'd taken down than about myself. If it had been an interrogation, they would certainly have been convinced that I was an authentic artist or an expert on art: I showed them how the red shades of the prominent round hat were reflected in the face and the whites of the eyes of the girl; how the light coming in from the window – a motif common to many of Vermeer's works – illuminated her face and made her nose almost translucent. I spoke of Vermeer's unique use of shadows, which were for the first time not black but just a little bit darker than objects near them, and I told them about the theory that Vermeer used a camera obscura to obtain the perfect perspective in his works. To finish off, I told them that despite the suggestion in Chevalier's novel – which had just been made into a film starring Scarlett Johansson – that the artist had a love affair with the maid who ostensibly was the model for *Girl with a Pearl Earring*, it was actually his daughter who posed for him, as far as was known.

Niki's parents, who had apparently been interested in publishing Chevalier's novel in Canada were surprised and even more surprised to hear that there was uncertainty as to Vermeer's first name – whether it was Jan, Johannes or Johan, and that some authorities added a "van" before his family name. The details of his life, which were overshadowed by those of other giants of Dutch art of his period, were vague.

Yoshima asked me about my military service. I told him a little about the work of the Engineering Corps and about mine clearing, a subject that turned out to interest both parents greatly. Much-publicized efforts were under way at the time to clear minefields from former battlefields, such as Okinawa, Cambodia, Vietnam and others. I refrained from mentioning the mines I had laid around our fortified positions in southern Lebanon, most of which remained in place when Israel finally withdrew in 2000.

Niki's parents liked what they heard, and were polite and sympathetic, but didn't really know how to react to the strange match their daughter had made. It'd be interesting to see how my parents would react to her, I thought.

Yoshima, I discovered during our conversation, had started off as a print worker, became the owner of a printing works, and had met Emily when she was a literature student. After she became a literary agent, he began printing work that she selected, along with the other print jobs. "Emily's ability to assure authors whom she selected that their books would be published without being dependent on other publishers' decisions gave her a lot of power," Yoshima said. "And some of that power has recently passed to Niki."

"In fact, since Niki's been working with me, we've become a combination of a literary agency and a small publishing house," Emily added. "Niki's got a really good eye for literature, and we don't pass on the writers she picks." I noticed that Niki had gone a little red in the face.

What her mother was hinting at was that they didn't want her to stray away from the family business.

After the meal, there was a surprise in store for me. Yoshima took me into a space which in Japanese homes serves as an internal garden, and which here housed a kind of dojo, a judo gym with a wooden roof. Yoshima said something to his daughter in Japanese, bowed, and she bowed back and disappeared into the house. Then he bowed to me and to Emily, who was standing next to me, and also entered the house, with measured paces. I guessed what was about to happen, and waited expectantly.

"This is in your honour. They haven't done this for years," said Emily, who seemed a little embarrassed.

When Niki and her father came back, they were in samurai garb, which resembled judo robes but were made of a different fabric, with silk patterns, and also cut differently. Vests made of some stiff material protected their chests. Both were carrying swords, about thirty inches long with grey steel blades and black hilts, the type known as katana, Niki told me later. I was more and more intrigued. Yoshima also had a wakizashi, a shorter sword with a hilt studded with precious stones, at his waist.

The sword fight between the two was stunningly beautiful. Yoshima was restrained but firm, his movements hard and strong. Niki hovered like the wind, delicate, fleet, agile, but her strokes and thrusts were very powerful. The blades clashed with great force and the metallic sound resonated in my ears like cymbals. She circled around Yoshima like a bird of prey, and he fought back like an ageing lion. Twice he trapped her in a corner of the room, his sword pressing hers down, but both times she escaped with a glorious wheeling leap. Once she managed to get her sword onto his chest. I watched them enchanted and mesmerized.

After what could have been between five and ten minutes – it was difficult to estimate – the two stood facing each other, their swords pointed downwards, and bowed deeply.

I looked questioningly at Emily, wondering if it was appropriate to clap, which is what I felt like. She understood and nodded, and she joined me in applauding the combatants.

Only after leaving the dojo did Yoshima embrace his daughter, and she kissed him.

"You're in great shape, my daughter," he said in what sounded to me like a Japanese style of address.

"And you're still as strong as ever, father," she replied in the same manner. They looked at each other lovingly.

"They like you," Niki told me as we left, her parents waving goodbye from the door. "That makes me even happier."

But a fine mesh of sadness that I could discern in her eyes told me she was already contemplating her separation from them, a separation that would be very difficult for her. I loved her enough to understand that she had no reason at all to prefer my life in my country and close to my parents, over her own life in her country and close to her parents.

When I wanted to express this, she put her finger on my lips.

There was something else that I wanted to do before returning to Israel. I fully grasped its implications. I also fully grasped that it would elicit great ire and that it was liable to block my way back to the Mossad, both because I'd be considered someone who wilfully harmed the organization, and because I would remain without the cover that Ron Friedlich had given me thus far. They would have to treat me as any other operative, without the added value of my resemblance to the dead Canadian. Mickey, as is, or Mickey and Niki, as a package deal.

Because it was a drastic, possibly life-changing step, for her as well as me, I decided to let my final decision hang fire. No one was pressurising me. The month of March had brought with it the first faint signs of the end of winter and I was free and happy, more than I'd ever been before. Niki and I were a couple madly in love.

Udi's phone call came when I was resolved. "I'm coming back," I said, "but naked and with a dowry."

"Translation, please."

"Without Ron and with Niki."

Udi was silent for a while. Then he said: "Hold your decisions. I may be able to be there next week."

"These two things are not up for discussion."

Again he remained silent, weighing my words.

"Nevertheless, wait. I'll try to get there and we'll talk."

I was glad that I had a few more blissful days with Niki, reaffirming each day and each night how essential it was for her to be the woman in my life, for the rest of my days.

Before a week had gone by, Udi called again.

"I don't know if you've heard what happened in Ashdod. In any case, I can't come but I need you."

"But only the way I said; with Niki, without Ron."

"I've already begun rolling the idea along the corridors. Anyway, if you don't come back, neither will Ron. I'd rather have you at peace with yourself, and without the rock that's weighing down your conscience. But you do not know the whole picture, and you mustn't make mistakes. And about your dowry – that's interesting. Interesting. Once I suggested something to you about her. You're apparently one of those people who, when they're asked for a glass of water, bring the whole well. And don't be offended now – I didn't say a glass of milk. Do what's good for you, and then we'll work something out. I hope you'll be here when I get back." I went to the TV and flicked through the news channels, but there was nothing about Ashdod. I went online, to Y-Net, and there found a full report about the double terror attack at the port. One suicide bomber from Fatah and the other from Hamas, both from the Jebaliya refugee camp in the Gaza Strip. Ten Israelis dead, thirteen wounded. In response the Air Force had attacked the metal workshops in Gaza, where the bombs had been made. The Jewish settlers were blaming the recent "disengagement" – the withdrawal of Israeli forces and removal of settlements from the Gaza Strip.

Once again, I was surprised at the extent to which I felt detached. The words on the screen and the few pictures had almost no effect on me, on the emotional level. Could I carry on here, with Niki, growing accustomed to the distance and the break with everything that had been close to me, living my life as an artist, with a beloved wife, living the present as if there had been no past, and building myself a totally different future?

I debated with myself for one more day, and asked Niki if she wanted to join me on a mission which I reckoned would be tougher than any of the missions I'd been on so far.

"Going to see Ron Friedlich's parents?" said my very smart sweetheart. "Ever since you asked about them after I told you I'd spoken to them, I've been waiting for you to suggest it." She hugged and kissed me. "Have I ever told you I love you?"

✧✧✧

Then she sat me down at the table and took a chair facing me.

"You really don't remember anything of your first night back here, do you? I decided back then to tell you about it and I did, but when I saw you didn't mention it again in the morning, I didn't repeat the full version."

I had no idea what she was talking about.

"Remember I told you I had a friend who looked like you?"

I remembered.

"I saw him soon after I began working at the university. He simply walked right past me, and I was in shock. It was a year or two after we met in Japan."

"Ron Friedlich . . .?" I stammered.

"Yes. I didn't think it was you for one moment, but the resemblance was amazing. I asked myself what I should do about it, and I decided to let the wind take me wherever it took me."

"Meaning?"

"To see what would happen."

"And?"

"I arranged for someone to introduce us. We went out a few times. It wasn't right."

"Which means?"

"You look alike, but that's all."

"You'll forgive me for wanting to hear more?"

"I knew I shouldn't have told you. But I don't want to leave any secrets between us. He was the pretty boy on the football team, who'd never made an effort to achieve anything, and when we met he'd already decided to give up sports, after he wasn't signed up by any pro team. And he'd begun taking the drugs that screwed him up in the end. The girls he was after were cheerleaders with nothing but their blonde hair. It was pretty clear from the first date that it wouldn't go anywhere, but I gave it a second chance. I even agreed to meet his lovely parents, but that was it."

I was supposed to be relieved, but I couldn't accept the idea that that was all there was to my Ron, my Canadian double. I asked her to tell me more.

"He was an easygoing guy, very self-confident, but I missed that combination of bashfulness and strength that I recognized in you back there, in Tokyo. I also didn't see a capability for dedicating himself, for fighting for something, like you had there. For him, everything was clear and simple. There was something shadowy about you that attracted me more."

"Shadowy?"

"Yes. It's something I love in you. Waiting in the rain outside the club in Asakusa, that was shadowy. Heavy. Hard. Even a little scary, don't you think? To get drunk at the bar and draw me was shadowy but equally attractive and charming, no? So is the fact that you can suddenly break away and disappear. Every day with you is a surprise – if I find you here when I come home in the evening, and it's a party if you stay the night, and I'm kept in suspense as to whether you'll still be here in the morning."

"That's how you feel, my darling?" I held her tight and my heart contracted. But then I asked her to go on telling me about Ron: "After that there was no contact between you?"

"We bumped into each other on campus. But nothing beyond that."

Our reunion in the registrar's office came into my mind. I asked her what had happened there, what she'd thought.

"When I saw you through my office door, I jumped. At first I thought you were Ron, but when I heard your voice and you mentioning the name Ron Friedlich, I wondered what was going on, so I came to take a look."

"And why . . ."

"Why did I help you? Somehow I knew you were involved in something that was not quite kosher and as I've told you, I had in my head the story about the Canadian passports the Israelis used in Jordan. I wouldn't have paid attention if I didn't know you from before. I thought that perhaps you were trying to appropriate Ron's identity due to your resemblance. I didn't give it too much thought right then, I simply thought you might get into trouble and I wanted to help."

"And then?"

"I was straight away in love again but I tried to suppress my feelings. But the way that you wanted to see a different part of the city each time we went out, and then that encounter with the stranger in the restaurant that you denied, convinced me of what was really going on."

"And then, when I vanished . . ."

"Somehow I expected it to happen. I saw you weren't altogether wholeheartedly here, that part of you was somewhere else. I was also worried of course and I tried to find you but after I realized that you hadn't been hurt, and the message you left confirmed it, I gave up. With a broken heart."

I thought about telling her how I had debated with myself before I left, about the times that I had raised the matter with my superiors, but that would have been trying to justify something that in truth wasn't justifiable, and I left it for another time. Instead I decided to bring up something that had bothered me ever since leaving her that message.

"I know I don't have the right to ask you this, but it bothers me. When I called you then, and you didn't pick up, it was two a.m. here ..."

Niki's expression hardened and an angry frown appeared between her eyebrows. "I'm sorry that you asked and this must be the last time that you ask and I answer. I was brought up with the belief that loyalty is the supreme value. But you left, and the moment you did that, the moment I realized that was what had happened, I owed you nothing. And don't ever expect me to be loyal if you walk away from me. Yes, with a broken heart I went to someone else. And that night I was with him. Exactly like the song you sang for me, about the candle that went out in the sailor's sweetheart's window."

My insides constricted from the intensity of the blow she had just dealt me but there was nothing I could say and nothing I had the right to say. But I knew I had to break the silence, before it led us to a bad place.

"If so, what happened when you got that call from Jordan? Why did you help me?"

Niki was also relieved that I'd changed the subject.

"At first, I thought it really was Ron Friedlich on the line. It seemed weird. Years had gone by, why should he be calling me out of the blue, and in the middle of the night too? I thought I wasn't hearing right. Luckily you reminded me about the transcripts and you mentioned the date, and I put two and two together. As soon as I came to, I realized you were using Ron's documents, and you were in trouble."

"I think you'll make a first class secret agent," I said, and pulled her close.

"We'll make a great couple of agents," she said, a very serious expression on her face.

"As for Ron's parents," she said, "I'd better go alone. It would be a pity to get Israel mixed up in this. When they see your resemblance to him it would only make them sadder and complicate things. I'll tell them I heard from a common friend that Ron was in Sinai with the Bedouin and he'd died there. It will be a lot easier for them to hear it from me and they also won't be able to ask any questions, because I can say I don't know anything else. By the way, this will not be coming at them like a bolt from the blue. There'll be pain, but when I spoke to them they told me he'd been hospitalized because of drugs, in India I think. My impression was that they'd given up on the hope that he'd ever recover and come home."

Niki, my love, my own samurai.

Part Two

Ruth and Boaz

I.

A Samurai in Tel Aviv

FALLING IN LOVE with an Israeli may be sexy, but deciding to go and live in Israel? Niki's family and friends could not fathom this move of hers. Her parents were trying to sway her against it, and I no longer felt comfortable visiting them.

Despite his busy schedule, Udi came to Toronto to hear directly from Niki that this was indeed what she wanted and to conduct an initial appraisal of her suitability. I remembered that he'd warned me not to bring him "some new immigrant", and here I was bringing him a complete foreigner, something that was considered an even greater security risk. Udi apparently received a favourable impression, as he stayed in town to oversee our preparations for departure and make sure we didn't do something dumb that would prevent us from coming back. He told me to keep up the lease on my rented apartment so that if required it could continue to serve as part of my cover down the road. We were still a long way from Niki's acceptance into our ranks.

Udi managed to talk me out of confessing to Ron's parents. "It makes no sense to lose this passport and the cover you've constructed, especially now when Niki may be joining us. So what if those Bedouin said that he was dead? Bedouin are natural liars, even polygraphs don't work on them. I wouldn't go and drop an atom bomb on Ron's parents just because some Bedouin said something, perhaps only to get a better price for the passport. Who knows?" It sounded convincing, so I conceded for the time being, and Niki was relieved.

Niki and I went to take our leave from her parents only on the day of our flight. Emily was distraught, and Yoshima was cold and restrained. This time, Niki's sister Mila was there. She'd come especially from Vancouver, where she was studying, to say goodbye. Unlike Niki, Mila was a replica of their father. She greeted me warmly, backed Niki's daring decision, and lightened the gloomy mood. She joined us on the drive back to Niki's place.

"Your parents may be right," I said to a glum Niki in the car, and I tried to cheer her up by cracking an old joke: "Moses stuttered, and when he said the People of Israel should go to Ca . . .Ca . . . Ca . . . – his brother Aaron misinterpreted him – and told them that their destination was Canaan. But Moses meant to say Canada."

They both giggled a little, but then Niki burst into a protracted bout of sobbing. We stopped at the roadside and I hugged her, almost regretting my decision to go back to Israel. But she took control of herself, dried her eyes and insisted on driving home. Then it was Mila who was weeping softly, in the backseat.

We had sent most of Niki's things on a few days before, and all we had now were two big suitcases. Niki, practical and reserved, gave her sister instructions about the apartment and the car, handed over the keys to both, and we went down to the waiting cab. To make it easier for Niki, Mila stayed behind in the apartment.

Avi, our case officer, was waiting as we came off the plane at Ben Gurion Airport. He leaned over and kissed Niki and then gave me a long handshake, as if he was rounding off our exchange of glances last time we met, in the hotel in Amman. He told us that an Office van was waiting to take us to a hotel.

"We didn't think you'd want to take her to your place. Perhaps you need a bit of time to fix it up."

I was grateful for the consideration. My apartment must have been pretty mouldy with dead plants, columns of ants feasting on particles of food and dirty items of clothing all over the place, not to mention the pictures of Dolly.

"Where's Udi?" I asked.

"With the crew, at work," he answered in Hebrew, and he whispered in my ear, "Yesterday in Athens we settled scores with some bad guys connected to the recent terror attacks." Then he said out loud, "It's beginning to get them down, what's going on around here. The prime minister, I mean. Soon you boys will start going to some more interesting places."

He walked with us to border control, and asked Niki for her passport. "Pity to contaminate it with an Israeli entry stamp," he told me. He showed the guard a document and led us through a side door. "Welcome to Israel," he said to Niki, and I thought it was also welcome to the Mossad. Operational thinking on the matter of Niki had already begun. They were taking it seriously.

Niki was in a state of shock during our tour of Tel Aviv. In the spring of 2004, the big city was celebrating almost a complete year of freedom from terror attacks since the bombing at Mike's Place, a pub on the beachfront promenade. Not very far away, places like Rosh Ha'Ayin, the Geha intersection and the hitchhiking stop outside the Tzrifin army base were in the metropolitan periphery but far enough away for the bombs there not to be heard in the city. Jerusalem, Haifa and Ashdod, which sustained heavy casualties during this period, also didn't really register on Tel Aviv's radar. The promenade was crowded and on sunny days people went down to the beach, and the brave few even went into the sea. Niki was captivated.

"You know, I've read a lot about Israel, but nothing described it as it really is," she said, thrilled and already in love with the place.

We travelled to Haifa to meet my folks. I thought it was better to get it over as soon as possible.

"Is a half-Japanese also a 'shiksa'?" I had asked my mother, preparing her for the upcoming encounter. "Oh, don't talk nonsense," she replied, taking a liking to Niki from the first moment. My father was also more friendly than usual. I didn't think that they realized that "this was it", that I loved Niki and that she was here to stay. They were disappointed when I told them we were heading back to Tel Aviv that same evening, but we said we'd come for Friday night dinner, with the whole family.

When we left, Niki mentioned that I hadn't said anything about what I'd been through in Jordan. "Odd, isn't it? I'm not supposed to tell them anything. That they don't know what I do is taken for granted. But it's strange I can go through such a momentous experience, and the people who are the most important in the world for me know nothing about it."

After a short silence, during which Niki was perhaps trying to work out the significance of this matter for her own relationship with my parents, she said, "But we'll know everything about each other, won't we?"

"Almost everything," I said to her. and explained that even within a small team there had to be compart-mentalization and that things were conducted on a "need to know" basis.

The Office gave me a week to get organized and, because I didn't want us to begin our life together in the shadow of my memories with Dolly, we rented an apartment on Rehov Ruppin, a quiet street a minute from the promenade. The three-roomed apartment with basic furniture on the top floor of a four-storey building had a balcony facing the sea. I removed everything out of my apartment and we bought what we still needed on two jolly shopping sprees at the IKEA store in Netanya. We were a typical young couple.

We drove to Jerusalem in a car the Office put at my disposal and, for the first time, I discovered the Christian side of Niki. She didn't define herself as belonging to any specific religion, as the daughter of a Shinto adherent and a Christian, but her excitement was evident at the various Christian sites we visited. I took her to the Holy Sepulchre, at the end of the Via Dolorosa, before we went to the Western Wall and other places of Jewish interest. Just as she had been in Tel Aviv, Niki was impressed by the cafés and bars in the narrow streets of the Nahalat Shiv'a area, places where her playgirl instincts came out.

Then we took a three-day trip around the Galilee: Niki yelped with delight when Lake Kinneret, the Sea of Galilee, came into view on the way down from the Galilee hills, against the background of the fields and pasturelands spread out around it. Here too we visited Christian sites, starting with the Mount of Beatitudes, where Jesus preached the Sermon on the Mount, and the pretty church built out of black basalt rock and limestone and with its copper dome. From there we hiked down to the Tabgha valley with its seven springs and visited the Church of the Multiplication of the Loaves and the Fishes and the Church of the Primacy of Peter. Niki was visibly moved, and I was worried that her connection to the country, as someone who was meant to be a Mossad operative, was beginning to be built on the wrong foundations. But I decided to leave it up to Udi to handle this. Our meeting with him had been set for the start of the next week and, for the time being, it was only Niki and me, the Kinneret, the Golan Heights and the Galilee, and all the love in the world.

In our cosy bed and breakfast room at Neveh Ativ, on Mount Hermon, I realized how much I loved her when even the little "plop" that I heard from the bathroom sounded really cute to me.

At the foot of Mt Hermon and along the border with Lebanon, Niki listened with interest and retrospective concern when I told her about my military activities there. It seemed to me that things only began to be real for her when we saw the fortified positions along the northern frontier road and the Hezbollah flags on the other side of the fence, the Humvees and armoured cars bristling with weaponry and soldiers in their combat vests all smeared with mud. "Samurais in camouflage uniforms," I said as we drove past a battle crew preparing for night activity, and she said, "Those very words were on the tip of my tongue."

After reaching Rosh Hanikra and its pretty rocky reefs on the Mediterranean shore, we headed south for the Friday night dinner at my parents' home. My sisters kissed Niki, and after a moment of embarrassment when Lital, Tzippi's eldest daughter, blurted out "But she hasn't got Japanese eyes," and pulled her own eyes to show what she meant, Niki burst out laughing and everyone relaxed. She was accepted into my family, and she accepted my family. That hurdle, at least, had been overcome.

Niki fell in love with Haifa. In my parents' apartment she said that the view of the port reminded her of the view from her apartment in Toronto, but when we drove along the Carmel ridge, stopping at the customary vantage points next to Stella Maris in one direction and the Louis Promenade on the other, she admitted that it was a long time since she'd been in such a lovely place and she couldn't understand why I'd left it.

After Saturday's day of rest in Tel Aviv, our meeting with Udi was awaiting us.

I'd been told to bring Niki to the small house in the Kirya but didn't know if I would be expected to stay or not. Because there was only one chair facing Udi at his desk, I gestured to Niki to sit and remained standing next to her. Udi didn't suggest that I draw up another chair so I understood that my presence wasn't wanted but, nevertheless, I stayed while Udi asked her what she thought of the country so far and how we'd settled into the apartment. After she gave an enthusiastic reply and I answered about the apartment, I asked if I was free to go. The reply was in the affirmative and I went downstairs to Orit the receptionist but all she could offer me was instant coffee, so I walked to the corner and came back with a large latte in a paper cup.

I waited for hours. This was probably the longest getting-to-know meeting in Mossad history, or at least in the history of Udi, the man of few words. For a time I was irritated at Udi for not giving me some kind of timetable and leaving me to dry out in tense anticipation. Then I got it: Udi had said he wanted to meet Niki on Sunday at ten. He hadn't said he wanted to meet Niki and me. He was creating a barrier between us, one that I would feel strongly further down the road, and perhaps he was doing the right thing. Just as a couple may be useful in an operation, an intimate connection outside the working framework was liable to be a nuisance and to do damage. Udi wanted to build Niki as an independent operative and not as my mate.

I remained tense until I heard the door upstairs creaking. What would happen if he'd decided she wasn't suitable? Would Niki be willing and able to live her life in Israel? Particularly if I remained in the Mossad and was travelling all the time. Or would we perhaps go back to Toronto and begin our lives as a normal couple, an artist and a book editor?

I finally heard Niki's sweet voice saying, "Thank you, I'll find my way out," and her legs, still pretty but not so crooked now, appeared at the top of the stairs. She glided nimbly down, with a smile on her lips and a gleam in her eyes, said goodbye quickly and warmly to Orit and pulled me outside, unable to suppress what she wanted to tell me.

"What a great guy," she gushed the moment we were through the gate. And between then and when we sat down in a nearby restaurant, she didn't stop speaking about the way he had managed to get into what she called "the depths of my being" and fathomed what made her tick – "what I want to be when I'm grown up" – and mainly, how much she wanted to be with me and how much she was ready to sacrifice for just that. Almost without taking a breath, she went on to express her amazement at the lively street with all its many restaurant, and, as soon as she saw the Cinémathèque, she wanted to find out if there was something interesting to see.

In turn, Niki had also made a good impression on Udi: her mobile phone rang while we were still in the restaurant, and she was asked to report the next day to undergo a series of tests.

"At least you'll be exempt from English lessons." I tried to smile, but in the pit of my stomach I felt a twinge, without really knowing where it came from or where it was leading. Here was Niki, finding her way into the Mossad without any help from me, and perhaps even without any connection to her relationship with me. Very quickly, without either of us noticing it, Udi had become the axis around which her life would now revolve as a trainee and later as an operative. Almost imperceptibly I had been cast aside. Udi, the old fox. There was no knowing now what was really hiding behind his paternal manner but Niki's enthusiasm for Udi shed new light on him. He was indeed someone who could make plans for us that would never cross my mind. His large head seemed to me to be full of schemes and thoughts compared to which my own seemed linear, binary, yes or no, clear and simple.

I felt strange during Niki's training period when I was in Israel, and it was intolerable when I was abroad. Most of my time was spent at the squad's base, training and preparing for upcoming missions. Udi was away a lot; I didn't know if he was with Niki or with other trainees and even when he came to the base he never gave me the slightest hint what was happening with her, not even whether I should hurry home in the evening because she was through for the day, or that there was no point in hurrying because she was on an exercise that would take all night. For him, I was the operative Boaz, and not Niki's boyfriend, and she was Niki the trainee: there was nothing to connect us.

The hours I spent waiting for Niki in our apartment were infuriating and, when she eventually arrived, full of adrenalin and happiness, I had to summon all of my very small acting talent to participate in her enjoyment. She felt free to tell me about everything she was doing and from her stories I grasped that she was an outstanding student. I knew of course that she was athletic and an expert at martial arts, and I wasn't surprised to hear that she was also a crack shot. She performed the exercises – in which I'd had to strain my brain for a suitable cover story – easily and naturally, almost casually. Where I'd had to think up all kinds of pretexts and exert myself to get into any site – be it a cinema or an industrial plant – Niki did it with a simple smile. She was so nice and natural that nobody ever suspected her when she was on lookout duty by day or break-ins by night. She was as transparent as the wind. Even her foreign-looking features didn't make people think they should keep an eye on her.

Throughout her training period, which was much shorter than mine, I took part in six or seven short operations abroad and each one involved a week of preparation, a week of travel and a week of debriefings, during which there was a distance between us that I didn't like. It was difficult for me to be without her when I was abroad, and coming home to the empty apartment was difficult for her. Niki was concerned about me and interested in what I was doing but Udi had ordered me to tell her nothing, because until she completed her training and was officially inducted, she "wasn't one of us", and this too was difficult.

My first mission came at the same time as Niki was on her first intelligence-gathering course. I had really wanted to be there, to hear about it and perhaps give her advice, but some Iranian nuclear scientists were due in New Delhi, on their way back to Tehran from a secret visit to North Korea, and we were tasked with photographing them and the materials they had with them, and copying everything on their laptops, if they had any. Their trip had been kept totally under wraps, and we didn't know what it was all about.

Because of the short notice, Jerry, Ronen and I flew directly from Israel to New Delhi and Udi was supposed to be joining us there later. Unlike the shock on my first landing in India, in Mumbai, arriving in New Delhi was easier: a modern airport, the imperial buildings and broad streets of the new city that the British had left behind, and a friendly atmosphere. At least that's what I felt, but not Ronen and Jerry. The ride from the airport to the city centre was like a roller coaster for them, with the insane overtaking, sudden stops, and incessant horn tooting. And when we arrived, the beggars caught their eyes, and the stench filled their nostrils. "Wait till you see Old Delhi," I told them. "The alleys and the slums – then you'll really have something to complain about."

We checked into three different hotels where the Iranians were likely to stay: Jerry at the Crowne Plaza, Ronen at the Hyatt Regency and I at the Hilton. If they surprised us and went to a different hotel, Udi would be following them and check in there as well. We were to meet the group at the airport and tail them but, before their arrival, we had a few hours to get to know the city. We began at Connaught Place, a park surrounded by a ring of shops named after Rajiv Gandhi, somewhat reminiscent of Tel Aviv in the 1970s, and then an outer ring named after Indira Gandhi. All the main roads led into this square, making it a convenient point of departure for familiarizing oneself with the city.

Jerry, the courteous former aircrew man, would rather have stayed inside the Crowne Plaza. He kept on complaining about the stench, the exhaust fumes and the atrocious racket made by the three-wheel auto rickshaws that filled the streets and he bemoaned the criminal neglect of what had once been handsome buildings. The ever-practical Ronen quickly located an optician's shop and stocked up with contact lens fluid at "a quarter of the price in Israel". Of the streets forking out of the square, I chose the one that would take us to the Main Bazaar, and gave my friends their first taste of being a pedestrian in India: narrow alleys, beggars who never give up, sharp-eyed pedlars and an abundance of colourful and amazingly cheap goods – shirts for a dollar that wouldn't survive the first wash, and knapsacks for five that would fall apart on your first hike.

To me, it was all a feast for the eyes, ears and nose, and I also knew how to use the word chalo, which means "let's go", but is actually used as a polite way of telling beggars and pestering kids to scram. Ronen also enjoyed the outing, but not Jerry. I could understand him; that was how I had felt on my first day in Mumbai a decade before. Happily for him, the time soon came when we had to head for the airport to meet our guests.

There was no prior intelligence about the number of members in the Iranian delegation, but the last message that we'd received from Israel said there were four people with Persian-sounding names on the passenger list of the North Korean airline flight. We were given the names but there was nothing we could do with them at the time. We got to Terminal B, where the flight was due to land, in a rented car which I drove. Jerry and Ronen had little bags, so they'd look like passengers who had just arrived. Our plan was for the two of them to join the Iranians if they took a train or airport shuttle to town, and for me to follow them in the car. If they took a cab, we'd have no choice but to tail them in the car.

It wasn't difficult to spot the Iranians from a distance, among the handful of Koreans and others from Southeast Asia and zero Europeans who came out of customs into the arrivals hall. They headed for the taxi rank, with Jerry after them hoping to hear the destination they'd give their driver. He heard "Hyatt Regency" clearly and reported this to us over our radio network. We agreed that he'd take the next cab to the hotel, while I'd try to get Ronen there in the car before the Iranians, so he could be at the reception desk when they checked in.

It was beginning to get dark and if driving in India in the daytime is a perilous affair, at night it is a true defiance of fate. For some unknown reason, in addition to all the other ills, the Indians don't use their vehicle lights and you have to guess, in the dark, what's moving ahead of you and what's coming towards you. I drove as fast as I could without causing an accident and reached the hotel two minutes after the Iranians and one minute after Jerry. Looking like any tourist, he stood behind them at the reception desk and managed to hear one of their room numbers. Ronen went straight to the elevators at the end of the hallway and waited for them there.

By the time Udi arrived later that night, we were able to give him the numbers of their rooms and also report that they'd booked a half-day tour, starting at seven a.m. the next morning. Udi took a room on the same floor as the Iranians. "They're likely to take the interesting stuff with them on the tour. I want to get organized for a break-in when they go down for breakfast," he told us.

Our plan was for Ronen to go to breakfast at the same time as the Iranians and to report to us when they left the dining room, for Jerry to guard the staircase and the housekeeping room next to it, with Udi and I executing the break-in and copying the material on the computers, first one room and, if there was time, the others afterwards. Using his room key and Ronen's, Udi made a master key to the Iranians' rooms, based on the identical teeth of the two in his possession.

It seemed that I had only just fallen asleep when the alarm went off and woke me from an especially deep slumber. I immediately inserted my earphone: Udi was already conducting a communications check. Without having breakfast, I drove to the Hyatt and went straight to Ronen's room, which was the departure point. We didn't want to bump into the Iranians needlessly, and only when we received a signal from Udi, who was watching the corridor with a miniature periscope that he'd slipped under his door, did we set out: Ronen, in a track suit, to the dining room, Jerry to the staircase and I to the elevator.

Udi was waiting for me in the corridor, and as soon as he got the all clear from Jerry, he opened the first door. In the room all we found was a suitcase full of clothes.

"Moving on to two," Udi said into his lapel mike, and moments after getting Jerry's OK we were in the next room. Here there was a locked briefcase and it took Udi a minute to pick the lock. Inside, there were dozens of sheets of paper in Persian and Korean.

"Photograph them. I'll go to the next room," Udi told me and, after checking with Jerry and Ronen, he was gone.

I snapped the pages rapidly, one after the other, taking into account that because of my haste I might miss a line at the edges and that they may not be returned to the case in the same order as they were before. Each one took a couple of seconds and a few minutes had gone by when I heard Ronen say, "They're getting ready to leave the dining room." Immediately afterwards Udi ordered, "Wrap it up, now."

I put the documents back in the briefcase, as tidily as I could, closed it and replaced it where we'd found it, next to the suitcase. "Coming out," I reported and, once more, Jerry gave the OK. I pressed the inside button, closed the door behind me, and saw Udi leaving the room at the end of the corridor.

"They're in the elevator," I heard Ronen saying. Udi went into his room on the same floor. Jerry signalled that the coast was clear, and I went to the emergency stairs at the other end of the corridor.

A few minutes later we were all in Ronen's room. My photographs looked quite good and we transmitted them to HQ in Israel on an encrypted phone call. Udi had managed to get into both of the remaining rooms. There was nothing of interest in the first, but in the second there was a laptop and he had downloaded all the material that appeared to be relevant. He encrypted it and relayed it to Israel.

"Time for breakfast," he said and for the first time I thought that I detected him suppressing a smile of satisfaction.

We all went to Jerry's hotel restaurant. I sat next to Udi and when the other two went to refill their plates at the buffet, I asked Udi how things were going with Niki.

"Niki who?" he asked, and the subject was closed.

Back in Israel, I found Niki exhausted after the intensive intelligence collection course, but also happy. This was the first time since our reunion that we'd been apart for longer than a day or two and during that evening and night, our pent-up longings for each other kept erupting right up until we had to leave and go our separate ways.

When I reached the base, I heard good things about her from the staff who didn't care as much about "need to know" as Udi. "I have never seen such agility in performing the phone drill," Avi told me. He was referring to a move involving surveillance of a target who was staying at a hotel but would regularly use a nearby payphone. The trainee's task was to slip a microphone-transmitter into the mouthpiece of the phone. As he or she was doing this, a cop was sent in to check up on them. Niki was just finishing replacing the cover of the mouthpiece, with the mike already installed, when she was surprised by the officer.

She greeted him with a smile and said, "Oh, hi officer, thank God you're here. Perhaps you can screw this mouthpiece on better. I'm not strong enough."

The cop, who didn't know what it was all about, helped her. Only after Niki had left the scene, when the officer was rebuked over his radio, did he hurry after her, and ask her why she'd been tampering with the phone, and why she had a screwdriver in her hand. "One can tell that you haven't used a payphone in a long time," she said. "Ever since the arrival of the mobile phone, no one maintains these things, and people who need them know they have to work on them a little."

He nodded and let her go.

Niki, my own champion.

I recalled how I had strained my brain for a cover story when I'd done the same drill and, in the end, had come up with a really pathetic pretext. I wondered if Udi also made such comparisons between me and her.

2.

Together and Apart

OUR TEAM'S NEXT missions were no less successful than the New Delhi caper. Relatively quiet months in Israel, as far as terror attacks were concerned, enabled Mossad intelligence to focus us more and more on activities connected to Iran and Syria's non-conventional arms acquisition, and their supply of weaponry to the terrorist organizations. The material from New Delhi yielded further operations that kept many other squads busy, and we also were assigned a small slice, which involved photographing the documents of a high-level North Korean official on a stopover in Beijing.

I knew Beijing from my trip there after my first year at art school but in the interim the city had changed astonishingly. A wide superhighway, the likes of which I could not recall, led from the airport to the city centre, and as we drew nearer I saw the stumps of a dense multitude of skyscrapers that hadn't been there ten years before. The city's multiple ring roads were wider than I remembered and it seemed to me that entire neighbourhoods of the traditional hutong alleys and small homes had been razed to make room for the highways and high-rises.

The break-in and photographing operation was fairly straightforward and went smoothly. This time, too, we got our hands on a laptop, the insides of which Udi was only too happy to replicate, giving plenty of fruitful work to the personnel of the department whose job was tracking non-conventional armaments.

The abundance of information that we'd brought in from Beijing, New Delhi and Warsaw also provided new missions for most of the operational squads. As for Udi's squad, we were assigned jobs in the Muslim republics of the former Soviet Union, intercepting consignments of missiles on their way to Iran. This was the route chosen by the Russians to avoid the risk of direct flights or marine shipments which could be vetted by the Western powers enforcing sanctions against Iran. Silent sabotage operations, the injection of a chemical agent into the launch mechanisms, had been decided upon as our modus operandi. No one would know or see anything until the order was given for firing the missiles when nothing would happen. In each case, we located the convoys, followed them to a spot where they parked for the night, and then stole into one truck after another and dealt with each missile, by removing the cap of its "brain", inserting the liquid and reassembling it. We took turns, Jerry and I keeping watch while Udi and Ronen were doing the job on the missiles, then switching roles.

These were relatively lengthy missions, taking a few nights each to neutralize all the missiles in each convoy, and we could only work between patrols of convoy guards. In the daytime, we drove some distance away from the convoys using a transponder that we'd fixed onto one of the trucks. At night we caught up with them and worked. We were exhausted after the first round on one of the convoys, more so after the second, and the third turned out to be the last.

On our last mission we began in Kazakhstan, continued in Uzbekistan and wound up in Ashgabat, Turkmenistan, close to the Iranian border. After completing the work, and as we were walking away from the convoy towards our vehicle, we were surprised by a Russian officer in a military jeep, who was apparently checking the parked trucks or the guards. We were a few hundred yards away from the convoy but also a similar distance from our car, and we didn't have any logical pretext for being there. The Russian could see this and he aggressively demanded that we identify ourselves. He got out of his jeep and menacingly placed his hand on the butt of his pistol.

What authority a Russian officer had in the independent republic of Turkmenistan wasn't clear, but, apparently, the Russian military still enjoyed quite a lot of freedom of action here and in the other ex-Soviet republics that allowed the convoys to pass through their territory. Udi never bothered to ask for his credentials. The punch he delivered to the throat of the Russian, who was every bit as burly as Udi himself, was so fast and so professional that the man immediately crumpled to the ground. He made gurgling choking sounds but with what was left of his consciousness he went for his handgun. Udi was quicker, and bending over, he reached the gun first, drew it out of the holster, gripped it by the barrel and smashed the butt against the officer's temple. There was a crackling sound of broken bone, and a black pool of blood spread on the ground.

Udi wiped the pistol, replaced it in the holster and mounted the driver's seat of the jeep. "Get in," he said, and drove us to our car.

"He's going to die out there," I said.

"You have my permission to go back and administer mouth to mouth resuscitation," Udi replied gruffly, "or, perhaps you want us to carry him with us to the nearest hospital?"

We got into our car and Udi sped away in silence, until we crossed the border into Azerbaijan. Only there did he report to HQ and request that a flight be laid on for us from Tashkent the next night. This meant another long day of speeding along the potholed roads. Some of the route covered part of the ancient Silk Road. I would have been happy to visit Bokhara or Samarkand, but knew that would have to wait for another opportunity. At least I could enjoy the scenery.

I wasn't supposed to tell Niki about the mission, and I didn't go into the details, but she saw how moody I was and I decided to tell her about the killing of the Russian officer. An unnecessary killing, to my mind. "I've already seen Udi in such situations. He turns into a machine. It's frightening," I said, and Niki patted my hand. When she tried to make the point that if the Russian had remained alive he would have given a description of us and we were likely to have been caught, I was angry. I knew she was right. But like in Warsaw, it was difficult for me to accept killing for purely tactical reasons, whatever they may be. It bothered me that she was defending it.

"It's not that he's a machine," Niki insisted. "I'm spending quite a lot of time with him, and I can read people. There's some kind of a secret there." Her words didn't console me, and her closeness to Udi didn't improve my mood.

In August, Hamas dealt Israel a painful blow: a double-suicide attack on two buses in Beersheba that left sixteen people dead. This time, the Mossad decided to send us to Khartoum to hit the Hamas office there which was still occupied with organizing arms smuggling from Iran into the Gaza Strip, through Egypt. When I complained that this was an attack "under the lamppost" at a second or third echelon target of the organization, Udi replied that we were not the only squad going on the offensive, and that this wasn't merely an act of retaliation but the prioritization of a pigeonholed operation that had only now been approved by the prime minister.

The mission had another interesting element: after we had got organized and rented a car, Udi would report to HQ and then we'd head for a dry riverbed near the seashore and rendezvous with a unit of naval commandos who would give us the explosive devices we were to use.

The night-time navigation job, from the moment we left the main road, was given to me. I spent many hours with Moshik, the intelligence officer, going over the route to the meeting place. Because I couldn't be carrying a detailed map when I entered Sudan, and the large scale maps necessary for navigation weren't available, I studied the route on aerial photographs that showed all the details but were not up to date, and which I could not, of course, take with me. I used a stereoscope and the 3-D pictures jumped out at me and engraved themselves on my memory – but in black and white. In any case, that's what it would look like at night . . .

This was my first mission in a Muslim country that, unlike Jordan, was openly hostile, and I confessed to myself that I derived a great deal of encouragement from the presence of Udi, Ronen and Jerry. From the window of the plane, a vast, flat, brown city spread out in all directions, with the confluence of the White and Blue Niles at its centre, a little to the north-west of the airport. I was reminded of Moshik's briefings, when he told me that the river divided the city into three: Khartoum itself, Omdurman beyond the White Nile, and North Khartoum across the Blue Nile. Some eight million people lived in the metropolitan area, with their mud dwellings stretching from horizon to horizon, and reddish desert mountains in the background. I didn't remember why one river was called white and the other blue, but both were brownish-green, with narrow strips of greenery along their banks.

Entry procedures weren't too complicated, with most of the talking done by Jerry, the head of our "safari group" and he did so with a relaxed charm. As soon as we left the obsolescent terminal, a cab took us to the Kanon Hotel, which Jerry had recommended, a little to the south-east of the airport. "Last time I was at the Hilton and I hated it," said Jerry. "It looks fine from a distance, a pink ten-storey building, but inside everything was falling apart. I moved here, and it was great."

The Kanon was a modern building in modern surroundings, something that, based on Moshik's briefing, I didn't think I'd see in Khartoum.

During the day, we surveyed the area around our target, and Udi decided on the way we would do the job. We would break into the office at night, place the explosive device in an inside room, and when the door to that room was opened, the blast would kill everyone in the offices. And we'd leave another bomb, with a time-fuse, for the first responders. When I objected, Udi replied in biblical terms: "'Woe to the wicked man and woe to his neighbour – especially if the neighbour accommodates and feeds him."

Udi didn't want to lose time, and he reported to HQ that from our point of view we could go ahead with the rendezvous with the navy the next night. We set out at noon, heading for the Red Sea coast, more than 300 kilometres to the east. The highway itself was in bad shape and at nightfall we had to go off the road for several dozen miles to the meeting place. I dozed most of the way in the air-conditioned Range Rover Jerry had provided for his safari, waking up only for my night-time navigation duty.

Udi established contact with the naval unit, received confirmation that they had left their mother ship and had begun sailing towards the beach, and I took over the steering wheel. I ascertained that we were at the right point for leaving the highway. The contours of the terrain were well fixed in my mind and fitted in with the dirt road we were now travelling on. Jerry told me what to say if we ran into a military patrol. The paucity of wild game in this area made our "safari" cover story more than dubious, but at most they would think we were rather silly. Jerry had all the necessary official papers.

It took us about two hours to reach our destination. Udi made sure that the surrounding sand was firm enough for our vehicle before I left the dirt road and stopped. We didn't want to be seen by anyone who happened to drive past on the dirt road, or by some Bedouin, but neither did we have any intention of sinking into the sand dunes. I switched off the lights and the engine. I walked a few hundred yards eastwards, Ronen went northwards and Jerry southwards, to make sure there was no one in the vicinity.

When I had gone far enough and my eyesight had adjusted to the dark I knelt and scanned the area around me. There was no one to be seen, but I could smell the sea, and it filled me with both gladness and longing. For a moment I thought I could also hear the roar of the waves. It was a peculiar feeling, to be alone in the desert, with the star-filled dome of the sky above me, a light breeze lapping at my face, and intermittent calls of nocturnal animals. I thought, in that silence, that this was a situation that no ordinary person could ever experience, and I felt blessed that I was in this place. Only Niki was missing, beside me, but soon . . .

We came back to the vehicle and started taking kit out as if we were preparing a camp site for the night. Udi contacted the navy and gave them our precise coordinates. They reported that they'd made a quiet landing and had begun their hike in our direction.

We had a relaxed but alert wait of about half an hour, with a warm desert wind caressing us, myriad stars lighting the sky, and the noises of the desert by night, made by small reptiles, insects and nocturnal birds all around us. The navy men walked for about two kilometres along the dry river bed from the beach up to where we were waiting. Just before they made contact, their commander reported to Udi by radio that they could see us with their night vision equipment, and he signalled with a quick flash of a torch.

Soundlessly their shapes emerged out of the dark, remaining part of it. Most of them knelt down a few dozen yards away from us and only three approached – the commander and two commandoes carrying the two explosive devices. Udi, Jerry and I walked towards them, with Ronen staying at the wheel of the Range Rover, in case of a hitch. Udi and the commander shook hands, Jerry and I took the bombs, and within moments they were gone, vanishing into the wadi as if they'd never been there.

"Great guys," I said.

"That's what they're saying about us now," said Udi nonchalantly, and he told us where to put the devices. We returned the rest of the stuff to the vehicle and, in keeping with procedures, we waited half an hour, until the commander of the navy unit radioed that they were back on the water. Then we set out on the long drive back.

I was a bit anxious about travelling with the explosives, not because I was afraid they'd go off, something I knew wouldn't happen, but because of the roadblocks deployed at the entrances to the city at night. The Mossad bomb-makers had thought of this and disguised the devices as

And so it came to pass, shortly before Christmas 2005, that we landed in a freezing Toronto and were greeted with enormous happiness by Niki's parents, who were unaware as to what they owed this joyful reunion.

With generous assistance from the Mossad, we rented a more spacious apartment, in the building next to the one where Niki had lived before. We loved the Old Town area and the outskirts of the centre, and had lovely memories from them and from the many cafés, pubs and restaurants that we knew and liked. I painted furiously, and distributed the pictures to various galleries. Niki told her mother that she wanted to work for another company for a while, so that she wouldn't break the routine of the small family company again and again. Her mother was surprised, and perhaps a little hurt, but we didn't want, and couldn't allow, Niki's cover story to lead to her parents' home. She registered a literary agency in her own name and printed business cards.

We'd been told to build a "marriage story", and we did so with pleasure and found it quite exciting. We weren't supposed to get married, and we didn't; nobody would take the risk of registering Ron Friedlich for marriage in Toronto before all the necessary procedures had been checked out.

Hand in hand, we went to City Hall, feeling like a bride and groom on their wedding day. In the circular entrance space, we went to the reception area to the left, and asked for the marriage application forms. A quick look at the form revealed that there were a few details that we'd have somehow to get hold of, such as the places of birth of the groom's parents and his mother's maiden name. These were items that I hadn't discovered in my break-in at the Friedlichs' and there was no way that I'd go there again. These things must be accessible in some data base, I thought. I was surprised to see that one of the spaces on the form was for religious affiliation. Niki was also surprised and said that in her entire life she'd never been in a situation where she'd been required to give that information.

We wanted to see the place where we would have tied the knot, where we would say we had done it if we were ever asked. A sign pointed us to the "Wedding Chamber, East Tower, 3rd floor, Elevators 1, 3, 4 East." From the elevator, a short corridor led us to a glass door with a black sign on it, giving the registrar of marriages' office hours. We pressed an intercom and were buzzed in. We found ourselves in a little hall, the description "chamber" was quite apt because it was no larger than the living room at Niki's parents' house. To the right of the entrance stood a simple table, and on it there was a vase of artificial flowers. Facing the table were three rows of chairs, about five in each row. Apart from oil paintings of flowers and guitars on the walls, two pot plants at the corners of the grey carpet that covered the floor, and curtains, there were no ornaments or decorations in the room, but nevertheless, we felt quite festive.

"Say hello to my parents," I gestured at the first two chairs on the left in the front row. "And you kiss my mother and father," Niki gestured at the chairs on the right, "and my sister Mila," pointing at the chair in the middle. I turned to the second row, "OK, if so, then thank you Tzippi and Aliza, for coming all the way here and it's a pity you left your husbands and the kids at home."

But then I was overwhelmed by a wave of sorrow. If we did get married here, my parents and my sisters wouldn't come. Niki sensed my sorrow straightaway, understood what had caused it, and whispered, "We'll have a big wedding in Tel Aviv . . ."

A secretary came down from the floor above us and in a friendly manner explained the procedure. I was surprised that there wasn't a place for refreshments or a little party, and she said that what happened there was a purely legal matter and everyone celebrated afterwards in their own way.

The Mossad had given us one month. Niki didn't need all this time but to establish cover as a couple we both needed it. We made sure to appear together at various events, to go to shows together and keep the tickets, walked around as much as the winter permitted, and took dozens of photographs of ourselves. It was the perfect honeymoon. It wasn't easy to imagine that as soon as it was over we'd be thrown into a series of complicated and dangerous operations. On the night before we flew back, Niki asked me, "Do you think that when all this ends, in two or three years' time, I don't know how long, we'll be able to go back to being what we really were meant to be? A painter and a literary agent?"

✧✧✧

There was another sad parting from her parents, and another silent ride to the airport, and flight to Israel. This time, Udi himself came to meet us at the arrivals gate and lead us through a side door. On the way to the base, he gave us a brief survey: After 232 deaths in terror attacks in 2002, the year I enlisted, and 140 in 2003, the number had gone down in 2004 to 55. The Intifada by the Palestinians seemed to be on the wane and we would be able to devote ourselves to dealing with the Iranian nuclear weapons programme, which was looming larger all the time. This was now the number one task of the Mossad in general, and of our squad in particular.

I felt a certain regret, almost unnoticeable even to myself, at having to give up waging the war on terrorism, without having satisfied my dormant urge for vengeance. However, the new peril facing Israel was clear to me, and I was ready to make the switch in my mind to the Iranian menace, which was now more concrete than the various terrorism threats.

I could see from Niki's face that she was still upset by the separation from her parents who repeatedly phoned us. Contrary to Udi's optimistic predictions, there was a terrorist attack on the Stage Club on Tel Aviv's promenade, and five people were killed. Emily and Yoshima, as well as Mila, had heard so much from Niki about that wonderful esplanade which was close to where we lived and where we spent a lot of time strolling, jogging and dining out. They were totally hysterical and insisted that she come home immediately. Nothing she said could have calmed them, and I had nothing to say. We tried to build a new routine, with the knowledge that terror was still alive and killing.

In one of the briefings with Moshik, I also learned that my own personal circle, or spiral, was still alive: the man who had headed the apparatus that ended up in the murder of Dolly, and that included Rumana, Sharitakh and Raddad, was a functionary by the name of Bassam al-Sultan, and he had left Hamas when it became primarily political, to join the ranks of the more militant Islamic Jihad. He had crossed into Jordan and from there to Syria, where he was building, from a distance, a military force in the West Bank and the Gaza Strip as an alternative to Hamas. "After Sheqaqi, Head of Islamic Jihad, was sent to join the virgins in Paradise, al-Sultan is the only one of the Jihad gang in Damascus who really understands how to recruit and train fighters, how to plan attacks, and how to transport weapons. And when Ramadan Shallah, Sheqaqi's successor, decides it's time for an attack, he's the one who plans it and issues the orders," Moshik told us. "He's someone we'd like to get our hands on sometime." He left me with musings that I knew I should not even fantasize about. But they cropped up on their own. If I was ever to be assigned to a mission in Damascus, I'd have my own private one to carry out while I was there.

Our neighbours in the building on Rehov Ruppin probably thought we were an ordinary couple. We left our apartment before eight a.m., sometimes in an embrace and still feeling the afterglow of our early morning sex, went down to the underground garage, where, on clear days we mounted our motorbike and on rainy days got into our car. We headed for our base near the city. In the late evening we came home together, and never went out. On dry nights, we'd take our coffee and sit on the balcony and gaze at the sea, or what we could see of it between the apartment buildings facing us. On wet nights, we sat in our little living room. Niki spoke to her family and her friends on Skype and answered the emails that had come in to her literary agency from young writers who wanted to submit manuscripts. I watched TV, painted – the pictures I didn't like I signed RF and shipped them to the galleries in Toronto – and we'd go to bed.

The need to keep Niki's enlistment in our service a secret, and the desire to avoid her having to tell a cover story to my friends, led me almost completely to cut off my relations with the limited social circles to which I'd been connected. For the same reasons, we didn't visit my family very often, and they also hardly ever came down from Haifa to see us. The members of Udi's squad became the only people we saw regularly, apart from each other. I was worried about how this would affect Niki. I had known new immigrants who settled in kibbutzim when they arrived here, and when the kibbutz dream failed them for whatever reason, the whole Israeli dream was also lost for them. Niki, however, from the very beginning never had an Israeli dream, she just had me.

❖❖❖

I never managed to explain to myself the mixture of serenity and arousal that spending time together with her during the day caused me. When we were prepped for the same mission, we were briefed together. Because each of us also had separate operations to perform, some briefings were separate too. But we were together in the dining room and the gym at the base, and when we had free time there, we went about our cover activities – Niki reading manuscripts and I painting. The distinction between professional and private life was completely blurred, and it all seemed unreal.

There were days when the other guys were on operations, and Niki and I were the only participants in the weekly hand-to-hand combat practice, and we had to fight each other. I knew that at home we would have ended up in bed, but when the instructor called an end to our fight, all we could do was bow to each other and move over to the edge of the mat. On some occasions the sexual tension was so unusually heightened that we didn't wait until we got home and instead we released it in our room at the base. Once when there were too many people at the facility, we made love in the car, at the far end of the car park.

It was worse when Niki was the opponent of another member of the squad. I already felt very close to Jerry and Ronen, but two new operatives had joined us, Dave and Philip, young and charming flirty types, very irritating. Neither did I like it when she was closeted in a briefing with an instructor or in a one-to-one meeting with Udi. I often had the notion that in another incarnation Niki could have been the partner of any one of them. Were it not for me, Niki's selection mechanism, which had apparently been programmed to home in on strong foreign types, would have zeroed in on someone else.

"How can you say such a thing," Niki remonstrated when I told her about this one evening. "You of all people, who claim that since meeting me in Tokyo you couldn't fall in love with anyone else? And I know that since that meeting, I also haven't been able to find anyone else! You really are infuriating!"

She's right, I thought, and that is indeed the way it is with us. Perhaps every pair of lovers believes they are unique but I know too many people who simply chose someone suitable from those who were available. I felt that ultimately I was a very lucky guy.

3.

A Couple in Stockholm

AT LAST WE were assigned our first mission together. A Swedish electronics manufacturer was clandestinely selling the Iranians components for its nuclear programme. Our team had to furnish the proof. In his briefing Moshik informed us solemnly that it was impossible to get into the tightly secured premises of the company, Gimbers, without being discovered. The lab area was out of bounds to everyone who didn't work there and over the last two years all efforts to get an agent inside or to recruit one of the workers had failed. This dovetailed with the suspicions that Gimbers was supplying Iran with computers for their uranium enrichment centrifuges, and perhaps even the centrifuges as well. However, an employee of the security firm that had fitted the Gimbers plant with its alarms and closed circuit TV had been recruited, and the information he'd provided wasn't particularly encouraging: the alarm system was highly advanced, with complete coverage of every last corner, and it worked in tandem with the CCTV, which transmitted a new image every five seconds. Anyone breaking in would both trigger the alarm and be photographed. "There is no other facility today that has a more efficient security system," said Moshik. The company knew it was breaking the international embargo, and didn't want to get caught.

With the help of this agent and the information he supplied, our tech branch had developed a jammer that would silence the alarm in any room it was taken into. Another device would delay, but not prevent, the transmission of CCTV images to the control centre. When it was taken out of range, the delayed images would be sent in a single burst.

"Of course we asked if the control centre personnel would notice that there was a delay but we didn't get an unequivocal reply," said Moshik. "It depends on the alertness and the intelligence of the operators. Every five seconds, when a new picture is relayed, there's a split-second flicker to which the brain generally grows accustomed and doesn't notice. But it's like when there's suddenly an unusual silence and it alerts you, so the lack of the flicker may alert an operator."

Udi made it clear that, "If they are very alert, they'll see there's a delay in transmission from the cameras next to the outer wall, outside the office building and inside the specific room where the break-in is to be carried out. The question is, will they realize that it's a break-in or think it's a technical glitch. That's something we won't know until they respond. We do know that they don't have a large force there but even if we can get in and out they'll still have images of us."

"OK, so this is why the ski-mask was invented," I said.

"That won't help with these systems," said Moshik. "We've obtained some of the data from the cameras, and our techies ran some tests with them. They have the same resolution as airport cameras, and they can undress you completely. Even if you wear wigs and sunglasses, moustaches and beards, their electronic identification technology will come up with pictures of you underneath all the accessories."

"You have to take into account that they'll reach you," said Avi, "and the answer to that situation must be found in your cover story."

Udi summed up the chances and the risks: "With the gadgets we have, the chances that we'll get the job done, fully or partially, are good. The chances that we'll manage to get clear of the place without being caught are reasonable. But the chance that we won't leave tracks behind is very low, and there's a risk that our faces will be exposed. I've taken this assessment to our Division chief, and he took it higher up, to the director, and we have a tentative approval. As the Mossad's director put it, exposing Gimbers's link with the Iranians and ending the transfer of the centrifuge components is at the moment more vital than preventing an operative or two getting burned. But because of this risk, we'll use the smallest possible crew."

"Are you saying that we may find the mission has succeeded, but we'll be burned? Out of the game?" I objected.

"The alternative is not to execute, and that's a non-starter with the director, as you know," Udi replied. "Certainly not when it comes to anything connected with the Iranian nukes."

We located a security installation with a similar layout to the Gimbers plant and made a lot of practice runs, climbing the wall and breaking into the office building and the inside rooms. Based on more info from the agent, the Mossad's stations in northern Europe acquired a number of the same type of locks as those used at Gimbers and the relevant tech team devised ways of opening them. We spent hours practising in both the light and the dark, until we could complete the job in seconds.

We then began practising the operational model, with the entire squad participating. Ronen and I were the break-in detail, Udi and Jerry the lookouts inside the facility, Niki was at the wheel of the getaway car, Dave was the lookout outside the wall, and Philip was driving the interference car that would block attempts to follow us. As we practised, it emerged that the job could and should be done with fewer operatives in order to reduce the number in danger of being burned. First to be dropped was Jerry – Udi would have to manage on his own if a security patrol turned up. Then came Dave and Philip. Ronen would drive the second car, because of his greater experience, and I would do the break-in by myself. If I were surprised, Udi would come to my assistance.

"As we know the break-in is almost certainly going to be discovered," I remarked, "wouldn't it make sense to simply take the file with us instead of wasting time photographing the contents? Especially seeing that I'll be doing it on my own?"

Udi said that he'd asked this question, and the reply he had received was that if there was any chance at all that the break-in not be discovered, that would be best. But even if it was, we didn't want the Gimbers people to know which of the thousands of files had been handled; if they did, they would be able to conceal the evidence and ship the goods to the Iranians before we could get the local police to raid them.

I didn't ask why I was chosen to be the operative most likely to be burned, but I was told anyway: from the point of view of cover, Niki and I were a very strong duo. I was the point man of the operation and the person most likely to be photographed because if I were to be identified and questioned, with Niki's help, I would have the best chance of getting out of trouble. This sounded reasonable to me.

Ronen was left without a role in the break-in, unless something went wrong, like police cars showing up at the site or chasing us. His job would be to enable us to escape. He would also be the one who would sneak Niki and me out of the hotel parking basement on the way to the target, and back again afterwards, and then get Udi out of Sweden.

A check of the ways of leaving Stockholm showed that it would be better for us not to depart the morning after the op because it was possible that photographs of Udi and me would reach airport security by then, and in any event the names of departing passengers would be registered as suspects in the break-in. Leaving by ferryboat too soon would also involve border formalities, with the same risks. Travelling to Norway across Sweden involved a 300-mile trip, and the local authorities were unlikely to suspect that anyone would escape that way. In the end it was decided that Udi and Ronen would take the overland route out to Oslo, and Niki and I would stay in Sweden for a day and go to the meetings that had been set up for us with gallery owners and publishers as part of our cover stories.

In discussions with Avi, it was decided that our cover stories would be stronger if Niki and I didn't turn up in Stockholm as a couple, but rather arrive at the hotel as strangers and stage a pick-up scene, to be witnessed by hotel staffers. This would make the conclusion by investigators that we'd come there as a team, intending to provide each other with cover, less apparent. Avi told us to forget all the "couple-cover" work we'd done in Toronto. My address would be the Beach apartment and Niki's the Old Town one. We practised a chance meeting of two Torontonians in a hotel lounge, and set out on our mission.

Thus, the Canadian artist Ron Friedlich found himself, towards the end of a frosty, gloomy winter, going from one Scandinavian gallery to another, with a portfolio of his work under his arm. For two days, I was in enchanting Copenhagen, where the cobbled streets behind the City Hall are lined with galleries: I could have sold all of my paintings there. In Oslo, where I spent the next two days, my success was partial at best, and I had to make do with the business cards of the snobbish curators. Then I travelled to even-colder Stockholm and took up residence in the Best Western Kung Carl hotel. The Best Western chain has four hotels in the city and I thought of choosing the Terminus, situated next to the railway station, something that might be useful for a getaway, but in the end picked the Kung Carl, which is right in the city centre. As I was to meet Niki in Stockholm, I thought we would be able to enjoy a little more of what Stockholm had to offer if we stayed there. It made sense for a Canadian artist to take a North American hotel that wasn't too expensive

– the Kung Carl had a four-star rating. It had a few other advantages, too. Despite its tall, pyramid-like structure, it was fairly intimate, with a small lobby and bar lounge, where Niki and I would be able to meet up, as planned.

Not a bad job, this, getting to visit a different country every few weeks I thought, as the train from Oslo arrived in Stockholm. Time and again I found myself in awe at the beauty of Europe's capital cities, and Stockholm was no less beautiful than any other imperial capital, with its splendid palaces and homes situated on the islands in the strait between Lake Mälaren and the Baltic Sea, where the city stands.

I waited for Niki to arrive before touring the city and in the meantime called several galleries from the hotel. Some of them wouldn't even meet me; they didn't operate in such a disorganized fashion and weren't ready even to consider accepting an unknown artist's work. But there were some who agreed to take a look, and at the set time, the owner, or the curator, or the artistic adviser was waiting for me to show my portfolio. Their reactions were not at all bad, and within two days four galleries, all of them in Drottninggatan, "Queen's Street", had agreed to buy my works. Drottninggatan is a busy pedestrianised shopping street in the heart of Norrmalm, in the northern part of the city, among buildings which were quite old, stone structures and the others which were more modern but all of which were of a reasonable height, five or six storeys. There was something ascetic about this city which had maintained its traditions and never chased after American-style progress.

I had only three RF pictures left when Niki came to the hotel. She'd spent four days in Berlin, where she found a brim-full literary scene, and another day of meetings in Finland, where she'd signed a contract with a well-thought-of young poet. In Stockholm, she'd set up four meetings in the first two days, after which our operation was scheduled to take place, and another one for the next day.

I was sitting in the hotel lounge, on a leather two-seater, its back to the wall, facing the bar. There were two leather armchairs next to the coffee table in front of me. The other seating groups in the lounge were occupied, and the set-up suited me. I had sat in the bar on the two previous evenings as well, and struck up a friendship with the young Turkish barman. This evening, I'd ordered a Campari and cola, half and half, in a tall glass. The brown of the cola and the red of the Campari gave the drink the colour of blood. After taking a healthy sip, I began looking at the catalogues of several galleries that I'd brought with me.

I smelled Niki's perfume before I saw her and looked up: her dyed-blond hair had startled me for a moment. She was wearing a dark dress with low-heeled shoes and her shoulders were covered by a shawl. Clearly she had come from her room and not from outside. She went straight up to the bar and asked for a Bacardi and soda. With the drink in her hand, she glanced around the lounge. All the groups of seats were occupied and the barman surveyed the space, trying to help her. When his eye caught mine, I nodded, indicating that it was OK for her to sit with me.

"Maybe near this gentleman here," he said, and gestured towards me. With feigned embarrassment, Niki asked me if that was all right and I said of course it was.

She sat on one of the leather armchairs, put down her glass, took a manuscript out of her bag, and began reading.

We'd been apart for a week, establishing our individual cover stories. Her eyes were immersed in the manuscript, the barman was dealing with some other people, and I could now study the features of my sweetheart without any distractions. They had something unfamiliar about them. The week's separation had created a slight distance between us that enabled me to observe her with a certain degree of detachment. She was so gorgeous. My gaze caressed the now fair hair, which intensified her glow; her ivory forehead, her fine eyebrows, and her eyes which, as she was looking downwards at the manuscript, seemed to be half-closed from where I was sitting. Her small, chiselled nose, her child-like lips slightly open, with the tip of her pen between them. Her high cheekbones and taut cheeks, which I knew would make the sound of a drum when I tapped them with my fingers. Her pointed chin. Her long and slender throat, with the deep hollow at the bottom, and on either side of the hollow, the two collarbones that seemed separate from her body, running on under the shoulder straps of her dress.

I can reconstruct every second of the tortuous process of our getting to know one another and becoming lovers, a process which made us one body and one soul, and yet then, in that hotel bar, with Niki playing the stranger, I felt I could start wanting her from the beginning again.

I finished my drink, and went up to the bar for another. I quietly asked the barman if he knew who she was, and he said he didn't. I asked for a dish of almonds for myself, and another for her, and when I placed it on the table in front of her and she raised her lovely eyes to look at me I asked her, aware of the inquisitive gaze of the barman, where she was from.

"Canada," she replied and I burst out laughing.

"Canada! So am I," and against the rules of correct etiquette I offered her my hand, and introduced myself, "Ron Friedlich."

Niki gave a little smile, brushed her hand against mine, and went back to her manuscript.

I exchanged a brief glance with the barman, a shared masculine objection to female reticence, and went back to my catalogues.

After a while, I asked the barman for a pen and paper, and drew her. I got up and left, leaving the drawing and my room number with the barman. "Give it to her when she leaves," I requested, and politely took my leave.

It was a little hell, trying to sleep alone a few doors away from each other, and after she called to thank me for the drawing, we couldn't restrain ourselves and she came to my room, violating the explicit instructions of the operational orders. The stolen sex was sweeter than ever, making up for the week of celibacy and of missing each other, but before daybreak, a moment before Niki slipped away to her room, she said with a grave expression, "I don't want this kind of life of lies and stolen love. I want us to be together, out in the open. You painting and selling your work, and me meeting young writers, editing and publishing their work in Canada. When will it be like that? When?"

And with a tear appearing in the corner of her eye, she vanished into the corridor.

I knew that her complaint was justified. Totally. I felt a wholeness when I painted and nothing else – except when I was making love with Niki – allowed me to immerse myself deeply into it, with my entire being, to ignore the world around, to be at one with my creations. I felt like the composer, the player and the conductor of a piece of music, all three together at the same time. When I looked at the completed work, I sometimes felt euphoric, and when my paintings were exhibited or sold I felt enormous happiness. It was absolutely clear to me that my artistic talent emanated from deep inside me. With utter clarity I saw how the fulfilment of my artistic talent gave me a sense of self-realization, satisfaction, and even serenity. And I knew that like any other strong inner urge, if it did not find release, I would feel unfulfilled and frustrated. I had to rate my inner abilities by their intensity, and to realize them accordingly, and with me, this meant that painting – and of course my love for Niki – had to have higher priority than the break-in to Gimbers the following night, and everything connected to that. And once again I was compelled to conclude that my order of priorities was all screwed up.

For a moment, the slight insult that I'd felt at being chosen to be "burned" was replaced by an odd hope: if I was in fact burned, I would at last be able to put my priorities in order. To be what I was meant to be by virtue of my inner, natural abilities.

I would try, at least, to eke out a few more hours of togetherness with my Niki and in the hotel dining room I initiated an exchange, "Didn't we meet in the bar last night?" and suggested we tour the city together. Surprised, she accepted.

We walked along the bridges that led to the parliament building, which was located on a small island on the strait that bisects the city. From there, we continued through the old city, passing the baroque royal palace and the opera house and then, in this compact city it wasn't far to the garden neighbourhoods, the southernmost of which are located on a cliff overlooking the archipelago that stretches out towards Finland.

In the late afternoon we met up with Udi, Ronen, Avi and Moshik in a restaurant. Moshik gave us the latest intelligence. Now it was definite that I had to get to Room 205 on the second floor of the Gimbers office building where the bookkeeping files were kept, and to photograph a file labelled "Checkmate." Avi had brought the jamming devices with him. The plan called for Niki to activate one of them from the car which would disrupt the cameras covering the wall and the alarm beam that passed along the top of it, while Udi and I climbed over the wall into the plant's grounds. Udi would remain in the yard to deal with any guards who turned up and would operate the second device to neutralize the cameras outside the building. I would use the third when I was inside to jam the cameras in the corridor and Room 205 and the alarms.

In the Mercedes with dark tinted windows that Moshik had rented, we drove around the plant and tied up the loose ends: where we would stop and dismount, where Niki would park and wait for us, where Ronen would wait in the second car. Back in town, Moshik handed to Udi the car that Niki would be driving. Avi had rented a Toyota Land Cruiser SUV for Ronen, big enough for him to be able to block, by any means necessary, vehicles that tried to interfere with or chase after us. The two of them drove off and Niki and I headed back to the Best Western Kung Carl to finish off establishing our cover story. Ronen checked into the same hotel.

When I entered the lounge, the barman told me that Niki was really wowed by the drawing and had said she'd call me. "She called," I confirmed, adding that we'd arranged to meet in the lounge that evening.

This time we made sure that snatches of our conversation would be heard by the bartender.

"St. George College? Really?"

"The Varsity Blues football team? You don't say!"

In a short while we were deep in animated conversation. Then we said goodnight to the barman, and I left him a very generous tip. We went up to Niki's room, where the Swedish investigators were meant to find me next morning, if things went wrong. We didn't pass up on a brief sexual interlude before ordering a late supper from room service. When it came, I opened the door clad in only a bathrobe and Niki made sure the waiter heard her saying something to me.

An hour later, we took the elevator down to the parking level where Ronen met us and took us – heads down to avoid being seen – in his SUV to the rendezvous with Udi. We moved to the Mercedes, and Ronen drove to his waiting place, a few hundred yards away from the plant where he would be listening in on our wavelength ready to deal with any number of contingencies, when and if they occurred.

Niki took the Mercedes's driver's seat, with the jamming device in her hand. Udi and I, wearing work overalls with all the implements we might need in the pockets, sat next to the doors, ready to jump out, Udi in front and I in the backseat. Fortunately, winter was almost over and we could make do with relatively light clothing. We donned specifically designed heavy plastic masks which would make the job of identifying us a little more difficult. Traffic on the road to Gimbers was sparse, and the moment came when we could stop close to the wall.

"Go! Go!" Niki shouted excitedly when she got the signal from the device indicating that the cameras and alarm were neutralized. I patted her left shoulder, the only sign of affection I allowed myself at this juncture, and just before we leaped out I saw Udi patting her on her right shoulder, and I couldn't help feeling a pang of jealousy. But he was the commander and that was his way of encouraging his young warrior.

Stopping and leaving the car took no more than three seconds, which we had established during the dry runs in Israel, and in another three seconds we were glued to the wall. Niki kept the jammer running, Udi made a "thieves' ladder" for me with his hands, heaving me onto his shoulders, so I could use clippers to snip the razor wire atop the wall and push it aside with the asbestos gloves I had donned. I switched my jammer on and pointed it at the building, shifted myself around and gave my hand to Udi, straining my muscles to their limit to lift his not-inconsiderable weight, and within a minute we were both on the plant's grounds. I heard Niki doing a U-turn. She had to keep her jammer on in order to prevent the transmission of the pictures of our break-in that had been stored in the camera.

Now it was Udi's turn to jam the cameras and the alarm on the outside and I hurried to the building. Getting through the door was easy with all the pre-adjusted gear I had in the pockets of my jumpsuit and all the practice runs I'd done. As soon as I was inside I activated my jammer, got the confirmation signal and in a few seconds I was up the stairs and at the door to room 205. Here too the lock gave way quickly. I silently blessed the techies' skills, neutralized the alarm and the camera, and found the filing cabinet.

Within a couple of minutes that seemed like eternity I located the Checkmate file. It was thicker than I thought it would be, and I realized that photographing the contents would take longer than we'd planned for. I regretted that Ronen wasn't with me because we could have divided the work. But I reported to Udi and began snapping the documents, one at a time. I hadn't even completed half the task when I heard Udi's voice.

"Patrol in the building. Get down where you are."

I marked my place, closed the file and returned it to the drawer. Then I hid in the space behind the filing cabinet that I had noted previously was out of the camera's view and pretty much hidden from the entrance to the room. Like Niki, I kept the jammer working, so that the footage that had backed up wouldn't be transmitted. I could now hear the guards' footsteps and voices. It took no time at all for them to reach room 205 and it seemed to me that they had headed straight for it. They opened the door, switched the light on and looked around. One of them went to the camera, checked it and tapped it a few times. The two exchanged some words in Swedish then left.

I waited until their voices and footsteps faded before coming out of my hiding place and resuming the job. I reported to Udi, but he didn't reply and I assumed the guards were passing close to him. A minute later I heard his voice in my earphone: "How much have you still got?"

"About half the file."

"Stop now and leave. Something's going on down here."

"Should I take the file with me?" I asked.

"No. The orders haven't changed," he replied.

I put the file back, but before I could leave the room, Udi came on again: "They're back with reinforcements. Go to the emergency staircase. When they get to the second floor, leave the building."

In line with our contingency plans, I left a simple jammer behind in the room that would delay the camera transmissions until it was found, in principle giving us enough time to get clear of the facility. I locked the door behind me, inactivated the cameras in the corridor and hurried to the emergency stairs. I heard the guards climbing the main staircase to the second floor, and Udi radioed: "There's a guard at the main entrance. Tell me when you approach, and I'll deal with him."

The man was lying face down on the ground when I left. We alerted Niki and Ronen, and Niki brought the car up. Her jammer had been working throughout the operation. Udi and I ran to the wall and climbed over where we'd cut the wire.

The moment our devices stopped jamming the cameras would transmit their backed-up contents to the control room: the car stopping, us climbing the fence, the break-in to the office building and into Room 205, me photographing a file – although they wouldn't be able to know which one – and our getaway would be seen. We hoped we'd be far enough away before the police were notified and roadblocks were set up. In any event, Ronen was ready to block the guards' vehicles if they gave chase. That didn't happen in the next few minutes and we were already close to the city centre when Ronen radioed that the plant's gates were opening and guards were inspecting the fence. Udi ordered him to join us.

Half an hour later, with our heads down again, Ronen drove us into the hotel garage, and five minutes later Niki and I were in bed in her room. The gadgets and work clothes we'd left in the Mercedes for Udi to get rid of. The hundreds of documents that I'd managed to photograph I sent to Tel Aviv on an encrypted line.

After dropping us, Ronen went to pick up Udi who'd parked the Mercedes – that had definitely been photographed and identified – in a residential area near his hotel. The paper trail would lead no further than Moshik's phoney documentation but Moshik had already disembarked from a ferryboat in Latvia, and Avi, who'd rented the SUV, was about to do the same in Estonia. After checking out of their respective hotels in an orderly fashion, Udi and Ronen set out on the long drive to Norway. The assumption was that they would be on the other side of the border before Udi's image was distributed to all remote border stations.

Later on, I worked out what had presumably happened after our getaway. After the plant's grounds were searched and nothing was found, the Gimbers' security staff saw that the CCTV cameras were now working and studied the images. They saw me and Udi doing what we had done, and they rushed with the material to the police, emphasizing that the photographs of the documents could harm national security and that the break-in had been a highly professional job. The unfortunate guard outside didn't know what had hit him, but Udi was seen "dealing with him" on the footage. The police took a sample image from each series and enhanced the figures: It took their laboratories some extra time, but at the end Udi and I were visible and identifiable, despite our strong masks. The pictures were distributed to all stations, airport security and hotels.

The Best Western night receptionist didn't know the guests well, and he showed the pictures to the bartender, who identified me at once, but said I couldn't possibly be connected because I was just an artist selling his pictures in Stockholm. The clerk told the young Turk that no one had asked for his opinion, and called the police. When the cops found my room empty, the barman was questioned and he told them about the romance that had blossomed between me and Niki. Minutes later, at six a.m., there was a knock on Niki's door.

We'd anticipated this visit, and discussed how Niki should react. Her performance was perfect. Naked under the hotel robe and her hair all tousled, she opened the door. The officers were embarrassed, and asked if Mr Ronald Friedlich, pictures of whom they showed her, happened to be in her room. Niki said she wasn't sure as the picture was not clear enough, and then let loose with a string of curses that I was amazed to hear coming out of her mouth. I was "woken up" by the ruckus, put a towel around my waist, and went to see what the commotion was all about. The cops were even more embarrassed. I looked at the pictures.

"That guy looks a bit like me," I said. "Where and when was this taken?"

"Tonight," said the officer, who didn't know many details.

"Here? In this hotel?" I asked.

"Of course not."

"Well then, it can't be me, and you are disturbing us for nothing."

"Please come with me," the officer requested, but Niki yelled that she'd make a major scandal out of it.

"I intend to go back to bed," I told him, "and at about nine I'll go down to breakfast. We can talk later." He requested that we not leave the hotel and I closed the door on him.

We couldn't go back to sleep of course, or even make love, but we lay in each other's arms, giving each other the warmth we both needed. The next stage was beyond our control, and that made for an unpleasant wait. The cops didn't come back, we didn't fall asleep, and we counted the minutes as time crawled by with infuriating slowness.

Just before nine, I went to my room, followed by an officer who had been standing guard outside all the time. I got dressed, took the last paintings I still had, and about which I had arranged in advance a meeting at a certain gallery at noon, and at the entrance to the dining room I met Niki, immaculately groomed and dressed in her best clothes. She had a meeting lined up with a young writer and his local publisher.

The cops waited patiently until we'd finished eating, and then they asked us to accompany them to the hotel manager's office.

"I have a meeting at twelve noon, so you'll have to finish your questioning by eleven. That's all the time I can give you, and I think it's more than enough, to question me about a stranger that looks a bit like me," I told them. It was almost ten, and Niki said she'd have to leave in half an hour.

The interrogation was very professional. Within the time we'd given them, the investigators received confirmation that Niki had indeed been holding meetings with writers and literary agents and that I had sold paintings at a number of galleries. We also gave them the names of the galleries in Copenhagen and Oslo, and the literary agencies in Berlin and Helsinki where we'd been before coming to Stockholm. We answered every question they had about what each of us did in Canada omitting, of course, anything that could indicate we'd known each other there. Our supper order to Niki's room came up on the computer and the room service waiter confirmed rather embarrassedly that Niki and I had been "in an intimate" situation when he brought us the late-night meal. Niki was allowed to leave but not before she repeated emphatically that I'd been with her all night.

I continued to answer their questions. The tape from the garage was played and we weren't seen either going or coming back, although I did see our hunched-over shapes in Ronen's SUV. The night receptionist testified that he, too, hadn't seen us leaving or returning during his shift. Then it was the turn of the poor barman, who was called from his bed after his night shift, and he confirmed our story about how we had met.

The investigator, rather shamefacedly, informed me that despite the resemblance, he concluded that it was apparently a coincidence, and he apologized for the inconvenience. He even offered to take me in his police car to my meeting, but I passed and called a cab.

We counted the minutes that night too, which we spent together in Niki's room to bolster our cover story, although there wasn't any hot sex. Niki looked at the clock every half hour, dozing off for a few minutes and waking in a panic, and the next morning we took our separate flights out, according to plan.

"The material is amazing," said Avi when he met me at the exit from the boarding bridge at Ben Gurion airport. "The plan is to hand it to the Swedish secret service and, if they shut off this channel, Military Intelligence says there'll be a delay of many months in the Iranian uranium enrichment project."

"Until they find another supplier," I said.

"Right, but that's why we have you guys."

At the preliminary debriefing in his office, Udi apologized to me for getting away that same night and sparing himself the grilling that we'd had to face. He assumed that the investigators had gone to his hotel as well and that he'd been recognized there. He and Ronen had crossed into Norway without a hitch, he said "but if we'd stopped for a coffee on the way we might have had to pay dearly if the pictures had turned up in the meantime. In the final analysis, we did all right. It was your combined cover that did it. I wouldn't have got away with it as elegantly as you two. We'll drink to our success here, with both of you and with the chief, when Niki gets back."

Niki arrived in Israel a few hours after me, and I insisted on going to the airport to meet her. She was dead tired. Her legs were shaking, and all she wanted was home and bed. "Who can celebrate now?" she fumed when I told her they were waiting for us at the base. "It's unbearable, this tension. How do people live their whole lives like this?"

I actually enjoyed the ceremony, which I'd gone through a few times now since joining the squad. For Niki it was new – and superfluous. To her, the toasts and the speech by the chief were part of an alien culture. She'd done what she'd been ordered to do, and she didn't think she deserved to be thanked for it. I knew that she was motivated by her samurai loyalty to me, and my heart was brimming with gratitude and love for this small, courageous woman, whom everyone there, or so it seemed, idolized. Especially when I recounted at the debriefing how she had yelled at the cops at her hotel room door. Nobody knew about the hours of fear and suspense she had gone through and the other operatives, who'd undergone similar experiences, tended not to ask or to speak about it.

Udi sent us for a five-day break in Eilat, and we really needed it. Niki fell in love with the red hills spilling into the blue sea. She enjoyed the promenade, with all the junky paraphernalia sold there, and I found out that she couldn't tell the difference between the common punks who congregate in Eilat and respectable kids. After she restored her hair to its original colour, she made herself fine plaits with coloured beads at the ends, although in a few days she'd have to unplait them again. She took a scuba diving lesson and loved swimming with the dolphins, we did a turn on a tandem paraglider high above the bay and Niki screeched with glee and waved like a little girl at the operator of the motor boat towing us. We swam in the cold sea and the heated pool, and more than anything else, we loved.

We almost didn't speak about the mission we'd just been on, but we couldn't help speaking about our future. "It felt like a dream, when we were playing at the real life we should be living," Niki said sadly. "All of a sudden, the cover story was like what our real lives should be, and the operation was just an interruption."

I didn't say a thing, just hugged her tight, something I hadn't been able to do when she'd said similar things in the hotel room in Stockholm and ran away crying. To be a samurai was a metaphor that wrapped loyalty in a certain ideology and in certain colours. But Niki was a young woman who certainly wanted to live a life of love, family and work uninterrupted by missions involving samurai loyalty.

How long would this loyalty endure? When would Niki say, "That's it", that as far as she was concerned the samurai chapter had ended, and now she wanted us to live like any other couple?

I knew that in Japanese culture, "no" did not exist. By means of "yes" they also express the negative, so as not to offend the person they are talking to. I had encountered it many times, when Japanese people couldn't answer my questions, even if I was simply asking for directions. Niki, so far, hadn't said no, but she told me about the wonderful meetings she'd had with young writers and their agents and publishers. Her eyes shone and I saw how happy this occupation made her. I knew that in these meetings she felt the same satisfaction that I felt when I had meetings in galleries, especially when they'd agreed to purchase my works.

Back in Canada, when she was working as an editor, she'd told me of the excitement of discovering an outstanding manuscript, that without her, a young writer might not be able to publish, and about the job of editing, during which she turned into a silent partner in the writing process, trying to be the optimal reader of the work, and very delicately directing the writer towards what in her eyes was missing from the story. "And what is more difficult, towards what is unnecessary in it, because a writer is in love with what he has written, and doesn't see the reader." And now, as a literary agent, she was happy with every discovery of a good book that without her would never be discovered by readers in the English language. She loved what she was doing, but she was being forced into doing it in a completely secondary way.

And what would I do when she said "No"?

In the meantime, all I permitted myself was to hint again at the deep place from where my commitment to Israel and the Jewish people sprang. When she talked about how much she had liked the young German writers, I told her that I still felt a barrier that made it difficult for me to look at a German and see only his nice side.

Miscomprehension was discernible in Niki's eyes.

"Let's try and see it from the way the brain works," I said, because I knew that any other explanation would come up against words I'd heard often before: but these are the grandchildren of the Nazis, and they've learned from history, and not all of their grandfathers were part of the Nazi war machine.

"Since I was a small child, whenever I heard the word 'German' it was in a negative context. The neurons in my brain ran from the word 'German' to the word 'Nazi' and created hardwiring between Germans and roundups, transports, concentration camps, death camps and the murder of millions of my fellow Jews. In my brain, very rigid patterns were formed that connect Germans to very negative feelings."

"But the people I met were really nice, and polite, and gentle!" Niki objected.

"I've also met Germans like that. I'm not blind, deaf or stupid," I replied in near anger. "That's why I'm talking to you about what goes on in my brain, involuntarily, subconsciously. Every meeting with a 'positive' German creates new connections, which are countered by fixed neural patterns. The brain's plasticity makes it possible for new connections, with new meanings, to be formed at every such meeting. But there would have to be thousands of meetings for the general pattern in me to change."

"So do you think that such patterns link you to the past, of your family and of your nation?"

Steel-trap smart, she had grasped precisely what I had wanted to tell her.

"I think so. I think that my consciousness, or my will, are not free of very powerful associations that link me to the history of my people in general, and of my family in particular."

"Do you mean that when your father's family was not in Israel it had no protection, and that the right place for Jews, as you have told me, is in Israel?"

"Yes, but that's only half the picture. Being here isn't enough."

"You mean that you have to be prepared to fight for this country."

"That's right, that's what I did in the army and what I'm doing now."

"How long for?"

"Just as many Christians continue to have a neural connection that leads from the word 'Jews' to the words 'crucifiers of Jesus,' and to negative stereotypes, so in the minds of many Muslims and Arabs we do not belong here. There is great hatred towards us and willingness to drive us away, to launch a Jihad against us. As long as this lasts, my commitment will last."

Niki pulled away from my embrace. "You have to understand. I do not have any such associations that connect me to your past and your country. I am connected only to you."

I reflected on her words for a moment. I had known that this was the way it was when we arrived in Israel together but I was not convinced this was still the case, after her long months of training, close to Udi and the other instructors, and after her brief time with our team. It seemed to me that Niki was beginning to feel at home, with the team and perhaps even without me.

Nevertheless, I tried to ease the situation. "But I am a package deal. I am all of these patterns that link me to my people and my country, and also to my great love for you, and each moment with you creates new connections that are becoming the most important pattern of my life."

"As long as I am here," said my wise Niki, "as long as the patterns in your brain elicited by the word 'Israel' and those that arise from the word 'Niki' dovetail with each other..." And she left it at that.

I also remained silent. What would I do if she forced me to choose? Was it at all possible to separate the two things without feeling like a person who had an arm amputated?

The meeting with the Swedish secret service took place while we were in Eilat, and Udi phoned us to give us a report of what was said. The head of the Mossad station covering Scandinavia, and the HQ officer responsible for the efforts to derail Iran's nuclear weapons project, showed the Swedes a few dozen of the documents I'd photographed which proved beyond doubt that Gimbers was supplying the Iranians with both uranium enrichment centrifuges and computers, in violation of the international boycott.

"So, I understand that it was your people who broke into Gimbers last week." The head of the Swedish service added, "You know, we are aware of their identities." He described what had happened after we made our getaway.

"What bothers us more," said the Mossad head, without admitting anything, "is that those photographs are in Gimbers' hands, and who knows if they won't be passed on. We'd be very grateful if you dealt with this."

"No problem," said the Swede. "We'll forget the names the hotels gave us, and no one else knows them. I'll immediately send people to confiscate all the CCTV pictures. We'll pass your material to the public prosecution department, which is the only body that can act on it."

The heads of Gimbers were arrested within a few days, and a shipment ready for dispatch to Tehran was seized. "But," Udi said, "there may still be a little problem. The cops didn't find our photos, and we're afraid that the bastards did pass them on, perhaps to the Iranians. We may be able to intercept them on the way. I'll talk to you about it as soon as you get back from Eilat. And when will that be, by the way? Perhaps tomorrow?"

4.

The Gentleman in Brussels

WE DECIDED TO give up our last day in Eilat, even though Niki was keen to have one more dive. Anything we could do to stop the Iranians from getting our pictures was far more valuable than another day of fun in the sun.

When we arrived at our base outside Tel Aviv, we found that the rest of the team was already in Europe. The Mossad station head in Scandinavia had obtained, from his Swedish counterparts, the identity of the middleman through whom Gimbers dealt with the Iranians. If the images had been passed on, the Swedes said, it was through this man, Yuri Gladstone. An international businessman with a trading company registered in Luxembourg but who apparently lived in Brussels. Gladstone was the nominal purchaser of the equipment on behalf of Iran, and his name had come up in the Swedish cops' grilling of the Gimbers's executives but they didn't know much more about him.

The next day, in the early afternoon, we landed at Zaventem airport, Belgium. We were to meet Udi in Brussels at eight p.m., and until then wouldn't know what our role in the operation would be or what our cover story was. For the time being, we decided to stay together and took a room at the Royal Windsor hotel in one of the narrow streets leading off the Grand Place. We spent the rest of the day wandering through the ancient side streets and in that magnificent square, one of the most beautiful in the world to my mind, surrounded as it is by palatial buildings, four or five storeys high, with pillared façades, ornate cornices and topped by steeply sloping roofs. The City Hall, at the centre of one side, was the most impressive of all, perhaps precisely because of a slight asymmetry in the number of pillars on either side of the façade, something which, legend has it, led the architect to take his own life.

We didn't want to stray too far from the square and its vicinity and in the time we had left walked around the nearby alleys full of seafood stalls and restaurants, and visited the famous Manneken Pis, the sculpture of a little boy peeing into a fountain, which surprised us by being so small, especially in relation to all the renown it enjoys. By sunset it was too cold to stay outside so we arrived early for the meeting with Udi. Our rendezvous turned out to be an elegant café, with its name in gilt lettering, with polished mahogany furnishings upholstered in green leather. Udi and Ronen were already there.

"I recommend the moules," said Udi, and then he took a look at Niki and said, "You've got a tan. The sun is good for you."

Ronen helped us get over the slight embarrassment over the personal compliment, so rare coming from Udi, and said, "And my recommendation is the oysters in white wine."

"Suits me," said Niki, with a slight blush on her cheeks following the very unexpected compliment, and we laughed because her reply was a response to both Udi and Ronen. Once again, I had to remind myself that for Udi she wasn't my sweetheart, but rather his operative. To gain time to sort my thoughts out, I ordered a coffee and asked for a menu.

"I visited the Luxembourg address, and Dave checked the registry of companies," Udi told us. "Yuri Gladstone's set-up is a straw company. There's an office services company at the address and from the mail we swiped from their box, we obtained two addresses in Brussels. We've done some recon around them, and one of them, the Place Louise, is a business address; the second in Avenue Molière is residential. Jerry's watching the apartments and Dave's on the offices."

"What's our job?" I asked.

"Firstly, to stop the pictures of you and me, and perhaps also of Ruth, getting to the Iranians. But in this matter, I'm afraid we're trying to close the stable door after the horses have bolted. It's been a week since our break-in and if he wanted to send them, it stands to reason he's already done so, by e-mail. Just to be sure, I've started growing a beard," and he rubbed his unshaven jaw. "Boaz, you'll grow a moustache, and Ruth will dye her hair darker."

Udi went on to tell us that our team's first task was to pinpoint the man and his business, because he was apparently the key figure in Iran's non-conventional weaponry acquisition efforts. Enquiries about his company had already led to other firms in Europe that manufactured tools and materials for the nuclear industry which he purchased and transported to Iran. Two other teams were already engaged in handling these leads, one in Norway and another in Russia.

"And once we've found him, what, specifically, are our orders?"

"When we've got more details, a decision will be made in Israel as to how to deal with him. It could be anything, from setting fire to his office to beating him up or intimidating him, right up to elimination. Whatever they decide."

"And at the same time to get our pictures back."

"If they're still there," Udi affirmed. "All signs are that Yuri's here in Brussels. But almost nothing is known about him. We'll have to link whoever uses the office with whoever lives at the apartment, make sure he's our man, and only then, as I've said, will the decision be made on what to do with him."

Udi had requested, but did not receive, permission for a break-in at the office and the flat. After the Stockholm episode, the man must have known there was a skilled burglary team after him, and he could easily booby trap either or both sites.

I found Place Louise to be a large square at the city end of the fashionable Avenue Louise, which leads from the square to the woods abutting the Uckle neighbourhood. The large buildings around the square provided us with several good observation posts. Niki chose the Häagen Dazs ice cream parlour, with its endless selection of flavours, while I preferred Quick on the opposite corner with its hamburgers swathed in mayonnaise, like everything else in Brussels.

Before or after her shift, Niki liked popping into the nearby Galeries Louise, an elegant mall of upmarket stores, or other shopping choices in the adjoining streets leading off the square. At the end of the Avenue Louise stood the vast and imposing Palais de Justice and opposite it, a memorial "To the glory of the Infantrymen who died for the country". I learned here that Belgium had throughout history been the main killing fields in the wars between Germany, France and Holland, and was actually established to serve as a buffer between them.

I spent the hours between my shifts paying quick visits to the major museums which are located on or near Rue Royal, which forks off the end of Avenue Louise. Some of the splendid treasures of Flemish art are exhibited in the Royal Museum of Fine Arts, but I enjoyed myself more in the Comics Art Museum in Rue des Sables. I had loved Belgian comics ever since the days I had tried to understand how Tintin and the Smurfs were made, and I borrowed some of their techniques for my Israman. Niki came with me on one visit, and when I told her about Israman, she was thrilled. "And I thought I knew all about you," she said, almost scolding me.

Uckle was the neighbourhood of choice for the European Union bureaucrats, perhaps because it offered a combination of quiet in the side streets, and the big city in the broad avenues which led to the centre and were lined with every sort of shop one could need. The neighbourhood was too expensive for many of its original inhabitants, some of whom rented their apartments out to EU people and, of course, it was well out of reach of the hundreds of thousands of migrants from North Africa who had taken over other areas, especially around the railway stations in the north and south of the city.

Avenue Molière, where we suspected Yuri Gladstone lived, was one of the quieter streets in Uckle, with typical Belgian residential buildings, each in a different architectural style and four to six storeys high, built up against each other, with common side walls. I soon learned that the only evident danger of keeping watch here was the many piles of poop deposited by dogs, which the locals preferred to raise rather than children, and whose droppings they didn't bother to pick up off the pavement.

My encounters with Belgians convinced me there was more than an iota of truth in the stories about their thick-headedness. There were, for example, salespeople who wouldn't sell me one package containing various kinds of chocolate cookies, although they were all priced the same, and insisted on weighing and packaging each kind separately. Perhaps there was something in the joke about the Belgian stuck in a lift with a tourist and telling him not to worry, because a few days before he'd been stuck for hours on an escalator that had stopped working.

Three frustrating days of lookouts in the Place Louise and Avenue Molière went by before we had a possible "target". He was a tall, handsome man of about forty, who wore a well-cut suit and left the apartment building every morning. It was only after scrutinizing the photographs taken by a camera we'd placed in a car opposite the office building, that we saw that he arrived there a little while later.

We'd noticed him from the outset, but because he didn't take the tram in the direction of Place Louise, we didn't follow him. Once we'd seen him entering the office building, we stuck to his tail for the next two days. It was clear that he was wary, performing an elementary kind of drill for detecting surveillance, and trying to shake off anyone who might be on his tracks. He got into a tram heading for the city centre, and there he changed to another tram that dropped him near the office building. He didn't go anywhere apart from his office and his home. It could be presumed that he wouldn't swallow any bait and he'd be suspicious of anyone approaching him. Phillip and Dave, who had accumulated dozens of hours of lookout duty near the two locations and were the least well-trained in our team, felt that they were already "cooked" by the curious glances they'd received from passersby, so Udi decided to move on to the next stage.

The plan was for Niki to establish contact with the target and try to dig up any details she could, and, if possible, to get invited into his office or his apartment. She'd then try to spot any alarm systems, identify the types of locks, and plant a miniature microphone-transmitter wherever possible.

The next two mornings, Niki was on Yuri's tram. After getting a message that he had left home, she boarded the tram at the stop on the cobbled Chausée d'Alsemberg, one stop before Avenue Molière, and stayed on when he got off. She sat facing the seat where he generally sat. But Yuri was completely indifferent to her presence, hid behind his *Guardian* and never exchanged either a word or even a glance with her. Elementary spycraft, of course, forbade her to take the initiative.

"A whole week's gone by," said an exasperated Udi, "and HQ is still ruling out a break-in, as long as we don't have more info. And we don't even have proof that he's our man, and not some British EU bureaucrat. Meanwhile, the two other teams have broken into plants in Oslo and Moscow and downloaded tons of material. They're working on it at HQ, and we shall see – perhaps it'll lead to a change in their thinking. At any rate, we have to be more aggressive, and Ruth, that's going to cost you a sterile cut on your thigh."

I wasn't even asked for my opinion, Niki didn't object, and that's how the next stage of our operation got started.

On the designated morning, I was on lookout outside Yuri's residence. I was standing in the doorway of a small clinic close to the corner of Molière and Alsemberg when I saw him leave and walk in my direction. I reported this and Niki left Udi's car, where she was being prepped, and stood in line at the tram stop.

Yuri ignored her again when he sat down facing her. A few stops later, close to the Gare du Midi and the Moroccan and Algerian neighbourhoods, a noisy group of four Middle-Eastern-looking youngsters boarded the tram. They left no doubts as to their origins, speaking in a mixture of French and Moroccan Arabic. One of them noticed Niki and made a remark about her semi-oriental appearance. They laughed and moved close to her.

One of them asked the "Voulez vous . . ." question. Niki looked down and didn't reply. This made them mad.

"Good fuck for good money," one of them said, in English, and they laughed again. Again not obtaining any reaction from her, he said, "You give me good fuck, I give you fifty euro, OK?"

Niki tried to shrink into her seat. None of the other passengers intervened, including Yuri, who went on reading his newspaper.

Niki's lack of response was driving the ruffian out of his mind, and he nudged her shoulder with his elbow.

"Why you no answer me? Arab not good? Arab good fuck!" And saying this he pushed his groin forwards and grabbed his crotch. This was too much for Yuri. He looked up from his paper, glared at the youngsters and demanded, "Leave the lady alone!"

Now the four turned on him in a mixture of Arabic and French, and the "English-speaker" among them said, "You want I fuck you instead?"

Yuri took a deep breath, folded his paper deliberately, and stood up. "Leave the tram now!" he commanded.

"Sit, old man," said the punk and tried to push him back into his seat.

But Yuri was tougher than the young roughneck thought and the resounding slap he delivered in return for the push was fast, hard, and perfectly accurate – a blow with a large open palm that hit the side of the young man's head with a force that must have torn his eardrum. He staggered in shock and crumpled to the floor, with a wail. It was a clear declaration of war. One of his friends leaned over to hold him, and the two others jumped on Yuri.

But Yuri defended himself and drove them off with a well-executed series of parries and punches. Then one of the hoodlums pulled a knife.

Now Niki got up to help. There was a flurry of punches and curses when all of a sudden the tram jerked to a halt. Everyone lost their balance and Niki let out a short yelp of pain.

The doors opened and the gang yelled to each other that the police were coming and ran away.

Niki and Yuri found their feet. Niki thanked him effusively, and Yuri said quietly, "You are bleeding," and pointed at her knee. Blood was trickling down her leg from under her dress. She instinctively pulled her skirt up, exposing a bleeding cut on her thigh.

The tram was moving again. Yuri collected from the driver a first-aid kit and Niki put a patch of gauze on the wound and bandaged it in a rather careless way.

At the next stop, she said, "I think I'll get off here, and take a cab to the hospital."

"My office is quite near," said our target. "If you wish I can bandage you properly there. I don't think it's a very serious cut. It's not worth the hundreds of euros you'll have to pay at the hospital."

Niki accepted gratefully.

She was surprised when he stopped a cab. "I usually change trams here, but I don't want to waste time now," he explained.

"Bingo!" said Udi when we saw, through the window of his car, the two alighting and then entering the cab. Since he'd picked me up and as we followed the tram in case something went wrong, neither of us had uttered a word.

A CCTV camera over the door to Yuri's office covered the whole hallway. He used two large Spyder keys to open the two separate locks and once inside he immediately reached behind the coat rack to turn off the alarm. His office suite comprised an entrance room with a kitchenette, a toilet and a simply furnished room with a desk, two arm chairs, a locked filing cabinet, a desktop computer, a fax machine and a telephone. On the wall was a thin plasma screen.

While Yuri was putting the kettle on and getting the first-aid kit, Niki surveyed the office. Two cameras were watching her from two opposite corners. She scoured all around her for a suitable place to plant the microphone she had in her bag without being filmed by the cameras. In the end she quickly pushed it into the space between the back of the chair and the cushion she was sitting on. Not ideal, but that was all she could do without being caught on camera.

Mishka Ben-David

Yuri came back with a cup of tea, a bandage and antibiotic ointment.

"It's stopped bleeding, and I don't know if it's a good idea to open it up now," said Niki.

"Yes, although it bled a lot, the cut looks shallow and clean," he agreed. "You were lucky."

His guard was apparently down by now: Niki's charm was working. They arranged to meet later at a restaurant where, she said, she'd have more time to thank him for saving her from "those Arab hooligans".

When she told us all this, an hour later in Udi's hotel room, she agreed with Udi that the incision he'd made in her leg wasn't deep enough, and the capsule of the blood-like liquid that she'd popped when removing the plaster over the cut during the brawl was too big.

"That's why I insisted on bandaging myself in the tram and why I didn't want to change the bandage in his office," she said.

As for the "hooligans", they showed up a little later at a pre-arranged café. They were smartly dressed now and on their way to the airport. For them it was a two-day break from the Mossad cadet course. They were full of spirits, except for the poor guy who had taken Yuri's slap and was still in pain and hearing bells. "I hope you gave it to him good," he muttered to Udi as they left.

Then Udi gave us the arrangements for the evening. Niki would wear a wire to transmit her conversation with Yuri. Udi and I would be keeping an eye on them in the restaurant, and Ronen and Jerry would be in a car in the car park ready to replace us if we aroused Yuri's suspicions. Dave would be waiting at the nearby taxi rank and Philip would be at the wheel of another car on the other side of the street, facing the direction which could not be taken from the restaurant.

The briefing was interrupted by a call from Jerry, who was in a car on Avenue Louise, close to the square and within range of the microphone in Yuri's office.

"Most of the time I could only hear mumbling," Jerry reported, "because the mike doesn't pick up voices from the desk area, but then he must have walked around the room with the handset, or he was speaking on his mobile and sitting in the armchair. Anyway, he spoke to someone called Hani about the police in Oslo calling in the executives of the Ziegelmeyer company and informing them that they were suspected of breaching the embargo on Iran. They'd been ordered to hand a bunch of documents to the cops, and they're consulting their lawyers over whether they are obliged to do so."

"Thanks. We have our connection. He's the man," said Udi, but Jerry continued: "This Hani was very upset. He told Yuri he was as full of holes as a Swiss cheese, and that he should check where he's leaking from."

"We know he's our guy. We know he'll be at the restaurant at eight, let's finish it off. No need for the date with Ruth," I said.

"You're saying this out of purely professional considerations, right?" Udi rebuked me sarcastically. "The meeting with Ruth will take place as planned. She may get more stuff out of him. That we have discovered his ties with Norway and Russia as well as Sweden doesn't mean he hasn't got more connections with another twenty places. Ruth has given us valuable pre-op intelligence on his office security, and back at the big Office – ours – they're getting organized to deal with it. She's good at this, and I've ordered her to go to his apartment with him, if he suggests it, and to get the same kind of info. Then perhaps they'll approve a break-in."

I felt that I was turning red in the face, but I had nothing more to say on the matter. Udi was acting correctly, and clearly my relationship with Niki couldn't be a reason for her not to meet Yuri that evening, nor to stop her from accepting an invitation to go home with him. Nevertheless, I was indignant. Her having dinner with a guy like him was in itself difficult enough for me to swallow. An invitation to go home with him afterwards had obvious implications. Even assuming that Niki would avoid going to bed with him, as she undoubtedly would, was I supposed to simply watch it happening and keep quiet?

"Have you also ordered her to sleep with him, 'if he suggests it'?"

"I had my doubts about whether it was right to employ a couple," said Udi ruefully. "After this mission, we'll have to draw our conclusions but for now we'll do what's best for the mission. Although I don't have to share this with you, I'll answer you, just to calm you down. We decided that if the subject comes up, she'll invite him to her hotel, and there we'll be waiting for him."

I gulped and looked down. But Udi didn't make do with having put my mind at rest. He also ousted me from the team carrying out the operation.

"And I've decided that the lead team for tonight's show will be Jerry and me. We'll be in the restaurant. You and Ronen will be back-up."

Whatever happened in the restaurant, and perhaps in the apartment, would be transmitted over the wire Niki would be wearing, and Udi didn't want me in earshot or eyeshot. In the unpleasant silence that reigned afterwards, I pictured the minutes before Niki had boarded the tram that morning: how she had lifted her skirt and bared her thigh, how Udi had bent over her with a surgeon's lancet and cut into her flesh. What had he said to her just before? Did he calm her and, if so, how? How he had caressed the place for the cut with alcohol-saturated gauze. And what had he done the moment after making the incision, when the white skin of her thigh was lacerated, and blood began oozing out? Did Niki cry out in pain? Perhaps he had kissed her – a fatherly kiss, of course. And then he had pushed the bloody lips of the wound together, and stuck on the broad Band-Aid containing the capsule that would be torn open when Niki pulled the plaster off. I remembered the way he'd gently patted her shoulder, almost caressed it, when we got out of the car at Gimbers. What had he done this time, when she left his car at the tram stop? Stroked her head? And what did Niki feel about him? He definitely was a significant figure in her life. For the entire duration of her course she'd spent more time with him than she had with me, and now he was her commander; our commander.

"Are you with me, Boaz?" Udi's voice interrupted my reverie.

"No, but let's speak about it another time."

"There won't be another time," said Udi. "We're on a mission here. No secrets."

"Don't fuck with my head," I heard myself blurting out. What had been seething inside me suddenly boiled over and I hadn't sensed at all that this outburst was imminent. "It's you who is compartmentalizing me all the time, keeping her a secret from me."

I got up and left the table.

We didn't return to the subject. I went to the bathroom and washed my face. While there, Jerry called again and said he'd heard strange noises from the office, a kind of electronic whistling sound, and then nothing more. Udi said he'd check it out with our technical department and soon received a reply: it was possible that some kind of a jammer had been activated, or a wavelength scanner, but "it could also be any other thing that puts out an electronic screen, even a TV."

A taxi dropped Niki at the restaurant. From our position in the car park we saw her slight form, stunning in a dress and high heels and a beautiful fur coat, all of which she'd bought that afternoon, using Udi's operational funds. I'd been with her when she shopped, but not at the briefing Udi gave her. Beyond what he'd told me, I didn't know what limits he'd set for her – or hadn't set. It was clear to me, as in the past, that at moments like this Udi had nothing but the mission itself on his mind. Ronen saw that I was upset, and put his arm around my shoulders.

"Don't worry, it's no big deal. No drama. Don't have porno movies in your head. We don't do things like that, it's time you got it. If it's necessary, we get local call girls, and pay them a bit more than usual."

That Mossad's kosher Jewish girls were kept out of the dirty games, I was aware, but who knew if Niki, a Gentile Canadian-Japanese, wasn't some kind of a call girl in Udi's eyes, someone who could be used for non-kosher assignments?

"Get over it, enough," Ronen scolded me. "But seriously, I don't understand you. I would never in my life ever have brought my girlfriend into the squad. Isn't it enough to have one in the family doing crazy stuff? There isn't one of us who's normal. We've each got our own loose screw, and that's why we're here. For you, it's the girlfriend who was killed by a terrorist. For me, it's the disaster that happened to my commando unit, when most of them were killed on that op in Lebanon, and I was saved because I stayed home with some stupid injury, and since then I've felt obliged. For Jerry, it's that he once shelled our forces, also in Lebanon, by mistake. For Udi, it's apparently some kind of family complications – there are all kinds of rumours but he doesn't talk about it, so no one knows. Your Niki was actually normal, I think, until you brought her into this. Tell me, what kind of kids will you two screw-ups have?"

Just then, we saw Udi and Jerry entering the restaurant. Niki had been told to arrive early, so she'd be seated at the table Yuri had booked. Udi and Jerry found a table from which she and Yuri could be seen, but far enough away to seem completely unconnected. Last of all, Yuri arrived in a cab, tall and elegant, in a long overcoat and a Borsalino hat.

"Looks like a cool guy," said Ronen, rubbing salt in my wounds.

Niki's wire transmitted only to Udi. He could talk to us and hear us on another wavelength.

A quarter of an hour after they started, Udi's voice came over our receiver: "They've finished the first course. Everything going nicely. No intelligence yet. Main course on the way. Out."

Five minutes later, Yuri put a little box next to Niki's hand. She opened it and found a ring inside.

Embarrassed and surprised, she looked at him but the expression she met with was not that of an ardent suitor. His face was cold and his voice hushed, when he said, "The reason you're still alive is not the two gorillas sitting in the far corner. If you do anything hasty, all three of you will die. I am armed. I will know precisely what you do and what you say, just as I know about the microphone you planted in the armchair in my office. I am now going to the bathroom, and then I'll leave. You will neither move nor say anything for at least five minutes. After that, do whatever you want to do."

He left the table. Niki assumed the ring was a microphone and that in any case Udi had heard Yuri's speech via her wire. She didn't want to move as long as Yuri was still on the premises, in case he drew his pistol and opened fire. Then, when Udi had still not reacted, she got up and headed for the exit, beckoning him with her hand. Udi followed her, surprised. When he grasped what was going on, he radioed me and Ronen to close off the exit.

Ronen got out of the car and ran to the restaurant door, and I manoeuvred the car out of the parking area. There was no trace of Yuri. Philip said he hadn't seen him going the other way. Yuri had apparently realized that apart from the "two gorillas" inside, there was also a lookout outside, and he had slipped away in the dark.

"Comb the streets around here," Udi told Ronen and me, pointing which way to go. "If he planned his getaway in advance, there may be a car waiting nearby. Don't go too far from the Gare Centrale, because that's the closest station, and he may be heading there. I'll take a cab to the Gare du Midi. Jerry take a cab to the Gare du Nord, and Ruth, you go into the Gare Centrale." He left Dave at the taxi rank, in case Yuri appeared there, and he sent Philip to another rank nearby.

"What about the office and the apartment?" Jerry asked.

"He won't go back there. He's aware that we know about them."

"What's with that ring?" asked Niki.

"I suppose it's a jamming device. That's why I didn't hear what he said to you. Take it off the table and dump it in the nearest bin. Pay the bill, so they don't send the cops after us."

—◦–◖◗–◦—

There was no sign of Yuri in the vicinity. We covered every street that led to the Gare Centrale. We saw Niki heading for the station in a cab, and going inside. Gare Centrale is a small station, faced in marble and built in a similar style to that of the surrounding neo-classical structures. It wasn't very crowded – if Yuri was there, she would likely spot him. Jerry had a less palatable job, at the Gare du Nord, in the heart of the Arab district which was full of brothels; the chances that Udi would spot Yuri in the gigantic Gare du Midi, with its additional TGV high-speed railway station, were very small. If Yuri wanted to disappear from Belgium in a hurry, the TGV to Paris would be a good way for him to do it.

I didn't think Niki was in danger in the well-lit station but, nevertheless, I decided to join her there. I drew up at the entrance, asked Ronen to take over the wheel and rushed inside. I went down to the platform level, heard a whistle and saw the doors closing, and the train began gliding soundlessly out of the station.

It was then that I saw him, framed in a window of one of the cars, as the train drew slowly away. He was taking his hat off and looking down at the platform. He had a hand on his hip, in a stance that could have indicated he was gripping the butt of a pistol. I followed his gaze, and I saw her.

Niki was sitting on a bench, only a few metres from the tracks. She was watching Yuri, without moving, as the train took him further and further away.

I looked up at the electronic notice board, just catching the name of the train and its destination before the information changed. "He's on the FC to Amsterdam," I radioed via the microphone on my lapel. "In coach number five. Just left Centrale. Jerry, he'll be at your station in three minutes."

"Just got out of the taxi, flying down," Jerry answered.

"Jerry, get on that train but keep your distance from Yuri," Udi's voice came in. "Report the situation in the coach, and wait for orders. Ronen, are you in the car?" Ronen replied in the affirmative.

"Speed to Zaventem, that's the next stop. Jerry'll tell you if Yuri's getting off there. If not, proceed to Mechelen. You've got a chance of getting there before the train."

Niki was watching the train being swallowed up by the dark tunnel. I sat down next to her.

I waited. After a long minute, she turned to me with a distant trace of an embarrassed smile.

"What happened?" I asked, although I already knew: she'd come down to the platform and Yuri and she had spotted each other. A glance at the board had told her the train would leave in four minutes. She had enough time to call us. She knew she could speak into the microphone at her throat without Yuri realizing what she was doing, if she turned her back to him. Yuri was watching her, his hand on his hip, but she knew he wouldn't draw a pistol and fire at her. There were several armed police officers in the station, and he may have presumed that Niki had a handgun in her bag. They held each other's eyes.

While she told me her story, I could imagine him standing there, upright, tall and handsome, with a shadow of a smile on his lips. The prey didn't look like prey, but like a man holding all the cards, and the hunter didn't look like a hunter, but like a confused woman who didn't know how to play her cards. I assumed that Niki recalled how he'd stood up to the punks, how he'd brought her the first-aid kit, first in the tram and then in his office, and the cup of tea. She remembered their friendly chat over their first course. His accent added a touch of gentleness to his elegant appearance, his deep voice and his polished manners. When they met in the restaurant, he already knew what she was, and if he'd wanted, he could have done away with her. She owed him.

"You know you'll have to give some very complicated explanations," I said after hearing her story.

But that, I felt, wasn't what was bothering me. It wasn't my operative-companion who had given in to the charms of a middleman. It was my sweetheart. Niki realized what was going on inside me, put her head on my shoulder and tried to intertwine her fingers with mine. But I remained frigid. Too many things were not looking right here.

Ronen didn't manage to catch the train at Zavantem or at Mechelen. His chances of reaching Antwerp before the train were zero, and the station after that was Breda in Holland. After Antwerp, Jerry reported that Yuri was now alone in his compartment. People from Antwerp who worked in Brussels and went home to sleep had disembarked, and only a few passengers were continuing on to Holland. Udi checked the timetable and saw that when the train got to Breda, another train heading from Amsterdam to Brussels was due at the opposite platform.

"You have permission to execute," we heard Udi's sharp, clear-cut message to Jerry. "Do it when the train begins slowing down before Breda. Make him look as if he's asleep. At the station transfer to the train to Brussels. Ronen will be waiting for you in Antwerp."

❖❖❖

Jerry fitted the silencer to his pistol and moved close to Yuri's compartment. But as the train slowed down Yuri suddenly stood up and walked along the corridor in the direction of the exit. He took his bag with him, and it looked as if he intended to get off the train. Perhaps he also knew about the train to Brussels. Jerry weighed up whether to shoot him in the back of the head, with everyone heading for the exit seeing the body in the corridor, or to follow him and wait for a better opportunity. But then Yuri opened the door to the toilet and went inside. As he turned around to close the door, the silencer on the barrel of Jerry's gun was the last thing he saw. There were two clicks, louder than Jerry would have preferred, and Yuri crumpled. Jerry fired once more, into the middle of Yuri's forehead, and only then did he see that Yuri had managed to draw his own pistol from his belt and was holding it in his hand. Jerry pulled the door closed as the train's brakes screeched. He didn't have the time to remove his silencer and shoved the pistol with its burning-hot barrel into the inside pocket of his jacket. Disembarking passengers were coming towards the exit, and Jerry mingled with them and got off, crossed to the opposite platform and climbed onto the Brussels train, with the gun searing his chest. Before Yuri's body was discovered by a terrified passenger just outside Rotterdam, Jerry was already well inside Belgian territory.

"Moving to standard getaway mode," Udi radioed after Ronen reported that Jerry was in his car, and we heard his brief report for the first time. Dave and Philip checked out of their hotels and took the fast night train to Paris, Ronen and Jerry picked up their belongings at their hotels and headed for Germany in the rented car. Udi ordered me to stay in my hotel until he completed debriefing Niki and to get ready to leave with her in the morning.

I waited restlessly in our room. I didn't even try to fall asleep. I scanned all the TV news stations, until there was a report about a man who'd been found shot dead in the toilet of the train from Brussels to Amsterdam. The dead man was said to be a British citizen and was not known to the police, and there was no indication who had shot him. The assumption was that it was either an espionage or a criminal situation, because the victim was holding a pistol. The investigators believed the assassins had got off the train at Rotterdam or Schiphol, and the security camera images from these stations were now being scrutinized. I reported this to Udi, who said there was no change in the departure arrangements, and added nothing about Niki's debriefing.

I had several nerve-racking hours before five a.m., when the door opened and there she was. I didn't know how to express to Niki all that had accumulated in my mind during those hours: the love, the fear, the jealousy, the frustration, and the uncertainty – about her future on the team, and perhaps even about our future as a couple.

I didn't know what to ask her or what to tell her. I sensed that she wanted only one thing, for me to hug her and shut up. But perhaps that's also what she'd wanted from Udi, in his room. A different hug, perhaps, fatherly and understanding, but still a hug, to console her for the difficult decision she had taken. I remained silent, and waited for her to speak. Niki's eyelids were so heavy that only a narrow slit remained open.

"We have tickets on the eleven a.m. TGV to Charles de Gaulle, and a flight from there to Israel at three thirty," she said at last. "I want to sleep in the little time we have."

The way she said "Israel" sounded jarring to me; the rest of us always used a codeword, or said "home". It also bothered me that she took off only her top clothes, got under the covers and pulled them over her head.

She never gave me an iota of information about what had come up during her session with Udi. He had probably instructed her to keep it all to herself but I felt I couldn't endure that. I told her quietly that the events of the day, with Yuri at the station and now with Udi, were a little too much for me to take. She must have heard the frustration in my voice but no answer came from under the blanket.

It wasn't Niki who would have to choose between life with me on the squad and her own normal life in Toronto, and it wasn't I who'd have to choose between life with her, as an artist, and the Mossad. The two of us would have to choose between life together and the squad. But between us, now, there was only silence.

5.

Artificial Respiration

I DIDN'T GET into bed with her and instead dozed in the armchair. We hardly spoke while we were packing our things, or on the way to the station, or in the fast train to Charles de Gaulle airport. It wasn't stress over whether we'd be caught. Niki could have been linked to Yuri, if investigators found out about their dinner together but the chances that would happen within a few hours were minimal. There was a sense of foreboding that our relationship was at a crossroads. I didn't know if Niki had anything to hide about the hours she'd spent alone with Udi the night before, or about their relationship in general, and my worries on that score seemed too unfounded and childish for me to mention them. But although I said nothing further, the soul-destroying jealousy that was gnawing at my insides must have been evident to her. We tried to be nice to each other while waiting for our flight, in the few necessary interactions that occurred, like when I asked her if I could get her anything from the café at the departure gate, or if she wanted the window seat on the plane. I didn't know if the cold I felt during the flight came from the air conditioning, the window, or from inside myself. The blanket that I requested from a stewardess didn't make it any better.

At night, in our apartment, I thought that if we made love, things might get back on track. Niki didn't refuse but it was the worst sex we'd ever had. She was dry, and the rocket that usually sprang out of my groin was not as hard as it always had been. I came, but only with difficulty, and Niki was ice cold. This time there wasn't even one "Yes" and the State of Israel didn't arise. We didn't speak about what was happening between us. When she turned her back towards me, I put my hand on her hip and remained awake after her quiet breathing indicated she was fast asleep.

Only in the morning, while we were sipping our bitterer than usual coffee, did I ask Niki what had happened at her meeting with Udi. And I quickly asked if he'd given her a tongue-lashing.

"No . . . Do you think he should have rebuked me? Do you think I developed some kind of special sympathy for Yuri? Or that I should have sparked off a gunfight in the railway station by acting myself or by speaking into my mike?"

She was right of course, and she also knew exactly how to take accurate aim at my secret fears about her and Yuri and to try to allay them. And as she went on to talk about her meeting with Udi, she did so with the intent of stopping up that crack in my heart: only now did it transpire that there had been someone else present at the meeting, a member of another squad who was there to question Niki about Yuri's office, the locks on the door, the location of the alarm control box, and of the cameras. She knew that this other team was going to work there, and she wasn't supposed to say anything about it to me.

Right after Niki's initial description of the office was received, HQ had decided that we would continue working on Yuri and another squad would move in to handle the office. They'd landed in Brussels at the same time as Jerry and Yuri set out on their train journey northwards, and an hour and a half later, after Jerry reported "mission accomplished", they were given one hour to get their job done. HQ estimated that it would take at least an hour before Yuri was identified and the Brussels police would get to his office.

Because of the short time at their disposal, the break-in team decided not to photograph the material but simply to take it all with them. Yuri's computer and several dozen files from his cabinet were duly packed and carried down to a waiting vehicle and from there shipped securely to Israel, that same night. They also dismantled the cameras that had transmitted to Yuri's computer, and took them along too.

"This guy was the veritable tycoon of Iranian non-conventional weaponry acquisition," said intelligence officer Moshik, who'd come to our facility straight from the technical department, where the contents of the computer and files were being scrutinized. "Meanwhile, links with dozens of other companies in most European countries have been discovered, almost all of them involved with equipment or materials used in the nuclear, missile and chemical industries. We don't know yet what deals he'd done with them, but that'll probably come out during the day."

The Dutch had conveyed Yuri's details to Interpol the same day he was killed and the first hints of his true identity were emerging. His real name was Eddie McMurphy and he was an MI6 veteran who had crossed the lines and had been living under an assumed identity in Europe for a decade. Even the British had no idea what he'd been up to since he'd retired. While still in their service he'd specialized in setting up straw companies and money transfers, which he'd now turned into a business.

"It may be that the Brussels operation was just the tip of the iceberg of what's in store for us," said Jack, deputy chief of the operations division, who'd come to congratulate our team. The chief himself was meeting with the break-in team, perhaps an implicit message that the Mossad saw their mission as more successful than ours. Jack said that Jerry's one-on-one pursuit of Yuri had been a "citation or demotion" matter, and I had some trouble in explaining the expression to Niki and the kind of culture that it reflected: if necessary, you take risks against standing orders, and if it works you're a hero, but if it fails you're screwed.

"We do not work like that," Jack said. "It went against all the rules, of both safety and security. We're not making a James Bond film and there were other ways to get the job done. Ronen's attempt to catch up with Jerry and Yuri was a correct move, Jerry's staying close to him was good but he should have stuck to his tail and aid should have been summoned from Holland. The job should not have been done by a lone operative. Yuri was a trained professional, and when he drew Jerry towards the toilet, it was a death trap. He already had his gun in his hand. Jerry beat him to it by a second, and that was pure luck."

But despite this, Jack praised us. "There's no doubt that neutralizing Yuri dealt a blow to the Iranian procurement effort. There's no sign that he had an assistant or that there's anyone who can step in and take his place. We're studying the material and trying to see if there are ways to get results by conferring with our counterparts in Europe, or if we'll have to prioritize new 'blue and white' all-Israeli ops. We don't have an infinite number of squads." That was supposed to be a joke but not one of us knew how many operational squads like us there actually were. When we spoke about it, Ronen guesstimated there were perhaps ten, but Jerry thought less. I had no idea.

The deputy chief wound up by saying that the mission had been accomplished only in part because the pictures of Udi and me, and perhaps of Niki, hadn't been found on Yuri's computer and could be flying around the world. There was no way of knowing who had them. It was also possible that the Dutch cops would get hold of the images of the man getting off the train at Breda and immediately taking the one back to Brussels, namely Jerry, and that they were doing the rounds at Interpol.

After the congratulatory part, we went on to our internal debriefing. I came out of it angry, because the reprimand I got for going into the train station without reporting and getting permission was at the same level as Niki's reprimand for failing to radio that she had her eyes on Yuri. This was seen as a purely operational decision: she didn't have approval for shooting him, and if she'd done so she'd have been caught; if she had reported in a manner that aroused his suspicion she might have been fired at by him, and in any case if she'd called us we wouldn't have got there before the train pulled out.

"I understand your reasons, but still I would have preferred you to have found a way to report and to leave it up to me to decide," said Udi, but he didn't indicate that he thought it was a grave error, especially after hearing her further explanations. In order to use her mike, she said, she'd have had to turn around, losing sight of the target, so we wouldn't have known if he'd boarded the train or not. He could have hidden somewhere along the platform and, had we rushed in, there could have been a blood bath.

I didn't know whether she was just selling Udi made-up pretexts that sounded professional and keeping her real reason, her debt to the English gentleman, to herself, or whether it was all in my head. I didn't ask her about it later, simply because we didn't speak later.

The material from Yuri's office, after it was sifted, pointed to fewer questionable companies than the experts had suspected. In order to disguise his illicit activities, he had also done a lot of legitimate deals, using only his fax and computer. But there were plenty of companies from which he'd purchased forbidden items, transferring them via his straw companies to Iran. Apart from the Norwegian and the Russian companies, there were also two companies in Austria and one each in Switzerland, Germany, Ukraine and Latvia. "As you see, it's easy to enlist the old anti-Semites, like the various German-speakers, Ukraine and Latvia, as well as the new anti-Semites who pose as anti-Israeli, and won't let themselves be outdone," Udi commented. Our team had been assigned to deal with the two Austrian companies. Other teams had been dispatched to the other countries where dialogue with the local services couldn't produce results.

I was pleased to work in Austria, a country that had not in any way paid for its hasty and eager identification with Nazi Germany. The Austrians managed to make the world forget the referendum that had shown almost unanimous support for the annexation of their country by Hitler and, since I was a boy, I had believed that their attempts to exonerate themselves and present themselves as victims were pathetic.

"Initial intelligence indicates that these are fairly easy assignments. Businesses that are ostensibly legitimate, with security precautions that are apparently nothing out of the ordinary," Udi said. "So we'll act simultaneously, with Ruth, Jerry and me in Salzburg and Boaz, Philip and Dave in Vienna."

There's no need to describe what I felt when I heard that Udi was separating Niki and me, and was taking her with him. I thought that at least I deserved to be informed in advance, before the whole team was told. Was he aware of what was happening between us? Had he told Niki in advance?

A kaleidoscope of different scenes and suspicions buzzed around in my head. Niki's admiration for Udi after their meeting in the little house in the Kiryah, her enthusing about him during her training, the way Udi excluded me from knowing anything about her, his hand on her shoulder as we left the car in Stockholm, the intimacy they must have experienced when he cut her thigh, the many hours she'd spent with him on our last night in Brussels, even if there was someone else there for some of the time. And now he was putting her on his team for Salzburg, and sending me hundreds of miles away, to Vienna. Why did he have to do that? What relationship would develop between them there? Would he send Jerry to one hotel and stay with Niki in another? I felt as if, under the surface, something was happening that I had no control over, and also no way of preventing, if I didn't want to look like an idiot. But in conditions like these, I didn't want to share the same apartment and the same bed with her.

Niki cried when I told her. She reiterated that she was doing everything for my sake, for my country and if I thought differently then, despite my overgrown physique, I had the mind of a foolish teenager. Even though I knew she was right, I couldn't overcome the jealousy pumping through my veins which was all the more frustrating because I didn't know if there was any real basis for it. I hoped, somehow, that Niki herself would take the matter up with Udi, that she would object to going with him instead of with me, but she was too disciplined a soldier. Or perhaps she wanted it that way.

I spent the night before the flight on the couch, stewing in my jealousy and unable to fall asleep. Niki, downcast, said nothing in the morning, but apparently she told Udi. When he called me to his office and tried to talk to me I cut him off with a rudeness that, once again, surprised me: "You're the last one who can open his mouth about this. What you've done to us is total 'divide and rule' – putting her in your crew, not bothering to explain why, and presenting me with a fait accompli, so now I'm saying that what happens between us is not your business, and I'm not prepared to discuss it with you."

"We'll talk when we get back," said Udi. "You two haven't yet honoured the promissory notes that you've signed."

I knew what he was talking about. In casual conversations over recent months, we'd heard over and over again references to what the chief and Udi had said at the outset: Niki and I were destined to carry out some assignment as a couple, in a dangerous target country. But right now, the "couple" part of that was something I could not really identify with. "Maybe you'll honour the note, with her," I blurted out. I really should not have said that, but couldn't help myself.

"Don't squander the credit that you've earned with me, Mickey," Udi said, using my real name, responding to my having shifted things onto the personal level. Instead of kicking me out he rose ponderously from his chair and walked out of his office, leaving me standing there.

✧✧✧

Our missions in Austria were straightforward and were over quickly. Udi decided we'd been working around the clock for too long, and he didn't want to take on complicated break-ins. Because they had been defined as "intimidation" and "alarm-bell" missions, meant to scare the companies in question and make the authorities aware of what was going on there, he decided that we'd suffice with placing incendiary devices in their premises, and with time fuses that gave us plenty of time to get away. We spent only one night on gathering pre-operational intelligence about night-time routines, their security arrangements and the frequency of police patrols, and the next night we executed. In Salzburg, Udi's crew broke into the grounds of the plant, put their firebombs at the entrances to the warehouse, the offices and the production facility. In Vienna, we set the devices in the office building and as "dessert" also in a number of trucks parked in the yard. At both places, we left press cuttings of news stories describing Yuri's demise.

The guards at the Salzburg plant called the fire brigade as soon as the warehouse bomb went off, earlier than it should have. When the other device exploded, the firemen were already on site, and it was extinguished immediately. The damage wasn't great but the police sealed off the area, not allowing even the company executives to enter, and confiscated hundreds of files and documents, leading to a cessation of the company's deals with Iran.

In Vienna, the offices were destroyed almost completely, something that we hadn't meant to happen. The fire brigade came across the blazing trucks first and decided to deal with them, summoning another unit to fight the office building fire.

The company got the message and here too the Iranian game was over, or at least that's what they said in an email to one of Yuri's firms, a message that elicited a cheer when it appeared on that firm's computer, which was now located in an office of the intelligence division of the Mossad in Tel Aviv.

Udi made sure that Niki and I would fly back to Israel together. He had apparently realized that his attempt to relate to us as two regular operatives and to ignore our relationship had harmed our common purpose. But it was too late. We checked in separately, sat a few rows away from one another, and didn't exchange a word.

Niki threw a glance at me every now and then but I had a block of ice lodged in my chest. She'd spent the previous night with Udi and Jerry. With Udi, as I saw it. The implications that this had for me were indelible and undeniable. I knew that jealousy was irrational and insane. Somewhere deep down inside me, inside all males, there were genes that made the possibility that someone else would impregnate their mate the equivalent of a death sentence: it was not their own genes which would pass on to the next generation, but the genes of another male. All the will in the world, all the common sense in the world, could not overcome the lunacy of jealousy, once it had been aroused.

When we landed in Tel Aviv, we were met by an Office driver who'd been instructed to take us to our apartment but I told him I was going to my parents in Haifa and he didn't have to bother about me. I'd take the direct train from the airport.

Niki gazed at me with an enormous sadness. Tears began running down her cheeks and she made no effort to hide them. Small and upright, she stood by the open door of the vehicle with her coat collar turned up, watching me without moving, without speaking.

Perhaps it was those tears that began to melt the block of ice jammed between my groin and my throat, while I was on my way to the station. They trickled and trickled in my mind, and a little while after the train was on its way, they reached the part of me that hadn't yet hardened, activated a secret mechanism there, and I felt that the block was melting. It began filling my throat and I needed to take deep breaths to stop it from bursting through to my eyes. How alone she had looked there, how miserable, and how very dear to me, still. After all there wasn't even an iota of blame that I could level at her, idiot that I was. All she had done was obey Udi's orders, and the whole situation could have been hurting her as much as it was hurting me. But she, and not I, was the one who knew whether anything had happened between them, and what. I felt helpless. All the things that I'd been afraid of were still there. Not as facts, but as possibilities, and no denial could simply wipe them away. In a certain sense, my woman had been taken away from me. But perhaps I was hallucinating? Perhaps jealousy was making me lose my mind? After all, she was here, in Israel and in the Mossad, for me. What else was there for her here, apart from me?

And apart from him, perhaps.

I'd meant to sleep at my parents' home but instead, as soon as I reached Haifa, I took the next train back to Tel Aviv. I needed to lay out before Niki all my fears and all my love. To find with her, a way of keeping us together. From my point of view, that would mean her being out of Udi's squad.

I arrived home just before midnight. Niki wasn't there. Her little trolley bag was in the entrance hall. I went down to the garage. Our car was gone.

The blood was hammering at my temples as I started the motorcycle and set out for the base. The parking lot there was visible through the fence and our car was standing there. So was Udi's. I felt as if my body was imploding. I hadn't slept for three days and nights but I had to know what was going on. I stayed there, standing next to my bike and watching, for over an hour, in the shadow of a deserted industrial structure opposite the entrance to the base, perspiring from suppressed tension.

At two a.m., Udi left the main building. He was stooped and walked with heavy steps to his car without looking left or right, threw his bag onto the backseat, laboriously plunked himself behind the wheel, and drove off. I expected Niki to follow immediately after him but she didn't. For about half an hour I kept on burning like a fire out there, debating whether to go in and have it out with her, but I knew that in my overheated state, I would ruin everything. What if she had simply gone back to sleep at the base because she didn't want to stay at home alone, after everything she'd been through? And what if Udi had simply been there to write up his mission reports, so they'd be with the division chief and the director of the Mossad next morning?

My bike's engine roared when I started it and I left my helmet off to let my head cool down as I rode back home.

The insistent ringing of the phone woke me a few minutes past eight. It took me a moment to realize where I was.

"Everyone's here already, waiting for you," I heard the voice of Irit, the secretary. Shit. I had collapsed onto the bed in my clothes and hadn't set the alarm. I looked around and saw Niki hadn't come home.

I quickly got myself organized to leave, and when I looked at my mobile phone I saw that I'd missed three calls, all of them from the apartment during the time I was on the train to and from Haifa.

This time again it was the deputy chief, Jack, who came to debrief us. The chief may have been with the squads that had gone to Ukraine or Latvia, Switzerland or Germany – we weren't given any information about them. There was some criticism of the methods we'd chosen to carry out our mission, to the effect that they were too simple and too open. We were told that two firemen had been injured, something we had not intended, and that prevented any dialogue with the Austrian authorities on the subject of the two companies.

"If they were people we could talk to from the start, then we wouldn't have needed this operation," Moshik remarked.

After the technical part of the debriefing, in which each operative described exactly where he had stood, what he had seen, where he had moved to, and all the others said whether they thought it could have been done better and more efficiently, Udi announced that the team would be on leave until the beginning of the next week – two days, plus the weekend. Then he told me to come to his office. I looked at Niki, who hadn't uttered a sound during the debriefing, apart from describing her part. She wouldn't let me catch her eye.

"Am I to understand that you two have broken up?" Udi let fly at me as soon as he'd closed the door and before he sat down at his desk. My heart dropped. Was this what Niki had told him?

"I didn't know we have to talk to you about what goes on between us."

"Boaz" – this time he made sure to let me know he was speaking as my commander, that this was a formal and not a personal conversation – "I am not a marriage counsellor. I have only one thing on my mind, operations. I am asking you because I have to know, for operational reasons."

"What's the connection? From your point of view, anyway, we are not a couple. Make whatever plans you have to."

"I asked you a simple question. Can you answer it?"

"I haven't spoken to her about it yet, so do you expect me to discuss it with you?"

"Don't worry, I do not take or deliver messages between the two of you. Tell her later whatever and however you want to tell her. I have to know . . ."

"If you don't deliver messages, how do you know precisely what is happening?" I interrupted. "Look, right now you're giving me a message from her."

"When the driver tells me you went to your parents, and then Ruth comes to sleep in her room at the base, one doesn't have to be a big genius to see something's gone wrong between you. And I also heard what you had to say before."

"'Something's gone wrong' is a correct description. And that's all I'm going to tell you."

"Does that mean I have to find another couple for the mission in Algeria?"

This destination was news to me. "I thought it was Tehran or Damascus?"

"That was urgent, we couldn't wait for you, and other teams have already set out. Right now we're prepping people for Beirut and Algiers, and I've made it clear that the state your relationship is in makes it impossible for me to give you Beirut. Algiers is a little easier for foreigners but the mission itself is a little complicated."

I grasped what Udi was telling me. There was an important mission, about which I still knew nothing, and there were other people who would execute it if I said no. And no, I did not want another couple to go there. I wanted to be there. I had to be there.

"You don't need us as a couple. You need us as two operatives with the cover of a couple. And that's what you have. All the rest is none of your business."

"It's more complex than the way you've put it. The mission requires you to behave like a couple, and at the moment it doesn't look like you can do it. I'm also looking to the future, beyond Algiers. I have to know what's happening between you."

"What's happening between us is not even clear to me," I said finally. "But I think that even if we do stay together, both of us won't remain part of this team."

"You're thinking about leaving?"

"Me?" I was astonished. "No. But I don't think I can go on when Ruth's here too." I could also be formal and use her codename.

"Because?"

"We've already spoken about it. Ask yourself."

"Don't think you're acting in a film here, Boaz. It doesn't suit you. Ruth is an outstanding operative. I do not want to lose either you or her."

"You'll have to choose."

Udi sighed. "Again, I'm not your marriage counsellor. As I see it, what you're saying now is that I don't have a couple for the Algiers operation. It's a pity but I'll have to live with it. The State of Israel will have to live with it. Whatever the case, I'll have to know where the thing stands. From her I have not heard any notions about leaving. For me, she is in. On Sunday, when we get back from leave, tell me where you stand."

I felt the ground trembling under my feet. This could be a twist in the plot that I hadn't thought of. Niki staying, with me or without me. I had perceived our relationship as her condition for joining and staying in the Mossad. Was there a substitute for that, for me? Namely Udi?

When I left his office, I felt that my ability to resolve the triangle of me-Niki-the Mossad, or me-Niki-Udi, was slight. And somehow I lacked the energy to have it out with Niki, now that I had been faced with the possibility that she would stay on in any case.

I slipped into Moshik's office when I saw him sitting there, to avoid having to go past the room where Niki was.

"What's the story with Algiers?" I asked him, without any preliminaries.

Moshik had seen me going into the meeting with Udi, and apparently assumed that Udi had briefed me. He wasn't the most discreet of men, as I had already learned, and he willingly filled me in.

"Since we wrecked the Iranian supply route to Gaza via Sudan with that air raid, and since you bumped off their Khartoum office staff, almost all their weapons assistance has been going through Damascus and from there to Beirut. Half stays with Hezbollah, and the other half is shipped by sea to El Arish, and from there in tunnels to Gaza. That route has also been given quite effective negative treatment, some of it by other Mossad squads and some by the naval commandos and the air force. You've heard of the attacks on convoys in the Bekaa valley in Lebanon, and the seizure of boats carrying arms. But recently alarming amounts have been coming in, and there are indications that the Iranians have found a new corridor – via Algeria and from there direct to Beirut."

"How come Algeria? It's a long way off the route."

"You know that in recent years there's been a civil war going on there, with about a hundred thousand dead, because the Islamic party won the elections and the army didn't let it take over the government. So the Iranians have hitched a ride on the situation there."

"Meaning what?"

"In the beginning they funded and armed the Islamist militias, who perpetrated worse acts of terrorism in Algeria than anywhere else in the world, but as it wasn't happening in Israel it didn't make the headlines here. When the Iranians saw that wasn't helping – because the Algerian army also massacres without thinking twice – they apparently did a deal with the army. If it permitted them to use Algeria as a hub for weapons shipments, they'd stop arming the militias. It's not altogether clear," he added when he saw the perplexed expression on my face, "but what is clear is that the situation is enabling them to ship arms via both air and sea, in the guise of innocent cargo. If it's by air, they change the planes' call signs, markings and flight numbers, and they continue on to Lebanon as if they were Algerian aircraft. We have to do something about it."

"What's that something?"

"First, to get a grip of what's actually happening. What planes or ships are bringing the stuff in, and how it is then sent on to Lebanon. Other units are trying to find out what exactly the Iranian involvement is in Algeria, and who in the government is working with them. Then it will be decided how to act and against whom."

"And what's our role?"

"After Udi made it known that you had potential as a couple, it was decided that part of the intelligence gathering would be up to you, and we've been waiting for you to be free and ready for it."

"When you say 'you,' you mean Ruth and me?"

"Correct. It needs impeccable cover, which she has, and when you're teamed up with her, it extends to you too."

"And aren't there any others like us in the other teams?"

"Each team is tailor-made according to the requirements of the mission and there are already teams doing what they have to do. After we analyzed the Algiers mission, it was clear that a couple was needed. You surely don't want Ruth to be teamed up with someone else," he chuckled, not knowing that he was treading on very sensitive ground.

"I don't get it."

"Well, you're taking me into matters of cover, which I don't know about and don't want to go into. But I'll tell you what I do know, intelligence-wise. We'll have operatives in Iran to report when a consignment is dispatched. Intelligence will keep track of the plane or the ship, and your job will be to keep a lookout on the airfield, or the port, or both, and to identify the arrival of this kind of cargo, and report when it departs. Then there'll be a team in Beirut to observe their arrival there and complete the puzzle."

"Sounds a bit far-fetched," I said. "How are we supposed to know precisely which plane or ship is the one."

"You don't know everything yet and you aren't familiar with all of our capabilities," Moshik put me in my place. "If it's a ship, there's no problem at all, because you'll be able to keep a lookout from your hotel room in Algiers. I've already located a suitable hotel. If it's a plane, you'll get exact intelligence on the time of departure, the model, the colours, and there will be a whole array of means of knowing exactly when it is due to land and ready for take-off. You'll just have to verify the flag change and so on. You don't need to know any more."

"It's still not clear why a couple's is needed, or particularly airtight cover."

"This is a job that will take time. For example, we don't know if the ships are unloaded in the port and the containers are then loaded onto other vessels, or if they change their names and flags and sail on from there, and that will require a stay of a few days in Algiers, in your hotel, or even recon patrols in the port itself. And if it's a plane that takes off in Iran, let's say in the afternoon or the evening, then you'll have to be at your lookout post at night, and our research has told us that's a place where no normal foreigner could have any logical reason for being and that there are security patrols there. From what I understand, the planners reached the conclusion that your cover is just about the only one that will work: an artist who has decided to paint the sunset from that point, or Algiers by night, and it's better that he's got a girlfriend with him so if they stay there until late at night they can pretend to be lovers who couldn't control their passion, or something like that."

Moshik noticed my dismay and saw fit to add: "Don't take me at my word. As I've said, I don't deal with cover stories. Just heard some things."

"Why does it have to be us? Surely the huge Mossad can find male and female operatives with cover that entails having sex before, during and after?"

"I agree with you that this is a dumb kind of moral code," Moshik bent over towards me and whispered, "because whenever we put a male and a female into the field with the cover of a couple, even when they don't have to fuck, they never pass up the opportunity." He burst out laughing. "But the huge Mossad has found original solutions, and I know of at least another two teams that have already had such missions, because they came up with the required operational tool. That is to say, they picked the right operatives and custom-built their cover according to the mission and the circumstances on the ground."

I exhaled the air that had been trapped in my lungs. The ship mission sounded simple, the aircraft one more complicated, and both seemed to be important. But so far I didn't feel a sense of compulsion or commitment. Moshik apparently detected this, and again he bent towards me.

"You still have to get the intelligence in an orderly fashion. But only so you're not in for a surprise, I'll tell you this: because of the situation in Jordan and Syria, all kinds of characters on our wanted list have been looking for places to take it easy, outside of the region. Algeria is accepting them with open arms. Bassam al-Sultan went there not long ago, and we know he's taken up residence in a nice house overlooking the sea in the Casbah."

While Moshik was imagining the hotel room overlooking the port or the slopes of the hill overlooking the airfield, I was now picturing the narrow alleys of the Casbah. There, living in relative peace and quiet, was Bassam al-Sultan, the top of the pyramid responsible for killing Dolly and five other people in that particular suicide bombing, and the deaths of dozens of others and the wounding of many hundreds in other terrorist attacks both before and after it. This was reason enough for me to do everything necessary to get there.

The tension between Niki and me wasn't a secret in the squad, and I saw the anticipation on the faces of my colleagues as I walked up to Niki, who was concentrating on some paperwork.

"I'm done here. You coming?"

She turned to me. Her downcast features lit up for a moment, and then darkened again. She had not seen in my face what she had hoped to see.

"I'm coming," she said, and tidied her desktop with a few absent-minded movements.

I'd arrived in a taxi that morning because it was raining heavily so we naturally went home together in our car, which was in the car park from the previous night.

There was no way that I could put off talking about the things between us that had to be cleared up.

"I don't know yet about the upcoming mission, but I want you to leave the squad after it's finished," I said. "This whole set-up, with you and me under Udi, with Udi manipulating us however he sees fit, with him teaming you up with himself – I can't live with it."

"I know. I've spoken to him about it."

"And . . .?"

Niki raised her beautiful eyes to look at me. "You are important to me. Our relationship is important to me. But if it has suddenly just about broken up about nothing, or perhaps about stuff that crossed your mind and that never actually happened, then I don't know. I don't know if my leaving the squad will solve anything. Something else will crop up to make you jealous. I think you have to learn to get over it."

She was talking like someone who'd been in psychological counselling.

"It is not exactly jealousy," I replied with the answer I'd worked out in advance over the past few hours. "It's knowing clearly that someone in my immediate surroundings is doing whatever he feels like doing with my woman."

Niki gaped at me.

"I don't mean actual sex. I mean that as the commander he does whatever he sees fit with you, without taking me into account at all."

"And as the commander he does whatever he sees fit with you, without taking me into account at all," Niki shot back. "Have you considered that when he put you in Vienna and me in Salzburg, he wasn't only taking me away from you, but also you from me? So why don't I feel the same way as you do? Why do I see it as part of a commander's legitimate considerations, exactly the same as separating Ronen and Jerry?"

"How is that the same? They aren't a couple."

"We are a couple to Udi when he needs a couple. Not when he doesn't."

I drove around the streets of Tel Aviv, as the rain poured down. I didn't want us to go home with empty hearts but there was also a gloomy silence in the car. When the rain died down, I stopped next to a small café.

We were alone there. I held my cup of latte tight in my hands as the rain started up again and rattled down onto the glass ceiling, and I told Niki what I knew about the Algiers mission.

"I know. Udi told me. And there are a few more under way, in Tehran, Damascus and Beirut."

Again my mood plummeted. I'd had to prise it out of Moshik.

"How come he told you?"

"I remembered what the chief said about us operating as a couple, and I told Udi I wasn't sure it would happen, because you'd walked out on me."

"I walked out?"

"So what do you call it, when before that last op you slept on the couch, and when we got back you went to your parents and didn't come home?"

"I still don't understand why he told you."

"Because I asked. I asked what I was missing because of it."

"So it's not me that you're losing out on, but the Algiers gig?"

Niki sighed. "I really do not know you. And you really don't get it. Algeria isn't an enemy that I was raised hating. It's all about you. It's all you."

We were not managing to get it together. This unfamiliar, unlikely tough-mindedness on Niki's part, her refusal to say she'd leave the team – I tied it all in with the special relationship that had evolved between her and Udi. Perhaps the two of them were only waiting for us to get back from Algiers, and then Udi would send me packing and stay with Niki? How could I know?

Again, we put off going back to our apartment. We went to a film that was supposed to be a romantic action film about a couple of married agents ordered to kill each other, but whose love triumphs (as it had between Brad Pitt and Angelina Jolie when they made the picture). But it turned out to be an idiotic comedy full of scenes of impossible sharpshooting, and didn't do anything to make happen what both of us wanted. It was close to midnight when we left the cinema. It was clear to me that anything I did now, apart from going home with Niki, would be a highly dramatic move and create a situation from which it would be difficult to retreat. We entered the apartment with empty hearts. We got into bed together, and we even held hands, but the mountain of problems dividing us and the memory of the terrible sex we'd had last time stopped us from going further.

Without becoming lovers again, we did decide one thing: we both wanted to go on the Algiers mission. To me it was very important, because it was perhaps the greatest contribution I could make, and to Niki – because it was so important to me. That, at least, was what she said, and I preferred not to think about the other possibilities. We'd work out the rest when the time came.

On Sunday, back at the base, we both lied to Udi.

"We want the mission," I told Udi in her presence. "We are all set to do it."

"I'll accept what you are saying but not necessarily because I truly believe it," Udi looked me in the eye first and then Niki, "but because I have no other option. Two other teams have already carried out similar jobs in Tehran and Damascus, with terrific results. A third team has been prepped for Beirut and they have been working on their cover for a long time: they are all set to go. Another team is also ready for Iran, and the Office needs all three to work together, in synchrony. I cannot lag behind.

"We have to reach a situation in which you'll be able to keep an airstrip under observation day and night, at short notice. If we don't tie up the loose ends, there can be no green light for hitting the weapons when they are unloaded, or being shipped in trucks out of Beirut airport. So I simply have to accept what you are telling me, even though the expressions on your faces are saying something else. But I will be able to assess the situation before the op, because I am going to be there with you."

When he saw the astonishment on my face, he quickly added, with a wry smile, "Don't worry, not in the same hotel room."

✧✧✧

Awareness of what we were to expect didn't make our faltering relationship any better. Circumstances had forced us to be together, but it was no more than an unsuccessful attempt at artificial respiration. With each night that went by without sex, and mostly without even affectionate hugs, the realization grew in me that this was going to be not only our last joint mission but also the end of the great love we had shared. If I hadn't known that leaving our home would mean cancellation of the operation, I would have walked out. Perhaps Niki felt the same. She was with me now only when she had to be, and for the rest of the time I didn't know where she was. Once, when I noticed that both she and Udi were away from the base, and I asked her about it, she narrowed her eyes and said: "As I told you in Toronto, that was the last time you ask me and the last time I answer that question. I also told you not to expect me to wait for you, if you decide to leave. Physically or emotionally."

And that's the way I was left, with a host of questions and doubts, living under cover in my own country and in my own home, trying to deceive my own commander – but perhaps deceiving no one but myself.

We soon entered the stage of intensive training, day and night, and we had almost no time alone together, especially not at our apartment, and no time to examine what was happening to our relationship.

We went through almost two weeks of training, working on details of our cover, and on how to use my camera's telescopic lens and the night vision device to make identifications of ships and planes in daylight and in the dark. We put a lot of time into learning the various types of cargo planes according to their shape and colour by day and their lights by night. We studied material on the city of Algiers, which I discovered was a metropolis with over two million inhabitants, and from the pictures and films Moshik showed us, it also looked like quite an exciting place. The old part, high on the hills, made up of steep narrow streets and antiquated buildings, known as the Casbah, was where Bassam al-Sultan had taken refuge. The lower part of the city which had been built by the French after they conquered the country in 1830 was more modern.

Situated in the middle of Algeria's long and jagged coastline – over 600 miles, between the borders with Tunisia and Morocco – the city boasted two ports. Because of the hilly range running parallel and close to the shore, the airfields were some distance away. According to Moshik's intelligence, the military cargo planes from Iran didn't land at the civilian Houari Boumediene airport, about twelve miles to the east of the city, but at a military airfield located in a sheltered valley in the hills to the west. We would be able to watch the port where the cargo ship could be expected to dock, but not the airfield. To do that we would have to scout out a good lookout position in the surrounding hills which had nice names like Mont Plaisant, and Djebel Koukou.

After we were well acquainted with the theoretical material, we drove out to the hills outside Jerusalem where Moshik had scouted locations as similar as possible to what we would encounter on the outskirts of Algiers, from the points of view of topography, terrain, and distance from the landing strip. We practised navigating up the slopes of the hills, keeping watch with the telescopic lens and night vision device, and retreating back down. On the last evening, when we had the technical stuff down pat, the HQ staffers began to stage troublesome situations, such as the arrival of a military patrol, or a bunch of ruffians showing up to harass us. There was no problem at all with anything to do with my painting but when it came to acting out our cover as lovers, things were awkward. If we were to be caught just after sundown, we could explain with the help of paintings that I would do in advance and finish off in Algiers, and say we were having a picnic supper. But if we had to wait for a landing or take-off later in the night, or in the early morning hours, the only reasonable explanation would be for us to have been making love, and deciding to spend the rest of the night there in each other's arms.

Our awkwardness was understood by the HQ people as embarrassment, unwillingness to perform a love scene just for their benefit. It was only on Udi's face that I saw doubt and dissatisfaction. He did not believe our relationship had returned to normal, but he drew the line at interfering.

All the prepping didn't leave us much time for sleep, and when we came home just before daybreak, we dropped exhausted into bed, almost without saying anything, and certainly without touching one another.

✧✧✧

Moshik summoned me to his office where there was a large optical machine through which aerial photographs were spooled and could be seen in 3D through a special eyepiece. The intention was for me to memorize the terrain as well as possible, including the point where we'd go off the road, how to navigate to the lookout position, and the places on the way where I could set up an easel and where we could lay out our picnic. Niki was supposed to take my place at the eyepiece when I was finished.

After I'd been there about an hour, Moshik announced that he was going to eat, but I said I wanted to keep going, and found myself alone in the intelligence officer's room. As had often happened in the past, I realized that there was a plan in my head even before I was conscious of it: I quickly went through the files in an open cabinet and discovered one labelled "Algiers – Casbah – Activists". I found Bassam al-Sultan's name in the index and on the page indicated, there was a photograph of the man and a description of his place of residence, as reported by an agent whose reliability was classified as "unknown"; a sketch of the way to get there, and an enlarged detail from an aerial photo on which his house was marked.

I knew I didn't have much time. I took a sheet of paper from the printer, and made a quick sketch of the aerial photo, trying to memorize the details I wouldn't manage to draw. The diagonal angle of the shot made it possible to see the façade of the little house, and I drew it, as well as some of the salient structures at the entrance to the alley and near the house, and then, rapidly, the man's face.

After I'd replaced the file and folded and pocketed the sketches, I knew the die had been cast. I would do what the state wanted me to do, but I would also do what my conscience compelled me to do.

In the remaining days, I studied the field files Moshik left with us and, as well as memorizing the ways of getting to the observation points, I worked out how to navigate through the alleys inside the Casbah. The maps, aerial photographs and reports of operatives who had been there enabled me to construct a reasonably good route to al-Sultan's house. On a tourist map I found that there was a pottery centre at one end of his street, and a jewellery centre at the other. That would give me an excuse for moving along the street and back again, and perhaps I could even order something and return the next day to pick it up.

When Udi notified us that we were leaving in two days' time, I was taken aback. There were still big holes in our cover story and we'd hardly spoken at all about contingencies and responses. Dozens of things could go wrong between the moment we landed in Algiers and the time we left, and especially during the time we were in the hills observing the landing strip. We were liable to be challenged at any given moment, but we had few alternative cover stories. Clearly, being discovered at night with the night vision device in our possession would demand one response, while being stopped on the road, with Udi a short distance away, would demand another. A different pretext would be needed for each set of circumstances, and my painting, or making out with Niki – the only options that had been prepared – would not be relevant or logical in all of them.

I remarked upon this to Udi. And to myself I observed that I had not prepared a contingency and response plan for my own private mission, or even the means of carrying out the kill and making a getaway.

"The new team is already on the way to Tehran, the Beirut team leaves tomorrow, and there is no alternative here – we leave the day after tomorrow. Whatever hasn't been tied up, we'll tie up in the field," he replied. I didn't like either his answer or the whole situation, and I didn't understand why they couldn't hold up the other teams, who'd been training for a long time, until we were also ready. I said so.

"The shipments are getting from Tehran to Beirut via Algiers at the rate of one plane a day. Every day's delay means another few hundred missiles that will drop on our country in the next war. The entire defence establishment is waiting for our information. There's no way that a suspicious aircraft, or an airfield, or a convoy can be attacked if there's a risk that we'll discover afterwards that we made a mistake. It can be done only if there is one hundred per cent solid info. And we can't wait any longer. We've held everyone up long enough."

I saw this as a personal reprimand and kept quiet but I felt a sense of foreboding, especially when I learned that only Udi would have a weapon concealed in his luggage. In my mind, I pictured all kinds of things that could go wrong that we hadn't even discussed, and then there was my own personal plan, for which I would need a weapon.

"I don't like the idea of us being on the hill without a weapon," I ventured.

"A handgun could not save you from an army patrol, only a good cover story, and having a gun would ruin that," Udi replied.

Niki listened to the argument with eyes wide-open and frightened.

I said: "You know as well as I do that if three or four soldiers come across us without suspecting that we are armed, I could take them all out in a matter of seconds."

"And then we'd have to try to make an insane getaway, with no chance at all of success. And if they come at you with loaded rifles at the ready, you may be able to kill one or even two, but then they'd mow both of you down. Argument over."

"I want to take it up with the chief. It's my ass – and Niki's – that you're putting on that hilltop without protection."

"These are the chief's own orders," said Udi. "Have no doubt, it's been discussed in depth, we've presented him with all the different possibilities, and this was the conclusion. But nevertheless, I'll pass your objections on."

6.

Algerian Nights

As we boarded the plane, and again as we approached our destination, I pulled Niki towards me and hugged her. She looked like a stranger, with her hair cut differently and dyed darker, and I probably seemed like a stranger to her, with the moustache I had grown. I didn't know if she was also experiencing the horrible wrenching feeling that I had, a feeling that wasn't quite fear and not quite excitement but an unpalatable cocktail of both, plus a whole lot of other emotions I couldn't define. The chief and Udi had said that the sense of adventure dies as you are about to board a plane for Tehran or Damascus, and what keeps you going is patriotism only. It was true, I found, even when the destination was marginally less perilous, like Algiers. Niki's face gave nothing away, but her response to my hug was immediate. I don't know which one of us needed it more. I think we were both pleased that the hug was even part of the operational orders. "At the departure point, on the flight and upon landing, you are to behave like a pair of lovers, without attracting too much attention." Someone was apparently worried that we'd stage a hot French kiss. That clearly wasn't going to happen.

As the Algerian shoreline emerged, we both tensed up. From a distance, the coast looked jagged, with green mountains rising nearby, and beyond them a brownish landscape. But when the plane circled before landing, I saw the picture that Moshik had described: a vast brown and white city that spread out along the shore extending to the north and east, and ascended into the green hills. To the west of the city, the hills became mountains, also green, with scattered neighbourhoods climbing up their slopes. We tried to spot the military landing strip hidden in a valley but couldn't. Our plane continued its descent, banked to the east and the city below thinned out, giving way to cultivated fields. Just before touching down we saw, to our left, the buildings of Dar El Beida, the white suburb on whose outskirts lies the international airport, with the sea beyond it, and fields stretching to the south, and the desert beyond.

The new terminal of the Houari Boumediene airport was still under construction, but we got an impression of a cluster of interconnected round structures, with boarding bridges protruding from them. Most were still raw concrete, but some had been faced in white stone, and green glass towers, apparently extensions of the stairwells and elevator shafts, rose above them.

My stomach wrenching intensified as we headed for passport control. At the security briefing before we left, Moshik and Udi had repeated the warning that the enemy had pictures of Udi and me, "and perhaps of Niki too". Which enemy wasn't clear but it was very likely that Yuri had received them from Gimbers and passed them on to the Iranians. What the Iranians had done with them, no one knew. They could have distributed them to their intelligence stations in Europe and to their allies in the "Axis of Evil", particularly the Syrian and Hezbollah intelligence agencies, and if the assessments of a new Iranian-Algerian connection were correct, the pictures could also be here.

"So why are you sending the three of us out there together?" I'd asked, although I was tempted not to do so, for fear of appearing overly anxious.

"Because we do not know," Udi answered, not exactly aptly. "And if we cancel operations or erase operatives because they may be recognized, we may as well shut down the business and emigrate to Canada."

Clearly, the mention of Canada had been a rebuke, and I'd dropped the subject, but now, in the arrivals hall in Algiers, it surfaced again in my thoughts. Our pictures could be right here, with the border control officer, on a "wanted" list. The moustache might deceive the officer, if he didn't closely examine the "wanted" picture or Ron Friedlich's passport photo. The chances that Niki had been caught by the CCTV camera as she sat in the car seemed slim to me, and the possibility that she'd be recognized from a shot like that was small indeed, especially with her new hairdo. It dawned on me that Niki had a clear advantage over me, and not only because of the photographs. She could be coming here as an innocent Canadian tourist, and the authorities would have no reason at all to suspect her. And just as she could serve as my life line, I could be her handicap. Despite all the preparations, the well-established cover, the authentic documentation, I was an Israeli. Someone who was born in Israel and had lived there some thirty years, a Jew, and it was impossible to gloss over that. I was relieved that, unlike Udi, I didn't have to cope with smuggling in a double-bottomed suitcase, with the dismantled pistol and night vision device hidden there: a slight compensation for having my demand to be armed turned down by the chief.

Niki went up to the border control booth just ahead of me. I'd decided it would be better not to be a stumbling block in this situation, so I dropped back a little. Her passport was stamped and returned to her. I stepped forward and gave the officer my passport. Would he check it against a wanted list? Would the moustache raise questions in his mind? He opened it casually, and gave Ron's picture and then me cursory glances, and stamped it. I exhaled in relief.

I told the taxi driver to take us to the Sofitel Hotel. A quite modern overpass at the exit from the airport put us on the N5 highway and we sped towards the sea until we reached the outskirts of the city itself, where the road ran along the shoreline and bore the impressive name of the Boulevard of the Army of National Liberation.

As we drove by the seashore, I was strongly reminded of the Arab part of Haifa, with the hills rising to our left and the old buildings covering them. Close to the port, the cab turned onto a narrow street and stopped at the entrance to the Sofitel.

Like most of the city, the Sofitel was white. It was an impressive, although not very large, building, four or five storeys high, with tall pillars at the front, and the floors above them presenting a uniform façade with blue-tinted windows. Nimble and polite bellboys took our luggage. The receptionist, backed by a wall of striking mosaics, was expecting our arrival and check-in was rapid. He asked us to leave our passports to be photographed and inspected, a routine procedure that nevertheless made me nervous. The elevator boy showed us to our room which was large and gleaming, with a parquet floor and gilt decorations on the walls and, as promised, it overlooked the port. As soon as I drew the curtains and saw the view I felt a slight relief – at least I was spared the need to ask for a room change.

If the planners at HQ had intended Niki and me to jump onto the bed immediately while the Mukhabarat agents on the hotel staff watched via cameras secreted in the mirrors, the lamps, the radio, wherever, that was not going to happen. We unpacked in almost total silence and, to relieve the uncomfortable tension between us, we went out to take a first look at the city.

In front of the hotel was a manicured garden and beyond that the imposing Martyrs' Memorial, honouring the vast numbers of Algerians who died in the country's bloody war to achieve liberation from French rule. The huge concrete monument was made up of what appeared to be three giant palm fronds forming a triangular structure, with an eternal flame at its centre.

If the Algerians could overcome their incalculable losses and the atrocities of the French colonial regime which dwarfed the injustices of Israel's occupation of Palestinian territories, perhaps there was a chance for peace, sometime, between us and the Palestinians, I thought, and I even mentioned it to Niki. The expression on her face clearly meant, that's not something to talk about here, and of course she was right.

From the memorial, we took a short cab ride to some of the other sights of the lower, French-built part of the city. Only a minute's drive away was the National Museum of Antiquities, where Niki enjoyed the beautiful Ottoman mansion which housed it, more than the artefacts. We saw the National Library and stopped to look at the presidential palace, a single-storey structure, painted brown and white and ornamented with pointed arches in the Moorish style, splendid in its simplicity.

The two main mosques of the city were the Jama'a al-Kebir, or the Great Mosque, which was almost a thousand years old, and what is known as the New Mosque, although it is some 300 years old. They are both situated in the Casbah which Niki and I could now visit like any other tourists.

Both buildings were impressive – the former because of its enormous size and because of the way its ancient component parts were preserved over a millennium: major renovation work a century ago had been sensitively carried out – and the second for the Ottoman architecture that gave it its four minarets.

The Casbah on the hill overlooking the Bay of Algiers was a city in itself and it was clear to me that I'd have to go back there to scout out the home of Bassam al-Sultan, my own private target.

I took photographs of Niki from all possible angles and I asked another tourist to take a picture of us together. I hugged her as any lovers would. We held hands as we walked along but the tiny hand in mine was cold, and when she enthused about various items in a souk we came across, I did not sense genuine joy or interest.

The combination of the old upper city and the lower city with its modern design and architecture and large numbers of French automobiles, created a cosmopolitan atmosphere that surprised us both. One site in the centre intrigued us in particular. A kind of rectangular plaza sloped up towards a hill, with the sea below on one side and a well-tended park with giant palm trees in the middle. It was fringed by gleaming white five- to seven-storey buildings in a style which I thought could be called colonial. They reminded me of the large, attractive Arab buildings in Jaffa. All had balconies with balustrades painted blue and, at pavement level, there were cafés and restaurants with colourful parasols. The central post office, five storeys tall with three gigantic Moorish arches, dominated the square. Like all the other buildings, it too was white.

"What a lovely place," said Niki. "Let's sit down in one of the cafés."

For the first time, I felt a little like a tourist. The Parisian atmosphere, the well-cared-for old buildings and everything else that wasn't Parisian but typically Algerian, gave the place a special touch that captivated us. We smiled at each other and for a moment, one brief moment, the old intimacy was back. But when Niki saw hummus on the menu, one of the few words she recognized, and wanted to order it, I signalled to her to drop it. As Canadians, we had no reason for ordering it. The spark that had lit up in her eyes a moment before went out.

Instead, I ordered a croque monsieur and a croque madame and as dessert, French toast that came swamped in a sickening amount of syrup and was topped by banana rings.

When I thought we'd done enough to bolster our cover, we returned to the hotel in silence. In the remaining hours of daylight I decided to conduct some preliminary recon up in the Casbah. Niki's eyes showed disbelief when I said I wanted "to walk around alone for a while in the main street," but she saw in my eyes that there was no point in arguing.

"Just like a pair of lovers would do," she said with sarcasm and pain, and I responded in a similar vein, saying, "So he can surprise her with an Algerian bracelet engraved with her name in Arabic."

The expression on her face softened. How much she needs me to show affection, I thought, and I also felt a light tremor of love, diluted by sorrow and helplessness, rising inside me. What a pity that I was lying. That I'd order a bracelet, yes, but in the jewellery centre in the Casbah as part of a cover plan and intelligence gathering for an operation that was likely to separate us forever.

✧✧✧

Steep streets led up to the Casbah, some paved and some loose gravel, lined by houses of one to four storeys with tidy courtyards adorned with colourful bougainvillea. Here too the dominant colour was white. As in many Arab towns, sewage ran through the streets, and there were hosts of children, pedlars, bicycle and tricycle riders and donkey-drawn carts. I remembered exactly where al-Sultan lived but I directed my cab driver to the pottery centre, at one end of his street. After buying a set of six coffee cups and a jug, I walked cautiously down the narrow alley and soon spotted the house. It was relatively large, surrounded by a high wall, with a broad gate. The Palestinian Islamic Jihad apparently took good care of its top activists.

As I stood in the entrance of the jewellery centre, waiting for Niki's name to be engraved on the gold bracelet that I'd bought without bargaining over the price, a black Pajero SUV drove by, entered the alley, and stopped at the entrance to al-Sultan's house. The driver got out of the vehicle, opened the gate, got back in and manoeuvred the Pajero into the property. I didn't see his face, and I wasn't sure if this was my target or not. I calculated that his action had left me enough time to cover the twenty-odd yards that had separated us, to enter the yard behind him, to make sure he was al-Sultan and to pump bullets into him. Bullets from a gun I didn't have. But I could stick a knife into him, I thought.

I glanced at my watch and looked around me. The man had probably come home after a day's work at the Islamic Jihad office. He was likely to do the same the next day and the one after. Then I'd be waiting for him right here, in the car that I was going to rent in any case, with the shabriyeh, the ornate Arab dagger that I'd buy in a shop in the main street, as no doubt many tourists did. As soon as he drove his car home, I'd close the gap between us and, perhaps, as I drove the curved blade into his heart I'd tell him, "This is for Dolly, No. 4 bus, Allenby Street, September 19,

2002." Or perhaps I'd say nothing, because this wasn't a Hollywood film, and I'd leave the shabriyeh in his body and hurry to my car and clear out, tossing the gloves that I'd buy for the occasion into a rubbish bin.

And because this really wasn't a Hollywood movie, I'd have to plan how to get out of Algeria before security at the airport was tightened. In the haste with which we'd left Israel, I had not managed to plan either the means of eliminating al-Sultan or the getaway. Killing him and then swinging at the end of a rope in the city square was not what I had in mind. Only now did it occur to me that if I did not want to endanger Niki and Udi, I'd have to stay behind after they left and then do the job. And to prevent them from interfering with my plan, I'd have to go to the airport with them, and disappear at the last moment, after they had checked in and couldn't come looking for me.

My head was bursting with ideas and plans. The voice of the jeweller presenting me with the engraved bracelet brought me back to reality.

On the way back to the hotel I went into a souvenir shop and bought a handsome shabriyeh with a slight curve to its blade, a decorative sheath and a handle studded with cheap white stones, like many of the ornaments for sale in the shop. It was undoubtedly a tourist souvenir, but also an effective weapon.

Niki was thrilled with the bracelet and immediately clasped it around her thin wrist. She kissed me and pressed her body against mine in a way that could have easily led to love making. I shuddered. My woman was indeed thirsty for a simple demonstration of her mate's love. With what cold practicality I had brought her what she saw as a lover's gift, but was in fact nothing more than a way of creating cover, cover for an act that was liable to lead to the end of our relationship. How wide the rift between us had become.

At first, I couldn't understand why I was not thawing out, not responding to Niki's small demonstrations of affection. Udi and HQ expected us, as hinted at in our operational orders, to make love that night, in case the Algerian intelligence services were secretly observing us. But this wasn't the right thing to do. I could not sleep with her at the same time as I was planning this deed that would in all likelihood terminate our relationship, and when it was my deceitful present that had aroused her.

We did cuddle and kiss each other when we got into bed although Niki was a little put off by my moustache. I kissed her on the neck, and she stroked my lower abdomen, but for the first time in my life, my organ did not respond, not even slightly.

I switched the lights off and we lay there in each other's arms. Enough time for whoever may have been watching us – I thought this was being done through the open jaws of a pair of lions that adorned the dresser – to surmise that something was happening. But nothing was. Niki's body trembled in my embrace with what could have been sobs, but I didn't ask. When she rolled off my chest and turned her back to me, she trembled again, but differently, and then I heard the moan of her orgasm, a deep sigh and then silence.

Why doesn't this stupid assignment, which Niki was taking so literally, come to an end, I thought to myself. Then I would be free to achieve my own personal closure.

And then what?

Would my great commitment be over and done with, and if I survived, would I be able to go back to Niki, body and soul? That large and solid obstacle in the form of Udi would still be there waiting for me. And Niki, even if she overcame my deception, and the hours of anxiety after it turned out that I'd vanished at the airport and imperilled myself in a pointless act of vengeance, would she still want me at all, after my manhood had wilted in her hands? Like any normal man, no matter how good looking or successful, I felt that my ultimate test was my performance in bed. It wasn't reason that determined the supremacy of this test, but millions of years of evolution. And that same evolutionary consideration stirred in Niki's genes too, as well as in those of every other female who wants the best genes for her children. We'd had some fantastic sex in the past, but now I'd shown she couldn't rely on that in the future.

Niki's shivering and groans did not mean I could assume she was merely carrying out the operational orders. She had really wanted me. And I, as a man, had crumbled away right next to her. The preplanned love that Udi had tried to tailor for us in Canada led me to clear out of there, and the preplanned sex act that he had tried to tailor for us in the orders for Algiers had destroyed our love completely.

Udi arrived the next day and checked into the El Aurassi Hotel, on the way to Mont Plaisant, the mountain from which we would have a view of the military airfield. On the way there Niki reminded me that this was also the name of the hill in northern Toronto where her parents lived. The hotel was built like Hyatt hotels, with all the floors overlooking the lobby atrium and, as we entered, she couldn't help whispering to me, "Just like the Office in Tel Aviv."

We met in the lobby, and this was the first time that the sight of Udi, with his silver goatee, didn't evoke the warmth and confidence that, in the past, I'd absorbed from him, but rather a sourness. That only increased when he kissed Niki and shook my hand. He led us to one of the seating clusters and ordered Arabic coffee, so we'd "get a taste of Algeria", he stressed for the benefit of the microphone that was likely to be secreted in one of the armchairs. He asked us a few pointless questions, such as how did the flight go, and also a more pointed "How was the night in the hotel", to which we both replied with a rather reserved, "All right."

Later on, we took a drive in his car. In order to put the Mukhabarat, which almost certainly had us under surveillance, off its guard, he drove into town past the parks with brief stops at the Bardo museum, the university campus and the enormous Notre Dame d'Afrique basilica in the north of the city. This massive brown structure, topped by a tower with a large silver dome, stood on a cliff overlooking the bay. I was surprised to see so prominent a Catholic site in this Muslim city, until Udi, who drove around with such confidence that I realized this wasn't his first visit here, reminded me that the French had annexed Algeria, and the basilica was built under French rule.

He took photographs of us outside the basilica and inside, with the blue mosaic walls behind us and the central dome with its vivid colours soaring above. Then he left us alone there and it occurred to me that from Niki's half-Christian point of view, this must be a peculiar situation: being inside such a magnificent Catholic church in an Arab country, as part of an Israeli-Jewish team operating against Iran and extremist Islam.

I let her be on her own for a while with the statue of the Virgin of Africa, and on the way out hugged her lightly and she responded with a thoughtful silence. We climbed into Udi's car and he drove off in the direction of Mont Plaisant. After a few minutes he stopped at an unexpected place: the Tomb of the Unknown Soldier, on the outskirts of the military city built on the mountainside. "We have to pay tribute to our hosts," he said, without even the ghost of a smile, and we went out into the cold wind to honour the memory of the nameless soldiers who had died in the bloody war against the French. Udi wanted us to make several stops before the place where he would brief us, and to take a few photos just in case, and this also enabled us to check the cars behind us. I noticed one that I thought I'd seen at the basilica, and Udi suspected another that had drawn closer when we began climbing the mountain road.

After we returned to our car, Udi headed for the western slopes of the mountain and stopped at the side of the road. One of the two cars that we'd noticed stopped a few hundred yards from us.

Spring had arrived, but a chilly wind was blowing on the mountainside. Despite this, Udi told us to leave our coats in the car. "I assume your clothing is clean but I don't know who shoved what into one of your coat pockets," he said without apologizing, and launched into concrete explanations of what we had to do. He indicated with a movement of his head where the airfield lay, mostly concealed from our view, with only one end of the landing strip visible, about three kilometres to the north west of where we stood. "From Djebel Koukou there'll be a better angle, but with this tail that we've picked up, I'd rather not go there now. We'll wait until just before the actual operation."

Udi repeated the briefing: We would travel on the road around Djebel Koukou, stopping at a point overlooking the airfield. We had a camera with a giant telephoto lens, enough for our needs during the daytime. If the action on the airfield began after dark, we'd make sure we weren't under surveillance and Udi would remove the night vision device from the secret compartment in his bag and give it to us. Also concealed there was a dismantled mini-Uzi whose parts had been treated in a way that ensured they wouldn't show up on airport security scans. The car would remain at the roadside as part of the cover story and Udi would move away, but he'd stay close enough to intervene if necessary while Niki and I would climb by foot until we reached the best vantage point.

Intelligence and the reports of operatives who had been there before informed us that at night, about once every hour, an armed military squad patrolled a track that crossed the path along which we would climb. The soldiers were equipped with torches and scanned the area, which was designated a closed military zone at night. Signs announcing this were posted on both sides of the road we were driving along but were in Arabic only, which Canadian tourists couldn't be expected to understand.

Udi continued: After we separate at the foot of the hill, we'll do exactly what we've done during our training in the Jerusalem hills and climb until we reach the point that has been selected by topographical analysis, "but you can use your discretion if you locate a superior site for observing the landing strip".

"In the daytime, and even in the evening, your painter's easel is good enough cover. But you have no good cover for being there at night," he continued. "The best way to get rid of an army patrol is to create an intimate scene. You've finished painting, you've drunk too much wine, and one thing led to another."

"Let's get back to the matter at hand," I tried to obviate his intrusion into our intimacy, although he was merely repeating the operational orders. "For example, what do we do with the NVD if we are discovered?"

I wasn't upset that Udi was leaving us without cover. Together with Avi, before we left Israel we'd prepared responses to several situations, all based on my painting and our relationship. We were to take with us a bag containing a blanket, wine, two glasses and bread and cheese, for a night-time picnic that we could say we'd planned. In addition, I'd have my easel and a sketchpad containing drawings of the landscape that I was to make in advance, so that I'd be able to say to anyone asking questions that "I started them here before the sun set." I was also aware that the risks Udi was taking were not small – there aren't many tourists who stop at the side of a deserted road armed with a mini-Uzi. It was clear he wouldn't be able to use the weapon against a suspicious patrol as long as we were performing our mission because, if gunshots were heard, the place would soon be crawling with security forces, putting us in danger too.

Udi ignored the resentment in my words, and calmly analyzed the hypothetical situation that I'd raised. The response we agreed upon was that as soon as I realized a patrol was approaching, I would hurl the NVD as far away as I could, and deny any knowledge of it if it was found.

"What if we can't positively identify the plane that lands as the one we are waiting for?"

"The couple in Tehran is supposed to be relaying the description of the aircraft and its take-off time. Our intelligence will track it all the way with radar and audio surveillance so we should know when it's due to land. It's likely you'll have enough info to make the identification."

We went over more last-minute questions and Udi provided reasonable answers.

"OK, let's say you see the plane land in the evening, and you wait until it takes off again in the middle of the night. What happens then?" he asked us.

"We report, pack up the kit and get the fuck outta there," Niki replied quickly.

This made Udi laugh, but the smile that crept onto my lips was soon erased when her choice of words reminded me of my last feeble attempt to make love to her.

I took a few photographs that I could use as a basis for the pictures I would make at the hotel, I also made a few sketches for the benefit of anyone watching us, and we drove away. On the way back we planned how we would check to make sure we were clear of tails as we drove in two cars to our destination.

Udi returned us to our hotel and informed us that, according to the latest intelligence, the ship that had been expected to dock had been held up, so we didn't have to waste time keeping an eye on the port from our room. "On the other hand, however, the aircraft is being loaded in Tehran right now."

We dined at the hotel's not very good Le Continental restaurant. Afterwards, Niki went up to the room and I picked up the car I'd ordered that morning, and bought the stuff for our picnic. Back in the room, I made some landscape sketches on the basis of the photos. I wanted to put Niki into the pictures, and when I turned around I saw she was sitting on the edge of the bed and hadn't said anything. As I watched I saw what seemed like a tremor in her back spreading slowly throughout her slight frame. Her arms and legs began shaking and her lips shivered. I hugged her and asked what was wrong but she couldn't speak. I took a miniature brandy from the mini-bar and gave it to her to drink. I thought she had calmed down a little but after a minute or two she rushed to the bathroom and threw up.

I bent over her, holding her forehead and neck with both my hands, as her small body writhed and expelled not just food but the juices of her stomach. The sounds she was making were awful.

"Fucking Algerian food," I said in frustration, but honest Niki shook her head. "I'm terrified that this is going to be our last day," she blurted out.

"So let's call it off then," I said.

"No way. I'll have to get over it," said my brave companion.

For the next hour we lay in bed hugging. Niki was still trembling, and now and again her stomach heaved. I wanted to call Udi but she stopped me.

"We don't know when it's going to happen, and in any case we'll have a few hours' prior notice. Let's see how I feel when the time comes."

I was reminded of Dudu, whose stomach also betrayed him on the eve of the mission in Sudan, and who was then ousted from the squad. I assumed that here, too, an element of fear was at play. Understandable fear. At border control, Niki was still a Canadian tourist with all the cover in the world. In a little while, she would be a Mossad operative who, for some time, would not have any logical cover for what she would be doing, deeds that could put her behind bars for many years. Perhaps a samurai does not tremble before a battle, but Niki was now a samurai without a master, preparing to do battle at the end of which, even if she was successful, she would not know what her fate would be.

Udi called and gave the code word that meant that the plane had taken off from Tehran. He said he'd pick us up in an hour's time. It was going to be a long night's work. The plane would land very late in the evening, and who could tell when it would leave again for Beirut.

I should also have been anxious but something happened to me that had happened before when I was getting ready for a mission. The anxieties that should have turned my stomach upside down were washed away by adrenalin and by mental focus, as if they weren't there at all.

I made Niki a cup of tea with a dash of brandy and ordered melba toast from room service, but mostly I hugged her close. The colour gradually returned to her cheeks and then she got up, stood in the middle of the room and began doing breathing exercises with her eyes closed. She added arm movements that looked like tai chi or chi kung – I couldn't tell the difference – and then she knelt on the carpet and went into a state of deep meditation.

When the time came for our rendezvous with Udi she stood up, smiled wanly and said, "I'm ready."

✧✧✧

We drove behind Udi to Celeste, a north-eastern suburb of Algiers. It really looked celestial, perched on a green hill from which both sides of the bay were visible as the sun set. I gave my hand to Niki, more in concern than in love, but she clasped it gratefully. I was a little too full of adrenalin to enjoy the view or the romantic aspects of the time and place.

We executed the moves we'd planned for detecting tails but our morning's activities had apparently allayed any suspicions the Mukhabarat may have had, and we were clean. I followed Udi to the fortress on the hilltop where we gave each other a last once-over and, when we were sure no one was following us, we headed for the spot where we were to leave our car. Udi stopped precisely where we had arranged and after yet another anti-surveillance check, he got out of the car with his little bag. From its double lining he removed the mini-Uzi which he had already assembled and put it into his belt, and the NVD, which he gave to us. He shook my hand with both of his, kissed Niki, said he was relying on us, and watched as we started our climb. We hurried away from the road, carrying the camera, the NVD, my folding easel, my sketchpad with its ready-made drawings, and a picnic basket which also held my brushes and paints. As the dark enveloped us, we heard Udi driving off, and half a minute later he stopped and we checked our radio contact.

Everything went according to plan, and no one interrupted us. We made our way to the prearranged observation point which turned out to be the only place from which there was an unobstructed view of the entire length of the landing strip. The runway was relatively short, well concealed among the hills, and I wondered how a cargo plane could manoeuvre its way to land there. At any rate, there was no air traffic so far, and I expected that when our plane arrived we'd have no special difficulty identifying it.

We set up camp, spreading out the blanket, taking out the wine, the glasses and smelly French cheeses. I hid the NVD in a hollow in a rock a few dozen yards away and tore one of the pictures I had prepared in advance out of the pad and fixed it to the easel. By the faint light from the moon, I adjusted the lines I'd made that morning to the view that was spread out before us now. I opened the box of watercolours, took out the brushes which I had hardly used at all since I had painted Niki in Toronto then poured a little water from the bottle I had brought into a plastic cup, dipped a brush into it, and began filling in the lines in shades of green and brown.

Niki spread herself out on the blanket and when I had stopped painting I sat down and she put her head on my thigh and her arm gently around my back. A chill was creeping up from the valleys, there was a slight breeze carrying with it the sounds of branches creaking, rustling leaves and small animals moving around, as well as jackals wailing and dogs barking in the distance. Niki held me tighter.

I shuddered and felt a need to pee but decided not to move. Spending a night outdoors in Israel was sometimes nice and sometimes not, depending on where you were and why you were there. I knew this from my army service and the many hikes I'd been on alone, especially after I returned from Japan and decided to spend vacations hiking the Israel Trail – all of its 840 km winding from its northernmost tip at kibbutz Dan down to its southernmost in Eilat – instead of taking more trips in Asia. Now, on that Algerian hillside, I felt a combination of the night I'd spent alone in the Dishon valley in the Upper Galilee, hearing wild pigs grunting and rooting around nearby, and the nights lying in ambushes in Lebanon.

While I was trying to sort out my feelings, the receiver in my ear came alive: Udi reported that the plane was approaching and I passed on the news to Niki. She stood up and I retrieved the NVD. I didn't know how the intelligence for our mission was set up but I was glad it was working.

I focused the device onto the airfield, all of which was clearly visible. The landing lights that we'd hardly seen before were now in plain view.

"Our friend is cleared for landing," Udi said.

With the scope glued to my eye, I could only see the space that the device was pointing at, and Niki was watching the sky and directing me.

"There it is, there it is," she said excitedly, just as the noise of the engines reached me. I followed her outstretched arm. The hours I'd put in studying the Iranian air force paid off. I saw immediately that it was an Antonov An-74, a smallish cargo plane immediately recognizable by the two jet engines perched on top of the high wings. Its landing gear was already down, and it was descending towards the runway. Painted on its tail fin was the Iranian flag with the emblem of four crescents around a line that looked like a sword at its centre; Moshik had told me that this was a way of writing the name of Allah in a special script. I could see no lettering on the fuselage. Once on the ground, the aircraft executed a turn at the end of the runway and stood there, ready for takeoff. I reported to Udi and felt a great sense of satisfaction. Half the puzzle was complete.

Niki and I spontaneously hugged each other. We decided there and then that we'd drink a toast to this initial success and I uncorked the wine and poured it into the glasses. "Here's to . . ." I began and observed enormous anticipation on Niki's face but I couldn't lie to either of us. "Here's to the mission," I said finally, and Niki pursed her lips in a sad smile, and took a sip. Now that the tense period of expectation was over and we had to wait to see when the plane took off again, we suddenly felt hungry and attacked the bread and cheese in the picnic basket.

We could see the plane with a naked eye, and from time to time I checked it through the NVD, but the only activity I noticed was refuelling, as the An-74 was designed for shorter distances. We now had an indefinite wait and it was getting colder, and the night noises were louder.

"Will you hug me? I'm cold," said Niki. I obliged, and we lay there cuddled in each other's arms on one half of the blanket, covered by the other half, trying not to make any unnecessary movements or any noise.

At short intervals, I sat up and focused my viewing device. I could see people on ladders propped against the tail and it soon became clear that they were sticking the Algerian flag, with the crescent and star in the middle, over the Iranian flag. I reported this to Udi, and he said we deserved a kiss.

Not long after that, he told us that the pilot had requested permission to take off. I felt a twinge of excitement at the thought that somewhere beyond the horizon unknown people were working with us and supplying us with intelligence. I wondered if they knew who and where we were and what we were doing. The mission had been easy. It was the only plane at the airfield, and a few minutes later it was taxiing down the runway, with the Algerian flag clearly discernible on its tail.

"Yallah, come to daddy," Udi told us when I reported that the plane had taken off. We packed up our equipment and began the walk down the hill.

I should have been full of pride and satisfaction. We had just completed a mission that the State of Israel had seen as highly important, and we were among the few who could have accomplished it. But, instead, I felt shrouded in a pall of gloom. Instead of celebrating our victory tonight, I would be busy tying up the loose ends prior to my private mission which, while closing the earlier chapter of my life, would also be the end of the present one. Even if I got out, Niki would never forgive me. The Mossad would never forgive me. And if I ever forgave myself, it would be because of the tremendous commitment I felt to doing this thing. I would not be able to live with the knowledge that Dolly's murderer had been within my reach and I'd let him get away and go on planning terrorist attacks that would take Israeli lives.

As far as I could see in the dark, Niki was also wrapped in gloom. She also apparently sensed that by doing this job I felt that I had ended not only my obligation to my country but also a chapter in our lives.

We were only about two hundred yards away from our car when Udi's voice came over the radio: "Patrol heading your way." Shit, I thought as I pulled Niki down onto a fairly flat patch, in the hope that the soldiers wouldn't see us. I quickly spread out the blanket and laid out the cheese, wine and glasses, the sketchpad and brushes. I didn't have time to put the easel up. I hid the NVD behind a big rock, a few yards away, and we lay hugging each other on the blanket. We heard footsteps and voices. Niki astutely put her hand into my trousers, but I moved it away gently. The sex had already occurred and now we were enjoying the afterglow, was the way I'd play it. At the last moment, I remembered to rip the receiver phones out of our ears and the tiny transmitter mics out of our coats and toss them into the bushes. This was a "contingency" for which we hadn't prepared a "response". Clearly we wouldn't want to be caught with radios, but it wasn't something that the planners had thought of when prepping us for the various things that could happen.

The footsteps came closer. I didn't move, still hoping the dark and the mist would keep us hidden. Then a powerful torch beam blinded me.

What had sounded reasonable around the table at the base – that anyone who came upon us intimately intertwined would be discreet and considerate enough to leave us alone – simply didn't hold water on the Algerian hillside. The four soldiers in the patrol aimed their rifles at us and barked orders in Arabic. What they saw may have spoken for itself but our attempts to explain didn't help because none of them could understand English. One of them knew enough to say, "Up, up!" gesturing skywards with his rifle.

I detached myself from Niki and got onto my feet. I hoped they wouldn't think of raping her and doing away with me there and then. In my mind I worked out how I would grab the rifle pointed at me and charge at them. I presumed that Udi, who wasn't hearing anything since I got rid of the radios, was coming closer. The soldiers had come from the west, and Udi was to the south-east of us, and this was why he had noticed them only at the last minute. Despite the very uncomfortable situation we were in, I derived some sense of security from the knowledge that he was close by, and at the same time I was angry and frustrated that things hadn't been planned better. No one had even thought of the possibility that we'd have no way of communicating. The soldiers indicated they wanted us to accompany them and I didn't know whether to try to play for time so that Udi could get within range for his mini-Uzi to be effective, or by staging an injury for example, giving him time to get closer, or just to obey the soldiers and rely on our cover story to get us out of trouble.

I began gathering together our things which would be useful corroborative evidence if we were brought before some officer but one of the men cocked his rifle and aimed it at my head. Another soldier picked up the sketchpad. At least we'd have that, I thought. Niki tried to say our car was down the hill, but a soldier shut her up with a brutal shove and a rasping shout of "uskoot" – "be quiet" in Arabic. Only the rifle barrel pointing at my head stopped me from intervening physically. We began walking along the path the soldiers had used, parallel to the road and some two hundred yards above it.

I was holding Niki's hand, this time not for cover but to try to cheer her up. Her fears had been realised. And why should she, this small, sweet Japanese-Canadian woman find herself so deep in such typically Israeli shit. Me, OK, I had all the reasons in the world, but why her? I was flooded with compassion, and perhaps love too, and I tried to convey it to her through the palms of our hands. When I sensed that it was working, I also put my arm around her, but this was too much for the soldiers, and one of them stuck the barrel of his rifle between us and separated us.

Another man was reporting something over his radio. We kept on walking, and every now and again one of them turned around, crouched and aimed his weapon in the direction we had come from. They had probably heard something that I hadn't. Perhaps it was Udi's footsteps, I thought and hoped.

After about ten minutes we reached a dirt road, and saw the lights of a vehicle approaching. It was a military pickup truck, and we were loaded onto it at gunpoint. Any hope of Udi helping us to end the affair there in the field was now dead.

7.

A Sunken Nipple and a Tiny Tattoo

ONCE AGAIN I was to be interrogated, and once again Niki was my only hope. But there was a difference: this time, I was also her only hope.

"Please let her go," I begged when we got to the base. "We're just a couple on holiday, and if we strayed into a forbidden area, I'm sorry but keep me here and let her go. It was my idea, a silly idea, to have a picnic up there."

The soldiers didn't seem to be paying any attention to what I was saying. When an officer showed up and told them to take Niki one way and me another, I repeated my plea to have her released. As they separated us at the entrance to their headquarters, she looked scared, scared to death almost. How wrong everything had gone! Between us, in the mission, in life. My feelings for Niki at that moment were so powerful that I went down on my knees to plead with them to free her. A rifle barrel was jabbed into my back and she vanished with her captors down the corridor.

The officer in charge of the patrol, an older man, was not a professional interrogator, and the place was not an investigation facility but rather a small base for the forces guarding the secluded airport, or so I deduced – I had no way of knowing it for sure. I didn't even know if it was within his authority to question us, or if this was merely a stage on the way to the Mukhabarat. He was, if I remembered the Algerian army insignia properly, a major. On the shoulders of his rather shabby uniform he wore gilt flowers on a green and white background with two yellow stripes, and his cap bore the Algerian emblem of a crescent and star over crossed swords and a wreath of leaves. He had apparently decided to enjoy to the hilt all the pleasure that the situation could give him. His dismal office had suddenly become an important investigation point, despite the blotches of mould on the walls. The damp had even encroached onto the photographs hanging there of President Bouteflika whom I recognized from the intelligence file, and his predecessor Boumediene, whose greatly enlarged picture I'd seen at the airport.

My wrists were tied together with bootlaces, as were my ankles – clearly the base wasn't equipped with handcuffs. I was seated on a chair a short distance from the officer's wretched desk, and in one corner two soldiers stood guard with Famas F-1 assault rifles at the ready. It was the first time I'd seen these French-made firearms which resembled the Israeli Tavor with their heavy-looking stocks and short barrels. One of the men, sloppily dressed, was holding a leg of his weapon's open bipod with one hand and had the index finger of the other on the trigger, and I thought that a hasty move on his part could put an end to my life. The officer's handgun was on the desk but, unlike the untidy soldier, he didn't seem frightened of me.

He scrutinized my passport and, after asking me where we were staying, he called the Sofitel and obtained confirmation that we were guests at the hotel. He spoke French to me, until it became clear that my French was worse than his English, after which he used a mixture of the two languages in a thick Arabic-French accent.

"You have de luxe hotel, dit moi pourqoi you make love on ze montagne where is interdit to be in ze nuit?" he asked, and luckily I still remembered some high school French.

"We did not know it was forbidden," I replied. "There is no fence or anything else there."

The officer, who was a hefty man of about fifty, with broad rounded shoulders and the thick arms of a farmer, rose slowly, walked around the desk, and slapped me with his roughened palm. The blow had little energy behind it and didn't hurt much as I managed to stiffen my jaw and neck muscles before it landed.

"You no answer ze question. Répondez vous!" he ordered, evidently enjoying this new role.

"We saw the spot during the day, while touring around Mont Plaisant. When it started to get dark, and we realized we had missed the sunset, we decided to have our picnic where I would have some scenery to paint in the twilight. So we stopped the car and climbed some of the way up the hillside."

Even to me, this prearranged response sounded a bit stupid. But the officer mulled it over for a while, and apparently didn't think my explanation totally unreasonable. He asked about the car, I told him where I'd rented it, and he called the company to confirm. Then he sent a patrol to check if it was where I said we'd left it.

While waiting for the patrol to come back he asked me about my occupation, why we'd come to Algeria, and what we'd done since arriving. I gave him full answers, and let him see on my digital Nikon the many pictures I'd taken at the mosques and Notre Dame and of the scenery, as well as the landscape sketches I'd made "up there" so that I'd be able to paint them later. The beautiful Niki figured in many of the pictures, and he asked me about her.

This reminded me, with a jolt, that she was nearby in the same situation as I was, and what felt like an electric shock of pain surged through me. I told him the story we had prepared of how we had met, and with each detail my heartache increased.

The officer was a lot less moved than I was by the story, and when I'd finished speaking, he ordered the guards to tie me to the chair and announced that he was going to hear Niki's version. While the slovenly soldier kept his rifle aimed at me, the other man wound a thick rope around me, pinning my upper body and arms to the back of the chair, my thighs to the seat and my calves to the legs of the chair. I was almost mummified, but my thoughts were about Niki. Why did she have to go through all of this? Even without any connection to the crisis in our relationship, or to my dumb machismo that had caused that crisis, how had I ever agreed to get her involved in this world? After all, when I did so, I had already been under detention and interrogation in Amman, and I was aware that this kind of thing could happen. Why had I allowed her to take these dangers upon herself? Why hadn't I done what Udi had suggested at the start – that we'd live as a couple and her role would be only to provide cover for me. I had brought her into this with my eyes wide open, succumbing far too easily and conveniently to her samurai codes.

The major spent a long time with Niki, but I couldn't say exactly how long because there was no clock in the room and I couldn't look at my watch. It was already very late at night, and I assumed that was why we were being questioned here and not taken to the Mukhabarat. This gave me some hope. If Niki gave him the same story, there was a chance we'd be released. Between these thoughts, I had visions of Udi finding us, entering the camp and freeing us, but I knew this was a fantasy. He couldn't know where we were or carry out a Rambo-type raid like that. For one thing, if it failed then we'd really be suspected and the investigation would become far more serious. All they had to do was to comb our picnic site and find the night vision device and radio gear, and we'd be in for many long years of imprisonment, or worse. Even a routine patrol the next day could happen upon the devices.

The hours went by. I wasn't wearing my coat, and the cold of the springtime night slowly penetrated my bones. But despite that, and despite all my fears and fantasies, my head drooped and I fell into a light doze, from which I was awoken by loud voices. My hopes that the affair would end with the major's interrogation were dashed. The door opened, and into the room came the major and a vigorous officer wearing another kind of uniform. He was about my age and height, but he was slim and agile and had a thick moustache. A Mukhabarat man, I guessed.

He took the major's chair, indicating his seniority, brought it closer, and sat with his knees touching mine and his face right in my face.

"I've just had a long talk with your girlfriend," he said in French, and when I said I'd prefer English he expressed surprise: "Aren't you bilingual there, in Canada?"

"In Quebec, perhaps. Not in Ontario," I replied and this seemed to satisfy him.

He continued in heavily accented but passable English: "Your petite amie sounds almost convincing. But we have made the gynaecological examination to her. You do not have the sexual intercourse there, on the mountain. I see no signs of the semen on her."

The thought of what they'd done to Niki demolished me. Did this mean they had stripped her, forced her thighs open and examined her vagina? Did this vigorous, crude officer facing me do it? Or the older major with those thick fingers? It was unlikely that they had a woman perform the examination properly, or that they had brought a doctor.

"We drank wine, we fell asleep . . ." I muttered. Would our crisis, which had made me impotent, bring about our downfall?

"In the meantime, everything you say, you and the woman, about your visit in Algeria and also about where you live in Canada has, how you say it, checked out. Luckily for you, it is the working hours there now. We have sent it to our consulate in Toronto, and they have checked and confirmed it."

I broke into a sweat over the possibility that the Algerians would contact the Toronto authorities and they'd get in touch with Ron Friedlich's parents. But the moustached intelligence officer's mind was elsewhere:

"So, even if you did not have the sexual relations tonight, you must know the intimate details about each other."

What kind of information was he expecting me to give him? What could he verify?

The investigator ordered a soldier to remove the rope binding me to the chair, and while this was being done he said: "She say you were stabbed once, before she meet you, in some kind of knife fight, and you have scars on your shoulder and your derrière. I am going to check that now."

In a minute the ropes were off me, but my wrists and ankles were still secured by the bootlaces. One of the soldiers was told to open my shirt and bare my shoulder and the intelligence officer took a close look at the old wound.

"That is not made by a knife," he said.

"Right. It was a broken bottle."

He told me to stand up and ordered the soldier to pull my trousers down. The first thing that entered my mind was my circumcision. They would see that my foreskin had been removed. That was also what their own Muslim penises looked like but why should Ron Friedlich, a Canadian, be circumcised? I dropped my trousers myself, shivering with cold and with anxiety that my Jewishness would be exposed. I could, of course, say I was circumcised for health reasons, but it would take me a few giant steps back.

Luckily, the officer didn't even look at that part of my anatomy. He went behind me and told the soldier to pull down my underpants.

"That is a knife," he said with authority when he saw the scar. He told the soldier to get me properly dressed again. No one had ever been so grateful as I was then for those fragments of shrapnel that had nicked my flesh.

"OK. Now you must to tell me something about her. Something that only you know."

I fell back into my chair. Here I was being ordered to tell them information that would mean they must undress Niki and ogle her body. "Of course there are such things. But there's no reason for me to tell you. The other officer has called Sofitel and confirmed that we were there together."

"Why are les dames always more clever than les hommes? What you think, this way you are protecting her? I can do with her whatever I wish, and you can do nothing about it. I ask you one simple question. So, answer, please, like she answer."

"The nipple of her left breast is inverted," I said, and both officers burst out laughing. The major even saw fit to translate what I'd said for the benefit of the soldiers, who didn't understand English.

"C'est tout? Perhaps also they cut off le clitoris," he looked at me mockingly.

If he had shoved his fingers into Niki's body to look for signs of my semen, perhaps he had also crudely examined that delicate spot. I tried to overcome the nausea that rose inside me and that tasted of the cheese I'd eaten before we were arrested.

"It is not a very rare thing, that the point of the nipple goes inwards," I said trying to make my voice sound matter of fact, so that this subject wouldn't obsess them. "And when it comes to the clit . . ." but I stopped myself before saying something derogatory about what some Muslims do to their women. I needed the sympathy of this disgusting creature, not his antagonism.

"Autre chose, please, something special, that only you know?"

"OK. She has a small tattoo of a sword, right under her navel."

"Vraiment? I have not gone so high," he laughed maliciously again.

If only the two of us were alone there. If only my wrists and ankles were not bound. If only I didn't have a rifle pointed at me. I knew I could shatter this slimy toad's skull and break every bone in his body.

"I go to look," he said and left the room. The major, who had noticed how upset I was, told his men to tie me down again, and followed him. He didn't want to miss the show.

I shuddered while the soldier was tying me to the chair, with rage, with horror at what Niki was going through now, with helplessness. This, I knew, was the lowest point in my life, and the thought that Niki was in an even lower place, made the situation intolerable.

When the door was opened again, the light of early morning poured into the room. My grilling had not taken so many hours, and I hoped that Niki's hadn't either. Where had the time gone? Perhaps while I had dozed off and they were waiting for the man from the Mukhabarat.

I thought I was hallucinating. In the light coming through the door, I saw the silhouette of Niki's slight frame. She was pushed into the room.

The major followed her inside. Niki looked exhausted but there was a soft glow on her white face.

"They are letting us go," she said as she came up to me.

The officer ordered the soldiers to untie me.

"You have ze bonne chance," he said. "He believe her."

I took a deep breath to gain control of the emotions stirring in my chest and to keep myself from crying.

When I got onto my feet, Niki put her head on my chest and hugged me. Then she took my arm and placed her hand over mine, in a calming gesture.

The major said a military vehicle would take us to our car.

He took his departure from us with some advice: "Pas plus de pique-nique."

We squeezed into the wide front seat of a Russian truck and, after a few failed attempts to get it started, for which I hardly had the patience, the engine finally responded and we left the base. I hugged Niki close and we didn't open our mouths until we reached the car.

On the way to the hotel we also sat very close, but remained silent, though Niki's tears flowed without stopping, and I breathed with difficulty, unable to contain all the emotions raging within me: the enormous swell of compassion and love for Niki; the hatred for the two Algerian officers; the anger at Udi and the hasty change in operating procedures that had left a pit for us to fall into; the frustration at now being under open scrutiny; fear that we could still be apprehended before we left, and refusal to accept that Dolly's killer was apparently going to remain alive. But I had not yet given up on that little dream. A new day had dawned, and who knew what to expect? Especially in our strange business.

When we got to our room, Niki hurried to the bathroom, and threw up again. This time, as I held her, she allowed herself to sob and moan. Then she filled the bath with hot water and foam, got undressed and immersed herself, body and head. I sat next to her and when she came up for air I held her hand. Then I saw a glimmer of something that I thought could possibly be a smile.

"You must need a bath too," she whispered. "Come on in."

8.

Home Again

DAYLIGHT WAS SEEPING through the curtains when we fell asleep in each other's arms, taking consolation from each other's exhausted bodies. I had barely the slightest conception of what Niki had been through and she wasn't yet ready to speak about it.

The ringing of the phone woke us. I had no idea what time it was. The caller identified himself as an Air Canada representative, and it took a few seconds for me to recognize Udi's voice. "As you requested," he said, "your departure has been brought forward and you will be leaving on an Air France flight at seven this evening to Paris and from there to Toronto on Air Canada, after a brief stopover. The tickets will be waiting for you at the airport."

So Udi was still here, and he knew we were back in the hotel. I didn't know what he'd been doing, and I didn't really care. He'd probably done whatever he could, but it hadn't helped us.

It was then that I remembered: Bassam al-Sultan! I still had an unfinished task and if I was flying out that evening, it would remain unfinished. But I did not want to let it go. All my hatred for the despicable interrogator of the night before was now channelled into that obscure figure up in the Casbah. It was unlikely that I'd be able to come back here in the future to do the job. But now the Mukhabarat would undoubtedly be shadowing us right up to the airport and it would be difficult for me to slip away from there as I'd planned, to execute the hit, and then to find another flight out. I needed time. Udi and Niki would have to leave without me.

"I'd prefer to spend another day here," I told Udi.

From the silence on the other side of the line I could picture the shock on his face. What, has the guy gone nuts? he must have been thinking. But he had to keep up the act, because of the people who were undoubtedly listening in.

"I don't think that it would be possible to make the change but I'll see what I can do. In the meantime, please be ready to take this evening's flight."

"I understand."

I looked at my watch. If my target were to come home a little earlier than he had when I'd seen him, I might yet manage to do the job and get to the airport at the last moment.

"Who was that?" Niki brought me back to reality.

"We fly out tonight, to Paris and then Toronto."

It was important for me to see how she reacted when she heard the destination. but all she did was close her eyes and pull me back into her embrace. She kissed me gently on my forehead, my eyes, my neck, and then she slithered down until she found the scar on my shoulder and kissed it and licked it and then she came back to my lips and I closed my eyes and surrendered all of myself to her mouth. Her tongue slid down my chest and belly and that was all that was needed to arouse me. But she went on loving and pampering me until I turned her onto her back and sucked at her inverted nipple and then tongued her little tattoo, and then between her thighs. We went on pleasuring each other until the very end, and the moment that this notion of "the very end" entered my mind, I was overcome by melancholy. This was perhaps the last time we'd be together.

I had to go now, if I wanted to get al-Sultan off my conscience. Niki was looking at me. My tensed-up state had caught her attention.

"What is it, my love?" she asked.

I couldn't lie. The night before, the interrogation, the last hour together, had created a new reality that I had to avoid ruining. I switched the bedside radio on loud and whispered into her ear.

"The man responsible for the suicide bombing that killed Dolly is here, in the Casbah. I have found his house. I don't want to go home before I've closed that chapter of my life."

Niki's eyes opened wide in shocked dismay.

"That means only one thing: that you haven't begun the second chapter, the one with me," said this so very wise woman of mine.

Her words bowled me over. Here I was, already preoccupied with tactical considerations – getting to the Casbah by car, shaking off surveillance, waiting for al-Sultan by the jewellery centre, following him, stabbing him with the shabriyeh as he opened the gate, getting to the airport – without even considering what it meant for my relationship with Niki. Beyond the chance that I'd get caught, or that she wouldn't forgive me, was it true that I had never devoted myself to Niki because I hadn't achieved closure on the episode with Dolly? But it had been Dolly who was supposed to be closing the unfinished episode with Niki that had begun in Japan!

The pointlessness of the act that I had planned was suddenly crystal clear: my inability to let go of the past and to devote myself to this wonderful part of my life that Niki had made possible, with all of her beauty, love, acceptance, and dedication.

Niki was sitting on the bed, with her girlish body, lovely face and eyes full of hurt.

"You have to choose, my love," she said in a tone that could not have been more gentle. "I am not talking at all about the unreasonable risk you would be taking. I am saying that your very readiness to take a risk like that shows that you haven't yet chosen me. That you haven't yet fully entered this chapter, our chapter."

"I'll be altogether free for our chapter if I manage to close that one," I said, not entirely sure of what I was saying.

"No." Niki shook her head, and began whispering again. "That chapter isn't the terrorist who killed Dolly. That chapter is Dolly. And if she did not die, for you, there, in that bombing, and also not after you found me again, she won't be dead when that bad guy dies. Look, there was someone above him too, and someone alongside him. I have chosen you. For good – and there's a lot of good – and for bad. That's why I'm here, with you, and not back in Canada. But you are only now facing the choice between your past, and your present and future. Between your dead love, and your living love. I do not intend to influence your decision. Just that you know it's all clear to me."

Her words were eating away at the state of operational alert that I'd worked myself into and that had almost blocked other voices from getting through to me. She was so right. How could I do it to her? Ask her to allow me to take an enormous risk that was all about my past, a past that had been shaped in order to help me get over the vacuum she herself had left when she vanished in Tokyo? And how could I do it, how could I give up on the once-in-a-lifetime love that Niki was for me?

I flopped down next to her, my head drooping. I covered my face with my hands.

"I don't know how I could even have thought about it," I muttered.

Niki's face was pale. "I am glad that this is what you have decided," she said, her eyes still expressionless. But inside me elation sprouted and spread and I surrendered to it joyfully. I had cast off a heavy burden, not only the burden of the solo operation which I had just forsaken, but the burden of all these years. The need to avenge Dolly had melted away and I had paid my debt to my country and to the Mossad. I am a free man, all of my being was cheering.

Niki put her arms around me. For the first time I was like a little boy with her. For the first time I was ready to devote myself to her alone, to give up all the bonds that had tied me to my life so far.

We stayed in bed for a long time, during which I shed all the episodes of the past, and my heart opened up to love and to the future and to this wonderful woman next to me, who would be woven into that future. She wasn't there with me in order to join with my past. She wasn't there with me to help me defend my homeland. She was there with me because she had chosen me. And now it was my turn to choose her, and not only because she was gorgeous, enchanting and unique. Nor because she had been prepared to accompany me back to my country and my people, this Ruth the Moabite of mine. I had to choose her, because that is what a man does when he finds his woman. And I had found her. And lost her and found her again. And I wasn't prepared to lose her again.

This insight had reached the roots of my being, and I was completely at peace with it.

On the way to the airport, Niki began shivering, whether because she was recalling the horror of the detention and the ordeal of the interrogation, about which she had still said nothing, or because she was anxious that our departure would go wrong. My stomach was also fluttering over that possibility. It would only have been that morning that the major and the Mukhabarat investigator would have filed their reports and only today that the details would have been analyzed in various departments by officials who had had a good night's sleep and had come to work fresh with clear heads. It was entirely likely that someone had said that the idiots who grilled us had been half-asleep, and that our story didn't hold water, not even a drop. And if there had been such a serious person, he might hold up our departure until everything was cleared up. It wouldn't need a bloodhound to sniff out the stuff we'd dumped at our picnic spot and lead investigators right to the night vision and radio devices.

Our arrest and detention were, from my point of view, over and done with but back in Israel we would certainly have to go very thoroughly into how we had gone into the operation without taking all contingencies into account. As for the interrogation, the slap I'd taken was no big deal but Niki's ordeal was still an open sore for me, and I had to know what had happened there. I cuddled her but her shivering didn't stop.

When we went up to the Air France counter, I saw Udi sitting on a bench, chewing on a roll. He acknowledged me with a slight nod of the head. That one intelligence agency had followed us when we were together did not mean that another service, the one that had interrogated Niki and me, knew about that. If they'd been following us, there was no reason to get Udi involved with us.

"Udi's here," I informed Niki, but she didn't turn her head to look for him.

At border control our passports were scanned and stamped. "I hope you had a nice stay in Algeria," said the woman officer who, surprisingly, knew at least that one sentence in English.

Niki's eyes met mine. What does one say in this situation?

"It was OK," I said and we moved on.

We had half an hour to get to the departure gate and take off was set for forty minutes later.

There wasn't much to do in the departure hall of the old Algiers international airport. There weren't even enough seats for waiting passengers. Everything had been put into the new terminal which was to be opened in the near future. Some passengers stood gazing out of the large windows while others sat either on the available seats or on the floor, around the broad pillars supporting the high roof.

I was hoping Udi wouldn't be on our flight. I hadn't yet digested the events of the previous night, nor the decision I had taken in the last few hours, and before I had done so I did not want to be either friendly or nasty to him. I sat next to one of the pillars, my back against it, and invited

Niki to sit on my lap. She did, resting her head on my shoulder, and I held her body which had stopped shivering. Our smooth passage through border control had apparently allayed her last anxieties.

My Niki. Everything was now open before us, or so it seemed. Here, in the airport in Algiers, after a night of operational activity, detention and interrogation, I felt light, alert and free, more so than I had for years.

"I was worried that you would end up like Udi," she said suddenly and quietly, and I tensed up again. She sensed it. "Didn't you know?" she asked.

"Didn't I know what?" I asked, almost impatiently.

"Udi's wife left him, with their son. They are living in England and they are not in touch with each other. He has lost them."

"What . . . when . . . and how do you . . . ?" I responded in utter confusion.

"Sorry. I thought you knew."

"No, but it makes no difference. How . . .?"

"Udi told me. When I told him you'd left our home, and he was trying to persuade me not to give up."

"Not to give up on what?"

"Not to give up on you, not to give you up, and not to give us up, because there are moments when this job of yours – he called it this 'malignant job' – is stronger than the things that are really important in life and sometimes, before you can get them into focus, it's too late."

As if spoken by my own lips. Here and there I'd heard hints about things that had to do with Udi's family life and his past, but no one spoke about it openly. Was it thanks to Udi, of all people, that Niki had remained faithful to me?

"He wasn't there when his son was born, or at his first two birthdays, and when the boy turned three Udi's wife threatened that if he wasn't there, she'd leave. And that's what happened. He was on some mission and when he got back they had already gone."

"And that was it? He gave up?"

"That's what I asked. He said he was angry that she didn't appreciate how important what he was doing was. And then he had to take international legal action to get her or the boy back, and" – here Niki's voice dropped to a whisper – "the Office told him that would mean public exposure and the end to his operational career. And that in any case as long as he remained operational no court would ever give him the boy back."

"And he chose the Office," I also whispered, stating the obvious.

"Évidemment," Niki replied in the French that she'd been forced to refresh not long ago with her interrogators. "It happened ten years ago. For ten years he hasn't seen his kid because, for all kinds of reasons, Udi can't go to England. His wife knows this and that's why she went there."

Some of the loose ends in Udi's personality, and in our relationship, were beginning to tie themselves up, but I wasn't in a hurry to buy this new Udi, and I couldn't stop myself from saying: "And despite everything he's been through, he didn't go out of his way to help us, until the talk with you. One could have expected a little more understanding and support from him."

"Right, but it was only after you left home that he got it, and that's also what he told me. You reminded him too much of himself, when he was starting off, and at times he found it was hard to see your happiness. He came to his senses only when he grasped that he'd gone too far with his envy of you and when he saw that our relationship was breaking down."

I couldn't restrain myself. "And you? Didn't you have any part in it?"

Niki sneaked a tiny smile. "There was not even a hint of that. But my feminine intuition did tell me that he was ever so slightly in love with me."

"He was in love with you, but nonetheless he tried to get us back together?"

"You are strange, you samurais of the Middle East. There's something you are loyal to more than to yourselves. Just like us, the samurais of the Far East."

Almost willy-nilly I turned my head towards that embittered, wise, cruel and complicated man. If he hadn't said what he'd said to Niki and given us the chance to rebuild our relationship through the mission, it is likely that I would have become exactly the same as him.

A man in uniform approached Udi. He had a piece of paper in his hand and was apparently ordering Udi to accompany him. They walked towards the offices at the other end of the departures hall.

"I think Udi's in trouble," I said to Niki. "Whatever happens, you get onto the plane."

Anxiety leaped into her eyes but I felt a surge of adrenalin, and walked along the hall, towards the door Udi and the man had passed through.

Once I was inside the anteroom, empty of people but full of closed circuit TV monitors, it wasn't difficult to deduce that this was the Mukhabarat's airport office. I heard Udi's voice arguing with someone through one of the doors. They were talking about some picture and I heard Udi saying something about "my friend". It did not sound good but, if he was speaking about me, I had nowhere to run to. I decided to go in.

Inside was none other than the moustached Mukhabarat investigator of the night before, and his colleague, the one who had led Udi to the room. Both of them wore pistols in holsters. It took me no more than a second to recognize the faces in the two pictures they were holding. They were of Udi and me – our recently scanned passport photos and the ones taken at Gimbers in Stockholm.

My entrance made both the Algerian officers turn away from Udi and when the one who had spent the night with Niki and me saw me, his jaw dropped. He had been hunting for me but I had found him.

The moment that he turned away was enough for Udi to deliver a not very stylish but accurate and powerful flying kick to the airport officer's ribs. I heard the crack of breaking bones and the air wheezing out of his lungs. My man didn't have time to close his mouth or realize what was happening before my fist crashed into his jaw. I felt his teeth breaking with the impact, and my fingers too, as I hadn't clenched my fist properly. With all my strength, I aimed a kick at his crotch and he emitted a sound as if his testicles were stuck in his throat, then he lost his balance and fell backwards. At the same time, Udi grabbed his victim's head and wrenched it sideways. The man dropped to the ground like a rag doll.

I still had my job to finish. I stood over the tormentor of Niki and me. His eyes were glued to me, expressing infinite anxiety as I raised my foot and brought it down, with all my weight, onto his throat, the way a Jewish bridegroom during a wedding ceremony smashes a glass with his shoe in memory of the destruction of Jerusalem, but this was in memory of what he'd done to Niki. And from the look in his eye a moment before he gave up the ghost, I knew that he knew. His Adam's apple crackled loudly under the impact, as did the vertebrae of his neck.

We dragged the two men behind the desk. Udi picked up the photographs that they'd dropped, gathered up a sheaf of papers and photographs from a fax machine and fed them into a shredder nearby. Then he straightened his tie, signalled to me to leave, removed the key from the inside of the door, locked it from the outside and dropped the key into his pocket.

It was pretty clear what had happened. When our passports were scanned at passport control and routinely transmitted to the Mukhabarat airport office, our interrogator had been on duty. Our hasty departure must have aroused his suspicion and he had decided to do some crosschecking. He sent our photos to his head office, which quickly identified me as the man photographed during the Gimbers break-in. The Iranians apparently had received the pictures and distributed them to their allies. The Mukhabarat HQ then sent the picture of Udi to the airport as well, and the officer saw that he too had just been through passport control. My moustache and Udi's goatee hadn't done what was expected of them. The man who went out to look for us spotted Udi first. What a surprise they got when I walked in of my own accord.

"There might still be someone out there looking for you, so you and Niki should hide in the toilets until boarding time," said Udi, and just before he walked away without any further ado, as if we'd just had hot dogs at a stand in Tel Aviv, he added, "Glad the two of you survived. See you in Paris."

I didn't like the idea of a Mukhabarat man with pictures of me, and perhaps of Niki as well looking for us in the departures hall, and when the call for our flight came over the loudspeakers almost immediately, I hurried to the gate, where I was greeted by a huge smile of relief from Niki. She jumped on me and hugged me as if I'd come back from hell, without even knowing how close I'd come to being there, or how close it still was. Later on I realized that she'd feared that despite everything I had left the airport to carry out my own private mission.

As we stood in line, I wondered why Udi hadn't joined us. Then an Algerian Airlines flight to Paris was announced, leaving at the same time as ours. I saw the line forming for that, and there was Udi, large, heavy, and slightly stooped. No one could have guessed that minutes before this big bear of a man had killed with his bare hands. Just as no one could have imagined the same about me.

As Niki and I handed over our boarding passes, and the stewardess tore off the stubs, a jarring, hysterical voice, speaking in Arabic, came over the public address system. I could only guess what it was saying but the stewardess motioned to us to continue towards the plane. Suddenly there was a lot of activity all over the terminal, with police and soldiers dashing around. Then an announcement came over in English saying that all boarding should cease immediately. The slain Mukhabarat colleagues had clearly been found.

In a minute Niki and I would be on French territory, in the Air France plane, but what about Udi? He was still in a queue with other passengers. It needed nerves of steel to book a flight on an Algerian plane when you are running for your life from Algeria. A moment before we were swallowed up by the gangway I glanced back and saw that he was nearing a welcoming Algerian Airlines stewardess, looking calm.

Niki and I were shown to our seats by a good-looking flight attendant. Udi had decided to pamper us: we were in business class. A smile of childish glee spread over Niki's face and right away she tried the comfortable seat that reclined almost all the way down and switched on the TV facing her. She knew nothing about what had happened minutes before or that the pandemonium outside was certainly connected to us. She couldn't guess, as I was assuming, that at that precise moment the pictures of Udi and me were being replicated and rushed to all the departure gates. I decided not to tell her anything until we took off, if we took off.

Our stewardess was charming, and when she asked if we'd like a drink, I ordered a double scotch and a glass of water with a lot of ice. She smiled and said, "Water, right away, but whisky after take-off. As long as we're on Algerian soil, alcohol is forbidden." Niki ordered orange juice, two glasses if possible. She was very thirsty.

I dipped my fingers into the glass of iced water, up to my knuckles. Niki's eyes opened wide. I sighed with a mixture of pain and pleasure, smiled to myself and closed my eyes. Niki was shocked to see how swollen my four fingers were. "He truly deserved it," I said with a half-smile when I saw her expression.

The ice eased the pain, but the story wasn't over yet. No other passengers had followed us on board, and clearly something was happening at the airport. The minutes went by as slowly as Chinese water torture. We were close to the cockpit, and when the door opened from time to time I heard the captain in angry exchanges with the control tower or airport authorities. I kept stealing glances at the entrance to the plane, where Mukhabarat men were likely to appear with our pictures. Perhaps the Air France ground stewardess had already identified us and reported we were on board. I debated with myself whether I should go to the captain and ask for his protection but realised that would have been a panicky, weak-nerved move. Time to grit teeth and wait.

Take-off time had come and gone. Through the window I saw the Algerian Airlines plane being towed onto the runway. Had Udi been arrested, and was that why they had okayed the plane for departure? Or did they assume that no foreign agent, especially a Mossad man, would leave the country on an Algerian airline? Something else that I wouldn't know until we reached Paris. If we reached Paris.

Niki saw that I was troubled, but I didn't tell her any more. Not even who I'd meant when I said he deserved being punched. Suddenly the jet engines started up. This was strange, because clearly the dozens of passengers who'd queued behind us hadn't boarded the plane. What was going on? I restrained myself from asking the attendant, but Niki did not.

"Algerian intelligence is searching for someone and wants to search all the aircrafts that were boarding but our captain, and those of British Airways and Lufthansa, who are also waiting to take off, have refused. After consulting IATA, the international airlines organization, they decided that if the local authorities stop the boarding process, they'll take off with whoever is on the planes."

The cabin attendant was staring at my hand in the glass. I realized how dumb I'd been: like pinning a sign on myself.

"Caught it in a taxi door," I volunteered without being asked, and she offered to bring me another glass.

"No thank you. It's not so bad," I said, trying not to catch Niki's eye.

Just then more passengers began entering the plane, the attendants hurriedly ushered them to their seats, and our gallant French captain began taxiing to the runway. Our attendant went through the standard safety routine and I closed my eyes. All I wanted was to feel that we'd taken off. From the air no one would get this proud Frenchman back on the ground.

The stewardess sat down, and the pilot accelerated. When the plane lifted off and banked to the north, I felt Niki's hand pressing on my left, uninjured hand. Through the slits of my eyelids I saw her staring out of the window as we flew over our mountain and, I knew, trying to identify the spot where we'd been. When the seat-belt sign went off, and we were over the Mediterranean, I got my whisky. I swallowed it in two gulps and ordered another.

"Are you sure you need it?" Niki asked.

"Yes, so I can tell you something," I said. "And I'd like you to get one too, so you can tell me about last night."

The attendant served the drinks with a light take-off snack, and then proceeded to tourist class. We were left alone. "I'll drink yours," Niki surprised me. And she told me. Quietly, detached, as if it wasn't she who had gone through the horror.

When she refused to spread her legs, the interrogator had ordered two soldiers to hold her. He wrenched down her trousers and shoved his brutal, invasive fingers into her.

"When I stopped resisting, the soldiers loosened their grip. His head was right between my legs. I knew that with one kick, maybe two, I could do him irreparable damage. I needed all the strength in the world to remain the innocent Canadian tourist, and not an operative."

Then she told me in the same quiet, detached way what had happened when he came back after questioning me, how he told the soldiers to take her blouse and bra off and how he stood and laughed, and they all laughed with him, at the sight of her inverted nipple.

"He's dead now," I whispered, and she sat up and asked me to say it again.

I took my bruised and swollen fingers out of the glass and held them up to her. "His jaw did this to me," I said.

What, how, when, Niki wanted to know.

I told her.

Only then did the weight on her heart lift, and she hid her face in my chest and sobbed.

"I know this may sound out of context," she said when she was calmer. Her head was still on my chest, her small hand gripping my arm. "I love you so much that you can't even begin to imagine. Everything I have done, even when I didn't agree with what I was doing, even when I knew you didn't like it, I did for you. In the days before this mission, when I didn't know what was happening with us, when I thought I'd lost your love, I wanted to die. I came here with you out of a readiness to die. If I had lost your love, I thought, at least I would die for the sake of a goal that you believed in and that I believed in for you."

Niki, my loyal Niki. With her unparalleled devotion. Complete devotion. Something I had never ever experienced, something that I did not believe even existed in the culture I came from. I'd never had a woman who was ready to die – in so many words – for a goal that I believed in, even if she had lost my love. And I, your common, everyday macho guy, insensitive, dull witted, had been ready to give up this sublime gift. Was I at all worthy of her? And how could I atone? What could I do for her that could compare with what she had done for me? What could I sacrifice that could compare with what she'd been prepared to sacrifice? Would giving up on Middle Eastern vengeance, infantile and idiotic, be enough?

At that moment, I knew. And when I knew, a part of me died and another part came to life.

Over and over again, I kissed the head resting on my chest, her fingers tightening on my arm. All her love was expressed in that grip, all her concern, all her anxiety about what lay ahead. As for me, my heart melted for the marvellous woman at my side and my feelings welled up inside me. Would this emotion, this part of me that had come to life for a new possibility that wasn't new at all, which we had discussed and dreamed of, would it manage to contain and carry the part of me that had died?

We landed at Charles de Gaulle airport in the early evening. It had occurred to me that the Algerians might have asked Interpol, or their friends in France, to detain us, but even if that did happen, I thought, the Office would surely get us off the hook. Be that as it may, I really didn't want to have to cope with thoughts like this right now.

Waiting by the baggage carousel, arms around each other, we heard a familiar voice behind us, saying "Bienvenue en France." Udi, who had landed just before us, had no suitcase, only a carry-on bag. I guessed that he had dismantled the mini-Uzi and hidden it on some Algerian hillside. He shook Niki's hand and I apologized that I couldn't do the same, showing him my swollen fingers. Addressing Niki, Udi said unsmilingly, "The other guy looked much worse last time I saw him."

"You've got tickets for an Air Canada flight to Toronto, leaving in two hours," he told us. "If you decide to use them, Niki won't have a problem. You, Ron Friedlich, can pick up Israeli documentation from Rafi, who is with our Paris station, in the transit hall. If you decide to come to Israel, there are seats for you on the El Al flight three hours from now. In that case, briefings start at the base at ten a.m." He allowed himself a little smile at last.

When we separated, Udi hugged Niki warmly and kissed the top of her head. Then he gave me a bear hug, letting me understand that he knew it wasn't clear if and when we'd meet again. As he headed for the transit hall, a sudden warmth enveloped me, as I watched the man who'd been so important to my life – for both good and bad – for almost all the last three years.

"Wait a moment," I called out after him. He turned back, and I said, "I don't know what we'll decide, but I do want to know what happened that night, before and after we were detained on the hill."

Udi let his carry-on bag drop to the floor. "For one moment, when you and Niki were holding onto one other, and were still apart from the patrol, there was a possibility of hitting all four of them. I was a few dozen yards behind you, about the maximum range of the mini-Uzi. But after they separated the two of you, and you were mixed together with the soldiers, it was over. I couldn't get any closer because they'd heard something. After they put you in the truck, I went to the spot where you'd had the picnic, took the gear and got rid of it. HQ directed me to the nearby base, and I kept it under observation until I saw you leave. You know the rest." Udi took a step towards me and patted me affectionately on the cheek. "You've done your bit, Mickey. I'd be happy if you came back. But if you decide not to, you can go on living with a good feeling. And by the way, there are already results."

Once again I was astonished at the way Udi accepted that I had options, and by the freedom he was giving me to decide. He didn't mean that now that I'd done this job, I wasn't needed any longer, "the Moor has done his work — the Moor may go." This was a reward. The ultimate reward. I watched him going up the escalator. A big man with an even bigger head, and a small bag.

We, too, made our way to the transit hall. A large electronic board showed that the Air Canada flight would be leaving from gate 35 and the El Al flight from gate 24. We waited in a café in the centre of the hall. I ordered an espresso, and Niki asked for a hot chocolate, with additional melted chocolate. She called it a Belgian chocolate, and the French waiter made a face. We both laughed.

"There's something I want to say to you, Niki. I made the decision on the flight and I've had two hours to think about it, to weigh it up and to change my mind, so now I am quite sure."

Niki eyed me, somewhat expectantly, somewhat amused.

"J'écoute," she said.

I took a deep breath. I knew that after I had spoken, there could be no retreat. The ball would be in Niki's court, for her to do with it whatever she wished.

"Do you remember when you were happiest?" I asked, thinking I knew the answer.

"With you?" she came back.

"With me," I replied, slightly deflated. Of course she could also have been very happy without me.

Her eyes lit up from a memory that seemed very far away now, like something taken from another era. "When you were painting and I was editing. In Toronto, in Tel Aviv, in Stockholm, even."

"Well, I'm willing for that to be our life from now on, Niki."

She narrowed her eyes and studied me. Her face was serious, and pale.

"We've already had this discussion," she said. "You can't."

"Things have changed. You made me choose, and I've chosen you. You deserve it, and so do I."

"Where?"

"Trans-Atlantic distance is the minimum that I need to overcome the enormous attraction of the Mossad."

"And your parents?"

"The same as yours. And I'll visit them often."

"Your sisters?"

"The same as your sister."

"And your past?"

"The past will not change. It will always be there for me."

"And will you also be there for it?"

"After we satisfy the present, and build a little bit of the future. The past will definitely go on whispering to me, inside me."

"And the Mossad?"

"It will also whisper to me, inside me."

"And burn you up, inside you?"

"Not if you'll be there all day long, to put the fire out. And not if I'm painting."

"Let's order another coffee and another chocolate, and this time I also want a slice of chocolate cake and ice cream."

"You'll put on weight."

"I want to, but not from chocolate."

We ignored the dozens of passengers waiting in the transit hall, locked together in a kiss full of promise.

"Jewish, Christian and Shinto wedding ceremony?" I asked.

"Or just the Toronto City Hall. In a simple white dress, holding a bouquet of white flowers."

And again our lips sealed the deal.

I'd taken into account that from his corner of the hall, somewhere near gate 24, Udi was watching us, and grasping which way the wind was blowing. I had no great regrets about our decision. Only great joy at what was about to be born now, long before our children.

After Niki had eaten her chocolate cake we moved out of the small café and sat on chairs at the centre of the hall. A young man with an Israeli look gave us a nod, and I understood that he was Rafi, who was there to give me an Israeli passport for my entry into Canada. I signalled that I'd seen him as Niki gripped my arm and drew my attention to the news on one of the TV screens located around the hall.

The image was one of a long line of burnt-out, blown- up trucks. A Lebanese government spokesman was speaking in fluent French, saying this was a grave violation of Lebanese sovereignty. He denied the Israeli claim that the convoy was carrying Iranian missiles from Beirut airport to Hezbollah. The Israeli foreign minister said in response that Israel was ready to give the UN unequivocal proof that the shipment had originated in Iran. The Israeli minister of security added that Israel would not allow this channel for the supply of missiles to exist, just as it had done in the case of other channels.

Niki's tight grip on my arm didn't weaken even after the news presenter moved on to report on calamities in other parts of the globe.

"Our buddies in Beirut also did their job," I told her and I felt a mixed sense of pride and of giving up something of great value.

"They didn't waste too much time, did they?" Niki whispered. No, they didn't waste time. "They" being "we".

"You know what," Niki said after some reflection. "It's possible to be a literary agent and a painter in Tel Aviv too, isn't it?"

"It's possible," I drew the words out. "But no."

Niki understood and said nothing.

Over the Atlantic, something else occurred to me: "You know, I don't want Tel Aviv to be our default option, and then there's something else. We owe a debt to Mr and Mrs Friedlich. Once we've paid it, I'll also know that I'm not a default option for the Mossad. If they want me, or us, they'll have to choose us again."

Epilogue

Epilogue

Leo's Story

OUR RENTED APARTMENT in Toronto was cold – we'd shut down the heating when we left – and there was nothing to eat there. I suggested we drove out to Niki's parents. They'd be happy to know we were back, and for good, but Niki put the visit off for some other time. Her acute senses had picked up my restlessness.

"You don't feel at home," she said.

"That's because this isn't really our place. It's a flat the Mossad is renting for us," was my excuse. "We'll have to find a home of our own."

"Don't you like it?" Niki wondered. True, from the large windows there was a magnificent view out over the shore of Lake Ontario, the Toronto islands, including nearby Olympic Island and its park, and many other green islands all the way out to the horizon. From the windows on the east, we could see dozens of the city's skyscrapers, where the lights were beginning to go on.

"Yes, I like it," I said.

"So, it's only a matter of procedure. They'll stop paying, and we'll start," said Niki, always practical.

At two a.m., ten in the morning in Israel, I woke up bathed in sweat. The debriefing was beginning at our squad's base in Tel Aviv. I took a shower and went back to bed, but couldn't fall asleep.

"Jetlag," I told Niki, who had woken up, worried.

"That happens only in the other direction, something's bothering you."

"In the morning we'll visit Ron's parents," I said. "I have to cut off all ties with the Office."

"OK, but we'll tell Udi before we do so," Niki responded, taking command. "I'm going to phone him right now." So saying, she dialled the base's open number.

Udi was on the line in a minute and she put him on speaker. There were triumphant voices in the background.

"Everyone congratulates you two. You were terrific," he said, "but if you're calling there must be something you want to say."

"Yes," I said. "I want to go and see his parents today. You know who I mean."

The background voices disappeared. Perhaps Udi'd left the briefing room.

"In principle, that's OK, but you don't know what to tell them. Things aren't exactly the way you see them. So I suggest you wait for me, and please don't do anything dumb that could cause a lot of grief."

"Unavoidable grief," I responded.

"You reckon you know the whole story but you don't. You'll see them, but not today. Niki, watch him for one more day, all right?"

"All right," she replied, and hung up.

"What is going on?" I asked. Clearly, Niki knew something that I didn't.

"I prefer to let Udi tell you. It's more complicated than you think."

"And you know the story?"

"Look, I know – knew – Ron, and his parents. It's complicated. Please, wait another day, and meanwhile come let's try to get some sleep."

She managed to fall asleep, with or without jetlag. I didn't, until much later.

When I woke up Niki told me Udi was on his way and that at his request she'd arranged a visit to the Friedlichs the next evening.

"Is he coming with us?"

"I don't know. He just asked me to set the visit up, and I did."

I decided not to question her any further. But now I knew, with even greater clarity, why I wanted to cut off any remaining ties between us, both of us, and Udi and everything he represented.

We spent the day shopping and visiting Niki's parents although she didn't tell them we were back for good, and they were happy enough that we were there at all. I also had a long talk with my parents, who were sorry to hear I was in Canada and that it would be some time before I got to see them. I collapsed into bed early and again woke up in the middle of the night, something that hardly ever happened to me. Udi hadn't been in touch – at least not with me – and I spent the day waiting impatiently for our meeting with the Friedlichs.

✧✧✧

My heart was beating faster than ever and only Niki's presence beside me calmed me a little. How was I going to feel when two elderly parents thought they were seeing their lost son standing in front of them, and right after that hear that he was actually dead? How would Niki and I introduce ourselves, bearing in mind that she had once been the girlfriend of their dead son?

"I don't want to lie to them," I said to Niki when I suggested that we refrain from speaking about our relationship. "This encounter is going to be very strange for everyone. We mustn't bring in things that could create a lack of trust in us."

As we stood before their front door, I hesitated. Perhaps this wasn't such a good idea after all? Niki watched me questioningly, or expectantly. I knocked. Footsteps were heard from inside. The door opened, and there was Leo. This close up, I could see that his beard partly covered a scar that ran from his cheek through his chin to his neck.

No one moved. We looked at each other in a friendly but anxious way, and then Leo's lower jaw started trembling. He couldn't hold himself back from crying and the tears began to flow. My own eyes were also teary but I knew that my own emotions were as nothing when compared to the depth of his own grief.

Then Leo extended his arms, placed his hands on my shoulders looked into my eyes and said, in Hebrew, with only a slight North American drawl, "Little Mickey, my how you've grown," and he pulled me to his breast and began sobbing.

My mouth dropped open. What was happening here? Hebrew? "Little Mickey"? I stole a glance at Niki. She was looking at me caringly and lovingly, and there were tears in her eyes too. But I also discerned the very slightest hint of a smile.

Leo stood back a little, wiped his tears, leaving a hand on my shoulder, and said, in Hebrew again, "Please come in. Diane is very eager to meet you."

How could she be "eager to meet" me? And wouldn't she think I was her son, coming back into her life?

Leo's hand slid gently to my back and he propelled me inside. Before us, I saw the diplomas and photographs on the wall, and at the end of the hall, with the staircase on the left, and two steps down to the living room on the right, stood the display case with the candlesticks and the menorah, and above them the Shalom plaque, which now, in the light, I could see was brightly coloured.

At the entrance to the living room stood Diane, Ron's mother, the good-looking woman I had glimpsed once before and who I knew from the photographs. She greeted me with shining eyes and a warm smile, holding her hands out to mine and offering me her cheek. This wasn't the way a mother welcomed her long-lost son. The gentle words she said to me, about how happy she was to meet me, were in English. She beckoned us into the living room, which was a little darker than the hall and escorted me down the two steps with her. Leo and Niki followed us. There, sunk into a deep armchair, sat Udi. I gasped. What was he scheming? What kind of trap had he laid for me?

He rose, ponderously. His goatee – like my moustache – was gone, but he was unshaven and looked as if he'd come here straight from the airport. He gave me his hand.

"You've got to listen now," he said quietly, holding on to my hand softly. "As I said, there's a lot you don't know. Let Li'or speak."

Li'or? Where had I heard that name?

Then it came back to me. "In the end it'll turn out that Li'or was right," I'd heard my mother telling my father but I was still too confused to see the whole picture.

We sat down, Niki and I on one sofa, Leo and Diane facing us, and Udi sank back into the armchair that suited his dimensions. Leo poured drinks from a new bottle of Alberta Premium that he'd opened in our honour. "Canadian whisky hasn't yet received the appreciation it deserves but it is good, really good," he said, mostly to break the silence.

Then he lifted his glass and said, "To our reunion. L'Chaim." He drank and pursed his lips.

The suspicion that had emanated from my gut the moment Leo uttered my name and hugged me, and had grown stronger as he spoke about Diane, and had nearly been resolved when I saw Udi, became a certainty when I'd finished my whisky: an absolute clarity spread through my mind.

"I'll speak English so Diane will also understand," Leo began, but Diane said quickly that it was fine if he practised his Hebrew because he'd "be needing it" and anyway she knew the story through and through. They exchanged a loving look, intimate and sad, in a way that only a couple who have lost a child can. Then Leo turned his attention to me and saw Niki, so he decided, nevertheless, to speak in English.

"I had no other option after the war, the Yom Kippur War. When I saw Tomer hovering between life and death, when I saw the bones of his leg where the flesh had been burned away. When I heard him screaming with pain, when I saw the enormous agony of your grandmother, and your grandfather, the most heroic man I've ever met in my life – a phoenix arisen from the ashes – weeping in despair, and when I saw the enormous anxiety on Riki's face, not knowing where her life would go from then on with this burned, half-dead husband of hers, with all the tubes that were keeping him alive and all the operations and skin grafts that still awaited him – I knew that I would not be able to endure it again."

Leo poured himself another shot and wet his gullet with the Canadian whisky, and I used the pause to tell Niki, "You know of course that Riki and Tomer are my father and mother." Leo added, "Yes, my sister-in-law and my twin brother."

I'd known it all, a moment before he began speaking. I'd begun to grasp it from the way he greeted me at the door, and now complete comprehension dawned on me. I saw the great resemblance to my father – the nose, the eyes, the forehead, everything that wasn't hidden by the beard and the scars. Nevertheless, his words, which he was speaking in an almost casual manner, as if I was already aware of it all, fell like hammer blows on my head. My father's dead twin brother had come to life, here in Toronto.

Everything was linking up in my mind. I realized how I had been misled, as a child, to think that my uncle – whose very existence had been concealed from me for a long time – was dead. When my father absolutely refused to speak about him. When he snatched the pictures of my grandparents with their twin babies out of my hands. I remembered the pictures that had been cropped, and where a dismembered child's hand could be seen. I understood how – with the logic of a child whose mind was replete with death and the smoke of the crematoria from which his grandparents had escaped, and the wars his grandfather and father had waged, and whose father had been so grievously wounded – I had decided that my uncle was dead. No other possibility had crossed my mind.

Leo kept on talking. "And on top of this came my huge disillusionment with the country. The way our intelligence failed to see that war was about to break out, with the writing so large on the wall but that no one wanted to read. The Army that didn't pass on the information to its troops on the borders. Golda Meir, the prime minister who was too scared of the Americans to approve a preemptive strike by our army. Moshe Dayan, the defence minister who turned from a lion into a pussycat. The wars of the generals, and their sheer arrogance in thinking that it would take them no more than a moment to knock 'the stinking Arabs' out."

The monologue continued: "I realized a malignant disease was spreading among us. And a malignant disease had broken out among the Arabs too. Their hatred, which until then had been suppressed to a certain extent, now erupted in full force. A localized cancerous growth can be removed surgically and the patient saved but you can't do anything if the disease has reached the glands and the bones. I saw on TV the Egyptians celebrating victory when our forces stopped only a hundred kilometres away from Cairo, and the victory celebrations in Damascus when we were only thirty kilometres away, shelling the city's outskirts, and I got it: the disease had spread to their brains. There'd be another war and another one after that, no matter how much stronger we'd be – because the tumour in their brains would always give them the feeling that they were on the brink of victory. When they look at the bigger picture – hundreds of millions of Arabs surrounding a few million divided and overconfident Jews, who also had over a million Arabs living among them – how could they not feel that it was only a matter of time? But I'm sorry, that's not the point." He swallowed what was left in his glass and poured himself yet another.

"The state was a secondary matter for me. I felt that I was betraying it, but mainly that I was betraying my family. I do not have to tell you where my parents came from and what they went through. I can't even imagine the hardships of bringing us into the world and raising us in the post-World War II conditions, during the Israeli War of Independence, and during the austerity of the first years of the state. After all that, I knew they wouldn't forgive me for losing my faith in the country and leaving, and neither would Tomer. He had never allowed me to lag behind him or to fail. He wanted me to be exactly like him – a fighter and a winner – and I wasn't like that. I was no hero. I didn't inherit those genes of my father's. Nothing to be done about that."

I comprehended exactly what he was saying. I felt so completely like him. I drank in his words, which were addressed directly to me.

"I knew they wouldn't forgive me, because of what had happened to Tomer, and despite the fact that I, too, had gone through quite a lot. Here, this," and he pointed at the scars hidden behind his wispy beard and that went on down his neck and under his shirt. "These were also burns that happened in a tank, at the beginning of the war, but they can't be compared to what happened to your father. These were second degree burns on my neck and chest. On my face, apart from a few spots, there were only first degree burns.

"When Tomer was also wounded, seriously, towards the end of the war, and it wasn't clear whether he would live or die, our parents broke down altogether. You see, when they began a new life, straight out of the camps, they didn't think that their lives and the lives of their children would be one long war. When the War of Independence was over, in which my father – your grandfather – had to fight again, and the state became a fact, and your father and I were tots of three or so, our parents decided that now they had reached a state of peace and plenty. They even changed our names to new, Israeli ones – Tomer and Li'or.

When he saw the surprise on my face he added: "Apparently you haven't seen documents from those days. When we were born we were named after our two grandfathers, who were both killed in the Holocaust. Moshe, our father's father, and Shlomo, our mother's father. If you look at your father's ID card, you'll see that his name is given as Tomer Moshe. Mine was Li'or Shlomo."

"They had high hopes but when those hopes were dashed they were still willing to carry on fighting for the dream. The way they saw it, there was no forgiveness for abandoning the motherland. In their eyes, and in my own eyes too, I was like a deserter from the battlefield, someone who in other places, is simply shot . . ."

"All you did was emigrate. That's not desertion," Diane said for our benefit, something she must have said to Leo many times before.

"No, no," Leo rejected this attempt to ease the verdict he'd handed himself. "The country was a battlefield, in the hospitals and on the borders. It is still a battlefield. You, Mickey, have also had to fight. When you were in Lebanon, I used to call your mother at work and she would keep me up to date about you."

Now I, too, swallowed my whisky and gave him my glass for a refill. I glanced at the others. Niki, whose hand was in mine, was pale. Diane was gently stroking Leo's back and her face was full of pity. Udi, a hunched figure in his armchair, sat grey, withdrawn.

"Tomer really cut me out of his life," Leo went on, choked, "and my father did also. I don't even know who incited whom." His voice broke up. Diane rose and hugged his head as he wept into her chest. Twice he tried to speak, but couldn't, and when he poured himself another drink, Diane took away the glass and the bottle, and returned with a bottle of water. I lowered my eyes. I could tell from Niki's trembling hand that she was crying, and I did not dare look Udi in the face. I wanted to believe that someone else, at least my commander, could view this melodrama from the outside.

Leo took a long draught of water, and began speaking again: "Your father, who was always quicker than me, already had a wife. And a little girl, Tzipi. And very soon you also made your appearance. How you were made, from all that charred flesh and pain, only Tomer and Riki could tell. My mother and father buzzed around Tomer like bees, and gave him all the love that they could, and anyone coming close was in danger of getting stung. He went through hell in the hospitals and rehab. More and more operations, more and more skin grafts. The infections kept returning and it wasn't clear whether he'd live or not and no one could say if he'd ever walk again – until they finished with the surgery he was forbidden to try to stand on his feet.

"Don't get me wrong; for months I sat next to Tomer's bed, taking shifts with my mother and father and Riki. I gave up completely on my own treatments. Tomer's condition was so bad that my scars seemed insignificant. Perhaps not to me, but to the people around me. My mother and father shut themselves off from me. All they could see was Tomer and they didn't think they had to relate to me as well. When I saw on Tomer what skin grafts looked like, I decided that instead of that I'd grow a beard. And when it thickened a bit and got longer and covered the scars where

hair didn't grow, they were hardly visible. Only Riki saw that I was also
going through hard times and was willing to listen to me. She was terrific.
But she had a little daughter to take care of, and her wounded husband,
and his parents, and she was pregnant. She didn't have much time for me.
I gradually withdrew to a point where there was only me and my
nightmares – about what had been and what would be.

"Our generation didn't run to headshrinkers, no one had heard of
post-traumatic stress disorder, and the term 'shellshock' was reserved for
soldiers who couldn't function. It wasn't applied to a guy like me, who'd
simply begun to think there wasn't any point to anything, not only because
of what had happened to him, but also because of what I saw clearly was
going to happen.

"I'd lost the will to live. I never went back to university, which
reopened as soon as the war ended. I was so shaken up that I even believed
the conspiracy theories about the war. You know them, don't you?" and
for the first time he looked at Udi, who returned a glassy gaze. "It may
have been nonsense, but the notion that Golda and Dayan had
collaborated with the Egyptians and the Americans was enough to make
me lose my last remnant of trust in the state. I felt completely alone."

An oppressive silence reigned. No one moved. It seemed that each and
every one of us was doing his own soul searching, and then my Uncle Leo-
Li'or-Shlomo, continued his monologue, almost whispering.

"When Tomer was discharged, after almost half a year in hospital, and
your small living room was turned into a hospital, my visits grew less and
less frequent. I felt as though I didn't belong there. And when you were
born, I really couldn't stand to be there any more. They needed me, I
know. Riki was running from you to Tzipi to your father's bed. And with
all the surgery he'd undergone, I'm not sure who was yelling more – you
or him. They needed me, but the new life that had been created there, the
intimacy between the wonderful woman, the wounded man, the little girl,
the new baby, the old parents, just as it drew them all together like a huge
magnet, it pushed me away. I had nothing but my anxieties. I decided to
escape, to run as far away as I could."

"And this is where my angel came in." Now his face softened, and a
wide smile appeared as he turned his eyes to Diane and took her hand in
his. "She could see the soul behind the scars. After a year, we got married
and a year later Ron was born. He was named after a good friend of mine

who was killed in the tank, next to me. Diane agreed, because it's a name that sounds all right here too, although she was worried that every time I said his name I'd think of my pal and that war and everything that she had worked so hard to liberate me from. She even exempted me from helping with the baby after I was accepted at dental school. Finally, I began living a new life."

"And my father? You never saw him again?" I asked, when the oppressive silence set in again.

"I saw him, but he never saw me," Leo smiled sadly. "The first time was after Sadat's visit to Israel. Diane and I sat and watched it on TV, holding hands and excited to the point of tears. I said that maybe I'd been wrong, maybe there was hope after all, and I wanted to go to Israel to see what was happening. And I did go. I called from the airport but Tomer hung up when he heard my voice. I called again and Riki answered. I heard them arguing whether they should speak to me. Riki asked me to give her time to prepare the ground for a family reunion, and in the meantime I would stay with our mutual friends, Ada and Kobi, you must know them. She succeeded, partly. My father and Tomer agreed, but only if I told them I'd come back for good. But I couldn't say that then. With my mother it worked, and we met in Ada and Kobi's apartment. My mother, your mother, your sister Tzipi and you. Riki was pregnant with Aliza. You were three. I don't believe you will remember it."

I didn't remember. But all at once, and very intensely, I realized the pain I would be inflicting on my father if it emerged that I was leaving Israel forever.

"I showed them new pictures of Ronnie. I'd been sending them pictures since he was born, and everyone spoke about how he resembled you. That's what the genetics produced. Your father and I were identical twins, you looked like him and Ron looked like me. My mother brought a sailor suit for him, the same as the one she had bought for you."

I remembered the pictures of Ron on the boat and me on Haifa beach.

"For me, it wasn't a successful visit, and I grasped how deep the rift was when Riki came to see me off at the airport and brought a bundle of photos that had been cut in half. In some of them I was with my father and in others with my mother, with Tomer cut out of all of them. I still have them. The other half must be with your parents."

As he spoke, Diane went over to a cabinet and took out an album where all the photographs had been neatly stuck in. I recognized them right away as the missing halves of the pictures I knew from home. In some of them there was a body with an amputated arm, which appeared in the photos at home, and in others there was a small hand belonging to my father or a large one, belonging to one of his parents, which had vanished from the pictures I knew.

"It was a great gift for me, but one that sliced through my heart," said Leo while Niki and I were studying the photographs. "You see, Tomer and I had been like this," and he clasped his hands together with the fingers intertwined. "We were never separated for a moment. As children, as teenagers, on youth movement hikes. Our mother even kicked up a fuss when they put us into different classes at school, but it didn't help. One time – can you hear me Diane?" he called out when she went to make coffee, " – one time, a young thug from another school, our age but known as the terror of the neighbourhood, came into our schoolyard looking for trouble. When the break began, I ran out first, straight into him, and he began beating me up. He didn't need a reason. Everyone was standing around and watching – no one dared to intervene and get beaten up too. He got me on the ground and was sitting on top of me, punching me. Suddenly, he was gone, and I really mean gone. Tomer had come out and, without thinking twice, grabbed him around the chest and hurled him away. In a second we were both on top of the thug, beating him up." He threw in a Hebrew phrase that translates literally as "cut him down" and looked at Udi, very pleased with himself. "Together we could have been a good Mossad team, no?"

The saliva dried up in my mouth. What did he know? But Leo was on a roll and I couldn't interrupt him.

"I tried once again two years later. This time, Diane came with me and Ronnie too. It was my last year at university, and we wanted to check out the possibilities of living in Israel. Before I called your parents, we visited all kinds of cities and neighbourhoods and met friends and Diane didn't rule it out. There was an optimistic atmosphere in the country. But your father and grandfather said, 'First let him say he's coming back to live here.' I took that as a slap in the face. That obstinacy, that lack of trust."

Perhaps I should have said something in their defence but I knew exactly what he was talking about, and painful as it was, I felt that I was on his side.

"I decided I would go to my parents' home. I thought that seeing Ronnie would soften my father. After all, he was his grandson. But it was awful. My father revealed himself as a fanatical, benighted old man. 'Look, I've brought you a little Friedlich, to keep the family name alive, what you wanted so much,' I yelled at him, but he said 'I need a little Simhoni. The Friedlichs died out in the Holocaust.' It was only after the Yom Kippur War that he and your father had taken the Hebrew name Simhoni. I don't know whether that was a Zionist act, a next step after they changed my name and your father's name to Hebrew names after the War of Independence, or if some rabbi had suggested it as a magical way of helping your father recover. You were born a Simhoni and my father and your father expunged the name Friedlich from every document where it had appeared. They decided that a new family had been founded there – a family of heroes, but that's my own observation. I felt excluded, rejected."

I remembered how happy my mother had been to tell me her maiden name, while my father had rebuffed me when I asked what our name had been, saying that those Jewish Diaspora names meant nothing, whether the Jews had chosen them themselves or the Gentiles had bestowed them. What was important, he said, was the Hebrew name we had chosen ourselves, in Israel. But in fact they had merely translated the "Diaspora" name Friedlich, which means happy, to the Israeli Simhoni, which derived from the Hebrew word for happy.

Leo, who had not only preserved the original family name but had also abbreviated his Hebrew name, Li'or, to a more typical American one, continued:

"At the end of that year I graduated and opened a clinic, and from then on my life steered its own course. I almost managed to disconnect myself, with great heartache, from my past, from my family. I felt as if a limb had been amputated but I pushed ahead, and built my own family. Nevertheless, when I heard Tomer had a new position in Ottawa, I was attracted there as if by some giant magnet. My information was only partial, and Diane advised me not to go," Leo paused and gazed at her adoringly. "She said that if your family was now living here and hadn't contacted us, it was a lost cause. For days I wandered around the vicinity of the Israeli embassy hoping to bump into him, as if by chance, and to renew the connection. And once I did see him. My heart leaped out of my breast and I began walking towards him but then immediately a young guy popped up next to me, a security man, and stopped me and asked for ID. Your father disappeared in the meantime and I returned to Toronto shamefaced, frustrated and exasperated.

"Years later, when I heard my parents' condition had deteriorated and they'd entered an old people's home, I visited them again. My father was almost blind by then, couldn't tell me from Tomer, and he held my hand. Instead of being happy, I felt like a thief. Like Jacob pretending to Isaac that he was Esau. I came back again during the shiva but I didn't want any drama so I told Riki I was coming and she told Tomer. He left as I was due to arrive: I saw him depart. You know, we are twins but, in addition to my beard, places also do things to people. I watched him. He looked hard, battle weary, introverted. Here, people tend to be open."

I understood, in the very depth of my soul, my uncle's pain and his need to unload his tale, but I wanted to get to the most important point. What seemed to me most important. I took a deep breath and asked, "And what happened to Ron?"

✧✧✧

Leo and Diane both sighed. Niki also sat up. "Ronnie was my American dream," said Leo. "I wanted him to grow up the way I would have if my father had chosen Canada instead of Palestine." I was astonished to hear my own thoughts coming out of his mouth. "And he didn't let us down. A good student, a well-brought up boy, an outstanding athlete – Niki can tell you about it, she was his girlfriend."

Niki paled. "I've already told him," she said, and it was clear from her tone that there was a gap between what she'd told me and whatever there had been between the two of them.

Diane took up the story: "Ronnie was, how should I put it, something of a free spirit. He loved sports, but wasn't good enough to be a pro. It was perhaps our fault that we never pushed him enough to excel at anything. We wanted him to take life easy. When he decided in high school that he wanted to be captain of the football team and began training for hours every day, Leo was even worried about it."

"Because that's not what's called taking life easy," Leo chimed in, and he again astonished me when he said "I was afraid that he'd want to get into some elite unit in the Israeli army, as an act of rebellion against his father." I felt that it was Leo's soul, my uncle's and not my father's, that was inside me and that his ideas were occupying my mind.

"In brief, no pro team drafted him from the Varsity Blues," Diane continued. "He'd studied a little environmental science and a little anthropology and comparative cultures and he liked people and places, but he didn't know exactly what to do with himself. I believe Niki thought the same, didn't you Niki?"

Niki blushed, and didn't answer.

"And then he took off on his grand tour of the world, saying 'Every Israeli guy goes on a long trip after the army,' so he'd do it after graduating. By the way, he had wanted to go to Israel and join the army, after graduating from high school and after his first year at university, and even after getting his BA, but Leo wouldn't hear of it."

"When he finished high school, the Israeli army was still in Lebanon," Leo justified himself. "I don't have to tell you about it, you were there. I spoke to your mother and I knew exactly what was happening. What had happened to me, and of course to my brother wasn't enough? Did I have to send my son as well? Forgive me for saying this, after what you went through in Lebanon," he said, as Diane pressed her hand on his thigh, "but I had made my choice, to run away from the wars. So I'm a coward. OK, and I have been paying for it every day since I got onto the plane out of Israel. So, should I have been a hero on my son's back?"

Leo was upset, Diane tried to calm him down. She continued talking.

"He left on his trip on the spur of the moment, as if he was running away from himself, and it dragged on and on. He was in China, Laos, Vietnam before he got to India, and the drugs . . ."

Leo picked up the narrative. "He dropped out of our lives. We knew he was in India. I made some inquiries and understood he'd got mixed up in drugs. I flew out there. It was too awful to see him like that. He didn't know me. Didn't remember or want to acknowledge that he was our Ronnie, my son. It's a terrible thing for a father. I saw that he was very confused, but he was independent enough to refuse to come back with me. I managed to persuade him to enter some rehab institution, and I left him there. My plan was to go back a month later – I couldn't stay there with him the whole time, I had patients here in the middle of treatments. But then he disappeared. When I inquired at the institution, all they said was that the problem wasn't drugs. He'd been cured of his addiction, but still hadn't got himself together."

It was easy to see that Leo was struggling with a serious guilt problem but when Diane wanted to speak instead of him, he put his hand on her arm and continued.

"It took us a long time before we discovered he was in Sinai. I flew to Egypt to look for him and spent more than a month in Sinai. I went from one Bedouin tribe to another with his picture. No one had seen or heard anything. There was no trace of him. After a while they became antagonistic towards me so I hired someone to carry on searching for me and returned to Canada."

"We faced a choice between devoting our lives to the search and losing our daughter and granddaughter, or paying professionals to do it for us and to carry on with our lives, as far as that was possible," said Diane, "and it really isn't possible."

"No, we never got back to being ourselves, and half a year ago I returned to Sinai but again, I drew a blank and felt that I had lost a son and it would have been better if it had happened in *milhamot Yisrael* — Israel's wars. Only last night, when Udi called, did what really happened begin to become clear."

"Let me take over from here," said Udi, speaking with uncharacteristic gentleness. Diane and Leo gave way to him. All eyes were on him as he sat up straight.

"Almost three years ago – there's no record of the actual date – a group of Bedouin from Sinai crossed into Israel north of Eilat. Ron was with them and they left him at the side of Route 12, the road that runs along the border with Egypt. People travelling along the road saw him and called the police. He had no papers on him. He was taken to the hospital in Eilat where he was diagnosed as being in a state of dissociation, presumably caused by a drug overdose. After a while, when he still couldn't remember anything about himself, his condition was described more precisely as a dissociative fugue, in which people detach completely from their identity. It can happen after a severe trauma, and drugs can pave the way for it."

So Ron was not dead! Ron was alive!

The realization sliced through my consciousness. My eyes opened wide, and I almost jumped out of my seat. Then I saw that none of the others was moving. I was the last to know. What was happening here? That Udi had lied to me I had already grasped but had Niki also been in on the secret? What was the true story?

Udi saw how upset I was, he had probably also expected it, as had Niki, who was gripping my arm harder, almost preventing me from moving or saying anything. Udi proceeded.

"He was transferred to a psychiatric institution near Haifa. After some months of treatment he began to communicate and it emerged that he spoke North American English but he still couldn't give his name. The change in his condition was very slow."

Udi wanted to continue with his chronological account but Diane wanted to know details of her son's current state, and where he was. Udi was quick to reply, telling her that Ron had recently had episodes of clarity, remembering who he was, and that he was apparently on the way to recovery. He was under good supervision.

Diane asked him to be more specific, and only then did I realize that Udi must have studied psychology. He gave a detailed explanation of dissociative fugue, a rare psychiatric disease in which patients lose touch with their previous lives and can leave their homes and occupations and begin wandering.

"That's exactly what happened to Ronnie," said Diane. She asked Udi how long it could go on for and he told her that, according to the professional literature he had read after speaking to the attending psychiatrist, it could be a matter of hours, weeks or months.

Leo wanted to know why it had happened. Udi explained that it was believed that the causes were psychological, such as the need to blank out a painful experience, or a severe inner conflict, finding expression in repression of feelings and detachment from one's identity.

"What painful experience could he have had?" Leo wondered, and when Niki suddenly squeezed my arm I realized that she was thinking about her having broken up with him as being a possible cause. Diane rescued her: "Perhaps it was disappointment at the fact that no pro team drafted him when he graduated, and your refusal to allow him to go to Israel and enlist there?"

Silence reigned after that.

After giving us breathing space, Udi continued. "At around the same time as Ron was brought into Israel, the Bedouin began selling his passport on the black market. It went from hand to hand and landed up in the Israeli underworld where some patriotic thief thought the country could make good use of it and gave it to one of the government ministries from where it eventually reached us."

"And then it was discovered that I resembled the picture in the passport," I interjected.

"It didn't happen quite so fast," said Udi and for the first time the hint of a smile appeared in the corners of his lips. "You asked if we reached you by chance and I replied that chance is your best friend and your worst enemy, but I didn't say that the connection was made by chance." I couldn't recall the details of that conversation back in the little house in the Kiryah but I assumed he was right. He had been speaking then with a goal in mind, and I'd been a tabula rasa, open to any interpretation.

"We checked the name Friedlich in our data bases. We found there were Friedlichs in Israel who changed their name to Simhoni and that's how we got to you. But resemblance isn't enough. As we didn't know if you would be suitable, we also sought out other men who matched the photo but in the end we chose you."

I shifted to Hebrew, with a tilt of my head to Leo and Diane: "Do they know what we are talking about?"

"They know we used Ron's passport for the benefit of Israel," he replied tersely. In his earlier talk with them he had apparently referred to this.

Udi took up the narrative again. "Nobody made the connection between the man picked up on Route 12 and the passport that reached us a few weeks later. It would have been almost impossible to make such a connection. Every night, dozens of people cross the border from Sinai without documents. Sudanese and Nigerians, Russians, Ukrainians and Lithuanians. Everybody wants to get to the Land of Milk and Honey."

"So how was the connection made?" I asked.

"Niki made it," said Udi. "Do you want to tell us how, Niki?"

For a moment I was frightened that Niki would say she had taken up with Ron because he looked like me – something that would bother his parents – or still worse, that she had resumed her relationship with me when I came to the university to get Ron's paperwork. It made me uncomfortable to be presented as having done that.

"I'd prefer you to do it, Udi," she said.

"OK. Niki knew that Mickey was using Ron's passport and, after joining the Mossad, she told us that she had known Ron. That was about a year ago," he said.

"But how did you tie that in with Ron himself, in the hospital," I wanted to know.

"I'll explain," said Niki, taking her hand out of mine and speaking to me without looking at me.

"When you asked for Ron's documents at Trinity College, and you came back into my life, I realized something wasn't kosher." Her use of the word "kosher" raised a smile with everyone except me. I was tense and jumpy. What other surprises were in store for me here?

"As I've already told you, I suspected that it had something to do with the things that Israel does with foreign passports, and because I knew that Ronnie was Jewish and loved Israel, I thought that perhaps it was being done at his initiative. I didn't want to ask too many questions.

"But then, later on, you told me Ron had died in Sinai and you wanted to tell his parents. I thought that was the right thing to do, and I even offered to do it myself because, after all, I know you," she said, glancing at Leo and Diane, who looked stunned. "And I also wanted to save them the shock of meeting you," she turned back to me, " you who are so like Ronnie. But then I thought about it again. I already knew who you were working for and I knew something about all the trickery and deception, and I thought – what if they'd misled you? What if they'd stolen or found Ronnie's passport and told you he was dead so that you would act confidently and wouldn't think that the real Ron Friedlich was wandering somewhere in the world?"

Niki's lateral or even manipulative thinking was far more developed than mine, I had to admit. I hadn't thought for a second that Udi was misleading me. Once again, I felt a wave of warmth and love for her spreading through me. Now I was gripping her hand and she sent me a quick smile of thanks, which also had a pinch of embarrassment at giving this sign of affection in full view of Leo and Diane. "I stalled for time and then Udi arrived and talked you out of it. Leo and Diane, I'm so happy I never went to see you then. That would have done you a terrible wrong. But I did decide to spend some time trying to solve the mystery. I spoke to Udi and it turned out that he too knew nothing about what had actually happened to the owner of the passport."

Udi took over.

"The people in our operational units do not have to know where their passports come from. I got it from the department that deals with documentation, with notification that its source was the Bedouin in Sinai and that there were rumours that its owner was a drug addict and had perhaps died as a consequence."

"I was told that he was dead," I blurted out, feeling an unconquerable need to settle this with Udi there and then.

"No. You were told that for all our practical purposes, he was dead. And also, that 'to know' would mean seeing the body with our own eyes, and that was something neither I nor you had done."

The ways Udi had found to deceive me without explicitly lying had been quite labyrinthine. He had apparently been able to live comfortably with the difficulty that I was having in believing that Ron was dead throughout my service, as long as his goal was being achieved and I had confidence in my assumed identity.

Now I understood why he'd been so agitated and had hurried to get to me after I broke into the Friedlich's house: not only could I have discovered that Ron was alive – nobody in the Mossad knew then what had happened to him – but also I could have found out that he was my cousin, and all the magnificent effort involved in recruiting and training me and sending me to establish cover would have gone up in smoke, because clearly there was no chance that I would have kept going if I'd known this. I also understood why they never kicked me out: my findings in the break-in only bolstered the assumption that the passport I was carrying didn't have the handicap of belonging to a living person, and it was worth their while to keep me on the job.

Either way, Udi wasn't interested in me right then. He was speaking to Leo and Diane.

"I asked those who handle documentation to check into the course the passport had taken, and I found out when it crossed from Sinai into Israel. Following Niki's request, I also looked into the people who had infiltrated at around that time. It took a few months but, in the end, we got to the story of the guy who had crossed over without any papers and who'd been taken to the hospital in Eilat. I asked for a follow-up on what had happened to him. That's how we discovered he was in the institution near Haifa."

"It was only a month ago that the information came in, and I went with Udi to see him," Niki took up the story. "We were busy with something important, so we couldn't manage any more than that one visit." She swallowed, nervous and embarrassed at saying this to his parents who would, perhaps, not be able to understand this negligence and forgive it. Already, the situation in which she had come to their home as my partner was in itself mortifying.

"It was an amazing visit, for me, and also because of what it did for Ron. For the first time, he began to connect events from the past and to relate to his true identity. But this clarity all at once turned into confusion which deteriorated into a psychotic episode. Ronnie began to scream, he locked himself in the toilet and ran amok. I'm so sorry, this is upsetting for you, but you should know what to expect. His nurse gave him a tranquilizing shot, and he went into a state that was very difficult for me to see," Niki said, and choked up.

Udi took up the thread. "The psychiatrist told us that Niki's visit and the reconnection with his identity created a breakthrough in his treatment. In his case, because of the drugs – and because there's no information on what drugs he'd taken and what he'd been through – recovery could take a long time. Seeing Niki renewed the link with his past but it also led to a disintegrative experience, and they have had to move slowly and carefully. The psychiatrist was even more optimistic after Tomer's visit."

"After what?" We all jumped up and blurted out, each one of us in their own language and manner.

"The shrink said the treatment had to proceed gradually. He wanted to wait at least another two weeks before we saw Ron again. We knew Niki wouldn't be able to visit him during that period, and he also didn't want it to be Niki because of the attack that her visit had sparked. Then I had the idea of putting Tomer into the picture. The doctor thought it might confuse Ron even more but, after deliberating, he decided that it was worth trying."

"And how did Tomer react?" Leo asked.

"I went to see him a couple of weeks ago. I introduced myself as Mickey's superior officer, and Tomer was surprised that I was familiar with the family history that he had hidden from his own son. Then he said, 'Well, over there you probably know everything about everybody.' I explained the situation and told him the doctor was keen on a visit from a family member. I said Mickey wouldn't be available any time soon, nor would Niki or I, that we were going abroad, and that you, Ron's parents, were totally unaware of what was going on, and at that point in time we couldn't put you in the picture. Tomer didn't hesitate for a moment."

"But what did he say?" Leo insisted.

"That family is family," Udi replied, and again there was a sticky silence.

I also had a question, which I preferred to ask in Hebrew. "Tell me, when you introduced yourself to my parents, when my father said what he said . . . What do they think, you know, about my exhibitions and all that?"

"Don't be a child," he spat out. "If they don't know exactly, they know more or less. Do you think your father would stay quiet about you spending so much time abroad, if he didn't get it?"

As soon as he'd jabbed me with this barb, Udi addressed the Friedlichs again.

"I spoke to the psychiatrist the day before yesterday. He told me that Tomer's visit went well. Ron remembered that his father had a twin brother in Israel and understood that Tomer was his uncle. The doctor said the time had come to bring close relatives into the picture. He also needs you to fill him in on Ron's medical history. He has to know, for example, if Ron ever had epileptic fits, or symptoms of depression or manic behaviour, or episodes of amnesia. It would help him come up with a precise diagnosis and, of course, the right treatment to get him out of it.

"As I told you yesterday, the Israeli government will pay for your flight and stay in the country. You have reservations on a flight tomorrow, if that suits you."

"We'll start packing right away, won't we love?" Leo said as he turned to Diane. "And you can tell your government that we are very, very grateful."

"The gratitude should be in the opposite direction. And it won't cost us as much as you think. I've spoken to Tomer and he says that the guest room in their home in Haifa is ready for you."

As we stood up to leave, I looked around me, taking in the American plenty, the designer furniture, the thick white rug, all very different from what they'd find in my parents' "guest room" which was nothing more than my sisters' room, or mine, ten feet by eight, with a bed, a teenager's desk and a wardrobe made of MDF.

Then my eye spotted the poetry book on the cabinet. Perhaps a copy of the one I had seen in the Friedlichs' bedroom when I broke in. I picked it up, as if it were the first time I'd seen it. In the background I heard Udi ordering a cab.

"Whose book of poems is this?"

Leo chuckled. "At one time, ages ago, when we were kids, I thought I'd be a poet, and your dad wanted to be an inventor. At school he'd design all kinds of spaceships. I became a dentist and he's a forester. All I ever wrote then were poems to girls but after all the traumas in Israel, the Yom Kippur War, the Gulf War, the Lebanon War – the words came flowing out, together with all the fears and the demons. And that book happened here, after fear made me run away. After I saw there was no hope there. After each of the traumas I wrote a number of poems and then I had them printed and bound. At the last minute, I decided to include a poem about peace, which I wrote after Rabin and Hussein made peace, or after the signing of the pact with Arafat at the White House, I don't recall which."

A poem about peace? I turned the book over, and there it was on the back cover, in very small print. Its not very original title was *And Perhaps*.

The footsteps of peace are muffled.
Peace steals secretively into the heart,
Confused, hesitant,
Self-effacing.
Without fanfares,
Without drum rolls.
As if ashamed of giving up:
Giving up on heroism,
Giving up on conquests,
Giving up on vengeance
For generations of injustice.
It has even given up
On justice, on truth,
And on what's rightfully ours.

"You can take it with you, a gift from me," Leo broke into my perusal of the poem. "In any case, I dreamed of showing it to your father so that perhaps he'd understand me. Both you and Ronnie are mentioned in it.

Not by name," he added when he saw my frown of surprise, "but you'll see there's a poem there about my sons, that is the sons of the poet who are fighting in the last war. I was thinking about you two when I wrote it. You're the older, he's the younger. Everything was so tangible to me. How could I have allowed him to go? And look where he's ended up."

And again he stood there, helpless. We kissed and hugged again and again. Udi exchanged thank yous with Leo and Diane, and we left.

When the door closed behind us, Udi placed one hand on my shoulder and the other on Niki's and pulled us together. "This may not be the right place to say it, or the right time, but I want you to have all the information you need to make the decision you need to make. The passport is still alive, because Leo and Diane will probably let us keep on using it, and Ron won't be needing it any time soon. But in the last few days, you've been on our table at HQ. We have analyzed all the implications of the fact that the three of us have been exposed. For most target countries, especially those directly or indirectly linked with Iran, we are burned."

"Meaning?"

"That as far as Arab countries are concerned, Algiers was our final stop," he watched our reactions. "We will apparently be able to function, but not in Arab countries. It's a pity, but the world's a big place and we have enemies everywhere so there's no lack of work. However, that's not all."

"What else is there?" I asked. Although I didn't intend to go back to the Mossad, I was interested in hearing what was graver than the fact that the career he'd planned for us had melted away and that even Udi himself was in many ways out of the game.

"Napoleon said he didn't want generals who were clever or bold, but generals with luck. You are both clever and brave but Mickey, the fact that in both of your last missions you were arrested shows that you are not lucky. It's been decided to release you from operational duties. If you wish, there are a lot of staff options for you at HQ."

"And Niki?" I asked with a quaking voice.

"Niki and you are a package deal." Looking at her, he added: "Without any connection to the fact that you were also detained, and we don't like that, if Mickey doesn't stay, neither will you."

So many options were now open to me, to us both. I didn't have to run away from my destiny any more – my destiny had stopped haunting me. Niki's sympathetic but unsurprised expression implied that she'd known all this, and was anxiously waiting to see my reaction. When she saw the relief on my face, the gleam returned to her eyes.

"I've booked seats for you as well, if you decide you don't want to miss the family celebration," said Udi.

I embraced Niki and answered, "We wouldn't miss it for all the money in the world."

Niki drove us back to town as questions ran through my mind. What would happen when we all met up in Haifa? And after that? What then? Leo's book was in my lap. I picked it up and read the rest of the peace poem on the back cover.

> *The footsteps of peace are silent.*
> *Lest someone lift his voice,*
> *Lest someone lift his weapon,*
> *Before peace finds its place*
> *Inside our hearts,*
> *Settles there and prospers*
> *And looks all around*
> *At the great light that will shine then.*
>
> *And we shall feel*
> *Conquered*
> *As if by a first love*
> *By a great hope*
> *By a new life.*
>
> *Peace comes stealthily*
> *And we wonder*
> *How is it that we didn't know*
> *That the day was near?*
> *And we rejoice*
> *And refuse to believe.*

✧✧✧

My eyes went back to the title, *And Perhaps.* A tiny bit of the hope that my uncle had harboured when he wrote the poem had trickled into my breast. And perhaps.

Niki drove on, without intruding, and I became absorbed in contemplation. In my imagination I pictured a scene:

My father and my uncle, Diane and my mother, Niki and I are standing at the entrance to a small pavilion. On a bench facing us, skinny, confused and smiling, sits Ronnie, my cousin and my double. The pavilion is painted white, and the sea winds and salt have peeled off the top layers. Around it, there is a withered lawn that all attempts to nurture and maintain have failed to revive but it seems that the people living here have not given up on the hope that they will be able to make the grass grow. There is a hot sun shining on our backs but a fresh breeze is keeping us cool. The sun is in Ronnie's eyes and he is squinting. Niki, a little apart from me, moves so that her slight body will shade his face. My father puts his arm around Leo's shoulders. My mother and Diane have tears in their eyes. I take a small leather pouch out of my coat pocket and from it extract a Canadian passport with the royal coat of arms on its worn cover. I take a last look at the photograph inside of the smiling, long-haired young man, with his strong face and square jaw, and I hand it to Ronnie. "You need it now more than I do," I tell him.

I erase the scene from my mind, so that I won't see Udi standing there, watching us.

Mishka Ben-David

This book is dedicated to the victims, both the dead and the wounded, of the terrorist attacks that are mentioned in the book and the many attacks that are not mentioned, but have not been forgotten; to the families of the victims, and also to all the people engaged in the Sisyphean task of preventing terrorism and stopping Iran from obtaining weapons of mass destruction, only a tiny part of whose activities has been hinted at here.

The terror attacks that are part of the narrative of this novel:
Dolphinarium nightclub, Tel Aviv, June 21 2001; 21 killed
Park Hotel, Netanya, March 24 2002; 30 killed
Matza restaurant, Haifa, March 31 2002; 16 killed
Hebrew University cafeteria, Jerusalem, July 31 2002; 7 killed
No. 4 bus, Allenby Street, Tel Aviv, September 19 2002; 5 killed
No. 37 bus, Haifa, March 5 2003; 17 killed
Maxim restaurant, Haifa, October 4 2003; 21 killed
No. 19 bus, Rehavia, Jerusalem, January 29 2004; 22 killed
No. 14 bus, Liberty Bell Park, Jerusalem, February 22 2004; 8 killed
Ashdod Port, March 14 2004; 10 killed
No. 7 and No. 12 buses, Beersheba, August 31 2004; 16 killed
Stage Club, Tel Aviv Esplanade, February 5 2005; 5 killed

Also mentioned:
In 2001: Sbarro restaurant, Jerusalem; Netanya; Nahariya; Hadera
In 2002: Rishon Lezion nightclub; Patt Junction, Jerusalem; Hadera, Megiddo,
In 2003: Old bus terminal, Tel Aviv; Moment Café, Jerusalem; Café Hillel, Jerusalem; Mike's Place, Tel Aviv; Tsriffin; Geha

Thanks are due to Yohanan Lakicevic for his advice on the subject of painting; to my daughter, Dr Shiri Ben-Naim, for advice on the state of fugue; to Irit Shmueli Cohen for advice on the subject of hostesses in Japan; to Amnon Jackont, Mattat Eshet, and Hava Lustig for their comments; to my wife Shina, Eitan Even, and Kobi and Ada Avshalom for reading the manuscript and their encouragement.